THE INHABITED ISLAND

THE

ARKADY AND BORIS STRUGATSKY

INHABITED

TRANSLATED BY ANDREW BROMFIELD

ISLAND

CHICAGO
REVIEW
PRESS

Published by Chicago Review Press Incorporated
814 North Franklin Street
Chicago, IL 60610
ISBN 978-1-61373-597-8

ИНСТИТУТ ПЕРЕВОДА

AD VERBUM

Published with the support of the Institute for Literary Translation, Russia.

Library of Congress Cataloging-in-Publication Data
Is available from the Library of Congress.

Cover photo and design: Jonathan Hahn

Typesetting: Nord Compo

Printed in the United States of America
5 4 3 2 1

CONTENTS

THE INHABITED ISLAND

PART I

ROBINSON CRUSOE

1

Maxim opened the hatch a little way, stuck his head out, and apprehensively glanced at the sky. The sky was low and solid-looking, without that frivolous transparency that hints at the unfathomable depth of the cosmos and a multitude of inhabited worlds; it was a genuine biblical firmament, smooth and impervious. And this firmament, which no doubt rested on the mighty shoulders of some local Atlas, was lit by an even phosphorescent glow. Maxim searched at its zenith for the hole punched through it by his ship, but there wasn't any hole, only two large black blots, spreading out like drops of ink in water. Maxim swung the hatch all the way open and jumped down into the tall, dry grass.

The air was hot and thick, with a smell of dust, old iron, crushed vegetation, and life. There was also a smell of death, ancient and incomprehensible. The grass came up to his waist, and there were dark thickets of bushes close by, with dismal, crooked trees haphazardly jutting up out of them. It was almost light, like a bright, moonlit night on Earth, only without any moonlight shadows and without any of that bluish moonlight haze; everything was gray, dusty, and flat. His ship was standing at the bottom of an immense depression with gently sloping sides. The terrain around the ship rose noticeably toward an indistinct horizon. And this was strange, because nearby a river, a large, calm river, flowed to the west, uphill across the slope of the depression.

Maxim walked around the ship, running his hand over its cold, slightly damp flank. He found traces of impacts where he was expecting them. A deep, nasty-looking dent below the indicator ring—that was when the ship suddenly jerked and flipped over onto its side and the cyberpilot took offense, so that Maxim had

3

to hastily override the controls. And there was a notch beside the right visual sensor iris—that was ten seconds later, when the ship was set on its nose and went blind in one eye. Maxim looked up at the zenith of the sky again. The black blots were barely even visible now. A meteorite strike in the stratosphere; probability zero point zero zero . . . But every possible event occurred at some time or other, didn't it?

Maxim stuck his head back into the cabin, set the controls to self-repair, activated the express laboratory, and walked toward the river. This is an adventure, of course, but it's still just routine. Boring. For us in the FSG, even adventures are routine. A meteorite strike, a radiation strike, an accident on landing. An accident on landing, a meteorite strike, a radiation strike . . . Adventures of the body.

The tall, brittle grass rustled and crunched under his feet, and the prickly seeds clung to his shorts. A cloud of some kind of midges flew at him, whining and droning, jostled about right in front of his face, and then left him alone. Serious, grown-up people don't join the Free Search Group. They have their own serious, grown-up business to deal with, and they know that all these alien planets are essentially tiresome and humdrum. Tiresomely humdrum. Humdrumly tiresome. But, of course, if you're twenty years old, if you don't really know how to do anything much, if you don't really know what you would like to do, if you still haven't learned to appreciate the most important thing that you possess—time—and if you don't have any special talents or the prospect of acquiring any, if the impulse that dominates your entire being at the age of twenty still emanates, as it did ten years ago, not from your head but from your hands and feet, if you are still primitive enough to imagine that on unknown planets you can discover some precious object or other that is quite impossible on Earth, if, if, if . . . Well then, of course—take the catalog, open it at any page, jab your finger at any line, and go flying off. Discover a planet, give it your own name, and determine its physical characteristics; do battle with monsters, if any such should be found there; establish contact, should there be anyone with whom to do so; or play Robinson Crusoe for a while, should you not discover anyone . . .

And it's not as if all this is pointless. They'll thank you and tell you that you have contributed to the best of your ability, and they'll summon you for a detailed discussion with an eminent specialist . . . Schoolchildren, especially the backward ones, and definitely those in the youngest classes, will regard you with respect, but when you meet your Teacher, he will merely inquire, *So you're still in the FSG, then?* He'll change the subject, and his expression will be guilty and sad, because he blames himself for the fact that you're still in the FSG, and your father will say, *Hmm* . . . and hesitantly offer you a job as a lab technician, and your mother will say, *Maxie, but you used to draw really well as a child*, and Oleg will say, *How much longer? Stop disgracing yourself like this*, and Jenny will say, *Let me introduce you to my husband*. And they'll be right, everyone will be right, apart from you. And you'll go back to the FSG central office and there, trying hard not to look at the other two blockheads just like you who are rummaging through the catalogs on the next set of shelves, you'll take down yet another volume, open it at random to any page, and jab your finger at it . . .

Before walking down the ridge to the river, Maxim looked around. Behind him the grass he had trampled down was straightening out, raggedly jutting back up, the crooked trees were black silhouettes against the background of the sky, and the open hatch was a bright little circle. Everything was very normal. Well, OK, he said to himself. So be it . . . It would be good to find a civilization—powerful, ancient, and wise. And human . . . He went down to the water.

The river really was large and slow, and to the naked eye it clearly appeared to flow down from the east and up toward the west (however, the refraction here was horrendous). It was also obvious that the opposite bank was shallow and overgrown with thick rushes, and a half mile upstream Maxim could see some kinds of columns and crooked beams jutting up out of the water and a twisted latticework of girders, entangled in shaggy, creeping plants. Civilization, Maxim thought without any particular enthusiasm. He could sense a lot of iron on all sides, and something else as well, something very unpleasant and asphyxiating; when he scooped up a handful of water, he realized that it was radiation, rather strong and pernicious. The river was carrying along radioactive substances from the east, and that made it clear to Maxim that there was little to be gained from this civilization, that once again this was not what was required. It would be best not to establish contact; he should just carry out the standard analyses, unobtrusively fly around the planet a couple of times, and clear out of here. And then, back on Earth, he would hand over his materials to the morose, worldly-wise gentlemen of the Galactic Security Council, and forget about all of this as quickly as possible.

He fastidiously shook his fingers and wiped them on the sand, then squatted down and started pondering. He tried to picture the inhabitants of this planet, which could hardly be thriving and trouble-free. Somewhere beyond the forests was a city, also unlikely to be thriving: dirty factories, decrepit reactors dumping radioactive gunk in the river; ugly, barbaric buildings with sheet-iron roofs, large expanses of wall, and not many windows; dirty gaps between the buildings, piled high with refuse and the corpses of domestic pets; a large moat around the city, with drawbridges over it . . . but, no, that was before reactors. And the people: he tried to picture the people, but he couldn't. He only knew that they were wearing a lot of clothes, that they were densely packed into thick, coarse material and had high, white collars that rubbed their chins sore . . . Then he saw the tracks in the sand.

They were the tracks of bare feet. Someone had come down off the ridge and walked into the water. Someone with large, broad feet, someone heavy, pigeon-toed and clumsy—definitely humanoid, but with six toes on each foot. Grunting and groaning, he had scrambled down the ridge, hobbled across the sand, plunged into the radioactive water with a splash, and swum, wheezing and snorting, to the opposite bank, into the rushes. All without removing his high, white collar.

Everything on all sides was suddenly lit up by a bright blue flash, like a lightning strike, instantly followed by rumbling, hissing, and crackling above the ridge. Maxim jumped to his feet. Dry earth came pouring down the ridge, and something shot up into the sky with a threatening screech, fell into the middle of the river, and sent up a fountain of spray mingled with white steam. Maxim started swiftly running up the slope. He already knew what had happened, he just didn't understand why, and he wasn't surprised when, at the spot where his ship had just been standing, he saw a swirling column of incandescent smoke, a gigantic corkscrew ascending into the phosphorescent vault of the heavens. The ship had burst, and its ceramite shell was flickering with a purple glow; the dry grass around it was merrily burning, the bushes were blazing, and smoky little flames were catching hold of the gnarled trees. The furious heat struck Maxim in the face, and he shielded himself with his open hand, backing away along the ridge—first one step, then another, then another, and another . . . He inched backward, keeping his watering eyes fixed on the magnificent beauty of this incandescent torch, this sudden volcano, scattering its crimson and green sparks, and the senseless frenzy of the rampaging energy.

No, it's obvious why, he thought in dismay. A big monkey showed up, saw I wasn't there, climbed inside, and raised the deck. I don't even know how to do that, but the monkey figured it out—it was a very quick-witted monkey, with six toes. Anyway, it raised the deck . . . What do we have in there, under the deck in our ships? Anyway, it found the batteries, took a big rock—and *wham!* A very big rock, weighing about three tons, and it took a swing . . . An absolutely massive, mega-huge kind of monkey . . . And it made a total wreck of my ship with its cobblestone—two hits up there in the stratosphere already, and now one down here too . . . An incredible story; I don't think anything like that has ever happened before. But what am I supposed to do now? They'll miss me soon enough, of course, but even when they do miss me, they're not very likely to believe that such a thing is possible—the ship has been destroyed but the pilot is still in one piece. What's going to happen now? My mother . . . My father . . . My Teacher . . .

He turned his back to the conflagration and walked away, moving quickly along the river. Everything around him was illuminated by red light, and his shadow on the grass in front of him kept shortening and lengthening by turns. On his right a sparse forest began, smelling of decaying leaves, and the grass turned soft and damp. Two large nocturnal birds cacophonously shot up from right under his feet and fluttered away, low above the water, toward the far bank. He fleetingly thought that the fire might overtake him and then he would have to escape by swimming, and that would be really obnoxious. Then the red light on all sides faded and went out completely, and he realized that, unlike him, the fire-fighting devices had finally figured out what had happened and performed their designated function with their usual dependable thoroughness. He vividly pictured to himself the smoke-blackened, half-melted cylinders, absurdly jutting up amid the blazing debris, belching out dense clouds of pyrophage and feeling very pleased with themselves.

Calmly now, he thought. The important thing is not to do anything rash. There's plenty of time. In fact, I've got heaps and heaps of time. They can search for me for all eternity; the ship's gone and it's impossible to find me. And until they understand what happened, until they're absolutely certain, they won't tell my mother anything. And I'll come up with something or other here.

He passed by a small, cool swamp, scrambled through some bushes, and came out onto a road, an old, cracked concrete road that ran off into the forest. Stepping over the concrete slabs, he walked to the edge of the ridge and saw the rusty girders, overgrown with creepers—the remains of some large latticework structure, half immersed in the water. And on the far bank he saw the continuation of the road, barely distinguishable under the glowing sky. Apparently there had once been a bridge here. And apparently someone had found this bridge a nuisance and had knocked it down into the river, which had not rendered it either more beautiful or more convenient. Maxim sat down on the edge of the ridge and dangled his legs. He carefully scrutinized his inner condition, reassured himself that he wasn't doing anything rash, and started thinking.

I've found the main thing I need. There's a road right here. A bad road, a crude road, and, what's more, an old road, but nonetheless a road, and on all inhabited planets roads lead to those who built them. What else do I need? I don't need food. That is, I could eat a bit, but that's just my primeval instincts at work, and we'll suppress them for now. I won't need water for at least a day and a night. There's plenty of air, although I'd prefer it if the atmosphere contained less carbon dioxide and radioactive filth. So I don't have any basic physical needs to appease. But I do need a small—in fact, to be honest, a quite primitive little—null-transmitter with a spiral circuit. What could be simpler than a primitive null-transmitter? Only a primitive null-battery. He squeezed his eyes shut, and the circuit of a transmitter based on positron emitters immediately surfaced out of his memory. If he had the components, he could assemble the little doodad in a jiffy, without even opening his eyes. He mentally ran through the assembly process several times, but when he opened his eyes, there was still no transmitter. There wasn't anything.

Robinson Crusoe, he thought with a strange feeling of curiosity. Maxim Crusoe, that is. Well, well—I don't have a thing. Just shorts with no pockets and a pair of sneakers. But I do have an island, an inhabited one. And since the island is inhabited, there's always hope that I might find a primitive null-transmitter. He earnestly attempted to think about a null-transmitter but didn't manage it very well. He kept seeing his mother all the time, as she was being informed, "Your son has disappeared without a trace," and the expression on her face, and his father rubbing his cheeks and confusedly looking around, and how cold and empty they felt . . . No, he told himself. Thinking about that isn't allowed. Anything else at all but not that, otherwise I'll never get anything done. I command and forbid. Command myself not to think about it and forbid myself to think about it. No more. He got up and set off along the road.

The forest, initially timid and sparse, gradually grew bolder, advancing closer and closer to the road. Several small, impudent young trees had already smashed through the concrete and were growing right there in the roadway. The road was obviously several decades old, or at least it had been several decades since it was used. The forest at the sides rose higher and higher, growing thicker and thicker, and in places the branches intertwined above Maxim's head. It got dark, and loud, guttural whoops started ringing out in the thickets, now on the left, now on the right. Something in there was stirring about, rustling and trampling. At one point something squat and dark, hunched down low, ran across the road about twenty steps ahead of him. Gnats droned.

It suddenly occurred to Maxim that this area was so neglected and wild, there might not be any people nearby, and it might take him several days and nights to reach them. Maxim's primeval instincts were roused once again, but he could sense that he was surrounded by plenty of live meat here and he wouldn't starve to death, that it probably wouldn't all taste great but it would be interesting to do a bit of hunting anyway. And since he was forbidden to think about the really important things, he started remembering how he and Oleg used to go hunting with the park ranger Adolph, with just their bare hands, cunning against cunning, reason against instinct, strength against strength, three days and nights at a stretch, chasing a deer through tangled, fallen trees, catching it, grabbing it by the horns, and tumbling it over onto the ground . . . Maybe there weren't any deer here, but there was no reason to doubt that the local game was edible; the moment he started pondering and got distracted, the gnats started ferociously devouring him, and everyone knew that you wouldn't starve to death on an alien planet if you yourself were edible there.

It would be fun to lose my way here and spend a year or two roaming through the forest. I could acquire a companion—some kind of wolf or bear—and we'd go hunting together and talk . . . only I'd get bored eventually, of course. And then, it doesn't look like I could get any pleasure out of wandering through these woods; there's too much iron everywhere, there's nothing to breathe . . . And anyway, first of all I have to assemble a null-transmitter . . .

Maxim stopped and listened. He could hear a hollow, monotonous booming from somewhere deep in the forest thickets, and he realized that he had been hearing this booming for a long time already but had only just noticed it. It wasn't an animal and it wasn't a waterfall—it was a mechanism, some kind of barbaric machine. It was snorting, bellowing, grating metal on metal, and scattering hideous, rusty smells. And it was getting closer.

Maxim crouched down and ran toward it without making a sound, sticking close to the side of the road, and abruptly stopped when he almost went darting out into an intersection. The road was intersected at right angles by another highway, a very muddy one, with deep, ugly ruts, and fragments of concrete slabs jutting up out of it. It was foul smelling and very, very radioactive. Maxim squatted down on his haunches and looked to his left, the direction from which the roaring of an engine and metallic rasping sounds were advancing. The ground under his feet began shuddering. It was getting even closer.

A minute later it appeared—nonsensically huge, hot, and stinking, made completely out of riveted metal, smashing down the road with its monstrous caterpillar tracks caked in mud. It didn't hurtle or trundle along, it barged its way forward, slovenly and hunchbacked, jangling sheets of iron that had come loose, stuffed full of raw plutonium and lanthanides. Moronic and menacing, with no human presence in it, mindless and dangerous, it lumbered across the intersection and went barging on, smashing the concrete, setting it crunching and squealing, and leaving behind a trail of incandescent, sweltering air as it disappeared into the forest, still lumbering and growling, until it moved away into the distance and gradually grew quieter.

Maxim caught his breath and brushed off the midges. He was astounded. He had never seen anything so absurd and preposterous in his entire life. Yes, he thought. I won't get hold of any positron emitters here. As he watched the receding monster, he suddenly noticed that the intersecting road was not simply a road but also a kind of firebreak, a narrow gap cut through the forest: the trees didn't cover the sky above it as they did above the first road. Maybe he ought to chase after the monster, he thought. Overtake it, stop it, and extinguish the reactor . . .

He listened closely; the forest was full of clamor, and the monster was wallowing about in the thickets, like a hippopotamus in a quagmire. Then the roaring of the engine started moving closer again. It was coming back. The same wheezing and growling, a surging wave of stench, clanging and rattling, and then it lumbered across the intersection again and barged back toward where it had just come from . . . No, said Maxim. I don't want to get involved with it. I don't like malicious animals and barbaric automatons. He waited for the monster to disappear from sight, walked out of the bushes, got a running start, and flew across the ripped-up, polluted intersection in a single leap.

For a while he walked very quickly, taking deep breaths in order to clear the iron behemoth's fumes out of his lungs, and then switched back to his hiking stride. He thought about what he had seen during the first two hours of life on his inhabited island and tried to assemble all these incongruous, chance events into a whole that was logically consistent. However, it was too difficult. The picture that emerged was fantastical, not real. This forest, stuffed full of old iron, was fantastical, and in it fantastical creatures called to each other in voices that were almost human. Just like in a fairy tale, an old, abandoned road led to an enchanted castle, and invisible, wicked sorcerers tried their damnedest to make life difficult for anyone who had ended up in this country. On the distant approaches, they had pelted him with meteorites, but that didn't work, so then they had burned his ship, thereby trapping their victim, and then sent out an iron dragon to get him. However, the dragon had proved to be too old and stupid, and by now they had probably realized their blunder and were preparing something a bit more modern.

Listen, Maxim told them. After all, I'm not planning to disenchant any enchanted castles and awaken your lethargic beauties. All I want is to meet one of you who is pretty bright and will help me with finding some positron emitters.

But the wicked sorcerers dug in their heels. First they set a huge, rotten tree across the roadway, then they demolished the concrete surface, dug a large pit in the ground, and filled it with rank-smelling radioactive slurry, and when even that didn't help, when the gnats grew disillusioned with biting him and abandoned him, as morning approached the sorcerers released a cold, wicked mist from out of the forest. The mist gave Maxim chilly shivers, and he set off at a run in order to warm himself up. The mist was viscous and oily, with a smell of wet metal and putrefaction, but soon it started smelling of smoke, and Maxim realized that a fire was burning somewhere nearby.

Dawn was breaking, and the sky was already almost bright with the grayness of morning, when Maxim saw the campfire at the side of the road, by a low, moss-covered stone structure with a collapsed roof and empty, black windows. Maxim couldn't see any people, but he could sense that they were somewhere nearby, that they had been here just recently and perhaps they would soon come back. He turned off the road, jumped across the roadside ditch, and set off, sinking up to his ankles in rotting leaves, toward the fire.

The campfire greeted him with its benign, primeval warmth, pleasantly agitating his slumbering instincts. Everything here was simple. Without having to greet anyone, he could squat down, reach out his hands to the flames, and wait, without saying anything, until the equally taciturn owner of the campfire handed him a hot dollop of food and a hot mug. Of course, the owner wasn't there, but a smoke-blackened cooking pot containing a pungent-smelling concoction was hanging above the campfire, and two loose coveralls of coarse material were lying a little distance away, beside a dirty, half-empty bag with shoulder straps that contained huge, dented tin mugs and some other metal objects with indeterminate functions.

Maxim sat by the fire for a while, warming himself up and looking into the flames, then got to his feet and went into the building. In fact, all that remained of the building was a stone box. He could see the brightening sky through the broken beams above his head, and it was frightening to step on the rotten boards of the floor. Bunches of bright crimson mushrooms were growing in the corners—poisonous, of course, but perfectly edible if they were well roasted. However, the thought of food immediately evaporated when Maxim spotted someone's bones, jumbled together with faded, tattered rags, lying in the semi-darkness by the wall. That gave him a bad feeling, and he turned around, walked down the ruined steps, folded his hands together into a megaphone, and yelled into the forest at the top of his voice, "*Ohoho*, you six-toed folks!" The echo almost immediately got stuck in the mist between the trees, and no one responded, except that some little birds or other started angrily and excitedly chattering above his head.

Maxim went back to the campfire, flung a few branches into the flames, and glanced into the pot. The concoction was boiling. He looked around, found something that looked like a spoon, sniffed at it, wiped it on the grass, and sniffed at it again. Then he carefully skimmed the gray scum off the concoction and shook it off the spoon onto the charred wood. He stirred the concoction, scooped up some of it from the edge, blew on it, then puckered up his lips, and tried it. It wasn't bad at all, something like tahorg liver broth. Then he looked around again and said in a loud voice, "Breakfast is ready!" He couldn't shake the feeling that his hosts were somewhere close by, but all he could see were motionless bushes, wet from the mist, and the black, gnarled trunks of trees, and all he could hear was the crackling of the campfire and the fussy chattering of the birds.

"Well, OK," he said out loud. "Suit yourselves, but I'm initiating contact."

He very quickly started enjoying the taste of it. Maybe the spoon was too big, or maybe his primeval instincts simply got the better of him, but he had lapped up a third of the pot before he even knew it. He regretfully moved a little distance away and sat there for a while, focusing on his gustatory sensations and giving the spoon another thorough wiping, but he couldn't resist it after all and took another scoop, from the very bottom, of those little, tasty, melt-in-your-mouth brown slices that were like sea cucumber. Then he moved well away, wiped the spoon yet again, and set it across the top of the pot. This was just the right time to appease his feeling of gratitude.

He jumped to his feet, selected several slim sticks, and went into the building. Stepping cautiously across the rotten floorboards and trying not to look over at the human remains in the shade, he started picking mushrooms and threading them on a stick, choosing the very firmest caps. If I could just salt you a bit, he thought, and add a bit of pepper too—but never mind, for first contact this will do anyway. We'll hang you over the fire, and all your active organic compounds will be dissipated as steam, and you'll be a delicious treat. You'll be my first contribution to the culture of this inhabited island, and the second one will be positron emitters. Suddenly it became a bit darker in the building, and he immediately sensed someone watching him. He managed to suppress his urge to abruptly swing around, counted to ten, slowly got up, and, smiling in advance, unhurriedly turned his head.

Looking in at him through the window was a long, dark face with large, despondent eyes and a mouth with its corners despondently turned down. It was looking at him without the slightest interest, with neither malice nor joy, as if it were looking not at a man from a different world but at some tedious domesticated animal that had once again clambered in where it had been told not to go. They looked at each other for several seconds, and Maxim could feel the despondency radiating from that face flood the building, sweep across the forest, across the entire planet and the universe surrounding it, and everything on all sides turned gray, despondent, and dismal. Everything had already happened, it had all happened many times over, and it would happen many more times, and there was no foreseeable salvation from this gray, despondent, dismal tedium. And then it became even darker in the building, and Maxim turned toward the door.

Standing there with his short, sturdy legs planted wide apart, and completely blocking the doorway with his broad shoulders, was a stocky man entirely covered with ginger hair and wearing a dreadful check coverall. Gazing at Maxim out of the riotous ginger thickets of his face were two gimlet-sharp blue eyes, very intent and very hostile, and yet somehow seeming equally jolly—perhaps by contrast with the universal despondency emanating from the window. This hairy roughneck had obviously also seen visitors from other worlds before, but he was used to dealing with these tiresome visitors abruptly, drastically, and decisively—without any contact-making or other such unnecessary complications. Hanging from a leather strap around his neck he had an extremely ominous-looking thick metal pipe, and with his firm, filthy hand he was pointing the outlet of this instrument for lynching alien visitors directly at Maxim's belly. It was immediately obvious that he had never even heard of the supreme value of human life. Or of the Declaration of Human Rights, or any other such magnificent achievements of progressive humanism, and if you told him about any of these things, he simply wouldn't believe you.

However, Maxim didn't have to make that choice. He held the stick with mushroom caps threaded on it out in front of him, smiled even more broadly, and enunciated with exaggerated clarity, "Peace! Friendship!" The despondent individual outside the window responded to this slogan with a long, unintelligible phrase, after which he withdrew from the zone of contact and, to judge from the sounds outside, set about heaping dry branches onto the campfire. The blue-eyed man's tousled ginger beard started moving, and growling, roaring, clanging sounds came darting out of that dense copper growth, instantly reminding Maxim of the iron dragon at the intersection. "Yes!" said Maxim, energetically nodding. "Earth! The cosmos!" He jabbed his thin stick up toward the zenith, and the ginger-bearded man obediently glanced at the smashed-in ceiling. "Maxim!" continued Maxim, prodding himself in the chest, "*Mak-sim*! My name is Maxim." For additional cogency, he struck himself on the chest, like an enraged gorilla: "Maxim!"

"*Mahh-ssim!*" the ginger-bearded man barked with a strange accent. Keeping his eyes fixed on Maxim, he launched over his shoulder a series of rumbling and clanging sounds, in which the word "Mah-sim" was repeated several times, and to which the invisible, despondent individual responded by uttering a sequence of sinister, dismal phonemes. The ginger-bearded man's blue eyes started rolling about, his yellow-toothed mouth opened wide, and he howled with laughter. When he was done laughing, the ginger-bearded man wiped his eyes with his free hand, lowered his death-dealing weapon, and unambiguously gestured to Maxim: *All right, come on out!*

Maxim gladly obeyed. He walked out onto the steps and proffered the stick with the mushrooms on it to the ginger-bearded man once again. The ginger-bearded man took the stick, turned it this way and that way, sniffed at it, and flung it aside.

"Hey, no!" Maxim protested. "Those will have you begging for more . . ."

He bent down and picked up the stick. The ginger-bearded man didn't object. He slapped Maxim on the back and pushed him toward the fire. Beside the fire he heaved down on Maxim's shoulder, making him sit, and started trying to din something into his head. But Maxim didn't listen. He was watching the despondent individual, who sat facing Maxim, drying some kind of broad, dirty rag in front of the fire. One of his feet was bare, and he kept wiggling the toes. And there were five of those toes—five, not six.

2

Gai was sitting on the edge of the bench by the window, polishing the badge on his beret with his cuff and watching Corporal Varibobu write out his travel order. The corporal's head was inclined to one side and his eyes were goggling out of it; his left hand was resting on the desk, holding down a form with a red border, and his right hand was unhurriedly tracing out calligraphic letters. It's great the way he does that, thought Gai, not without a certain envy. The inky-fingered old buzzard, twenty years in the Guards and still a pen pusher. Just look at him glaring, the pride of the brigade—any moment now he'll stick his tongue out . . . There, he's done it. Even his tongue is all inky. Bless you, Varibobu, you cracked old inkwell. We'll never meet again. And in general it's a sad business, this leaving—we got a fine set of men together, and real gentlemen officers too, and it's useful service, meaningful . . . Gai sniffed and looked out the window.

Outside the wind was blowing white dust along the wide, smooth street without sidewalks, paved with old hexagonal slabs. The walls of the identical long administrative and engineering staff buildings were glowing white, and Madam Idoya, a portly and imposing lady, was walking along, shielding her face against the dust and holding up her skirt—a brave woman, she hadn't been afraid to bring her children and follow the brigadier to these dangerous parts. The sentry outside garrison HQ, one of the rookies, wearing a new duster that was still rigid and a beret pulled right down over his ears, gave her the "present arms" salute. Then two trucks carrying educatees drove past, no doubt taking them for vaccination . . . That's right, give it to him, get him in the neck. He shouldn't go sticking his head over the side, he's got no business doing that here, this isn't some kind of public thoroughfare.

"Exactly how is your name written?" Varibobu asked. "'G-a-a-l'? Or can I simply write 'G-a-l'?"

"No way," said Gai. "My surname is Gaal. G-a-a-l."

"That's a shame," said Varibobu, pensively sucking on his pen. "If I could write 'G-a-l,' it would just fit on the line."

Write it, write it, inkpot, thought Gai. Forget the nonsense about saving lines. And they call you a corporal . . . Buttons all covered with green tarnish. Some corporal you are. Two medals, but you never even learned to shoot straight, everybody knows that . . .

The door abruptly swung open and Cornet To'ot briskly strode in, wearing the duty officer's gold armband. Gai jumped to his feet and clicked his heels. The corporal lifted his backside slightly but didn't stop writing, the old fogy. Call him a corporal . . .

"Aha," said the cornet, tearing off his dust mask in disgust. "Private Gaal. I know, I know, you're leaving us. A shame. But I'm glad for you. I hope you'll continue to serve with equal fervor in the capital."

"Yes, sir, Mr. Cornet, sir!" Gai said with true feeling. The exaltation even set his nose itching on the inside. He was very fond of Mr. Cornet To'ot, a cultured officer and a former high school teacher. And apparently the cornet appreciated his qualities too.

"You may be seated," said the cornet, walking in past the barrier to his own desk. Without bothering to sit down, he took a cursory glance at his documents and picked up the phone. Gai tactfully turned away toward the window.

Outside in the street nothing had changed. His own beloved squad tramped past in formation on the way to lunch. Gai watched them go with a sad air. Now they would reach the canteen, and Corporal Serembesh would give the command to remove their berets for the Word of Thanksgiving, the guys would roar out the Word of Thanksgiving with all their thirty throats—and meanwhile the steam is already rising above the cooking pots, and the bowls are gleaming, and good old Doga is all set to deliver that hoary old gag of his about the private and the cook . . . Really and truly, it was a shame to leave. Serving here was dangerous, and the climate was unhealthy, and the rations were really monotonous—nothing but canned stuff—but even so. Here, at least, you knew for certain that you were needed, that they couldn't manage without you. Here you faced that pernicious pressure from the South full on, taking it on the chest, and you really felt that pressure. Gai had buried so many of his friends here—over on the other side of the settlement there was an entire grove of poles with rusty helmets on them . . .

On the other hand, he was going to the capital. They wouldn't send just anyone there, and if they were sending him, it wasn't for a vacation . . . They said that from the Palace of the Fathers you could see all the Guards' parade grounds, so there was certain to be one of the Fathers observing every formation. Well, it wasn't an absolute certainty, but he might take a look every once in a while. Gai felt a sudden, feverish flush; completely out of the blue, he imagined himself being been called out of formation, and on his second stride he slipped and crashed down, flat on his face, at the commanding officer's feet, his automatic rifle clattering on the cobblestones, gaping open, and his beret wildly flying off into the air . . . He took a deep breath and stealthily looked around. God forbid . . . Yes. The capital. Nothing escaped their eyes. Well, never mind—after all, there were other men serving. And Rada, his dear sister . . . and his funny uncle with his ancient bones and primeval skulls. Oh, I miss you so badly, all my dearest ones!

He glanced out the window again and opened his mouth in bewilderment. Two men were walking along the street toward the garrison HQ. One of them was familiar: that ginger roughneck Zef, one of the especially dangerous educatees, the master sergeant of the 134th Sappers' Unit, a condemned man who earned his life by keeping the roads clear. But the other man—well, he was some kind of bogeyman, and a creepy kind of bogeyman at that. At first Gai took him for a degenerate, but then he realized that Zef wouldn't be likely to drag a degenerate into garrison

HQ. He was a really husky young guy, brown all over, as strong as an ox, and naked: all he had on was a short pair of some kind of underpants made out of some shiny material. Zef had his gun with him, but it didn't look like he was escorting this stranger; they were walking side by side, and the stranger kept trying to make Zef understand something, extravagantly waving his arms around all the time. But Zef was just letting him rattle on, and he had a totally bemused look on his face. He's some kind of savage, thought Gai. Only what was he doing out there on the highway? Maybe he was raised by bears? There have been cases like that. And he fits the part all right—just look at those muscles and the way they ripple.

He watched as the two men walked up to the sentry, and Zef, wiping away his sweat, started trying to explain something. But the sentry was a rookie; he didn't know Zef, and he prodded him under the ribs with his automatic, obviously telling him to move back to the regulation distance. Seeing this, the naked young guy got involved in the conversation. His hands flew backward and forward through the air, and his face was really strange now; Gai couldn't understand his expression at all. It was like mercury, and the man's eyes were dark, and they were shifting about rapidly . . . That was it—now the sentry was totally confused too. Now he would raise the alarm. Gai turned around.

"Mr. Cornet," he said, "permission to speak? The sergeant of the 134th Unit has brought someone in. Will you take a look?"

The cornet walked over to the window, took a look, and his eyebrows shot up. He pushed the window frame open, stuck his head out, and shouted, choking on the dust that came pouring in. "Sentry! Let them pass!"

Gai was just closing the window when there was a tramping of feet in the corridor and Zef edged into the office with his bizarre companion in tow. Tumbling in behind them, and jostling them on, came the officer of the guard and another two guys from the duty watch. Zef stood at attention, cleared his throat, fixed the cornet with his brazen blue eyes, and wheezed,

"Master sergeant of the 134th Unit, educatee Zef, begs leave to report. This man here was detained on the highway. All the signs indicate that he is insane, Mr. Cornet: he eats poisonous mushrooms, doesn't understand a word that is spoken to him, speaks in an incomprehensible fashion, and goes around, as you might be pleased to observe, naked."

While Zef was reporting, the detainee ran his agile eyes around the room, smiling at everyone there in a strange, sinister manner—his teeth were even and as white as sugar. The cornet clasped his hands behind his back, moved closer, and looked the man over from head to foot. "Who are you?" he asked.

The detainee smiled in an even more sinister manner, slapped his open hand on his chest and uttered something unintelligible; it sounded like "mah-sim." The officer of the guard guffawed, the sentries started giggling, and the cornet smiled too. Gai didn't immediately get the joke but then he remembered that in thieves' slang "mah-sim" meant "knife-eater."

"Apparently he is one of your company," the cornet remarked to Zef.

Zef shook his head, scattering a cloud of dust out of his beard. "Absolutely not," he said. "'Mah-sim' is what he calls himself, but he doesn't understand thieves' argot at all. So he isn't one of ours."

"A degenerate, probably," the officer of the guard suggested, and the cornet gave him an icy look. "Naked," the officer of the guard ardently explained, backing away toward the door. "Permission to carry on, Mr. Cornet?" he barked.

"Go," said the cornet. "And send someone to get the headquarters medical officer, Mr. Zogu. Where did you catch him?" he asked Zef.

Zef reported that the previous night he and his unit had been combing quadrant 23/07. They had destroyed four self-propelled devices and one automated device, purpose unknown, losing two men in the explosion, and everything was in order. At about seven in the morning, this unknown individual had approached

Zef's campfire from out of the forest. They had spotted him from a distance and followed him, concealing themselves in the bushes, and then chosen a convenient moment to detain him. At first Zef had taken him for a fugitive, then decided that he wasn't a fugitive but a degenerate, and was on the point of shooting him, but had changed his mind because this man . . . At this point Zef jutted out his beard, at a loss for words, and concluded, "Because it became clear to me that he wasn't a degenerate."

"From what did that become clear to you?" the cornet asked. The detainee just stood there motionless, his arms folded across his powerful chest, glancing at the cornet and Zef by turns.

Zef said it would be hard for him to explain. In the first place, this man hadn't been afraid of anything, and he still wasn't. And in addition, he had taken the soup off the fire and eaten precisely a third of it, exactly as a comrade was supposed to do, and before that he had shouted into the forest, evidently calling to Zef's men, sensing that they were somewhere nearby. And furthermore, he had tried to feed them mushrooms. The mushrooms were poisonous, and they didn't eat them or let him eat them, but he had obviously felt an urge to give them some kind of a treat, clearly as a sign of gratitude. And furthermore, everyone knew that no degenerate possesses physical abilities that exceed those of an average, frail person. But on the way here, this man had worn Zef out as if Zef were a little kid, strolling through patches of underbrush and fallen trees as if they were flat ground, jumping across ditches, and then waiting for Zef on the other side. And also, for some reason—maybe out of sheer bravado?—he had sometimes taken Zef in his arms and run two or three hundred strides with him like that.

The cornet adopted a pose of intense concentration while listening to Zef, but the moment Zef stopped speaking, he abruptly turned to the detainee and barked point-blank at him in Hontian, "Your name? Rank? Assignment?"

Gai was delighted by the adroitness of the move, but the detainee clearly didn't understand Hontian either. He bared his magnificent teeth again, slapped himself on the chest, and said "Mah-sim," then jabbed his finger into the educatee's side and said "Zef," and after that he started talking—slowly, with long pauses, pointing up at the ceiling or down at the floor, or running his hands through the air around himself. Gai thought that he picked up several familiar words in this speech, but those words had nothing at all to do with the matter at hand, or with each other. "Bedstead," the detainee said, and then "Hurly-burly, hurly-burly . . . Squirm . . ."

When he fell silent, Corporal Varibobu piped up. "I think he's a cunning spy," the old inkpot declared. "We should report him to the brigadier."

However, the cornet took no notice of him. "You may go, Zef," he said. "You have demonstrated zeal, and that will be credited to your account."

"Most obliged to you, Mr. Cornet," Zef barked, and he had already turned to go when suddenly the detainee gave a quiet whoop, leaned over the barrier, and grabbed the bundle of blank forms lying on the desk in front of the corporal. The old fogy was frightened to death (how about that for a guardsman!), and he recoiled, flinging his pen at the savage. The savage deftly caught the pen in midair, propped himself against the barrier where he was standing, and started sketching something on a form, taking no notice of Gai or Zef, who had grabbed hold of his sides.

"As you were!" the cornet ordered, and Gai willingly obeyed; holding this brown bear was just like trying to stop a tank by grabbing hold of its caterpillar tread. The cornet and Zef stood on each side of the detainee and looked at what he was scribbling.

"I think it's a diagram of the World," Zef said uncertainly.

"Hmm . . ." the cornet responded.

"But of course! There in the center is the World Light, and this here is the World . . . And as he understands things, we are here."

"But why is it all flat?" the cornet skeptically asked.

Zef shrugged. "Perhaps it's a child's perception. Infantil-
ism . . . Look here, see? This is how he shows the way he got
here."

"Yes, possibly. I've heard about that kind of insanity."

Gai finally managed to squeeze between the firm, smooth
shoulder of the detainee and Zef's prickly ginger thickets. He
thought the drawing he saw was funny. It was how schoolchildren in the first grade represented the World: a little circle at
the center, signifying the World Light, a large circle around it, signifying the Sphere of the World, and on its circumference, a thick
black dot. You only had to add little arms and legs to it and you
had "This is the World, and this is me." The unfortunate freak
hadn't even shown the circumference of the World correctly, he'd
drawn some sort of oval. Well, he clearly was deranged . . . And
he'd also drawn a dotted line leading from under the ground to
that dot, as if to say, *Look, that's how I got here!*

Meanwhile the detainee took another form and rapidly
sketched two little Spheres of the World in opposite corners,
joined them together with a dotted line, and then drew in some
kind of squiggles. Zef whistled hopelessly and asked the cornet,
"Permission to retire?"

But the cornet didn't let him go. "*Uhhh* . . . Zef," he said. "As
I recall, you used to be active in the area of . . . uh . . ." He tapped
a bent finger against his temple.

"Yes, sir," Zef replied after a pause.

The cornet started striding around the office. "Could you not
perhaps . . . *uhhh* . . . how can I put it . . . formulate your opinion
concerning the individual in question? Professionally, if I might
express myself in that way."

"I couldn't really say," said Zef. "Under the terms of my sentence, I have no right to act in a professional capacity."

"I understand," said the cornet. "That's quite correct. I com-
mend you. *Buuut* . . ."

Zef stood there at attention, with his blue eyes open wide.
But the cornet was clearly experiencing a certain degree of

discomfiture. Gai understood him very well. This was an important incident, of national significance. (What if this savage turned out to be a spy after all?) And HQ medical officer Zogu was a fine guardsman, of course, a brilliant guardsman, but he was only the HQ medical officer. Whereas the ginger roughneck Zef, before he became involved in criminal activities, had been very good at his job and was actually a great celebrity. But it was possible to understand him too. For, after all, everyone, even a criminal, even a criminal who has acknowledged his crime, wants to live. And the law was ruthless with regard to those already condemned to death: the slightest violation meant execution. On the spot. It was the only way; in times like these, leniency turned out to be cruelty and the only true leniency lay in cruelty. The law was ruthless but wise.

"Well then," said the cornet. "There's nothing to be done . . . But, speaking strictly personally—do you really think he's insane?"

Zef hesitated again. "Speaking strictly personally?" he repeated. "Well, of course, in speaking strictly personally, a man is inherently inclined to make mistakes . . . Well then, speaking strictly personally, I am inclined to regard this as a clear case of dissociated personality, with displacement and replacement of the genuine ego by an imaginary one. And, speaking strictly personally, on the basis of my own experience of life, I would recommend electroshock and phlcofcrous medication."

Corporal Varibobu stealthily noted all of this down, but the cornet couldn't be fooled that easily. He took the sheet of paper with the notes from the corporal and stuck it in the pocket of his field jacket. Mah-sim started talking again, addressing the cornet and Zef by turns—there was something he wanted, the poor fellow, something that he thought wasn't right—but at that point the door opened and the HQ medical officer walked in, apparently having been torn away from his lunch.

"Greetings, To'ot," he sullenly declared. "What's the problem? I see that you are alive and well, and that is some comfort to me. But who is this character?"

"'The educatees caught him in the forest," the cornet explained.
"I suspect that he's insane."

"He's a malingerer, not a madman," the medical officer
growled, pouring himself a glass of water from the carafe. "Send
him back into the forest and let him work."

"He's not one of ours," the cornet objected. "And we don't
know where he came from. I think the degenerates must have
captured him at some time; he went crazy while he was with
them and defected to us."

"That's right," the medic growled. "You'd have to be crazy to
defect to us." He walked over to the detainee and immediately
reached out to grab hold of his eyelids. The detainee gave a spine-
chilling grin and gently pushed him away. "Hey, hey!" said the
medical officer, deftly grabbing hold of his ear. "You just stand
still, my fine stallion!"

The detainee yielded. The medic turned back his eyelids, pal-
pated his neck and throat while whistling to himself, bent the
detainee's arms and straightened them out again, leaned down
and struck him below the knees, then went back to the carafe
and drank another glass of water.

"Heartburn," he announced.

Gai looked at Zef. The ginger-bearded man was standing off
to one side, with his gun set beside his legs, gazing at the wall
with emphatic indifference. The medical officer drank his fill and
went back to the freak. He felt him and tapped him all over,
looked at his teeth, punched him twice in the stomach, and then
took a little flat box out of his pocket, unwound a wire, plugged
it into a socket, and started applying the little box to various parts
of the savage's body.

"Right," he said, coiling up the wire. "And he's mute too,
is he?"

"No," said the cornet. "He talks, but in some kind of bear's
language. He only uses our words sometimes, and even then
they're distorted. He doesn't understand us. And these are his
drawings."

The HQ medic looked at the drawings. "Well, well, well," he said. "Amusing." He grabbed the corporal's pen and rapidly drew a cat on one of the forms, the way that children draw cats, all sticks and circles. "What do you say to this, my friend?" he asked, handing the drawing to the freak.

Without pondering for even a second, the freak started scratching away with the pen, and a strange animal, with a thick coat of fur and a heavy, menacing look in its eyes, appeared beside the cat. Gai didn't know any animal like that, but he did understand one thing: this was nothing like a child's drawing. It was drawn really well—quite wonderfully, in fact. Just to look at it was frightening. The medical officer reached out his hand for the pen, but the freak moved back and drew a different animal, a totally bizarre one, with huge ears, wrinkly skin, and a thick tail instead of a nose.

"Wonderful!" the medic exclaimed, slapping his sides.

However, the freak didn't stop at that. And what he went on to draw wasn't an animal but clearly some kind of machine—it looked like a large, transparent shell. He deftly drew in a little figure sitting inside the shell, tapped his finger on the figure, then tapped himself on the chest with the same finger, and said, *"Mah-ssim."*

"He could have seen that thing by the river," said Zef, who had walked up without being heard. "We burned something like that last night. But those monsters . . ." he shook his head.

The medical officer seemed to notice him for the first time. "Ah, professor!" he exclaimed with exaggerated delight. "So that's it, I thought there was an odd stink in the office! Would you be so kind, dear colleague, as to pronounce your wise judgments from that corner over there? You would greatly oblige me . . ."

Varibobu giggled, and the cornet said in a severe voice, "Stand by the doors, Zef, and don't forget yourself."

"Well, all right," the medic said. "What are you thinking of doing with him, To'ot?"

"That depends on your diagnosis, Zogu," the cornet replied. "If he's a malingerer, I'll hand him over to the prosecutor's office, and they'll get to the bottom of things. But if he's a madman—"

"He's not a malingerer, To'ot," the HQ medical officer said emphatically. "The prosecutor's office is definitely not the place for him. But I know a place where they will be interested in him. Where's the brigadier?"

"The brigadier is out on the highway."

"Well, that doesn't matter anyway. You're the duty officer, aren't you, To'ot? So you just dispatch this extremely curious individual to this address . . ." The medic propped himself against the barrier, shielding himself from everyone with his shoulders and elbows, and wrote something on the back of the last drawing.

"But what is this?" the cornet asked.

"This? It's a certain department that will be grateful to you for your freak, To'ot. I warrant you that."

The cornet uncertainly twirled the form in his hands, then walked over to the farthest corner of the office and beckoned the medic with his finger. They talked there for a while in low voices, so that only isolated phrases spoken by Mr. Zogu could be made out: ". . . The Department of Propaganda . . . Send him with a man you can trust . . . It's not so very secret! . . . I warrant you . . . Order him to forget the matter . . . Damn it, why, a snot-nosed kid won't understand anything anyway! . . ."

"All right," the cornet said eventually. "Write a cover letter, Corporal Varibobu!"

The corporal lifted his backside off his seat a little.

"Is the travel order for Guards private Gaal ready?"

"Yes, sir."

"Add prisoner under escort Mah-sim to the travel order. He is to be escorted without handcuffs and is permitted to travel in a public car . . . Private Gaal!"

Gai clicked his heels and drew himself erect. "At your command, Mr. Cornet!"

"Before presenting yourself at your new duty station in our capital city, deliver the detainee to the address indicated on this sheet of paper. After discharging these instructions, hand the note to the duty officer at your new station. Forget the address. This is your final assignment, Gaal, and you will of course carry it out as befits a fine young guardsman."

"Your word is my command!" Gai shouted in a rush of indescribable rapture. A surge of joy, pride, and happiness, a hot wave of ravishing devotion, swept over him, lifting him up and bearing him onward toward the heavens. Oh, these sweet moments of ecstasy, these unforgettable moments, these moments that shook him to the core of his being, these moments when he sprouted wings, these moments of sweet contempt for everything coarse, material, and corporeal . . . These moments when he thirsted for the fire and the command, when he yearned for the command that would unite him with the fire, hurl him into the fire, against a thousand enemies, against gaping gun muzzles, against millions of bullets . . . and that was still not all, it would be even sweeter still, the ecstasy would blind and consume . . . Oh, the fire! Oh, the glory! The command, the command! And there it is, there it is! . . . He gets to his feet, this fine, strapping, handsome fellow, the pride of the brigade, our Corporal Varibobu, like a flaming torch, like a statue of glory and loyalty, and he starts singing, and we all take up the refrain, every one of us:

> The Battle Guards advance with fearsome cries,
> Battle medals gleaming, faithful to their pledge,
> Sweeping all hostile fortresses aside, their blazing eyes
> Glinting as bright as blood-drops on a sharp sword's edge.

And they all sang. The brilliant Cornet To'ot sang, that very model of a Guards officer, for whom Gai wanted so badly, at this very instant, to lay down his life, his soul, and everything, to the strains of this very march. And the HQ medical officer Zogu sang, the very model of a brother of mercy, as coarse as a genuine soldier and as gentle as a mother's hands. And our Corporal Varibobu, ours to the very marrow of his bones, an old war dog, a veteran turned gray haired in battle. Oh, how the battle medals glitter on his distinguished threadbare tunic; for him there is nothing else but service, nothing apart from devotion.

Do you know us, our Unknown Fathers? Raise your weary heads and look on us, for after all you see everything, and then surely you must see that we are here, on the distant, barbarous outskirts of our country. We will die in rapture and in torment for the happiness of our motherland!

> *Our iron fists all barriers obliterate*
> *The Unknown Fathers are well satisfied!*
> *Our foes bemoan their dire, inexorable fate!*
> *Forward, oh gallant Guards, advance with pride!*
>
> *Indomitable guardsmen, the law's incisive blade,*
> *When Guards appear upon the battle scene,*
> *Swift into combat, and valiant in the fray,*
> *The Unknown Fathers' hearts are tranquil and serene!*

But what is this? He isn't singing, he's just standing there, with his legs sprawling, leaning against the barrier, and turning his idiotic brown head to and fro, with his eyes darting around, and he keeps grinning, he keeps baring his teeth . . . Who is that blackguard grinning at? Oh, how I'd love to walk up to him, uttering a fearsome cry, and take a swing with my guardsman's fist at that abominable white grin . . . But I mustn't, I mustn't, that's not the Guards' way. He is only a poor freak, a pitiful invalid, true happiness is unachievable to him, he is a blind nonentity, a pitiful fragment of humanity . . .

But this ginger-haired bastard, doubled over in the corner in agonizing pain . . . Ah no, that's a different matter: You always get headaches when we labor for breath in our rapture, when we sing our battle march and are prepared to rupture our lungs in order to sing it through to the end! You lousy educatee, you hideous criminal, you ginger bandit, I'll grab you by your chest and by your foul beard! Get up, you bastard! Stand to attention when guardsmen are singing their march! And I'll smash you across your head, across your head, across your filthy mug, across your insolent, goggling eyes . . . Take that, and that . . .

Gai flung the educatee away, clicked his heels, and turned toward the cornet. As always after a fit of rapturous exhilaration, he felt a ringing in his ears, and the world was sweetly drifting and swaying in front of his eyes.

Corporal Varibobu, blue from the strain, was feebly clearing his throat. The HQ medical officer, sweaty and crimson, was voraciously drinking water straight from the carafe and tugging a handkerchief out of his pocket. The cornet was scowling with a vacant expression, as if he was trying to remember something. By the door, ginger-haired Zef was squirming about in a dirty heap of check rags. His face was smashed and bloody, and he was feebly groaning through his teeth. And Mah-sim wasn't smiling any longer. His face had frozen, becoming entirely like an ordinary human face, and he was gazing round-eyed at Gai, with his mouth hanging open.

"Private Gaal," the cornet said in a cracked voice. "*Uhhh* . . . I wanted to say something to you . . . or have I already said it? . . . Wait, Zogu, leave me at least a sip of water, will you . . ."

3

Maxim woke up feeling sluggish and heavy headed. The room was stifling; the window had been closed at night again. But then, opening the window didn't make much difference. The city was too close; during the day he could see its motionless, reddish-brown cap of repulsive fumes, which the wind carried this way, and neither the distance nor the height of his room on the fifth floor nor the park down below were any help. What I could do with right now is an ion shower, thought Maxim, and then dart out naked into the garden—not this lousy, half-rotted garden, all gray from the fumes, but our garden, somewhere outside Leningrad, on the Karelian Isthmus—and then run about nine miles around the lake at full speed, and swim across the lake, and then walk along the bottom of it for about twenty minutes to exercise my lungs a bit, clambering over the slippery underwater boulders.

He jumped up, swung the window open, stuck his head out under the fine drizzle, took a deep breath of the damp air, and started coughing—the air was full of all sorts of stuff that shouldn't be there, and the raindrops left a metallic aftertaste on his tongue. Cars hissed and whistled as they hurtled along the express highway. Down below the window, wet foliage glistened and broken glass glimmered on top of a high stone wall. A man in a wet cape was walking around in the park, scraping fallen leaves together into a heap. Through the pall of rain Maxim could vaguely make out the brick building of some kind of factory on the outskirts of the city. As always, thick streams of poisonous smoke were slowly creeping out of its two tall chimneys and drooping back down toward the ground.

A stifling world. A troubled, sickly world. It's absolutely dreary and unappealing, like that official building where the men

34

with the bright buttons and bad teeth suddenly, completely out of the blue, started howling, straining their voices until they went hoarse, Gai, that likable, handsome young fellow, started beating that red-bearded Zef's face to a bloody pulp, and Zef didn't even try to resist. A troubled world . . . A radioactive river, an absurd iron dragon, polluted air, and disheveled passengers in a lumbering, three-story metal box on wheels that pours out bluish-gray carbon monoxide fumes. And another savage scene—in that very same passenger car—when those coarse men, who smelled of poorly refined alcohol for some reason, reduced an elderly woman to tears with their crude laughter and gestures, and no one stuck up for her; the car was absolutely jam-packed, but everyone looked the other way. Only Gai jumped to his feet, pale-faced with fury, or perhaps fear, and shouted something at them, and they cleared off . . . An awful lot of fury, an awful lot of fear, an awful lot of resentment.

Everyone here is resentful and repressed—either resentful or repressed. Gai is obviously a good-natured, likable kind of person, but sometimes he would suddenly fly into an inexplicable rage and start frenziedly quarreling with the people beside him in the car, and giving me surly looks, and then just as suddenly he would relapse into a profound stupor. And nobody else in the car behaved any better. They sat or lay there perfectly peacefully for hours, talking quietly, even smiling and quietly laughing, and then suddenly someone would start cantankerously griping at the person next to him, and the other person would nervously snap back, and instead of trying to calm them down, the people around them got sucked into the quarrel, and the fracas expanded until it engulfed the entire car, and then everybody was yelling at everybody else, threatening and jostling, and somebody was reaching over somebody else's head, waving his fists about, and somebody was grabbed by the collar, children were wailing at the tops of their voices, and somebody angrily tweaked their ears, and then everybody gradually quieted down, and they were all surly with each other, reluctant to talk, turning their faces away . . .

But sometimes the ruckus turned into something absolutely outrageous, with people's eyes goggling out of their heads, their faces breaking out in red blotches, and their voices raised to bloodcurdling shrieks, while some roared with laughter, some sang, and some prayed, raising their trembling hands above their heads. An insane asylum . . . And those cheerless, melancholy gray fields drifting by outside the windows, stations blackened with smoke, squalid villages, ruins of some kind that hadn't been cleared away, and gaunt, ragged women watching the train go by with their hollow, dismal eyes . . .

Maxim moved back from the window, limply stood in the middle of the cramped little room for a while with a feeling of apathy and mental exhaustion, then forced himself to gather his strength and limber up a bit, using the unwieldy wooden table as his apparatus. It won't take long before I get completely out of shape like this, he anxiously thought. I can probably cope with another day or two, but then I'll have to hit the road and roam around in the forest for a while . . . It would be good to head for the mountains—the mountains they have here look glorious, really wild. It's a fairly long distance, of course; I couldn't do it in one night . . . What was it that Gai called them? "Zartak." I wonder if that's their name or just mountains in general. But anyway, the mountains are out of the question. Not on my agenda. I've been here for ten days already, and nothing has been done yet . . .

He squeezed into the shower stall and spent several minutes snorting and rubbing himself down under the heavy artificial rain, which was every bit as repulsive as the genuine kind. It was a little bit colder, but the water was hard and limy, and what was more, it had been chlorinated, and it had also been run through metal pipes.

He wiped himself off with a disinfected towel, and then, feeling dissatisfied with everything—this murky morning, and this suffocating world, and his own idiotic situation, and the fatty breakfast that he would have to eat now—he went back into the room in order to make up the bed, an ugly contraption of iron bars with a greasy, striped pancake of a mattress under the clean sheet.

His breakfast had already been brought in and it was steaming and stinking on the table. Fish was closing the window again.

"Hello," Maxim said to her in the local language. "Mustn't. Window."

"Hello," she replied, clicking the numerous bolts shut. "Must. Rain. Bad."

"Fish," Maxim said in Russian. In fact her name was Nolu, but from the very beginning Maxim had dubbed her Fish—for the general expression of her face and her imperturbability.

She turned around and looked at him with unblinking eyes for a moment. For the umpteenth time, she set her finger to the tip of her nose and said "Woman," then she prodded Maxim with her finger and said "Man," and then she jabbed her finger in the direction of the loose coverall that he was so sick of, hanging on the back of a chair. "Clothes. Must!" For some reason she couldn't bear to see a man in just his shorts. For some reason she needed a man to swaddle himself all the way from his feet right up to his neck.

He started getting dressed and she started making his bed, although Maxim always told her he would do that himself. She moved the table, which Maxim always set against the wall, back into the middle of the room, and resolutely turned the valve of the heating system, which Maxim always set as high as it would go, right back down low again, and Maxim's monotonous repetitions of "Mustn't" all shattered against her equally monotonous repetitions of "Must."

After fastening the coverall at the neck with its single broken button, Maxim went over to the table and prodded at his breakfast with a two-pronged fork. The usual dialogue ensued.

"I don't want. Mustn't."

"Must. Food. Breakfast."

"I don't want. Tastes bad."

"Must. Breakfast. Tastes good."

"Fish," Maxim said to her with sincere feeling, "you're a cruel person. If you ended up with me on Earth, I'd run myself ragged in order to find you food that you liked."

"I don't understand," she regretfully said. "What is 'fish'?"

As he queasily chewed on a fatty morsel, Maxim took a piece of paper and drew a bream, viewed head-on. She carefully studied the drawing and put it in the pocket of her robe. She collected all the drawings that Maxim made and carried them off somewhere. Maxim drew a lot, and quite voluntarily. He enjoyed it; during his free time and at night when he couldn't sleep, there was absolutely nothing to do here. He drew animals and people, traced out tables and diagrams, and reproduced anatomical cross sections. He drew Professor Megu, looking like a hippopotamus, and a hippopotamus looking like Professor Megu. He set out the universal tables of Lincos, Freudenthal's invented language, and plans of machines, and diagrams of historical sequences; he used up masses of paper, and it all disappeared into Fish's pocket, but without any apparent consequences for the process of contact. Professor Megu, a.k.a. Hippopotamus, had his own method, and he had no intention of departing from it.

Hippopotamus had taken absolutely no interest in the Lincos universal table, the study of which was supposed to be the starting point for any first contact. Fish was the only one who taught the new arrival the local language, and she only did that in order to make it easier to deal with him, so that he would close the window and not walk around without his coverall. No experts in first contact were involved at all. Maxim was handled by Hippopotamus and only Hippopotamus.

However, Hippopotamus did have at his disposal a rather powerful research tool—mentoscopic technology—and Maxim spent from fourteen to sixteen hours a day in the scanning chair. Moreover, Hippopotamus's mentoscope was a good one; it allowed him to penetrate rather deeply into a subject's memories, and it had extremely high-resolution capability. Possessing a machine like this, it might perhaps have been possible

to manage without any knowledge of language. But Hippopotamus used his mentoscope in a rather strange manner. He
quite categorically, even rather indignantly, refused to display
Maxim's mentograms, and dealt with those mentograms in a
quite extraordinary manner. Maxim had deliberately developed
an entire program of memories that should have given the indigenous population here a fairly adequate impression of the social,
economic, and cultural life of Earth. But mentograms of that
kind entirely failed to rouse Hippopotamus's enthusiasm. He
contorted his features into a morose grimace, mumbled, walked
away and started making telephone calls, or sat down at the
desk and started tediously nagging his assistant, in the process
frequently repeating the succulent little word "massaraksh." But
when the screen showed Maxim blowing up an immense ice
boulder that had pinned down his ship, or blasting an armored
wolf to shreds with his scorcher, or recapturing an express
laboratory from a gigantic, stupid pseudo-octopus, it was literally quite impossible to drag Hippopotamus away from the
mentoscope, even by the ears. He quietly squealed, gleefully
slapped his hands on his bald patch, and menacingly yelled at his
exhausted assistant, who was keeping an eye on the recording
of the images. The spectacle of a chromospheric prominence
threw the professor into raptures as intense as if he had never
seen anything of the kind in his life, and he really enjoyed the
love scenes, which Maxim had mostly borrowed from movies,
in order to give the indigenous population here some impression
of the emotional life of humankind.

This absurd attitude to the material reduced Maxim to cheerless speculation; it gave him the impression that Hippopotamus
was not a professor at all but merely a mentoscope operator,
preparing material for the genuine contact commission, whom
Maxim still had to meet, and when that would happen remained
unknown. Which meant Hippopotamus was a rather primitive
individual, like the little kid in *War and Peace* who was only interested in battle scenes. And that was galling. Maxim represented

Earth, and—honestly and truly!—he really had every right to expect a more serious contact partner.

Of course, he could suppose that this world was situated on an intersection of certain unidentified interstellar highways, and that aliens were a common occurrence here. Such a common occurrence, in fact, that they no longer bothered to set up special, authoritative commissions for every new arrival but simply pumped the most impressive information out of him and left it at that. One argument in favor of such an assumption was the efficiency that had been demonstrated by the men with bright buttons, who were clearly not specialists, in coming to grips with the situation and dispatching the new arrival to the appropriate destination. Or perhaps some nonhumanoids who had been here earlier had left such bad memories behind them that now the local population regarded any alien visitor with categorical distrust, and in that case all the ballyhoo being kicked up over Professor Hippopotamus's mentoscope was no more than a facade, a pretense at contact, a way of dragging things out until Maxim's fate was decided by certain higher authorities.

One way or another, this is a total disaster for me, Maxim decided, gagging on his final piece of food. I have to learn the language as quickly as possible, and then everything will become clear.

"Good," said Fish, taking away his plate. "We go."

Maxim sighed and got up. They walked out into the corridor. It was a long, dirty-blue corridor, with long rows of closed doors, exactly like the door of Maxim's room, on the right and the left. Maxim had never met anyone here, but on a couple of occasions he had heard strange, agitated voices from behind doors. Perhaps other aliens awaiting their fate were kept here too?

Fish walked in front with a broad, male stride, as straight as a ramrod, and Maxim suddenly felt very sorry for her. This country clearly still had no concept of the beauty industry, and poor Fish was left entirely to her own devices. With that sparse, colorless hair protruding from under her white cap, those huge shoulder blades bulging under her white coat, and those hideously skinny legs, it must be impossible to put a brave face on things—except perhaps with beings from other planets, and even then only with the nonhumanoids. The professor's assistant treated her disdainfully, and Hippopotamus took absolutely no notice of her; the only thing he ever said to her was *"Yyy,"* which was probably his version of the intercosmic *"Ehhh . . ."* Recalling his own far-from-generous attitude toward her, Maxim felt a sudden pang of conscience. He hurried to catch up with her, stroked her bony shoulder, and said, "Nolu a fine girl. Good."

She glanced up at him with her dry face, looking more than ever like a startled bream face-on. She removed his hand, knitted her almost invisible brows, and declared in a severe tone of voice, "Maxim not good. Man. Woman. Mustn't."

Feeling embarrassed, Maxim dropped back again, and they walked to the end of the corridor like that. Fish pushed open a door and they found themselves in the large, bright room that Maxim had dubbed the "reception area." The windows here were tastelessly decorated with rectangular grilles of thick iron bars, and there was a tall, leather-upholstered door that led into Hippopotamus's laboratory. And also, for some reason, there were always two strapping, rather slow-moving representatives of the local population who sat by that door, without responding to any greetings and appearing to be in a permanent state of trance.

As usual, Fish walked straight through into the laboratory, leaving Maxim in the reception area. As usual, Maxim said hello, and as usual, the men didn't reply. The door into the laboratory was left slightly ajar, and Maxim could hear Hippopotamus's irritated voice and the loud clicking of the activated mentoscope. He walked over to a window and looked out for a while at the misty, wet landscape and the forested plain, dissected by the express highway, and at a tall metal tower that was barely visible in the rain, but he quickly grew bored and walked into the laboratory without waiting to be asked.

Here, as usual, the air had a pleasant smell of ozone, the duplicate screens of the mentoscope were flickering, and the bald-headed, overworked assistant with a name that was impossible to remember and the new Russian nickname Floor Lamp was pretending to adjust the apparatus while in fact intently listening to the ruckus. Sitting in Hippopotamus's chair at Hippopotamus's desk was a stranger with a square, peeling face and red, puffy eyes. Hippopotamus was standing in front of him with his feet planted wide and his hands on his hips, leaning slightly forward. He was yelling. His neck was bluish-gray, his bald patch was blazing a bright sunset purple, and spray was flying out of his mouth in all directions.

Trying not to attract attention, Maxim quietly walked through to his work seat and said hello to the assistant in a quiet voice. Floor Lamp, a nervous, hassled kind of individual, recoiled in horror, his foot slipped on a thick cable, and Maxim only just managed to grab his shoulders in time. The unfortunate Floor Lamp went limp, his eyes rolled back and up, and the blood completely drained from his face. He was a strange man, and hysterically afraid of Maxim. Fish appeared out of nowhere with a little bottle, already opened, that was immediately held up to Floor Lamp's nose. Floor Lamp hiccupped and came back to life, and before he could slip back into oblivion, Maxim leaned him against a metal cupboard and hastily moved away.

On taking his place in the scanning chair, Maxim discovered that the stranger with the peeling face had stopped listening to Hippopotamus and was instead intently studying him. Maxim amiably smiled. The stranger inclined his head slightly. At this point Hippopotamus slammed his fist down onto the desk with an appalling crash and grabbed the phone. The stranger took advantage of the pause that followed to utter several words, of which Maxim could only make out "must" and "mustn't." The stranger picked up a sheet of thick, bluish paper with a bright green border off the desk and fluttered it in the air in front of Hippopotamus's face. Hippopotamus peevishly waved it aside and instantly started barking into the phone. "Must," "mustn't" and the incomprehensible "massaraksh" gushed out of him like the bounties flooding out of a horn of plenty, and Maxim also caught the word for "window." It all ended with Hippopotamus angrily flinging down the receiver and bellowing at the stranger several more times, spraying him with saliva from head to foot, before shooting out of the room and slamming the door behind him.

The stranger mopped off his face with a handkerchief, got up out of his chair, opened a long, flat box that was lying on the windowsill, and took some kind of dark clothing out of it.

"Come here," he said to Maxim. "Get dressed."

Maxim looked over at Fish.

"Go," said Fish. "Get dressed. Must."

Maxim realized that the long-awaited turning point in his destiny was finally arriving: someone somewhere had decided something. Forgetting Fish's admonitions, he immediately pulled off the ugly coverall and arrayed himself, with the stranger's help, in the new attire. To Maxim's mind, this attire was not remarkable for either its beauty or its comfort, but it was exactly the same as what the stranger himself was wearing. He could even have surmised that the stranger had sacrificed his own spare set of clothes, since the sleeves were too short while the trousers hung down behind like a sack and kept slipping off Maxim's hips. However, everyone else present found Maxim's appearance in his new clothes very much to their liking. The stranger muttered something approving and Fish, softening the features of her face—as far as that is possible for a bream— stroked Maxim's shoulders and tugged the jacket down on him, and even Floor Lamp flashed a pallid smile from his refuge behind the control desk.

"Let's go," the stranger said, and set off toward the door through which the enraged Hippopotamus had rushed out.

"Good-bye," Maxim said to Fish. "Thank you," he added in Russian.

"Good-bye," Fish replied. "Maxim good. Healthy. Must."

She seemed to be moved. Or perhaps she was concerned because the suit didn't fit very well? Maxim waved to poor Floor Lamp and hurried after the stranger.

They walked through several rooms cluttered with ponderous, antiquated apparatuses, rode down to the first floor in an elevator that rattled and clanged, and arrived in the spacious, low vestibule to which Gai had brought Maxim several days earlier. And just like several days earlier, they had to wait while documents of some kind were written out, while a funny little man in a ludicrous hat scratched something on pink forms, and the red-eyed stranger scratched something on green forms, and then a young woman with optical enhancers on her eyes applied violet impressions to these forms, and everybody exchanged forms and impressions, in the process getting confused and shouting at each other, and grabbing the phone, and eventually the little man in the ludicrous hat took two green forms and one pink one for himself, tearing the pink form in half and giving one half to the girl who had applied the impressions, and the stranger with the peeling face was given two pink forms and a piece of thick blue cardboard, as well as a round metal counter with words stamped on it, and a minute later he gave all of this to a tall, strapping man with bright buttons who was standing by the exit, only twenty steps away from the little man in the ludicrous headgear, and as they were already walking out into the street, the strapping man started hoarsely shouting, and the red-eyed stranger went back again, and when he came back explained to Maxim that he had forgotten to take the square of cardboard, which he stuffed inside his jacket with a deep sigh. Only after that was Maxim, who was already streaming with sweat, allowed to get into an irrationally long automobile, taking a seat to the right of the red-eyed man, who was extremely agitated and panting hard and kept reciting Hippopotamus's favorite mantra: "massaraksh."

The car started growling and smoothly moved off, winding its way out through a motionless herd of other cars, all empty and wet, before driving across the large, asphalted square in front of the building, around an immense flower bed with withered flowers, past a high yellow wall with broken glass scattered along its top, and finally rolling up to the turn onto the express highway, where it braked to a sharp halt.

"Massaraksh," the red-eyed man hissed again, and switched off the engine.

A long column of identical trucks, with bodies made of crookedly riveted, bent iron, painted in blotches, stretched out along the highway. Rows of motionless round objects with a damp metallic glint protruded above the sides of the trucks, which were moving at a leisurely pace and maintaining the correct intervals, with their engines smoothly murmuring, and diffusing an appalling stench of organic combustion products.

Maxim examined the door on his side, figured out what did what, and raised the window. Without looking at him, the red-eyed man uttered a long phrase that was absolutely incomprehensible.

"I don't understand," said Maxim.

The red-eyed man turned toward him with an expression of surprise and, if his intonation was anything to go by, asked a question.

"I don't understand," Maxim repeated.

The red-eyed man seemed even more surprised by that. He reached into his pocket and took out a flat box filled with little white sticks, stuck one of them in his mouth, and offered the others to Maxim. Out of politeness Maxim took the little box and stated examining it. The box was made of cardboard and had a pungent smell of dried plant matter of some kind. Maxim took one of the little sticks, bit off a small piece, and chewed it. Then he hastily lowered the window, stuck his head out and spat. It wasn't food.

"Mustn't," he said, handing the little box back to the red-eyed man. "Tastes bad."

The red-eyed man looked at him with his mouth half-open and the little white stick adhering to his lip and dangling from it. Following the local rules, Maxim touched the tip of his own nose with one finger and introduced himself: "Maxim." The red-eyed man muttered something and a little flame suddenly appeared in his hand; he lowered the end of the little white stick into it, and immediately the car was filled with nauseating smoke.

"Massaraksh!" Maxim exclaimed, and indignantly flung the door open. "Mustn't!"

He had realized what the little sticks were. In the passenger car that he traveled in with Gai, almost all the men had been poisoning the air with exactly the same kind of smoke, only they hadn't used little white sticks to do it but long or short wooden objects that looked like children's whistles from some ancient era. They were breathing in some kind of narcotic—undoubtedly an extremely injurious habit, and at that time, in the train, Maxim's only consolation had been that the likable Gai was clearly also categorically opposed to this custom.

The stranger hurriedly tossed the little narcotic stick out the window and for some reason flapped his hand in front of his face. Just to be on the safe side, Maxim also flapped his hand and then introduced himself again. The red-eyed man turned out to be called Fank, and that was as far as the conversation went. They sat there for about five minutes, exchanging affable glances and taking turns pointing at the endless column of trucks and repeating "massaraksh" to each other. Then the interminable column finally came to an end, and Fank drove out onto the highway.

He must have been in a hurry. In any case, he immediately revved up the engine to a velvety roar, switched on some device that broadcast an abhorrent howling, and set off—in Maxim's opinion completely disregarding every rule of safety—racing along the highway, overtaking the column, and barely managing to dodge the cars hurtling toward him.

They passed the column of trucks and then, almost flying out onto the roadside, passed a wide red carriage with a solitary, very wet driver; they slipped past a wooden cart on wobbling wheels with spokes, drawn by a wet fossil of an animal, drove a group of howling pedestrians wearing canvas cloaks into a ditch, and then flew under the sheltering branches of huge trees with spreading crowns, planted in neat rows on each side of the road. Fank kept increasing speed, setting the oncoming stream of air roaring through the streamlined cowling, and vehicles ahead of them, frightened by this roaring, squeezed up close against the side of the road, making way. It seemed to Maxim that the car hadn't been designed for this kind of speed—it was too unstable— and he felt rather anxious.

Soon buildings sprang up, flanking the road on both sides, the car hurtled into the city, and Fank was forced to reduce speed. The first time, with Gai, Maxim had traveled through the city in a large public vehicle, crammed unbelievably full of passengers. His head was jammed against the low ceiling, people on every side were swearing and smoking, and the ones standing next to him kept callously stepping on his feet and jamming sharp corners of some kind into his sides. It was late evening, the windows hadn't been washed for a long time, and they were splattered with mud and caked with dust. And, in addition, they reflected the light of the little lamps inside the vehicle, so Maxim hadn't seen anything of the city. But now he was a given a chance to see it.

The streets were disproportionately narrow and completely choked with traffic. Fank's automobile barely even crept along, boxed in on all sides by vehicles of every possible kind. The rear wall of a van, covered in gaudy, brightly colored inscriptions and crude images of people and animals, towered up in front of them. On their left two identical cars crawled along, neither overtaking nor falling back, crammed with gesticulating men and women. Beautiful, striking women, not like Fish. Farther to the left some kind of electric train trudged along with a rattling and rumbling of iron, constantly scattering blue and green sparks; it was completely choked with passengers, who were hanging out of all the doors in bunches. On the right there was a sidewalk, a motionless strip of asphalt where traffic was forbidden. People wearing wet clothes in various tones of black and gray were walking along the sidewalk in a dense stream, colliding with each other, overtaking each other, dodging away from each other, forcing their way forward with their shoulders, continually running in through open, brightly lit doorways and mingling with the seething crowds behind immense misted-up windows, and sometimes suddenly gathering into large groups, creating blockages and whirlpools, craning their necks and peering at something or other. There were very many thin, pale faces, very similar to Fish's face, and almost all of them were unattractive, morbidly scrawny, excessively pale, haggard, and angular. But they gave the impression of contented people; they laughed frequently and willingly, they acted spontaneously, their eyes glowed, and their voices rang out, loud and lively, on all sides. Perhaps this is a fairly successful world after all, Maxim thought. In any case, although the streets are dirty, at least they're not piled high with garbage, and the buildings look quite cheerful; almost all the windows have a light in them because the day is overcast, and that means they obviously have no shortage of electricity. The advertising announcements glitter quite merrily, and as for the haggard faces, with this level of street noise and this level of air pollution, you could hardly expect anything else. It's a poor world, poorly organized, and not entirely healthy . . . but outwardly at least it appears to be fairly successful.

Suddenly something about the street changed. Agitated shouts rang through the air. A man climbed up a streetlamp, hung there, and started strenuously shouting, waving his free hand around. The crowd on the sidewalk started singing. People stopped, tearing off their hats, rolling up their eyes, and singing, shouting themselves hoarse, raising their narrow faces toward the huge multicolored inscriptions that had suddenly blazed into life across the street.

"Massaraksh," Fank hissed, and the car abruptly swerved.

Maxim looked at Fank. He was deathly pale and his face was contorted. Shaking his head around, he lifted one hand off the oval of the steering wheel with a struggle and stared at his watch. "Massaraksh," he groaned, and added several more words, but the only ones Maxim could recognize were "I don't understand."

Then Fank looked back over his shoulder, and his face contorted even more agonizingly. Maxim looked back too, but there was nothing special behind them. Just a completely enclosed bright yellow vehicle, like a square box, moving along the street.

The shouting in the street was completely unbearable now, but that wasn't what bothered Maxim. Fank was obviously losing consciousness, but the car was still moving. The van in front of them braked, its signal lights lit up, and the brightly daubed wall suddenly leaped toward them; there was a repulsive scraping sound and a dull thud, and the car's warped hood stood up on end.

"Fank!" Maxim shouted. "Fank! Mustn't!"

Fank lay there with one hand and his head lowered onto the steering wheel, groaning loudly and frequently. All around them brakes squealed as the traffic came to a standstill and horns sounded. Maxim shook Fank by the shoulder, then let go of him, swung his own door open, stuck his head out, and shouted in Russian, "Over here! He needs help!" A singing, yelling, clamoring crowd of people had already gathered by the car, energetically gesturing and brandishing their fists in the air above their heads. Maxim saw dozens of pairs of glaring, bloodshot eyes rolling around in their sockets. He didn't understand anything at all; either these people were outraged by the accident, or they were delighted to distraction about something, or they were threatening somebody.

It was pointless to shout—he couldn't even hear himself—and Maxim turned back to Fank, who was lying slumped back with his head dangling, kneading his temples, cheeks, and cranium with all his might, and there was saliva bubbling out between his lips. Maxim realized that Fank was suffering intolerable pain; he took a firm hold of Fank's elbows, hurriedly bracing himself in order to transfuse the pain into himself. He wasn't sure that it would work with a being from a different planet—he couldn't find the nerve contact he was looking for—and then Fank suddenly tore his hands away from his temples and started pushing Maxim in

the chest with what little strength he had left, desperately muttering something in a tearful, wailing voice. The only thing Maxim
could understand was: "Go, go . . ." Fank was obviously raving.

At that point the door beside Fank swung open and two
flushed faces, crowned by black berets and surmounting rows of
glinting metal buttons, were thrust into the car. Immediately a
multitude of firm, strong hands grabbed Maxim by his shoulders,
sides, and neck, tore him away from Fank, and dragged him out.
He didn't resist—there was no menace or evil intent in these
hands, quite the opposite in fact. He was dragged away into the
crowd, and from there he saw the two men in berets leading
Fank, doubled over, to the yellow vehicle, and another three men
in berets driving the people who were waving their arms around
away from him. And then the crowd roared as it closed around
the crippled car, which awkwardly stirred, rising up and turning on its side, so that Maxim briefly glimpsed its wheels slowly
turning in the air, and then it was already lying on its roof, and
the crowd was clambering onto it, and everybody was shouting
and singing, and they were all in the grip of some strange, rabid,
frenzied merriment.

Maxim was forced back toward the wall of a building and
pressed up against the wet glass of a shop window. Craning his
neck to look over people's heads, he saw the square yellow automobile, covered with a multitude of bright, glittering lights, start
moving with a brassy screech, force its way through the crowd
of people and vehicles, and disappear from sight.

4

Late that evening Maxim realized he had seen quite enough of this city, and he didn't want to see any more, but he did want to eat something. He had spent the entire day on his feet and seen a quite extraordinary number of things, without understanding very much at all, but simply by listening he had learned several new words and identified several of the local letters on signs and posters. The unfortunate incident with Fank had bewildered and startled him, but overall he was glad to have been left to his own devices once again. He liked his independence, and he had missed it all the time he was stuck in Hippopotamus's five-story termite hill with its poor ventilation. After thinking for a while, he had decided to temporarily get lost. Politeness was all very well, but information was more important. Of course, the first contact procedure was a sacred business, but no better chance to gather independent information was likely to come his way.

The city had astounded him. It was huddled down close against the ground. All the traffic here moved either across the ground or under the ground, and the gigantic spaces between buildings and above buildings were left empty, abandoned to the smoke, rain, and mist. The city was gray, smoky, colorless, and somehow the same everywhere—not because of the buildings, which included some rather beautiful ones, not because of the uniform teeming of the crowds on the streets, not because of the incessant dampness, and not because of the incredible life-lessness of its unrelenting stone and asphalt. Its sameness sprang from something more basic than all that. It was like a gigantic clockwork mechanism, in which none of the component parts are identical but everything moves, turns, engages, and disengages in a unified, endless rhythm, any change in which signifies

51

only one thing: malfunction, breakdown, and stoppage. Streets with tall stone buildings were succeeded by small streets with little wooden houses; swarming crowds were succeeded by the magnificent emptiness of broad public squares; gray, brown, and black suits under elegant capes were succeeded by gray, brown, and black rags under tattered, faded cloaks; regular, uniform droning was succeeded by the sudden, frenzied blaring of car horns, howling, and singing; all of this was interconnected, rigidly interlinked, and predetermined since time immemorial by certain unfathomable, internal functional correlations, and nothing had any independent significance. All the people looked just the same, they all acted in exactly the same way, and the moment you could get a close look and grasp the rules of crossing the streets, you vanished, dissolving into all the other people, and you could move along in the crowd for a thousand years without attracting the slightest attention. This was probably a complicated world, controlled by many laws, but Maxim had already discovered one of them, the main one: do what everybody else does, and do it in the same way as they do it. For the first time in his life he wanted to be like everybody else.

He saw some individuals who behaved differently from everybody else, and these people filled him with a keen sense of revulsion—they barged their way across the flow, staggering and grabbing at people coming toward them, slipping and falling, they had a repulsive and surprising smell, and other people shunned them but left them alone. Some of these individuals even lay stretched out beside walls in the rain.

Maxim also did as everybody else did. Moving with the crowd, he flocked into the echoing public emporiums under dirty glass roofs; moving with everybody else, he emerged from these emporiums; moving with everybody else, he went down under the ground, squeezed into overcrowded electric trains, and went hurtling off somewhere with an incredible rumbling and clatter-ing; swept onward with the torrent, he then came back up onto the surface, into new streets exactly like the old ones; when the flow of people divided, Maxim chose one of the streams and went whirling away with it . . .

Then evening came, the feeble streetlamps came on, hanging high up above the ground and not illuminating anything, and the large streets became completely congested. In the face of this congestion Maxim retreated and found himself in an almost empty, dimly lit side street. That was where he realized he'd had enough for today and stopped.

He saw three glowing golden spheres, a blinking blue sign woven out of gas discharge tubes, and a door leading into a semi-basement area. He already knew that as a rule three golden spheres were used to indicate places where food was served. He walked down the chipped steps and saw a small dining area with a low ceiling, ten empty tables, a floor that had just been sprinkled with fresh sawdust, and a glass buffet laden with brightly lit bottles of liquids in all the colors of the rainbow. There was almost no one in this café. A pudgy elderly woman in a white jacket with the sleeves turned up was sluggishly moving around behind a nickel-plated barrier beside the buffet; a little distance away a diminutive but sturdy man with a pale, square face and a thick black mustache was sitting at a round table in a casual pose. There was no one here shouting, or teeming, or emitting narcotic fumes.

Maxim walked in, chose a table in a niche as far away as possible from the buffet, and took a seat. The pudgy woman behind the barrier looked in his direction and said something in a hoarse, loud voice. The man with the mustache also glanced at him with vacant eyes, turned away, picked up a tall glass containing a transparent liquid that was sitting in front of him, took a sip, and set it back down. Somewhere a door slammed and a pretty young woman in a white, lacy apron appeared in the room, looked around to find Maxim, walked over to him, leaned on the table with her fingers, and started looking over his head. She had clear, delicate skin, a light down on her upper lip, and beautiful gray eyes. Maxim debonairly touched the tip of his nose with his finger and said, "Maxim."

The girl looked at him in astonishment, as if she had only just noticed him. She was so sweet that Maxim couldn't help smiling from ear to ear, and she smiled too, pointed to her nose, and said, "Rada."

"Good," said Maxim. "Supper."

She nodded and asked something. Maxim nodded too, just to be on the safe side. He smiled as he watched her walk away—she was slim and light, and it was pleasant to recall that this world also had beautiful people in it.

The pudgy woman at the buffet uttered a long, querulous phrase and retreated behind her barrier. They adore barriers here, thought Maxim. They have barriers everywhere. As if everything here were high voltage. At this point he realized that the man with the mustache was looking at him, and looking at him in an unpleasant, unfriendly kind of way. And on closer inspection, the man himself had a generally unfriendly air about him. It was hard to say exactly what the issue was, but for some reason he aroused associations with either a wolf or a monkey. So let him stare. We won't worry about him . . .

Rada appeared again and set down a plate of steaming meat-and-vegetable mush and a thick glass mug of frothy liquid in front of Maxim.

"Good," said Maxim, and slapped the chair beside him in invitation. He very much wanted Rada to sit there for a while as he was eating and tell him about something, so that he could listen to her voice for a while, and she could sense how much he liked her and how good he felt being beside her.

But Rada only smiled and shook her head. She said something—Maxim made out the word "sit"—and walked away to the barrier. A pity, thought Maxim. He took the two-pronged fork and started eating, trying to compose a phrase expressing friendliness, liking, and a need for companionship out of the thirty words that he knew.

Standing there, leaning back against the barrier with her arms crossed, Rada kept glancing at him. Every time their eyes met, they smiled at each other, and Maxim was rather surprised that every time Rada's smile became paler and more uncertain. He himself was experiencing very mixed feelings. He enjoyed looking at Rada, but this sensation was mingled with a growing sense of disquiet. He had a feeling of satisfaction from the food, which proved to be surprisingly delicious and quite hearty, but at the same time he could sense the sidelong glance of the man with the mustache and unmistakably discern the pudgy woman's disapproval emanating from behind the barrier . . . He took a cautious sip from the mug—it was beer, cold and fresh, but rather too strong. Not for everyone.

The man with the mustache said something, and Rada walked over to his table. They struck up a muted conversation, ill tempered and hostile, but at that point a fly attacked Maxim, and he had to do battle with it. The fly was brawny, blue, and brazen, and it seemed to come flying at Maxim from all sides at once; it buzzed and droned as if it were making a declaration of love to him; it refused to fly away, it wanted to be here, with him and his plate, walking over them and licking them; it was obstinate and garrulous. The whole business finished with Maxim making a false move and the fly crashing into his beer. Maxim fastidiously moved the mug to another table and set about eating the stew.

Rada came over and asked him something without smiling, looking off to the side. "Yes," said Maxim, just to be on the safe side. "Rada is good."

She glanced at him in undisguised fright, walked away to the barrier, and came back, carrying a shot glass of brown liquid on a saucer.

"Tastes good," said Maxim, giving the girl an affectionate, concerned look. "What's bad? Rada, sit here, talk. Must talk. Mustn't go away."

This carefully thought-out oration produced an unexpectedly bad impression on Rada. Maxim actually thought she was going to burst into tears. In any case, her lips started trembling, and she whispered something and ran out of the room. The pudgy woman behind the barrier uttered several indignant words. I'm doing something wrong, Maxim anxiously thought. But he absolutely couldn't imagine what it was. All he understood was that neither the man with the mustache nor the pudgy woman wanted Rada to "sit and talk" with him. But since they were obviously not representatives of public authority or guardians of the law, and since Maxim was obviously not breaking any laws, there was probably no need to take the opinion of these disgruntled individuals into consideration.

The man with the mustache muttered something under his breath but with a distinctly unpleasant intonation, finished his glass in a single gulp, took a thick, black, lacquered cane out from under the table, got up, and unhurriedly walked across to Maxim. He sat down facing him, set the cane across the table, and, without looking at Maxim but clearly addressing him, started straining slow, heavy words through his teeth, frequently repeating the word "massaraksh." His speech seemed as black and polished by frequent use as his ugly cane; this speech contained a distinct, black threat, and a challenge, and animosity, and all of this was strangely blurred by the indifference of his intonation, the indifference on his face, and the vacancy of his glassy eyes.

"I don't understand," Maxim said angrily.

Then the man with the mustache turned his pale face toward Maxim, seeming to look straight through him, slowly asked a question, enunciating every word separately, then suddenly whipped a knife with a long, narrow, glittering blade out of the cane. Maxim was actually caught unawares. Not knowing what to say or how to react, he picked up the fork off the table and twirled it in his fingers. That had an unexpected effect on the man with the mustache, who softly sprang back, knocking over his chair, but without standing up; he awkwardly squatted down, holding the knife out in front of him. His mustache rose up, revealing his long, yellow teeth.

The pudgy woman behind the barrier gave an ear-splitting squeal, and Maxim jumped to his feet in surprise. The man with the mustache was suddenly right up close to him, but at that very second Rada appeared out of nowhere, set herself between the man and Maxim, and started shouting loudly and vehemently— first at the man with the mustache and then, turning around, at Maxim. At this stage Maxim understood absolutely nothing at all, but the man with the mustache suddenly gave a gruesome smile, picked up his cane, hid the knife in it, and set off toward the exit. In the doorway he looked back, flung out a few words in a quiet voice, and disappeared.

Pale-faced, with her lips trembling, Rada picked up the fallen chair, wiped up the spilled brown liquid with a napkin, collected the dirty dishes and took them away, then came back and said something to Maxim. Maxim replied, "Yes," but that didn't help. Rada repeated the same thing, and her voice sounded angry, but Maxim sensed that she was less angry than frightened. "No," Maxim said, and the woman behind the barrier immediately started yelling, with her cheeks quaking, and then Maxim finally confessed, "I don't understand."

The woman darted out from behind the barrier and flew across to Maxim, without stopping yelling even for a second. She planted herself in front of him with her hands propped on her hips, still yelling. Then she grabbed hold of his clothes and started crudely rifling through his pockets. Maxim was dumbfounded and didn't try to resist. He simply kept repeating, "Mustn't," and plaintively glancing at Rada. The pudgy woman shoved him in the chest and, as if she had made some terrible decision, rushed back to her place behind the barrier and grabbed the receiver of the phone there. Maxim realized that he had been discovered not to have all those pink and green pieces of paper with lilac imprints, without which it was apparently not permitted to appear in public spaces here.

"Fank!" he declared with feeling. "Fank is unwell! Go. Bad."

But then the situation was unexpectedly defused. Rada said something to the pudgy woman, who dropped the phone, carried on clucking for a little longer, and calmed down. Rada sat Maxim in his old place, put a new mug of beer down in front of him, and, to his indescribable delight and relief, sat down beside him. For a while everything went very well. Rada asked questions, Maxim, glowing with delight, replied, "I don't understand," and the pudgy woman muttered in the distant background. Focusing intensely, Maxim constructed another phrase and declared that "rain falls massaraksh bad mist." Rada burst into laughter, and then another young and rather pretty girl arrived and said hello to everybody, she and Rada left the room, and a little while later Rada appeared without her apron, wearing a glittering red cape with a hood and carrying a large check bag.

"Let's go," she said, and Maxim jumped to his feet. But they weren't allowed to leave just like that. The pudgy woman raised a hue and cry again. There was something else she didn't like, and she started demanding something. This time she was waving a pen and a sheet of paper in the air. Rada argued with her for a while, but the second girl came up and took the woman's side. They were making an obvious point of some kind, and Rada eventually conceded defeat. Then all three of them started pestering Maxim. At first they kept asking one and the same question separately and in chorus, and Maxim, naturally, didn't understand. He merely shrugged. Then Rada told everyone to be quiet, gently patted Maxim on the chest, and asked, "Mak Sim?"

"Maxim," he corrected her. "Maxim. Mak—mustn't. Sim—mustn't. Maxim."

Then Rada set her finger to her nose and said, "Rada Gaal. Maxim . . ."

Maxim finally realized that for some reason his surname was required, which was strange in itself, but he was far more surprised by something else. "Gaal?" he blurted out. "Gai Gaal?"

Everyone fell silent. They were all astounded.

"Gai Gaal," Maxim happily repeated. "Gai is good."

There was uproar, with all the women speaking at once. Rada started pestering Maxim, repeatedly asking him about something. She was obviously terribly interested in how Maxim knew Gai.

Gai, Gai, Gai—the name kept surfacing in the torrent of incomprehensible words. The question about Maxim's own surname was forgotten.

"Massaraksh!" the pudgy woman finally exclaimed, and burst out laughing. The girls started laughing too, and Rada handed Maxim her check bag and took him by the arm, and they walked out into the rain.

They walked to the end of that poorly lit side street and turned into an even more poorly lit side street, with crooked little wooden houses along the sides of a dirty road that was unevenly paved with cobblestones, then they turned another corner, and another. The crooked little streets were empty and they didn't meet a single person along their way, lampshades of various colors glowed behind curtains in the weak-sighted little windows, and every now and then they heard muted music—choral singing in poor voices.

At first Rada chattered away in a lively fashion, often repeating the name Gai, and Maxim kept confirming that Gai was good, but he added in Russian that you shouldn't punch people in the face, that it was strange and he, Maxim, didn't understand it. However, as the streets became narrower and narrower, darker and drizzlier, Rada's chatter broke off more and more often. Sometimes she stopped and peered into the darkness, and Maxim thought she was choosing the driest route, but she was searching for something else in that darkness, because she didn't see the puddles, and every time Maxim had to gently tug her over onto the dry spots, and where there weren't any dry spots, he took her under his arm and carried her across. She liked it, and every time she swooned in delight, but then immediately forgot about it, because she was afraid. The farther away they went from the café, the more afraid she was; at first Maxim tried to establish nerve contact with her, in order to transmit a little courage and confidence, but it didn't work, just as it hadn't worked with Fank. And when they left the slums behind and came out onto a completely muddy, unpaved road, with an endless, wet wall surmounted by rusty barbed wire running along on the right, and a pitch-black, foul-smelling wasteland without a single light on the left, Rada's courage failed her and she almost started crying. In order to lift the mood at least a little, Maxim started singing the most cheerful songs he knew one after another at the top of his voice, and that helped, but not for long, only as far as the end of the wall, and then there were rows of buildings again—long, yellow two-story buildings with dark windows that gave off a smell of cooling metal, organic lubricant, and something else stifling and smoky. The sparse streetlamps glowed nebulously, and there were men in the distance, sullenly loitering under a tawdry sort of blind archway. Rada stopped.

She clutched Maxim's arm and started speaking in a fitful whisper, full of fear for herself and even more for him. Whispering, she tugged him back, and he complied, thinking it would make her feel better, but then he realized it was simply an unreasoning act of despair, and dug his heels in. "Let's go," he gently told her. "Let's go, Rada. Nothing bad. Good." She obeyed him like a child. He led her on, although he didn't know the way, and suddenly realized that she was afraid of those wet figures, and he was very surprised, because there was nothing terrible or dangerous about them—they were just ordinary members of the indigenous population, huddled up under the rain and shivering from the damp. At first there were two of them, then a third and a fourth appeared from somewhere with the little glowing lights of narcotic sticks.

Maxim walked along the empty street between the yellow buildings, straight at those figures, and Rada pressed herself closer and closer against him, and he put his arm around her shoulders. It suddenly occurred to him that perhaps he had been mistaken and Rada was trembling not in fear but simply from the cold. There was absolutely nothing dangerous about those wet men, and he walked straight past them, past those hunched-over, long-faced, chilled-through men with their hands stuck deep in their pockets, stamping their feet to warm themselves up, those pitiful men poisoned by their narcotic, and they didn't even seem to notice him and Rada, they didn't even raise their eyes, although he walked by so close that he could hear their morbid, irregular breathing. He thought that now at least Rada would calm down, now that they were already under the archway—and then suddenly another four men appeared out of thin air up ahead of them, as if they had detached themselves from the yellow walls, and stood across the path, blocking it; they were as wet and pitiful as the others, but one of them had a long, thick cane, and Maxim recognized him.

Under the flaking dome of the grotesque archway a naked lightbulb dangled, swinging to and fro in the draft. The walls were covered with mold and cracks, and the cracked concrete under their feet bore the dirty tracks of innumerable feet and car tires. There was a sudden hollow tramping behind them, and Maxim looked back—the first four men were pursuing them, breathing fitfully and irregularly, keeping their hands in their pockets and spitting out their repulsive narcotic sticks as they ran. Rada gave a muffled cry and let go of his arm, and suddenly the space was crowded: Maxim was forced back against the wall, and the men were standing just a hair's breadth away, but they didn't touch him, they kept their hands in their pockets, they didn't even look at him, they just stood there, not allowing him to move, and over their heads he saw two of them holding Rada by the arms, and the man with the mustache strolled over to her, unhurriedly transferred the cane to his left hand, and in the same leisurely style lazily slapped her on the cheek with his right hand.

This was so barbarous and impossible that Maxim lost his sense of reality. Something shifted out of kilter in his consciousness. The men disappeared. There were only two people here, himself and Rada; the others had all disappeared. Their place had been taken by fearsome, dangerous animals, trampling in the mud with clumsy, terrifying movements. The city disappeared, together with the archway and the lightbulb above his head. This was a region of impassable mountains, the country of Oz on

Pandora; this was a cave, an abominable trap set by naked, spotted monkeys, and the blurred, yellow moon was indifferently peering into the cave, and he had to fight in order to survive. And he started fighting just as he had fought that time on Pandora.

Time accommodatingly slowed down and stretched out, the seconds became very, very long, and in the course of each one it was possible to make very many different movements and strike many blows while seeing everything at once. They were heavy-footed, these monkeys, they were used to dealing with different quarry, and they probably simply weren't quick thinking enough to realize that they had made the wrong choice, that the best thing for them would have been to run, so they tried to fight . . . Maxim grabbed one wild beast by the lower jaw, jerked up the yielding head, chopped the edge of his hand hard against the pale, pulsating neck, and immediately turned to the next one. He grabbed, jerked, and chopped, then grabbed, jerked, and chopped again—in the cloud of their stinking, predatory breath, in the hollow silence of the cave, in the yellow, weeping semi-darkness—and filthy talons tore at his neck and slipped off, yellow fangs sank deep into his shoulder and also slipped off . . . There was no one near him any longer, and the leader with the club was hurrying toward the exit of the cave—because, like all leaders, he had the fastest reactions and had been the first to realize what was happening—and Maxim fleetingly pitied him, because his fast reactions were so slow. The seconds stretched out, becoming even slower, the fleet-footed leader was barely even moving his legs, and Maxim, slipping between the seconds, drew level with him and chopped him down as he ran, and immediately stopped.

Time returned to its normal rate of movement, the cave became an archway, the moon became a lightbulb, and the land of Oz on Pandora turned back into an incomprehensible city on an obscure planet that was even more incomprehensible than Pandora . . .

Maxim stood there, resting, with his itching hands lowered. The leader with the mustache was laboriously crawling around at his feet, and blood was flowing from Maxim's wounded shoulder.

Then Rada took him by the hand and sobbed as she ran his palm across her own wet face. He looked around. The bodies were scattered about like sacks on the concrete floor. He instinctively counted them—six, including the leader—and thought that two of them had gotten away. Rada's touch felt pleasurable beyond words, and he knew he had acted as he had to act, and done what he had to do—not a jot more and not a jot less. So let the ones who had managed to get away, get away. He didn't pursue them, although he could have caught up with them—even now he could hear the panic-stricken clattering of their shoes at the end of the tunnel. As for those who had not managed to get away, they were lying here, and some of them would die, and some of them were already dead, and now he realized that they were men after all, and not spotted monkeys or armored wolves, although their breath was rank smelling, their touches were foul, and their intentions were predatory and hideous. Nonetheless, he had a certain feeling of regret and sensed a loss, as if he had forfeited some kind of chastity, as if he had lost a small, integral part of the soul of the previous Maxim, and he knew that the previous Maxim had disappeared forever, and that gave him a slightly bitter feeling, which roused an unfamiliar kind of pride in him.

"Let's go, Maxim," Rada told him in a quiet voice.

And he docilely followed her.

"YOU LET HIM GET AWAY . . ."

"In short, you let him get away."

"There was nothing I could have done. You know yourself the way things happen—"

"Damn it, Fank! You didn't even have to do anything. It would have been enough just to take a driver with you."

"I know it's my fault. But who could have expected—"

"That's enough about that. What measures have you taken?"

"As soon as they let me go, I called Megu. Megu doesn't know anything. If he comes back, Megu will inform me immediately. Beyond that, I've put all the insane asylums under observation. He can't get very far,

he simply won't be allowed to, he sticks out like a sore thumb. He doesn't have any documents. I've given instructions that I must be informed about everyone who is detained without documents. He doesn't have any chance of hiding, even if he wants to. In my opinion, it's a matter of two or three days . . . A simple matter."

"Simple . . . What could have been simpler: get into a car, drive to the telecenter, and bring a man here. But you couldn't even manage that."

"I'm sorry. But a set of circumstances like that—"

"I told you, no more about the circumstances. Is he really like a madman?"

"It's hard to say . . . He's like a savage more than anything, I'd say. Like a well-washed and well-groomed Highlander. But I can easily imagine a situation in which he would appear to be insane. And then there's that perpetual idiotic smile, and that cretinous babbling instead of normal speech. And in general he's some kind of simpleton."

"I see. I approve of the measures you've taken. But there's one more thing, Fank. Get in touch with the underground."

"What?"

"If you don't find him in the next few days, he's bound to turn up in the underground."

"I don't understand what a savage would be doing in the underground."

"There are plenty of savages in the underground. And don't ask stupid questions, just do as I tell you. If you let him get away again, I'll fire you."

"I won't let him get away a second time."

"I'm glad for your sake . . . What else?"

"A curious rumor about Blister."

"About Blister? What, exactly?"

"If you don't mind, Wanderer . . . If you'll permit me, I'd prefer to whisper it in your ear . . ."

PART II

THE
GUARDSMAN

5

When he had completed the briefing, Cornet Chachu gave the following instruction: "Corporal Gaal, remain behind. The others are dismissed."

After the other section commanders had filed out, each with his nose to the nape of the man in front, the cornet examined Gai for a while, swaying on his stool and whistling the old soldier's song "Cool It, Mama." Mr. Cornet Chachu was nothing at all like Mr. Cornet To'ot; he was stocky and swarthy, he had a large bald patch, and he was much older than To'ot. In the recent past he had been an active duty officer, a tankman, and had been involved in eight coastal incidents; he held the Fiery Cross and three badges "for fury under fire." He had told them about his fantastic duel with a white submarine, when his tank took a direct hit and caught fire but he carried on firing until he passed out from his terrible burns; they said he didn't have a single patch of his own skin anywhere on his body, nothing but transplants from other men, and he had three fingers missing on his left hand. He was direct and coarse, like a genuine old war dog, and unlike the reticent Cornet To'ot, he never felt it necessary to conceal his mood from either his subordinates or his superiors. If he was in a jolly mood, the entire brigade knew that Cornet Chachu was in a jolly mood today, but if he was in a sour mood and whistling "Cool It, Mama" . . .

Looking into his eyes with a regulation glance, Gai felt despair at the thought that in some manner as yet unknown he had managed to anger and upset this remarkable man. He hastily ran through his memories of his own actions and the actions of the guardsmen in his section. But he couldn't recall anything that hadn't already been brushed aside with a casual gesture of that hand with three fingers missing and the hoarse, testy phrase "All right then, this is the Guards, after all. To hell with it."

The cornet stopped whistling and swaying on his chair. "I don't like idle talk and scribble, Corporal," he declared. "Either you recommend the candidate Sim or you don't recommend him. So which is it?"

"Right you are, sir, I recommend him."

"Then what am I to make of these scraps of paper?" The cornet extracted two folded sheets of paper from his breast pocket with an abrupt, impatient movement and unfolded them on the desk, holding them down with his mutilated hand. "I read, 'I recommend the aforementioned Mak Sim as a loyal and capable . . .' *weeell*, and then there's all sorts of idle blather . . . 'to be confirmed in the exalted station of a candidate private in the Battle Guards.' And here is your second little screed, Corporal: 'In connection with the above-mentioned, I consider it my duty to draw the attention of the command to the need for a thorough review of the previous life of the designated candidate for the rank of private in the Battle Guards, M. Sim.' Massaraksh! What exactly do you really want, Corporal?"

"Mr. Cornet!" Gai exclaimed in an agitated voice. "But I really am in a difficult situation here! I know candidate Sim to be a capable, competent individual who is devoted to the goals of the Guards. I am sure that he will be very useful to us. But I really don't know anything about his past! And as if that weren't enough, he doesn't even remember it himself. On the assumption that the Guards is a place for only those of unassailable integrity—"

"Yes, yes!" the cornet said impatiently. "Unassailable integrity, wholehearted devotion, to the very last drop, heart and soul . . . Let me put it in a nutshell, Corporal. You will retract one of these pieces of paper and tear it up this very moment. You have to think straight. I can't report to the brigadier with two scraps of paper. It's either yes or no. We're in the Guards, not a college of philosophy, Corporal! Two minutes for reflection."

The cornet took a thick folder of work documents out of the desk and flung it down in front of himself with an air of loathing. Gai bleakly glanced at the clock. This was an appallingly difficult choice to make. It was dishonorable and unguardsmanly to conceal from the command that he didn't know enough about the recommendee, even when it was a matter of Maxim. But on the other hand it would be dishonorable and unguardsmanly to dodge responsibility by saddling the cornet with the decision; he had only seen Maxim twice, and that was in the company formation.

Well, all right. One more time. Pro: He has passionately embraced and accepted the goals of the Guards to liquidate the consequences of war and eliminate the intelligence network of the potential aggressor. He passed the medical examination at the Department of Public Health without the slightest hitch, and after Cornet To'ot and the HQ medical officer Zogu sent him to some kind of secret department, clearly for assessment, he successfully passed that check too. (Of course, that's Maxim's own testimony—he lost the documents—but how else could he possibly have turned up, entirely free of all surveillance?) And finally, he's brave, a born warrior—he single-handedly dealt with Rat Catcher's gang—and he's amiable, easy to get along with, good-natured, and absolutely unselfish. All in all, he's a person of genuinely exceptional abilities.

Con: We have absolutely no idea who he is or where he came from; he either can't remember anything about his past or he doesn't want to tell anybody . . . and he doesn't have any documents. But is all of this really so very suspicious? The government only controls the borders and the central region. Even now two-thirds of the country's territory is rife with anarchy, famine, and epidemics; people flee from those places, none of them have any documents, and the young ones don't even know what documents are. And there are so many of them who are ill, or have lost their memory, or are even degenerates . . . In the final analysis, the most important thing is that Maxim isn't a degenerate.

"Well, corporal?" the cornet inquired, leafing through his papers.

"Right you are, Mr. Cornet, sir," Gai said in a despairing voice. "With your permission . . ." He took his own statement about the need to check on Maxim and slowly tore it up.

"A *corrrrect* decision!" the cornet barked. "That's the guards-man's way! Scraps of paper, ink, checks . . . Combat will check everything for us. When we get into our trucks and advance into the zone of nuclear traps, we'll see soon enough who is our man and who isn't."

"Yes indeed, sir," Gai said without any real confidence. He understood the old war dog very well, but he also saw very clearly that this war veteran and hero of coastal incidents was rather deluded, like all veterans and heroes. Combat was one thing, and unassailable integrity was another. But then, that didn't apply to Maxim. Maxim's integrity was crystal clear.

"Massaraksh!" the cornet exclaimed. "The Department of Health passed him, and everything after that is our business." After coming out with this rather mysterious proposition, he gave Gai an angry look and added, "A guardsman has absolute trust in his friend, and if he doesn't trust him, then he's not a friend and he should be sent packing. You surprised me, Corporal. All right then, quick march to your section. There's not much time left . . . During the operation I'll keep an eye on this candidate myself."

Gai clicked his heels and went out. Outside the door he per-mitted himself a smile. The old war dog hadn't been able to hold back after all, and he had taken responsibility. Well, what was good was always good. Now Gai could consider Maxim his friend with a clean conscience. Mak Sim, that was. His real surname was unpronounceable. Either he had made it up while he was delirious, or he really must be one of those Highlanders . . . What was it that their ancient king was called . . . Zaremchichakbesh-musaraili?

Gai walked out onto the parade ground and looked around for his section. The indefatigable Pandi was driving the guys through the upper window of a mock-up of a three-story building. The guys were streaming with sweat, and that was bad, because there was only an hour left until the operation.

"*Aaas you weeere!*" Gai shouted from a distance.

"*Aaas you were!*" Pandi yelled. "Fall in!" The section quickly formed up. Pandi gave the command "Atten*tion!*" strode over to Gai in quick time, and reported, "Mr. Corporal, the section is engaged in negotiating the assault course."

"Fall into line," Gai ordered, trying to express dissatisfaction with the tone of his voice, in the same superlative way that Corporal Serembesh always managed to do it. He walked along in front of the formation with his hands clasped behind his back, peering into the familiar faces.

Those gray, light blue, and dark blue eyes followed his every movement, expressing a readiness to carry out any command by slightly bulging. He felt how close they were to him, and how dear, these twelve great hulks—six active privates of the Guards on the right flank and six candidates on the left, all wearing smart black one-piece coveralls with brightly polished buttons, all wearing gleaming boots with short tops, all wearing berets dashingly tugged down to the right eyebrow . . .

No, not all of them. At the center of the formation, on the right flank of the candidates, the candidate Mak Sim towered up above the others, a really fine, well-built figure of a man, Gai's favorite, deplorable as it was for a commander to have favorites, but . . . hmm . . . Those strange brown eyes of his weren't bulging. Well, never mind that, he would learn in time. But that . . . hmm . . .

Gai walked up to Maxim and fastened his top button. Then he went up on tiptoe and adjusted Maxim's beret. That seemed to be all . . . Maxim was grinning from ear to ear in formation again. Well, never mind. He'd get out of the habit. He was a candidate, after all, the most junior man in the section . . .

In order to preserve the appearance of fairness, Gai adjusted the buckle of the man next to Maxim, although there was no need to do it. Then he took three steps back and gave the command "At ease." The section stood "at ease"—moving their right feet slightly to the side and clasping their hands behind their backs.

"Guardsmen," said Gai, "today we and our company go into action in a regular operation to neutralize the intelligence service agents of the potential enemy. The operation is carried out in accordance with format number thirty-three. No doubt the active privates among us remember their assigned functions under this format, but I consider it useful to remind our candidates who forget to fasten their buttons. Our section is assigned one entrance. The section divides into four groups— three groups of three men and an external reserve. The groups of three, consisting of two active privates and one candidate, go around the apartments in sequence, without kicking up a racket. On entering an apartment, each group of three acts as follows: the candidate guards the front door; the second private, allowing nothing to distract him, occupies the back entrance; and the senior private carries out an inspection of the premises. The reserve of three candidates, led by the head of the section—in this particular case by me—remains downstairs in the entrance, with the aim, first, of preventing anyone from leaving the building during the operation and, second, of immediately rendering assistance to any group of three that requires it. You know the composition of the groups of three and the reserve . . . Attention!" he said, taking another step back. "Into groups of three and the reserve group—divide!"

A brief multidirectional movement occurred and the section rearranged itself. Nobody took the wrong place, nobody got their automatic rifles tangled together, no one slipped, and no one lost his beret, as had happened in previous drills. Maxim towered up on the right flank of the reserve, still grinning from ear to ear. Gai suddenly got the wild idea that Maxim regarded all of this as just an amusing game. That wasn't the case, of course, because it simply couldn't be the case. Undoubtedly that idiotic grin was to blame . . .

"Pretty good," Gai growled, imitating Corporal Serembesh, and cast a benign glance at Pandi as if to say, *Well done, old man, you drilled them into shape.* "Attention!" he said. "Section, fall in!"

Another brief multidirectional movement that was splendid and quite beautiful in its impeccable precision, and once again the section was standing there before him in a simple, single rank. Good! Simply wonderful! That actually gave him a chilly kind of shudder inside. Gai clasped his hands behind his back again and started walking up and down.

"Guardsmen!" he said. "We are the state's buttress and its only hope in these difficult times. The Unknown Fathers have nobody but us on whom they can unhesitatingly rely." This was the truth, the simple, plain truth, and there was both allure and self-abnegation in that. "The chaos resulting from the criminal war may have blown over, but its consequences are still painfully felt in the present day. Guardsmen, brothers! We have a single objective: to tear up by the roots everything that drags us back toward chaos. The enemy on our borders remains ever vigilant, he has attempted repeatedly and unsuccessfully to draw us into a new war on land and at sea, and it is only thanks to the courage and fortitude of our soldier brothers that the country is able to enjoy peace and repose. But no efforts by the army can lead us to our goal if the enemy within is not broken. And breaking the enemy within is our task, and only ours, Guardsmen. For the sake of this, we accept many sacrifices, we shatter the peace of our mothers, brothers, and children, we deprive the honest worker, the honest functionary, the honest merchant and manufacturer of their well-earned rest. They know why we are obliged to intrude into their homes, and they greet us like their best friends, like their defenders. Remember this, and do not allow yourselves to get carried away in the noble passion of carrying out your mission. A friend is a friend, and an enemy is an enemy . . . Are there any questions?"

"No!" roared the section, all twelve throats in unison.

"Atten*tion*! Thirty minutes to relax and check your equipment. Dismissed!"

The section scattered, and the guardsmen headed for the barracks in groups of two or three. Gai unhurriedly followed after them, feeling pleasantly drained. Maxim was waiting for him a little farther on, smiling in anticipation.

"Let's have a game of words," he suggested.

Gai inwardly groaned. If he could just call him to order somehow! What could be more unnatural than a candidate, a dull blockhead, pestering a corporal with familiar comments half an hour before the start of an operation!

"This isn't the time," he said as drily as he could manage.

"Are you nervous?" Maxim asked in a sympathetic voice.

Gai stopped and raised his eyes to the sky. What could he do, what could he do? It had turned out to be absolutely impossible to reprimand a good-natured, naive giant like this, who was also his sister's rescuer, and in addition—at the end of the day—a man who was in every respect, apart from discipline in formation, far superior to Gai himself . . . Gai looked around and said in a pleading voice, "Listen, Mak, you're putting me in an awkward situation. When we're in barracks, I'm your corporal, your superior—I give the orders and you obey them. I've told you a hundred times—"

"But I'm willing to obey, give me an order!" Maxim protested. "I know what discipline is. Give me an order."

"I've already given you one. Get on with checking your equipment."

"No, I'm sorry, Gai, that isn't the order you gave. You ordered us to relax and to check our equipment, have you forgotten? I've already checked my equipment, and now I'm relaxing. Let's have a game, I've thought up a good word . . ."

"Mak, try to understand, a subordinate has the right to address a superior officer, first, only in the prescribed form, and second, exclusively on service business."

"Yes, I remember. Paragraph nine . . . But that's during duty time. And right now we're relaxing."

"What gave you the idea that I'm relaxing?" Gai asked. They were standing beside a mock-up of a wall with barbed wire, in a spot where, thank goodness, nobody could see them—nobody could see this huge tower of a man slumped against the wall and repeatedly trying to catch hold of his corporal's button. "I only relax at home, but even at home I wouldn't allow any subordinate to— Listen, let go of my button and fasten your own."

Maxim fastened it and said, "One thing on duty and another at home. What's the point?"

"Let's not get into talking about that. I'm tired of telling you the same thing over and over again . . . By the way, when are you going to stop smiling in formation?"

"It doesn't say anything about that in the regulations," Maxim immediately responded. "And as for repeating the same thing over and over again, I'll tell you this. Don't take offense, Gai, I know that you're not a speecher . . . not a declaimer . . . "

"Not who?"

"You're not a person who knows how to speak beautifully."

"An orator?"

"An orator . . . Yes, not an orator. But all the same. Today you gave a speech to us. Correct words, good words. Only when you talked to me at home about the objectives of the Guards and the situation in the country, it was very interesting. It was very much in your style. But here you say the same thing seven times, and not in your style. All very correct. All very identical. All very boring. Eh? You're not offended?"

Gai wasn't offended. That is, his vanity had been pricked by a cold little needle: until now he had thought that he spoke just as convincingly and smoothly as Corporal Serembesh or even Cornet To'ot. But then, if he thought about it, Corporal Serembesh and the cornet had also spent the last three years repeating the same things. And there was nothing surprising, let alone blameworthy, about that—after all, during those three years, no substantial changes had taken place in either the internal or the external situation.

"And where in the regulations does it say," Gai chuckled, "that a subordinate can correct his superior?"

"It says just the opposite there," Maxim admitted with a sigh. "But I don't think that's right. You listen to my advice when you're solving ballistics problems, don't you? And you listen to my comments when you make mistakes in the calculations."

"That's at home!" Gai heatedly exclaimed. "Everything is possible at home."

"But what if you give us the wrong aim at firing practice? What if you haven't properly corrected for the wind? Eh?"

"No, under no circumstances," Gai adamantly declared.

"So we fire inaccurately?" Maxim asked in amazement.

"You fire as ordered," Gai said in a stern voice. "In these last ten minutes, Mak, you've said enough for fifteen days in the punishment cell. Do you understand?"

"No, I don't understand. What about in combat?"

"What about what in combat?"

"What if you give an incorrect aim? Eh?"

"Hmm . . ." said Gai, who had never commanded in combat. He suddenly remembered how Corporal Bahtu had gotten in a muddle with the map during a reconnaissance operation and herded the section into close-range fire from the next company. He didn't come back, and he got half the section killed, and we knew that he'd gotten confused, but nobody even thought of correcting him.

For crying out loud, Gai suddenly thought, why, it could never even have occurred to us that we could correct him. A commander's order is the law, and even higher than the law—laws are sometimes discussed, after all, but you can't discuss an order; discussing an order is outrageous, harmful, simply dangerous when you get right down to it . . . But Maxim doesn't understand that, and it's not even that he doesn't understand it—there's nothing here to understand—he simply doesn't accept it. It's happened so many times already: he takes something self-evident and rejects it, and there's no way I can convince him—in fact, the very opposite happens. In fact, I start doubting, my head starts spinning, and I end up totally stupefied. Yes, he really is an extraordinary person . . . a rare, totally unique kind of person . . . he learned our language in a month. He mastered the grammar in two days. And in another two days he read everything that I've got. He knows math and mechanics better than our teachers, and we have genuine specialists teaching our courses.

Or take Uncle Kaan, now. Just recently the old man had been directing all his monologues at the dining table exclusively at Maxim. More than that, he had made it plain on more than one occasion that in these hard times Maxim was probably the only person who demonstrated such impressive abilities and such a lively interest in fossil animals. Gai's uncle sketched some terrifying animals for Maxim on a sheet of paper, and Maxim sketched some even more terrifying animals for him, and they argued about which of those animals was more ancient, and who they were descended from and why it happened. The scholarly books from the old man's library were even brought into play, but there were still times when Maxim didn't give the old man a chance to open his mouth. Gai and Rada didn't understand a word of what they were saying, but their uncle either shouted himself hoarse or tore the sketches into scraps and trampled them underfoot, calling Maxim an ignoramus, worse than that fool Shapshu, or suddenly started furiously raking both hands through his sparse gray hair and muttering with a dumbfounded smile, "That's audacious, massaraksh, audacious . . . You have a vivid imagination, young man!" One evening in particular had stuck in Gai's memory, when one of Maxim's pronouncements had struck the old man like a lightning bolt. Maxim said that some of these primordial monsters used to walk around on their hind legs, and apparently that proposition very simply and naturally resolved a protracted dispute that went back to before the war . . .

He knows math, he knows mechanics, he has a superlative knowledge of military chemistry, and he knows paleontology—good grief, who knows about paleontology these days, but he knows paleontology too . . . He draws like an artist, sings like a professional performer . . . and he's good-natured, unnaturally good-natured. He scattered those bandits, massacred all eight of them, completely on his own, with his bare hands. In his place anybody else would have acted like the cock of the walk and gone around looking down on everybody, but he was in torment, he couldn't sleep at night, and he was upset when people praised him for killing . . . Good grief, what a problem it was to persuade him to join the Guards! He understood everything, he agreed with everything, he wanted to join. "But I'll have to shoot there," he said. "At people." I told him, at degenerates, not at people, at scum, worse than gangsters . . . Thank goodness, we agreed that at first, until he got used to it, he could simply disarm them . . .

It's funny, and somehow frightening at the same time. Yes, no wonder he sometimes starts jabbering about coming from a different world. I know that world. My uncle even has a book about it: *The Misty Land of Zartak*. It says that the valley of Zartak, where happy people live, lies in the mountains to the east of here. According to the descriptions, everyone there is like Maxim. And the amazing thing is that if one of them ever leaves their valley, he immediately forgets where he's from and what happened to him before; he can only remember that he comes from a different world. Of course, my uncle says there isn't any such valley, that it's all made up, there's only the Zartak mountain range—and then, he says, during the war they blasted that mountain range with megabombs. So the Highlanders had their memories totally zapped out of them anyway . . .

"Why don't you say anything?" Maxim asked. "Are you thinking about me?"

Gai looked away. "I tell you what," he said. "There's only one thing I ask of you: in the interests of discipline, never show that you know more than I do. Watch how the others behave, and behave exactly as they do."

"I'm trying," Maxim said in a sad voice. He thought for a while and added, "It's hard to get used to it. Everything's different where I'm from."

"How's your wound coming along?" Gai asked to change the subject.

"My wounds heal up quickly," Maxim absentmindedly replied. "Listen, Gai, after the operation, let's go straight home. Well, why are you looking at me like that? I really miss Rada a lot. Don't you? We'll take the guys back to the barracks and then go home in the truck. We'll let the driver go . . ."

Gai drew as much air into his lungs as he could. But at that moment the silvery box of a loudspeaker on a pole almost right over their heads started growling, and the commanding voice of the brigade duty officer rang out, "Sixth company, turn out and form up on the parade ground! Attention, sixth company . . ."

And Gai only barked, "Candidate Sim! Stop talking and quick march into formation!" Maxim made to dart off, but Gai caught hold of the barrel of his automatic. "I implore you," he said. "Like everybody else! Act like everybody else! Today the cornet himself will be keeping an eye on you."

Three minutes later the company had already formed up. It had turned dark, and a floodlight flared to life above the parade ground. The motors of trucks murmured gently behind the formation. As always just before an operation, the brigadier, accompanied by Cornet Chachu, silently walked along the formation, inspecting every guardsman. He was calm, with his eyes narrowed and the corners of his lips amiably raised. Afterward, still not having said anything, he nodded to the cornet and walked away. The cornet, walking with a waddling gait and brandishing his maimed hand in the air, walked out in front of the formation and turned his dark, almost black face to the ranks of guardsmen.

"Guardsmen!" he croaked in the voice that sent shivers running up and down Gai's spine. "We have an assignment to carry

out. And we shall perform it in worthy fashion. Company, attention! To the trucks! Corporal Gaal to me!"

When Gai ran up and snapped to attention in front of him,
the cornet said in a low voice, "Your section has a special assignment. On arriving at the destination, stay in the truck. I shall take
command myself."

6

The truck had terrible shock absorbers, which was very noticeable on the terrible cobbled roadway. Candidate Maxim, clutching his automatic rifle between his knees, considerately held Gai by his belt, thinking that it would be inappropriate for the corporal, who was so concerned about his authority, to bounce and hover above the benches like some Candidate Zoiza. Gai didn't object, or perhaps he didn't notice his subordinate's attentiveness. Since his conversation with the cornet, Gai had been seriously preoccupied with something, and Maxim was glad the schedule meant they would be close beside each other and he would be able to help if necessary.

The trucks drove past the Central Theater, trundled along beside the foul-smelling New Life Canal for a long time, turned onto long Factory Street, which was empty at this time of day, and started winding their way through the crooked little side streets of a workers' district where Maxim had never been before, although recently he had been in many places and given the city very thorough and thoughtful study. In general, he had learned a great deal during these last forty-something days and finally figured out the situation, which proved far less reassuring and far more bizarre than he had expected.

Maxim was still at the stage of poring over his spelling primer when Gai accosted him with the question of where he came from. Drawings didn't help; Gai responded to them with a strange kind of smile and carried on repeating the same question: "Where are you from?"

Then Maxim had tetchily jabbed his finger at the ceiling and said, "From the sky."

To his surprise, Gai had found this perfectly natural and started peppering him with a barrage of words spoken with an interrogative intonation; at first Maxim took them for the names of planets in the local system. But Gai spread out a map of the world in the Mercator projection, and it turned out that they weren't the names of planets at all but the names of countries on the far side of this world. Maxim shrugged, uttered all the expressions of negation and denial that he knew, and started studying the map, and that was where the conversation temporarily ended.

About two days later, Maxim and Rada were watching television in the evening. The program being shown was a very strange one, something like a movie without any beginning or any end, without any definite storyline, and with an interminable cast of characters—rather sinister characters who acted rather barbarically from the viewpoint of any humanoid. Rada watched, enthralled, sometimes crying out or grabbing hold of Maxim's sleeve, and twice breaking into tears, but Maxim quickly got bored and was about to doze off to the dismal, menacing music when he suddenly caught a glimpse of something familiar on the screen. He actually rubbed his eyes in surprise. There on the screen was Pandora, with a morose tahorg trudging through the jungle, trampling down the trees, and then suddenly Oleg appeared, holding a decoy whistle in his hand, very intent and serious, walking backward; suddenly he stumbled over an exposed root and went flying, landing on his back in a swamp. Maxim was absolutely flabbergasted to recognize his own mentogram, and then another, and another, but there was no commentary, the same music just kept on playing, and Pandora disappeared, to be replaced by a blind, haggard man who was crawling across a ceiling, tightly wrapped in a dusty cobweb.

"What is this?" Maxim asked, jabbing his finger at the screen. "A program," Rada impatiently replied. "It's interesting. Watch." He didn't manage to get a sensible answer, and suddenly the strange idea occurred to him of dozens and dozens of different aliens, all diligently recalling their own worlds. However, he quickly rejected this idea; the worlds were too terrible and too uniform—small, poky, airless rooms; endless corridors crammed with furniture that suddenly sprouted gigantic thorns; spiral staircases winding their way down into the impenetrable gloom of narrow well shafts; barred-off basements packed with writhing bodies, motionless faces peering out between them through ghastly, motionless eyes, like in the pictures of Hieronymus Bosch. It was all more like delirious fantasy than real worlds. Against the backdrop of these visions Maxim's mentograms shone with a bright realism that, owing to his unique temperament, verged on Romantic Naturalism. Programs of this kind were shown every day, under the title *Magical Voyage*, but Maxim never did completely understand what the point of it all was. Gai and Rada responded to his questions with baffled shrugs and said, "A program. To keep things interesting. *Magical Voyage*. A story. Just watch it, watch! Sometimes it's funny, sometimes it's frightening." And extremely serious doubts arose in Maxim's mind about the goal of Professor Hippopotamus's research being first contact, and about his research really being research at all.

This intuitive conclusion was indirectly confirmed about ten days later, when Gai passed the exam to join the correspondence school for guardsmen wishing to apply for the initial officer's rank and began cramming math and mechanics. The diagrams and formulas of the elementary course in ballistics perplexed Maxim. He started pestering Gai, who didn't understand at first, but then, with a condescending smirk, he explained the cosmography of his world to Maxim. And then it turned out that the inhabited island was not a globe and not a geoid—in fact, it was not a planet at all.

The inhabited island was the World, the only world in the universe. What lay beneath the feet of the indigenous population here was the firm surface of the Sphere of the World. What hung above the heads of the indigenous population was a gaseous sphere of absolutely gigantic but finite volume; its composition was not yet known and it possessed physical properties that were not yet entirely clear. A theory existed that the density of the gas rapidly increased toward the center of the gaseous bubble, where certain mysterious processes occurred that gave rise to regular changes in the brightness of the so-called World Light, and this gave rise to the regular succession of day and night. In addition to short-term, diurnal changes in the state of the World Light, there were also long-term changes, which gave rise to seasonal fluctuations in temperature and the succession of the seasons of the year. The force of gravity was directed out from the center of the Sphere of the World, perpendicular to its surface. In short, the inhabited island existed on the inner surface of an immense bubble in an infinite firmament of solid matter that filled the rest of the Universe.

Totally dumbfounded by this surprise, Maxim tried to launch into a debate, but it very soon became clear that he and Gai were speaking different languages, and it was far more difficult for the two of them to understand each other than it would have been for a convinced Copernican and a follower of Ptolemy. The whole problem lay in the amazing properties of the atmosphere of this planet. First, its exceptionally powerful refraction hoisted up the horizon, and from time immemorial this had implanted in the heads of the indigenous population the idea that their land was not flat and quite definitely, absolutely not convex—it was concave. "Stand on the seashore," the school textbooks recommended, "and follow the movement of a ship that has pulled away from the quayside. At first it will appear to move across a flat surface, and the farther away it moves, the higher it will rise, until it is concealed in the atmospheric haze that screens off the remainder of the World." Second, this atmosphere was extremely dense, and it phosphoresced by day and by night, so that nobody here had ever seen the starry sky, and the incidences of observation of the planet's sun that were recorded in chronicles had only served as a basis for attempts to create a theory of the World Light.

Maxim realized that he was caught inside a gigantic trap, that first contact would only become possible when he managed to turn natural conceptions that had been formed over the course of millennia inside out. Apparently some attempts had already been made to do this here, judging from the common expression "massaraksh," which literally meant "the world inside out." And in addition, Gai had told him about a purely abstract mathematical theory that took a different view of the world. This theory, which arose in ancient times, had been persecuted by what was once the official religion, and it had its own martyrs. It had been given mathematical consistency by the works of brilliant mathematicians of the past but had remained purely abstract, although, like most abstract theories, it had finally found practical application very recently, when super-long-distance ballistic shells had been created.

After thinking over and collocating everything that he had learned, Maxim realized, first, that all this time he must have seemed like a madman here, and it was no accident that his mentograms had been included in the schizoid TV program *Magical Voyage*. Second, he realized that for the time being he would have to keep quiet about his alien origins if he didn't want to go back to Hippopotamus. This meant that the inhabited island was not going to come to his rescue and he had only himself to rely on, that the construction of a null-transmitter was indefinitely postponed, and he was obviously stuck here for a long time, or perhaps, massaraksh, forever. The hopelessness of the situation had almost floored him, but he had gritted his teeth and forced himself to think in a purely logical fashion. His mother would have to survive a very difficult time. She would be immensely wretched, and that thought was enough in itself to dispel any wish to think logically.

Curse this second-rate, self-contained world. But I have only two options: either carry on pining for the impossible and wallowing in bitter regret, or pull myself together and live. Live a genuine life, the way I have always wanted to live—loving my friends, achieving my goals, fighting, winning and losing, taking it on the chin and giving as good as I get—anything at all except wringing my hands in despair . . . He had stopped talking about the structure of the universe and started asking Gai about the history and social order of his inhabited island.

As far as history was concerned, things were not that easy. Gai had only a fragmentary knowledge of it, and he didn't have any serious books. And there weren't any serious books in the city library either. But it was clear that right up until the latest ruinous war, the country that had given Maxim refuge had been considerably more extensive and was governed by a bunch of bungling financial economists and depraved aristocrats who had driven the people into poverty, established a corrupt state apparatus, and eventually become involved in a large colonial war unleashed by their neighbors. This war had engulfed the entire world, millions and millions of people had been killed, and thousands of cities had been reduced to ruins. Dozens of small states had been annihilated, and chaos had engulfed the world and the country. A period of appalling famine and epidemics had set in. The bunch of bloodsucking exploiters had suppressed attempts at a popular uprising by using nuclear warheads. Both the country and the world were on course for total destruction.

The situation had been saved by the "Unknown Fathers." As far as Maxim could tell, these were an anonymous group of young officers from the General HQ who, one fine day, when they had at their disposal only two divisions, highly incensed at being dispatched into the nuclear meat grinder, had organized a putsch and seized power. That had happened twenty-four years earlier, and since then the situation had stabilized to a significant extent and the war had died down of its own accord, although nobody had concluded peace with anybody else. The energetic, anonymous rulers had restored relative order and straightened out the economy with harsh measures—at least in the central regions—making the country into what it was now. The standard of living had increased quite substantially, life had settled into a peaceful groove, civic behavior had improved to a level never previously seen in history, and in general everything had become rather good.

Maxim realized that the political order in the country was very far from ideal and represented a species of military dictatorship.

But it was clear that the Unknown Fathers enjoyed an extremely high level of popularity, and moreover in all strata of society. The economic basis for this popularity remained a mystery to Maxim; after all, half the country was still lying in ruins, military spending was huge, and the overwhelming majority of the population lived in conditions that were modest, to say the least . . . But the important point was clearly that the military elite had managed to rein in the appetites of the industrialists, which had made them popular with the workers, and also to subjugate the workers, which had made them popular with the industrialists. However, all of this was only guesswork. This way of posing the question seemed outlandish to Gai, for instance; for him, society was a unitary organism, and he couldn't conceive of any contradictions between social groups.

The external situation of the country still remained extremely tense. Two large states lay to the north of it—Hontia and Pandeia, both of them former provinces or colonies. Nobody really knew much about these countries, but it was known that both of them harbored extremely aggressive intentions; they continually sent in spies and saboteurs, contrived incidents on the borders, and were making preparations for war. The goal of this war was unclear to Gai, and in fact he had never even wondered about that question. There were enemies to the north, he was fighting their secret agents to the death, and that was quite enough for him.

To the south, beyond the border forests, lay a scorched desert produced by nuclear explosions; it had been formed on the territory of a whole group of countries that were most actively involved in the hostilities. Nothing was known about what had happened and what was happening now on those millions of square miles, and nobody was interested. The southern borders of the country were subject to continuous attacks by colossal hordes of half-savage degenerates—the territory on the far side of the Blue Serpent River was teeming with them. The problem of the southern borders was regarded as just about the most important one of all. Things were very difficult there, and that was where the elite units of the Battle Guards were concentrated. Gai had served in the South for three years, and he told Maxim some quite incredible things.

To the south of the desert, at the other end of the only continent on the planet, some states might possibly have survived, but they gave no indications of their presence. However, the so-called Island Empire, established on the two immense archipelagoes of the other hemisphere, constantly provided disagreeable evidence of its existence. The World Ocean belonged to the Empire; the radioactive waters were furrowed by an immense fleet of submarines, provocatively painted snow white and equipped with the latest word in combat technology, with gangs of specially trained cutthroats on board. As sinister as ghosts, these white submarines held the coastal regions in a state of ghastly agitation and anticipation, carrying out unprovoked bombardments and landing piratical assault forces on the shore. The Guards confronted this white threat too.

Maxim was stunned by this picture of universal chaos and destruction. He was dealing with a graveyard planet, on which the flame of rational life was just barely flickering, and that life was on the point of finally extinguishing itself at any moment.

Maxim listened to Rada's calm and terrible stories about her mother receiving the news that Rada's father had been killed (an epidemiologist, he had refused to leave a region stricken by plague, and at that moment the state had neither the time nor the capability to fight the plague by regular means, so a bomb had simply been dropped on the region); and about the time, ten years ago, when insurgents had approached close to the city, an evacuation had begun, and Rada's grandmother, her father's mother, had been trampled to death in a crowd that was storming a train; and about how, ten days after that, her youngest brother had died of dysentery; and about how, after her mother died, in order to feed little Gai and the completely helpless Uncle Kaan, she had worked for eighteen hours a day as a dishwasher at a military reconsignment point, then as a cleaner in a luxurious hangout for speculators, then competed in "women's sweepstake races," and then spent some time in jail, although not very much, but after jail she had been left without a job, and for several months she had lived by begging . . .

Maxim listened as Uncle Kaan, who was once a prominent scientist, told him how the Academy of Sciences was dissolved in the first year of the war and His Imperial Majesty's Academy Battalion was formed; how the originator of the theory of evolution went insane during the famine and hanged himself; how they had boiled up watery soup out of glue scraped off wallpaper; how a starving crowd had ransacked the zoological museum and seized the specimens preserved in alcohol for food . . .

Maxim listened to Gai's artless stories about the building of ADTs, or antiballistic defense towers, on the southern border, and about cannibals creeping up to the construction sites and abducting the educatee workers and the guardsmen on watch; about merciless ghouls, half men and half bears, or half dogs, attacking without a sound in the night. Maxim also listened to Gai's ecstatic praise of the system of ADTs, which had been constructed at the cost of incredible deprivations in the final years of the war, had essentially put an end to the military action by protecting the country against attack from the air, and even now was the only guarantee of safety from aggression by the country's northern neighbors . . . But, said Gai, those bastards organized attacks on the defense towers—those sell-out rats, murderers of women and children, who had been bought with Hontia's and Pandeia's dirty money, those degenerates, that scum worse than any Rat Catcher . . . Gai's high-strung face contorted in hatred. "The most important business is here," he said, hammering his fist on the table, "and that's why I went into the Guards and not into a factory, not into the fields or into a business but into the Battle Guards, who bear the responsibility for everything now . . ."

Maxim listened avidly, as if it was all some terrible, impossible fable, only all the more terrible and impossible because it was real, because so very much of it was still happening, and the most terrible and impossible things in all of this could be repeated at any moment. It seemed absurd and shameful to think about his own anxieties and problems, which suddenly became tiny—petty concerns about first contact, a null-transmitter, homesickness, wringing his hands . . .

The truck took a sharp turn onto a rather narrow street of brick buildings, and Pandi said, "We're here." People on the sidewalk drew back against the walls, shielding their faces from the light of the headlights. The truck halted and a long telescopic antenna extended to its full height above the driver's cabin.

"Disembark!" the commanders of the second and third sections barked in unison, and guardsmen scrambled over the sides of the truck.

"First section, remain where you are!" Gai commanded.

Pandi and Maxim, who had jumped to their feet, sat back down.

"Divide up into groups of three!" roared the corporals on the sidewalk.

"Second section, forward march."

"Third section, follow me!"

Steel-tipped boots clattered, a woman's voice squealed rapturously, and someone yelled from the top floor in a piercing howl, "Gentlemen! The Battle Guards!"

"Hoorah!" shouted the pale-faced people, who were pressing themselves back hard against the wall in order not to get in the way. It was as if these passersby had been waiting here for the guardsmen and, now that they had arrived, were as glad to see them as if they were their best friends.

Candidate Zoiza, sitting on Maxim's right, was still a complete boy, a long, skinny beanpole with white fluff on his cheeks. He nudged Maxim in the side with his sharp elbow and joyfully winked at him. Maxim smiled back. The other sections had already disappeared into their entrances, and only the corporals were left at the doors, standing there firmly and dependably, their faces immobile under their cocked berets. The door of the driver's cabin slammed, and Cornet Chachu's voice croaked, "First section, disembark and fall in!"

Maxim vaulted over the side of the truck. When the section had formed up, Cornet Chachu gestured to stop Gai, who had run up to report, then the cornet walked up close to the formation and commanded, "On helmets!"

The active privates seemed to have been waiting for this order, but the candidates hesitated. The cornet waited, impatiently tapping his heel, until Zoiza finally mastered his chin strap. Then he gave the orders "Right turn!" and "Forward on the double!" He himself ran ahead, with an awkwardly nimble gait, strenuously waving his maimed hand in the air as he led the section through a dark archway between iron containers of rotting refuse and into an inner yard that was as narrow and dark as a well shaft, crammed with stacks of firewood, before turning under another archway, as gloomy and foul-smelling as the first one, and stopping in front of a peeling door below a dim lightbulb.

"Attention!" he croaked. "The first group of three and Candidate Sim will go with me. The others will remain here. Corporal Gaal, at the whistle bring the second team of three upstairs to me, on the fourth floor. Do not let anyone out, take them alive, and shoot only as a last resort! First group and Candidate Sim, follow me!"

The cornet pushed the scruffy door open and disappeared inside. Maxim overtook Pandi and followed the cornet in. Behind the door was a steep stone stairway, narrow and dirty, with clammy iron banisters; it was illuminated by a sickly, sordid kind of light. The cornet friskily ran up it, three steps at a time. Catching up with him, Maxim saw a pistol in his hand and took his own automatic from around his neck as he ran, feeling nauseous for a second at the thought that now, perhaps, he would have to shoot at people, but he drove the thought out of his head: these weren't people, they were animals, worse than Rat Catcher with his mustache, worse than spotted monkeys—and the repulsive sludge under his feet and the walls covered with gobs of spittle confirmed and supported this feeling.

The second floor. A suffocating reek of kitchen fumes and a frightened old woman's face in the crack of a half-open door covered in tattered burlap. A demented cat meowed as it shot out from under their feet. The third floor. Some blockhead had left a bucket of kitchen slop in the middle of the landing. The cornet kicked over the bucket and the slop went flying into the stairwell. "Massaraksh," Pandi growled below them. A young guy and a girl with their arms around each other had squeezed back into a dark corner with expressions of frightened delight on their faces. "Get out, down the stairs!" the cornet croaked as he ran. The fourth floor. A hideous brown door with peeling oil-based paint, a scratched tin plaque with the inscription GOBBI, DENTIST. CONSULTATIONS AT ANY TIME. On the other side of the door someone was shouting—a long, drawn-out yell.

The cornet stopped, with sweat coursing down his dark face, and wheezed, "The lock!" Maxim didn't understand. Pandi ran up, pushed him aside, set the muzzle of his automatic to the door just below the handle, and fired a rapid burst. There was a shower of sparks, chunks of wood went flying into the air, and immediately, on the other side of the door, the protracted yell was punctuated by the popping sound of shots, splinters of wood went flying into the air again, and something hot and dense went hurtling just over Maxim's head with an atrocious screech. The cornet threw the door open; it was dark inside and the yellow flashes of shots lit up eddying billows of smoke.

"Follow me!" the cornet wheezed, and charged in headlong, straight toward the flashes. Maxim and Pandi dashed in after him; the door was too narrow, Pandi was squeezed, and he gave a brief moan. A corridor, fuggy air, powder fumes. Danger on the left. Maxim flung out his hand, grabbed a hot gun barrel, and jerked the weapon upward and away from himself. Someone's wrenched joints cracked with a quiet but appallingly distinct sound, and a large, soft body froze and limply fell. Up ahead in the smoke, the cornet croaked, "Don't shoot! Take them alive!"

Maxim dropped his automatic and burst into a large, well-lit room containing a lot of books and pictures, but there was nobody there to shoot at. Two men were writhing around on the floor. One of them kept shouting; he had already gone hoarse, but he kept on shouting. Lying in a faint in an armchair with her head thrown back was a woman, so white that she was almost transparent. The room was full of pain. The cornet stood over the shouting man and looked around, thrusting his pistol into its holster. Pandi shoved Maxim hard in the back as he burst into the room and was followed in by the other guards, dragging the corpulent body of the man who had been shooting. Candidate Zoiza, soaking wet and agitated, handed Maxim the automatic that he had abandoned.

The cornet turned his terrible, dark face toward him. "But where's the other one?" he croaked, and at that very moment a blue curtain dropped to the floor and a long, thin man in a soiled white doctor's coat clumsily jumped down off the windowsill. He walked toward the cornet like a blind man, slowly raising two huge pistols to the level of his eyes, which were glazed with pain. "Aiee!" Zoiza screamed.

Maxim was standing sideways and he had no time to turn. He jumped with all the strength in his body, but the man still managed to pull the triggers once. Maxim's face was scorched and powder fumes filled his mouth, but his fingers had already closed on the wrists in the white coat, and the pistols clattered to the floor. The man went down on his knees and lowered his head, and when Maxim let go of him, he gently tumbled forward onto his face.

"Well, well, well," the cornet said in an unfathomable tone of voice. "Put that one here too," he ordered Pandi. "And you," he said to soaking-wet, pale-faced Zoiza. "Run downstairs and tell the section commanders where I am. Tell them to report on how they're doing." Zoiza clicked his heels and dashed toward the door. "Oh yes! Tell Gaal to come up here . . . Stop yelling, you bastard!" he shouted at the groaning man, and prodded him in the side with the toe of his boot. "Ah, a waste of time. Flimsy garbage, trash . . . Search him!" he ordered Pandi. "And put them all in a row. Right here, on the floor. And the woman too, she's sprawled out in the only chair."

Maxim walked over to the woman, cautiously lifted her up, and moved her onto the bed. He had an uneasy feeling. This wasn't what he had expected. But now he didn't even know what he had expected—yellow fangs bared in a snarl of hatred, baleful howling, a ferocious skirmish to the death? He had nothing he could compare his feelings with, but for some reason he recalled how he once shot a tahorg, and the immense beast, so fearsome to look at and reputedly absolutely merciless, tumbled into an immense pit with its spinal column broken, and wept quietly and mournfully, muttering almost articulately to itself in its dying despair . . .

"Candidate Sim!" the cornet croaked. "I said on the floor!"

He looked at Maxim with his terrifying, transparent eyes, his lips twisted as if in a cramp, and Maxim realized it was not for him, Maxim, to judge or determine what was right here. He was still an outsider; he didn't know their hates and their loves . . . He picked up the woman again and put her down beside the corpulent man who had been shooting in the corridor. Pandi and the second guardsman puffed and panted as they painstakingly turned out the arrested group's pockets. But the prisoners were unconscious. All five of them.

The cornet sat down in the armchair, tossed his peaked cap onto the table, lit up a cigarette, and beckoned Maxim over to him with his finger. Maxim walked across and gallantly clicked his heels.

"Why did you drop your automatic?" the cornet asked in a low voice.

"You ordered us not to shoot."

"Mr. Cornet."

"Yes, sir. You ordered us not to shoot, Mr. Cornet."

Narrowing his eyes, the cornet released a stream of smoke up toward the ceiling. "So if I'd ordered you not to talk, you would have bitten off your own tongue?"

Maxim didn't say anything. He didn't like this conversation, but he remembered Gai's admonitions very clearly.

"What does your father do?" the cornet asked.

"He's a nuclear physicist, Mr. Cornet."

"Alive?"

"Yes, sir, Mr. Cornet."

The cornet took the cigarette out of his mouth and looked at Maxim. "Where is he?"

Maxim realized that he'd put his foot in it. He had to extricate himself from this situation somehow. "I don't know, Mr. Cornet. That is, I don't remember."

"But you do remember that he's a nuclear expert . . . And what else do you remember?"

"I don't know, Mr. Cornet. I remember a lot of things, but Corporal Gaal thinks they're all false memories."

There was the sound of hurrying footsteps in the corridor, and Gai entered the room and snapped to attention in front of the cornet.

"Take care of these half corpses, Corporal," said the cornet. "Do you have enough handcuffs?"

Gai glanced over his shoulder at the prisoners. "With your permission, Mr. Cornet, I'll have to get one pair from the second section."

"Go ahead."

Gai ran out. There was the sound of boots tramping in the corridor again, and the other section commanders appeared and reported that the operation was proceeding successfully: two suspicious individuals had already been detained, and as usual the residents were rendering active assistance. The cornet ordered them to finish up as soon as possible and to relay the password "Pedestal" to headquarters when they were finished. After the section commanders went out, he lit up another cigarette and said nothing for a while, watching the guardsmen take books down off the shelves, leaf through them, and throw them onto the bed.

"Pandi," he said in a quiet voice, "you deal with the pictures. Only be careful with that one, don't damage it—I'll take it for myself." Then he turned back to Maxim. "How do you like it?" he asked.

Maxim looked at the picture. It showed the seashore at twilight, a high expanse of water with no horizon, and a woman emerging from the sea. It was fresh and windy. The woman was feeling cold.

"A good picture, Mr. Cornet," said Maxim.

"Do you recognize the place?"

"Negative. I have never seen that sea."

"Then what sea have you seen?"

"A quite different one, Mr. Cornet. But that's a false memory."

"Rubbish. It's the same one. Only you were looking at it not from the shore but from a bridge deck, and the deck below you was white, and behind you on the stern there was another bridge, only a bit lower. And it wasn't this woman on the shore but a tank, and you were directing its aim at the base of a tower . . . Do you know, you young whelp, what it's like when a solid shot hits the base of a tower? Massaraksh . . ." He hissed and crushed out his cigarette end on the table.

"I don't understand," Maxim said in a cool voice. "I have never directed any fire at anything."

"But how can you know that? You don't remember anything, Candidate Sim!"

"I remember that I have never directed anybody's fire, Mr. Cornet. And I don't understand what you are talking about."

Gai walked in, accompanied by the other two candidates. They started putting heavy handcuffs on the prisoners.

"They're people too," the cornet suddenly said. "They have wives, they have children. They loved someone, someone loved them . . ."

He said it in a way that was clearly mocking, but Maxim said what he really thought. "Yes, sir, Mr. Cornet. It turns out that they are people too."

"You didn't expect that?"

"No, Mr. Cornet. I was expecting something different." Out of the corner of his eye, he saw Gai looking at him in fright. But he was already sick to death of lying, and he added, "I thought that they really were degenerates. Like naked, spotted . . . animals."

"You naked, spotted fool," the cornet emphatically exclaimed. "You bumpkin. You're not in the South now . . . here they're like people—dear, kind people who get bad headaches when they're really anxious. God marks the scoundrel. Do you get a pain in your head when you're anxious?" he unexpectedly asked.

"I never get a pain anywhere, Mr. Cornet," Maxim replied, "How about you?"

"*Whaaat?*"

"Your voice sounds irritated," said Maxim, "and so I thought—"

"Mr. Cornet!" Gai called out in a strange, trembling voice. "Permission to report . . . The prisoners have come around."

The cornet looked at him and chuckled. "Don't worry, Corporal. Your little friend has shown himself to be a true guardsman. If not for him, Cornet Chachu would be lying here with a bullet in his head." He lit up a third cigarette, raised his eyes to the ceiling, and let out a thick stream of smoke. "You have sound instincts, Corporal. I'd promote this fine young man to active private right here and now . . . Massaraksh, why, I'd promote him to officer's rank! He has the manners of a brigadier, he simply adores asking officers questions . . . But I understand you very well now, Corporal. That report of yours had every justification. So . . . we'll wait for a while before we make him an officer." The cornet got up, clumsily stomped around the table, and stopped in front of Maxim. "We won't even promote him to active private yet. He's a good soldier, but he's still wet behind the ears, a bumpkin. We'll take his education in hand . . . Attention!" he suddenly bellowed. "Corporal Gaal, lead out the prisoners! Private

Pandi and Candidate Sim, collect my picture and everything here that's made of paper! Bring them to me in the truck!"

He turned around and walked out of the room. Gai gave Maxim a reproachful look, but he didn't say anything. The guardsmen got the prisoners up, setting them on their feet with kicks and jabs, and led them to the door. The prisoners didn't resist, their legs were rubbery, and they swayed on their feet. The corpulent man who had fired in the corridor kept loudly groaning and swearing in a whisper. The woman soundlessly moved her lips. Her eyes had a strange glimmer in them.

"Hey, Mak," said Pandi, "take that blanket off the bed and wrap the books in it, and if it's not big enough, take the sheet too. When you've got everything, lug it all downstairs, and I'll take the picture . . . And don't forget your rifle, dimwit! You can't just go dumping your gun! And in action too . . . Eh, you bumpkin . . ."

"Cut the talk, Pandi," Gai said angrily. "Take the picture and go."

In the doorway he turned back toward Maxim, tapped his finger on his forehead, and disappeared. Maxim could hear Pandi singing "Cool It, Mama" at the top of his voice as he walked down the stairs. Maxim sighed, put his automatic on the table, and walked over to the heaps of books dumped on the bed and the floor. It suddenly struck him that he had never seen such a large number of books anywhere here, except perhaps in the library. The bookshops also had more books, of course. But only by the number of items, not by titles.

The books were old, with yellowed pages. Some of them were scorched, and some, to Maxim's surprise, were palpably radioactive. There was no time to examine them properly, so Maxim hurriedly stacked the neat piles on the spread-out blanket, reading only the titles. Yes, the book *Kolitsu Felsha, or The Insanely Brave Brigadier Who Performed Daring Exploits in the Enemy's Rear* wasn't here; the novel *A Sorcerer's Love and Devotion* wasn't here; the thick narrative poem *A Woman's Ardent Heart* wasn't here; and the popular leaflet *The Tasks of Social Hygiene* wasn't here. But Maxim did see the thick volumes of the serious works *The Theory of Evolution, Problems of the Workers' Movement, Financial Politics and the Economically Sound State, Famine: Stimulus or Obstacle?*, and various kinds of "Critiques," "Courses," and "Fundamentals," accompanied by terms that Maxim didn't know. There were collections of medieval Hontian poetry, the folktales and ballads of peoples unknown to Maxim, a four-volume collection of the works of a certain T. Kuur, and a lot of fiction: *The Tempest and the Grass, The Man Who Was the World Light, Islands Without Azure*, and many more books in unfamiliar languages, then once again books on math, physics, biology, and then more fiction . . .

Maxim packed up the two bundles and stood there for a few seconds looking around the room. Empty, warped bookcases, dark patches where pictures used to hang, and the pictures themselves, torn out of their frames and trampled underfoot . . . and no signs at all of any dentist's equipment. He picked up the bundles and walked toward the door, but then remembered and went back for his automatic. Two photographs were lying under glass on the table. One of them showed the transparent-looking woman with a boy about four years old, sitting on her knees with his mouth wide open in amazement, and the woman was young, contented, and proud. The other photograph showed a beautiful spot up in the mountains, dark clumps of trees, and an old, half-ruined tower.

Maxim swung his automatic behind his shoulder and went back to the bundles of books.

7

In the morning after breakfast the brigade formed up on the parade ground for the reading out of orders and assignment of activities. This was the most painful procedure of all for Maxim, if you didn't count the evening roll calls. The reading out of any orders always concluded with a paroxysm of absolute ecstasy—a blind, senseless, unnatural ecstasy, for which there was no justification, and which therefore produced an extremely unpleasant impression on an outsider. Maxim forced himself to suppress his instinctive abhorrence of this abrupt fit of insanity, which swept through the entire brigade, from the commander to the lowliest candidate. He tried to persuade himself that he simply was not capable of displaying the same passionate enthusiasm for the activities of the brigade administration as the guardsmen; he rebuked himself for possessing the skepticism of an alien and an outsider and tried to seek inspiration by repeating to himself over and over again that in difficult conditions such outbursts of mass enthusiasm were no more than an expression of people's solidarity, of their unanimity and readiness to completely devote themselves to the common cause. But he found it very difficult.

Having been raised since his childhood to take a restrained and ironic attitude toward himself, to feel distaste for all high-flown words in general and for triumphal choral singing in particular, he felt almost angry at his comrades in formation, these good-hearted, guileless, basically quite excellent guys, when suddenly, after an order had been read out, sentencing Candidate Somebody or Other to three days in the punishment cell for an altercation with Active Private Such and Such, they opened their mouths wide, cast off their intrinsic amiability and sense of humor, started enthusiastically roaring "hoorah" and singing

"The March of the Battle Guards" with tears in their eyes, and then repeated it for a second, third, and sometimes even fourth time. When this happened, even the cooks came pouring out of the brigade kitchen—fortunately for them, they weren't standing in formation—and enthusiastically joined in, boisterously brandishing their ladles and knives. Bearing in mind that in this world he had to be like everybody else, Maxim also sang and also tried to lose his sense of humor, and he managed to do it, but it felt obnoxious, because he didn't feel even the slightest enthusiasm—all he felt was a sense of awkward embarrassment.

This time the outburst of enthusiasm came after order number 127, concerning the promotion of Active Private Dimba to the rank of corporal, order number 128, concerning an expression of gratitude to Candidate for the Rank of Active Private Sim, for bravery demonstrated in the course of an operation, and order number 129, concerning the assignment of the barracks of fourth company to refurbishment status. The moment the brigade adjutant thrust the pages of the orders into his leather map-case, the brigadier grabbed his cap off his head, filled his lungs with air, and shouted out in a squeaky falsetto, "The Battle! Guards! Advance!" And then it went on and on . . .

Maxim felt especially awkward today, because he saw tears streaming down Cornet Chachu's dark cheeks. The guardsmen roared like bulls, beating out the time with their rifle butts on their massive belt buckles. In order not to see or hear any of this, Maxim squeezed his eyes as tightly shut as he could and started bellowing like an enraged tahorg, and his voice drowned out all the other voices—or at least, so it seemed to him. "Forward, fearless Guards," he roared, no longer hearing anybody but himself. What incredibly stupid words. Probably some corporal or other had written them. You had to really love your cause to go marching into battle with words like that. He opened his eyes and saw a flock of startled black birds darting about above the parade ground. "No diamond carapace will save you, our enemy! . . ."

Then everything ended as abruptly as it had begun. The brigadier ran his bleary eyes over the formation, remembered where he was, and commanded in a sobbing, broken voice, "Gentlemen officers, divide up the companies for exercises!" The dazed guys blearily squinted at each other, shaking their heads. They didn't seem able to grasp anything, and Cornet Chachu had to shout "Dress right dress!" twice before the ranks assumed the required appearance. Then the company was led off to the barracks, and the cornet gave his commands: "The first section is appointed to escort duty. Other sections commence exercises in accordance with the normal routine. Dismissed!"

The sections separated, and Gai lined up his section and assigned postings. Candidate Maxim and Active Private Pandi were given the posting in the interrogation room. Gai hurriedly explained Mak's responsibilities to him: "Stand to attention on the right of and behind the prisoner, and if the prisoner makes the slightest attempt to get up off the stool, prevent him from doing so by force. Obey the direct orders of the brigade commander. Private Pandi is the senior man—in short, watch Pandi and do everything he does. I wouldn't have assigned you to this posting for anything, but the cornet ordered me to. You just keep your eyes peeled, Mak. I don't really get what the cornet is up to. Either he wants to promote you as soon as possible—he really liked the look of you in action, yesterday at the review of the operation with the section commanders, he spoke well of you, and he put you in the order of the day—or he's checking up on you. I don't know why he's doing it, maybe it's my fault, with that report of mine, or maybe it's your fault, with those little conversations of yours . . ." He anxiously looked Maxim over. "Give your boots another polish, pull in your belt, and put on your dress gloves—no, you don't have any, candidates aren't provided with them . . . OK, run to the store, and look lively, we go on duty in thirty minutes."

At the store Maxim ran into Pandi, who was changing a cracked beret badge. "Look at this, Corporal!" said Pandi, addressing the store commander and slapping Maxim on his shoulder. "How about that? The guy's only been in the Guards eight days, and he has an expression of gratitude already. They've put him in the interrogation room with me . . . I reckon you must have come running for a pair of white gloves, right? Issue him some good gloves, Corporal, he deserves them. This guy's as tough as a nail."

The corporal started discontentedly muttering, reached into the shelves piled high with official-issue clothing, tossed several pairs of white, string-knit gloves on the counter in front of Maxim, and said with a scornful grin, "A nail . . . you and these crazies are all nails. Of course, when the pain has completely pulverized his innards, you can just take him and put him in a sack. My old granddad would be a nail here like that. No arms, no legs . . ."

Pandi took offense. "Your old granddad with no arms and no legs would have gone scuttling off on his eyebrows," he said, "if someone leaped out at him with two pistols. I thought the cornet was a goner."

"A goner, a goner . . ." the corporal grouched. "In six months, when you get dumped on the southern border, then we'll see who'll go scuttling off on his eyebrows."

When they walked out of the store, Maxim asked, with all the respect he could muster (good old Pandi liked respect), "Mr. Pandi, why do these degenerates get such bad pains? And all of them at the same time. How come?"

"It's from fear," Pandi replied, lowering his voice for greater solemnity. "They're degenerates, you see. You need to read more, Mak. There's this pamphlet called *Degenerates: Who They Are and Where They Come From.* You read it, or you'll always be the same ignorant bumpkin you are right now. Bravery on its own won't get you very far . . ." He paused for a moment. "Take us now: we get all agitated, for instance, or, say, we get a scare—but that's OK for us, except we'll maybe break into a sweat or, say, our knees will start trembling. But their bodies are abnormal, degenerate. If one of them gets angry with someone or, say, he gets in a funk, or whatever . . . then right away he gets bad pains in his head and all over his body. Bad enough for him to black out, understand? That characteristic is how we recognize them, and of course we detain them—grab them . . . Those are good gloves, and just my size. What do you reckon?"

"They're a bit too tight on me, Mr. Pandi," Maxim complained. "Why don't we swap? You take these, and give me yours that have already been worn in."

Pandi was very satisfied. And Maxim was very satisfied. Then suddenly he remembered Fank, the way he had writhed in the car, squirming about in pain . . . and then the guardsmen on patrol had grabbed him . . . Only what could Fank have been frightened by? And who could he have been angry with there? He wasn't agitated, was he? He was calmly driving the car, whistling, there was something he wanted very badly . . . probably to have a smoke . . . Of course, he did look back and he saw the patrol vehicle . . . or was that later? Yes, he was in a great hurry, and there was a truck blocking the road . . . maybe he got angry? Ah, no, I'm imagining things! You never know what kind of fits people might suffer from. And he was arrested for the accident. Though I wonder where he was taking me and who he was. I ought to find Fank . . .

He polished his boots and spruced up, putting himself into absolutely perfect order in front of the big mirror, hung his automatic around his neck, took another look in the mirror—and just then Gai gave the order to fall in.

After casting a critical eye over everybody and checking their knowledge of their duties, Gai ran over to the company office to report. While he was gone, the guardsmen played a game of "soap" and three stories of army life were told, but Maxim didn't understand them because he didn't know certain specific expressions, and then they started pestering Maxim to tell them how come he was so ginormous—that had already become a standing joke in the section—and they begged him to bend a couple of coins into little tubes as trophies. Then Cornet Chachu came out of the company office, accompanied by Gai.

He also cast a critical eye over everybody, stepped back, and told Gai, "Lead the section on, Corporal," and the section set off toward the HQ building.

In the HQ building the cornet ordered Active Private Pandi and Candidate Private Sim to follow him, and Gai led the others away. The three of them walked into a small room with tightly curtained windows and a smell of tobacco and eau de cologne. There was a huge empty table at the far end of the room with soft chairs arranged around it and a darkened painting of some ancient battle hanging on the wall: horses, close-fitting uniforms, unsheathed sabers, and lots of clouds of white, eddying smoke. Ten paces away from the table, to the right of the door, Maxim saw an iron stool with holes in the seat. The single leg of the stool was screwed to the floor with massive bolts.

"Take up your places," the cornet commanded, then walked forward and sat at the table.

Pandi carefully set Maxim behind and to the right of the stool, then stood on the left of it and commanded in a whisper: "Atten*tion*." And he and Maxim froze. The cornet sat there with his legs crossed, smoking and casually examining the guardsmen. He seemed entirely indifferent and disinterested, and yet Maxim could sense quite clearly that the cornet was very intently observing him, and not only him.

Then the door opened behind Pandi's back. Pandi instantly took two steps forward, a step to the right, and made a left turn. Maxim gave a jerk too, but he realized that he wasn't standing in the way, and this didn't concern him, so he simply goggled even harder. There was something infectious about this grown-up game after all, despite all its primitiveness and its obvious inappropriateness in the catastrophic conditions of the inhabited island.

The cornet got up, stubbing out his cigarette in an ashtray and lightly clicking his heels to greet the men walking toward the table: the brigadier, an unfamiliar man in plainclothes, and the brigade adjutant with a thick folder under his arm. The brigadier took a seat behind the table at the center. His expression was sour and peevish, and he thrust one finger in under his embroidered collar, pulled it out a bit, and twisted his head about. The plainclothes man, a nondescript little individual with a flabby, yellowish, poorly shaved face, took a seat beside him, without making any sound as he moved. Without sitting down, the brigade adjutant opened his folder and started sorting through his papers, handing some of them to the brigadier.

Pandi, after standing where he was for a while, as if he was feeling uncertain, moved back to his place with the same crisp, precise movements. The men at the table started quietly talking.

"Will you be at the meeting today, Chachu?" the brigadier asked.

"I have business to deal with," the cornet replied, lighting another cigarette.

"That's not good. There'll be a dispute there today."

"They caught on too late. I've already expressed my opinion on that matter."

"Not in the best possible manner," the plainclothes man gently remarked to the cornet. "And in addition, circumstances are changing, and opinions are changing."

"That's not the way it is here in the Guards," the cornet icily remarked.

"Really and truly, gentlemen," the brigadier said in a peevish voice, "let's get together today at the meeting after all."

"I heard they've brought fresh shrimp," the adjutant announced, still rummaging through his papers.

"With beer, eh, Cornet?" said the plainclothes man, backing up the adjutant.

"No, gentlemen," said the cornet. "I have only one opinion, and I have already expressed it. And as for beer . . ." He added something in an indistinct voice, the entire company burst into laughter, and Cornet Chachu leaned back in his chair with a satisfied air. Then the adjutant stopped rummaging in his papers, leaned down to the brigadier, and whispered something to him. The brigadier nodded. The adjutant took a seat and declared, apparently addressing the iron stool, "Nole Renadu."

Pandi pushed open the door, stuck his head out, and spoke loudly into the corridor. "Nole Renadu."

There was a sound of movement in the corridor and an elderly, well-dressed, but oddly creased and crumpled man walked into the room. His feet stumbled slightly. Pandi took him by the elbow and sat him on the stool. The door clicked as it closed. The man loudly cleared his throat, propped his hands on his parted knees, and proudly raised his head.

"Riiight, then . . ." the brigadier drawled, examining his papers, and suddenly started speaking in a rapid patter: "Nole Renadu, fifty-six years of age, property owner, member of the magistracy . . . riiight . . . Member of the Veteran Club, membership number such and such . . ." (The plainclothes man yawned, putting his hand over his mouth, pulled a brightly colored magazine out of his pocket, placed it on his knees, and started leafing through it.) "Detained at such and such a time at such and such a place; during the search the following items were confiscated . . . riiight . . . What were you doing at building number eight on Street of the Buglers?"

"I own that building," Renadu said with a dignified air. "I was consulting with my manager."

"Have the documents been checked?" the brigadier asked the adjutant.

"Yes, sir. Everything is in order."

"Riiight," said the brigadier. "Tell us, Mr. Renadu, are you acquainted with any of the prisoners?"

"No," said Renadu, with a vigorous shake of his head. "How would I be? However, the surname of one of them . . . Ketshef . . . I believe there is a Ketshef who lives in my building . . . But then, I don't remember. Perhaps I'm mistaken, or perhaps it's not in this building. I have another two buildings, one of them—"

"I beg your pardon," the plainclothes man interrupted, without looking up from his magazine. "But what were the other detainees talking about in the cell, did you happen to notice at all?"

"*Uhhh . . .*" Renadu drawled. "I must admit . . . You've got . . . *uhhh* . . . insects in there. So we mostly talked about them . . . Someone was whispering in the corner, but I must admit that I didn't pay any attention . . . And then, I find these people extremely distasteful, I'm a veteran . . . I'd rather consort with the insects, heh-heh!"

"Naturally," the brigadier agreed. "Well then, we are not apologizing, Mr. Renadu. Here are your documents, you are free to go . . . Escort officer!" he added, raising his voice.

Pandi opened the door and shouted, "Escort officer to the brigadier!"

"There can be no question of any apologies," Renadu solemnly declared. "I, and I alone, am to blame . . . And not even I, but my cursed genetic heritage. May I?" he asked, addressing Maxim and pointing to the table where his documents were lying.

"Sit down," Pandi said in a quiet voice.

Gai walked in. The brigadier handed him the documents, asked him to return Mr. Renadu's confiscated property to him, and Mr. Renadu was allowed to go.

"In Aio Province," the plainclothes man mused, "they have this custom: every degenerate who is arrested—I'm talking about the legal degenerates—pays a tax, a voluntary contribution to support the Guards."

"That is not customary here," the brigadier replied in a dry voice. "In my opinion, it is illegal . . . Let us have the next one," he ordered.

"Rashe Musai," the adjutant said to the iron stool.

"Rashe Musai," Pandi repeated through the open door.

Rashe Musai turned out to be a thin, completely jaded little man in a tattered night robe and one slipper. As soon as he sat down, the brigadier, with his face flushed bright red, yelled at him, "So, lying low, are you, you scum?"—at which Rashe Musai started verbosely and confusedly explaining that he wasn't lying low at all, that he had a sick wife and three children, that he worked in a factory, as a cabinetmaker, and that he wasn't guilty of anything.

Maxim was already expecting them to let him go, but the brigadier abruptly stood up and announced that Rashe Musai, forty-two years of age, married, a worker, with a record of two arrests, having violated the terms of the decree concerning exile, was sentenced, in accordance with the law concerning preventative measures, to seven years of educational labor with a subsequent prohibition on residence in the central regions of the country.

It took Rashe Musai about a minute to grasp the meaning of this sentence, and then a terrible scene was played out. The wretched cabinetmaker wept, incoherently begging forgiveness, and attempted to go down on his knees while carrying on shouting and crying, until Pandi eventually dragged him out into the corridor. And Maxim sensed Chachu's probing glance on him once again.

"Kivi Popshu," the adjutant announced.

A broad-shouldered young guy, whose face was disfigured by some kind of skin disease, was shoved in through the door. He turned out to be a habitual house burglar, a repeat offender who had been caught red-handed at the scene of the crime, and he acted in a manner that was simultaneously insolent and ingratiating. Sometimes he started imploring the gentlemen bosses not to condemn him to a ferocious death, and then he suddenly started hysterically giggling, cracking jokes and telling stories from his own life, which all began in an identical manner: "I'm breaking into this building . . ." He didn't give anyone a chance to speak.

After making several unsuccessful attempts to ask a question, the brigadier leaned back in his chair and looked to the left and the right with an indignant air. Cornet Chachu said in a flat voice, "Candidate Sim, stop his mouth."

Maxim didn't know how mouths were stopped, so he simply took Kivi Popshu by the shoulder and shook him a couple of times. Kivi Popshu's jaws clattered, he bit his tongue, and he stopped talking.

Then the plainclothes man, who had been observing the prisoner with keen interest for a long time, declared, "I'll take that one. He'll come in useful."

"Excellent!" said the brigadier, and ordered Kivi Popshu to be sent back to his cell.

When the young guy had been led out, the adjutant said, "That's all the trash. Now we'll start on the group."

"Begin straightaway with the leader," the plainclothes man advised. "What's his name—Ketshef?"

The adjutant glanced into his papers and spoke to the iron stool. "Gel Ketshef."

They brought in someone Maxim recognized—the man in the white doctor's coat. He was wearing handcuffs, and therefore held his hands unnaturally extended in front of him. His eyes were red and his face was puffy. He sat down and started looking at the picture above the brigadier's head.

"Is your name Gel Ketshef?" the brigadier asked.

"Yes."

"A dentist?"

"I was."

"And what is your relationship with the dentist Gobbi?"

"I bought his practice."

"Why are you not practicing?"

"I sold the equipment."

"Why?"

"Straitened circumstances," said Ketshef.

"What is your relationship with Ordi Tader?"

"She is my wife."

"Do you have children?"

"We did. A son."

"Where is he?"

"I don't know."

"What did he do during the war?"

"He fought."

"Where? In what capacity?"

"In the southwest. First as the head of a field hospital, than as the commander of an infantry company."

"Injuries? Decorations?"

"He had all of that."

"Why did you decide to engage in anti-state activity?"

"Because in the entire history of the world there has never been a more abhorrent state," said Ketshef. "Because I love my wife and my child. Because you killed my friends and depraved my people. Because I have always hated you. Is that enough?"

"Yes," the brigadier calmly said. "More than enough. Why don't you tell us instead how much the Hontians pay you? Or are you paid by Pandeia?"

The man in the white coat laughed. It was spine-chilling laughter, the way a corpse might laugh. "Drop this comedy, Brigadier," he said. "What do you need it for?"

"Are you the leader of the group?"

"Yes. I was."

"Which members of the organization can you name?"

"Nobody."

"Are you certain?" the plainclothes man suddenly asked.

"Yes."

"Listen, Ketshef," the plainclothes man said in a gentle voice. "You are in an extremely difficult situation. We know everything about your group. We even know something about your group's contacts. You must realize that we received this information from a certain individual, and now it depends entirely on you what name this individual will have—Ketshef or something different . . ."

Ketshef said nothing, keeping his head lowered.

"You!" Cornet Chachu croaked. "You, a former combat officer! Do you understand what you are being offered? Not life, massaraksh! But honor!"

Ketshef laughed again and started coughing, but he didn't speak. Maxim could sense that this man wasn't afraid of anything. Neither death nor dishonor. He had already been through all of that. He already regarded himself as both dead and dishonored . . .

The brigadier looked at the plainclothes man, who nodded. The brigadier shrugged, got to his feet, and announced that Gel Ketshef, fifty years of age, married, a dental practitioner, was sentenced to execution in accordance with the law concerning the protection of public health, the sentence to be carried out within forty-eight hours. The sentence could be commuted if the condemned individual consented to provide testimony.

After Ketshef was led out, the brigadier remarked to the plainclothes man with a discontented air, "I don't understand you. In my opinion, he was speaking quite willingly. A typical blabber—according to your own classification. I don't understand."

The plainclothes man laughed and said: "Well that, old man, is why you command a brigade, and I . . . and I am where I am."

"All the same," the brigadier said in a resentful tone of voice. "The leader of the group . . . inclined to philosophize a bit . . . I don't understand."

"Old man," the civilian said, "have you never seen a philosophizing corpse?"

"Ah, nonsense."

"But really?"

"Perhaps you've seen one?" the brigadier asked.

"Yes, right now," the civilian said. "And this is not the first time, note . . . I am alive, he is dead—what is there to talk about? That's how Verbliben puts it, I think?"

Cornet Chachu suddenly got up, walked right up to Maxim, and hissed up into his face: "What way is that to stand, Candidate? Which way are you looking? Atten*tion*! Eyes to the front! Stop shifting those eyes around!" He scrutinized Maxim for several seconds, breathing heavily, with his pupils narrowing and expanding at a furious rate—then he went back to his place and lit a cigarette.

"Right," said the adjutant. "That leaves: Ordi Tader, Memo Gramenu, and another two, who refused to give their names."

"Then let's start with them," the civilian suggested. "Call them out."

"Number Seventy-Three Thirteen," said the adjutant.

Number Seventy-Three Thirteen walked in and sat down on the stool. He was also wearing handcuffs, although one of his hands was artificial—a lean, sinewy man with unnaturally thick lips, swollen from repeated biting.

"Your name?" the brigadier asked.

"Which one?" the one-handed man merrily asked. Maxim actually shuddered—he had been certain that the one-handed man would remain silent.

"Do you have a lot of them? Then give us the real one."

"My real name is Number Seventy-Three Thirteen."

"*Riiight* . . . What were you doing in Ketshef's apartment?"

"Lying in a faint. For your information, I'm very good at doing that. Would you like me to show you?"

"Don't bother," said the plainclothes man. He was very angry. "You'll be needing that skill later."

The one-handed man suddenly broke into laughter. He laughed with a loud, resounding laugh, like a young man, and Maxim was horrified to realize that he was laughing sincerely. The men at the table sat and listened to that laughter as if they had turned to stone.

"Massaraksh!" The one-handed man eventually said, wiping away his tears on his shoulder. "Oh, what a threat! . . . But then, you're still a young man . . . They burned all the archives after the coup, and you don't even know just how petty you've all become . . . That was a great mistake, eliminating the old cadres—they would have taught you to take a calm approach to your duties. You're too emotional. You hate too much.

"But your job has to be done as drily as possible, formally—for the money. That makes a tremendous impression on a prisoner. It's terrible when you're being tortured not by your enemy but by a bureaucrat. Look at my left hand here. They sawed it off for me in good old prewar state security, in three sessions, and every action they took was accompanied by extensive correspondence. The butchers were doing a laborious, thankless job—they were bored, and while they sawed off my hand, they swore and grumbled about their miserly rates of pay. And I was terrified. It took me a great effort of will to stop myself from blabbing.

"But now . . . I can see how much you hate me. You hate me, I hate you. Wonderful! But you've been hating me for less than twenty years, and I've been hating you for more than thirty. Back then you were still walking in under the table and torturing the cats, young man."

"I get it," said the plainclothes man. "An old bird. The workers' friend. I thought they'd killed you all off."

"No chance!" the one-handed man retorted. "You need to get a bit more clued-in about the world you live in . . . but you still imagine that they canceled the old history and started a new one . . . What terrible ignorance, there's nothing to talk to you about—"

"That's enough, I think," said the brigadier, addressing the plainclothes man, who made a rapid note of something on the magazine and let the brigadier read it. The plainclothes man was smiling.

Then the brigadier shrugged, thought for a moment, and turned to the cornet. "Witness Chachu, how did the accused conduct himself during the arrest?"

"He lay sprawled out, with his toes turned up," the cornet somberly replied.

"That is, he didn't offer any resistance . . . *Riiight* . . ." The brigadier thought for another moment, got up, and announced the sentence. "The accused, number Seventy-Three Thirteen, is hereby condemned to death, but no term is set for the sentence to be carried out, and until such time as the sentence is carried out, the prisoner shall be employed in educational labor."

An expression of contemptuous bewilderment appeared on Cornet Chachu's face, and the accused quietly laughed and shook his head as he was led out, as if to say, *Well, would you believe it!*

After that Number Seventy-Three Fourteen was led in. He was the man who had been shouting while writhing around on the floor. He was full of fear, but he acted defiantly. He shouted out from the threshold that he wouldn't answer questions and wasn't looking for leniency. And he really did remain silent, without answering a single question, even when the plainclothes man asked if he had any complaints about bad treatment. It all ended with the brigadier looking at the plainclothes man and clearing his throat in a tone of inquiry. The plainclothes man nodded and said, "Yes, send him to me!" He seemed very pleased.

Then the brigadier looked through the remaining sheets of paper and said, "Let us go and get something to eat, gentlemen. This is impossible." The court retired and Maxim and Pandi were permitted to stand at ease.

When the cornet had also left, Pandi said, "How do you like those creeps? Worse than snakes, so help me! And what's the worst thing about it all: if their heads didn't hurt, how could you tell they were degenerates? It's terrifying to think what would happen then."

Maxim didn't answer. He didn't feel like talking. The picture of this world that had seemed so logical and clear only a day ago had become blurred and murky now. And in any case, Pandi didn't need an answer from him. After removing his gloves to avoid staining them, the active private took a paper bag of sugar candy out of his pocket, treated Maxim to a piece, and started telling him how much he hated this posting. In the first place, he was afraid of catching something from the degenerates. And in the second place, some of them, like that one-hander, came on so cocky, it was almost more than he could do not to thump them. There was one time he stuck it out for as long as he could, and then did thump one—he was almost demoted to candidate. The cornet had stood up for him though: he only gave him twenty days, and another forty without leave . . .

Maxim sucked on his sugar candy, listening with half an ear and not saying anything. Hate, he thought. This side hates that side, and that side hates this side. For what? The most abhorrent state of all time. Why? Where did he get that from? They've depraved the people. How? What could that mean? And that man in plainclothes—he couldn't have been hinting at torture, surely! That was a long, long time ago, in the Middle Ages . . . But then again, fascism. Yes, I recall now, it wasn't only the Middle Ages. Maybe this is a fascist state? Massaraksh, just what is fascism? Aggression, racial theory . . . Hitler. No, Himmler. Yes, yes—a theory of racial superiority, mass exterminations, genocide, world conquest . . . lies, elevated to a basic principle of politics, the state's lies. I remember that very clearly, that was what staggered me most of all. But I don't think there's any of that here. Is Gai a fascist? And Rada? No, it's something else here—the aftermath of war, explicitly cruel manners and behavior as a consequence of the difficult situation. The majority intent on suppressing the opposition of the minority. Capital punishment, penal servitude. This is all repulsive to me, but what else could you expect?

And what exactly does the opposition consist of? Yes, they hate the existing order. But what do they actually do, in concrete terms? Not a single word was said about that. It's strange . . . As if the judges had conspired in advance with the accused, and the accused had no problems with that. Well, it certainly looked very much that way. The accused are endeavoring to destroy the antiballistic defense system, and the judges know that perfectly well, and the accused know that the judges know that perfectly well—everybody sticks to his own convictions, there's nothing to talk about, and all that remains is to officially confirm the existing state of their relations. They eliminate the first one, dispatch the second one to be "educated," and the third one . . . for some reason the plainclothes man takes the third one for himself. It would be a good thing now to understand what connection exists between a pain in the head and a partiality for opposition. Why is it only degenerates who endeavor to destroy the system of ADTs? And not even all degenerates, at that?

"Mr. Pandi," he said, "the Hontians, are they all degenerates, have you heard?"

Pandi started thinking hard. "How can I put it? . . . You see," he eventually said, "we mostly deal with internal business concerning the degenerates, the urban ones and the ones they have down in the South. But what's up there in Hontia or wherever else, they probably teach the army men about that. The most important thing you have to know is that the Hontians are the most vicious external enemies our state has. Before the war they had to knuckle under to us, and now they're getting their own back, out of spite . . . And the degenerates are our internal enemies. That's all there is to it. You got that?"

"More or less," said Maxim, and Pandi immediately handed him a reprimand: in the Guards you didn't answer like that; in the Guards you answered "affirmative" or "negative," while "more or less" was a civilian expression. The corporal's sister could answer you like that, but you were on duty here, so you couldn't do that.

Probably he would have carried on pontificating for a long time—it was a gratifying subject, close to his heart, and he had an attentive, respectful listener—but at this point the gentlemen officers came back in. Pandi broke off midword, whispered "Attention," and after performing the requisite maneuvers between the table and the iron stool, froze in his position. Maxim also froze.

The gentlemen officers were in an excellent mood. Cornet Chachu was telling the others in a loud voice, with a disdainful air, about how in the Eighty-Fourth they stuck raw dough straight onto red-hot armor plating, and it was really tasty. The brigadier and the plainclothes man objected that the spirit of the Guards was all very fine, but the Guards' cuisine should be well up to the mark, and the fewer canned goods, the better. Narrowing his eyes, the adjutant suddenly started quoting some cookbook or other verbatim, and all the others fell silent and listened to him for rather a long time, with a strange, tender expression on their faces. Then the adjutant swallowed his own saliva the wrong way and started coughing, and the brigadier sighed and said, "Yes, gentlemen . . . But nonetheless, we have to finish up here."

The adjutant, still coughing, opened his folder, rummaged in the papers, and announced in a strangled voice, "Ordi Tader."

And the woman came in, just as white and almost transparent as the day before, as if she were still in a swoon, but when Pandi reached out in his customary manner to take her by the elbow and sit her down, she pulled sharply away, as if reacting to some kind of vermin, and Maxim fancied that she was going to hit Pandi. She didn't hit him—her hands were shackled—she merely enunciated very clearly, "Don't touch me, you lackey," then walked around Pandi and sat down on the stool.

The brigadier asked her the usual questions. She didn't answer. The plainclothes man reminded her about her child and about her husband, and she didn't answer him either. She sat there, holding herself erect, and Maxim couldn't see her face; all he could see was a tense, thin neck under tousled blonde hair.

Then she suddenly spoke in a calm, low voice. "You are all brain-dead blockheads and dopes. Murderers. You will all die. You, brigadier, I do not know you, this is the first and last time I shall see you. You will die a ghastly death. Not at my hands, unfortunately, but a very, very ghastly death. And you, you bastard from secret state security. I have already liquidated two like you myself. I'd kill you right now if not for this lackey standing behind me . . ." She caught her breath. "And you, you black-faced lump of cannon fodder, you butcher, you will fall into our hands. But you will die simply. Gel missed, but I know people who won't miss. You'll all die a long time before we knock down your cursed towers, and that's good. I pray to God that you won't survive your towers, because then you might wise up, and those who come later will feel pity for you and be loath to kill you."

They didn't interrupt; they attentively listened to her. Anyone might have thought they were willing to listen to her for hours, but she suddenly got up and took a step toward the table. However, Pandi caught her by the shoulder and flung her back down onto the stool. Then she spat with all her strength, but the gobbet fell short of the table, and she suddenly went limp and started crying.

For a while they watched her crying. Then the brigadier got to his feet and sentenced her to execution within forty-eight hours, and Pandi took her by the elbow and flung her out through the door, and the plainclothes man energetically rubbed his hands and told the brigadier, "Good job. An excellent outcome."

But the brigadier told him, "Thank the cornet."

And Cornet Chachu said only "Informers," and they all fell silent.

Then the adjutant summoned Memo Gramenu, and they didn't stand on ceremony with this prisoner at all. He was the man who was shooting in the corridor. His case was absolutely clear—he had offered armed resistance to arrest—and they didn't ask him any questions. He sat there on the stool, corpulent and hunched over, and while the brigadier read out his death sentence, he indifferently looked up at the ceiling, using his left hand to cradle his right, with its dislocated fingers swaddled in a rag. Maxim fancied he detected a strange, unnatural calm in this man, a kind of no-nonsense confidence, a cold indifference to what was happening, but he couldn't figure out his own feelings . . .

Before they had even led Gramenu out, the adjutant was already packing his papers away in his folder with an air of relief, the brigadier had struck up a conversation with the plainclothes man about the procedure for promotion, and Cornet Chachu had come across to Pandi and Maxim and ordered them to leave. In the cornet's transparent eyes Maxim detected a clear hint of derision and menace, but he didn't want to think about that. He thought with a strangely abstracted sense of commiseration about the man who would have to kill the woman. It was iniquitous, it was inconceivable, but somebody would have to do it in the next forty-eight hours.

8

Gai changed into his pajamas, hung his uniform in the wardrobe, and turned toward Maxim. Candidate Sim was sitting on his camp cot, which Rada had set up for him in a free corner; he had already pulled off one boot and was holding it in his hand but hadn't set about tackling the other one yet. His eyes were directed straight at the wall and his mouth was half open. Gai crept up on him from the side and tried to flick him on the nose. And, as always, he missed—at the last moment Mak jerked his head away.

"What are you pondering?" Gai playfully asked. "Are you grieving because Rada's not here? That's just your bad luck, brother. She's on the day shift today."

Mak gave a faint smile and started pulling off his other boot. "Why do you say she's not here?" he absentmindedly asked. "You can't fool me." Then he froze again. "Gai," he said. "You always told me that they work for money."

"Who? The degenerates?"

"Yes. You've often talked about it—to me, and the guys. Paid agents of the Hontians. And the cornet harps on about it all the time, the same thing day after day."

"What else do you expect?" said Gai. He thought Mak must be launching into his old conversation about monotony again. "You're a queer fish, after all, Mak. How could we start saying anything new, if everything always stays the same old way? The degenerates are still the same degenerates they always were. And they still get money from the enemy, the same way they always have. Last year, for instance, this crew outside the city was raided—they had an entire basement there stuffed with sacks of money. Where could an honest man get money like that from? They're not industrialists and not bankers . . . and right now bankers don't have that kind of money anyway, not if the banker's a genuine patriot."

Mak neatly set his boots down by the wall, stood up, and started unbuttoning his coverall. "Gai," he said, "does it sometimes happen that people tell you one thing about a person, and you look at that person and feel that it just can't be right? It's a mistake. A mix-up."

"Yes, it happens," said Gai, knitting his brows. "But if you mean the degenerates . . ."

"Yes, that's exactly who I mean. I watched them today. They're people just like any others—some better, some worse, some brave and some cowardly, and not animals at all, not like I was thinking, and like you all think—Wait, don't interrupt. And I don't know if they do harm or they don't—that is, from the look of things, they do, but I don't believe that they've been bought."

"What do you mean, you don't believe it?" said Gai, knitting his brows even tighter. "Look, let's accept that you can't take my word for it, I'm only a little man. But what about the cornet? And the brigadier? And the radio, if it comes to that. How is it possible not to believe the Fathers? They never lie."

Maxim took off his coverall, walked over to the window, and started looking out at the street, pressing his forehead against the glass and clutching the frame with both hands. "Why do they have to be lying?" he eventually said. "What if they're mistaken?"

"Mistaken . . ." Gai repeated in bewilderment, gazing at Maxim's bare back. "Who's mistaken? The Fathers? You crackpot . . . The Fathers never make mistakes!"

"Well, maybe not," said Maxim, turning around. "But we're not talking about the Fathers right now. We're talking about the degenerates. Let's take you, for example . . . You'd die for your cause if you had to, right?"

"I would," said Gai. "And so would you."

"Exactly! We'd die. But we'd be dying for a cause—not for a guardsman's rations and not for money. You could give me a billion of your banknotes, but I wouldn't agree to die for that! And would you?"

"No, of course not," said Gai. What a weirdo Mak was, always coming up with something.

"Well?"

"Well what?"

"Well, it's obvious!" Mak said impatiently. "You're not willing to die for money. I'm not willing to die for money. But the degenerates, it seems, are willing to. What sort of bullshit is that?"

"That's just it, they're degenerates!" Gai said with passionate feeling. "That's what degenerates are like. For them, money's more important than anything else; nothing's sacred to them. For them it's nothing to strangle a child—there have been cases like that . . . You must understand, if someone's trying to destroy the system of ADTs, what kind of human being can he be? He's just a cold-blooded killer!"

"I don't know, I don't know," said Mak. "Look at the ones who were interrogated today. If they had named their accomplices, they could have stayed alive, they would have gotten off with hard labor . . . But they didn't name them! So their accomplices mean more to them than money? More than life?"

"We don't know that yet," Gai objected. "By law they're all condemned to death, without any trial—you've seen the way they're tried. And if some of them are sent off to do hard labor, do you know why? Because we don't have enough men in the South . . . and let me tell you, educational labor is even worse than death."

Looking at Mak, Gai saw that his friend was hesitant and perplexed. He has a good heart, but he's still green, he doesn't understand that cruelty is necessary with the enemy, that right now kindness is worse than treason . . . I'd love to just smash my fist down on the table and shout, tell him to shut up and stop this idle talk, stop spouting all this crap and listen to his elders and betters until he learns to figure things out for himself. But Mak isn't some kind of blockhead, is he? He only needs things to be properly explained and he'll understand.

"No!" Mak stubbornly exclaimed. "It's impossible to hate for money. But they do hate . . . The way they hate us, I didn't even know people could hate that fiercely. You hate them less than they hate you. And what I'd like to know is: What for?"

"Just listen here," said Gai, "and I'll explain it to you again. In the first place, they're degenerates, they hate all normal people anyway. They're malicious by nature, like rats! And then, we get in their way. They'd like to just do their job, take the money, and live high on the hog. But we tell them, *Stop! Hands behind your head!* So are they supposed to love us for that?"

"If they're all as malicious as rats, then why isn't that . . . property owner malicious? Why did they let him go, if they've all been bought?"

Gai laughed. "The property owner's a coward. There are plenty of that kind too. They hate us, but they're afraid. The useful degenerates, the legal ones. It's more convenient for them to live as our friends . . . And then, he's a property owner, a rich man—he can't be bought that easily. He's not just some dentist or other . . . You're funny, Mak, just like a child! People aren't all the same, and degenerates aren't all the same—"

"I already know that," Mak impatiently interrupted. "But take that dentist, for instance. I'd stake my life that he hasn't been bought. I can't prove it to you, I just feel it. He's a very courageous and good man—"

"A degenerate!"

"All right. He's a courageous and good degenerate. I saw his library. He's a very knowledgeable man. He knows a thousand times more than you or the cornet. Why is he against us? If our cause is just, why doesn't he know that—an educated, cultured man like that? Why, on the brink of death, does he tell us to our faces that he is for the people and against us?"

"An educated degenerate is a degenerate to the second power," Gai sententiously declared. "As a degenerate, he hates us. And his education helps him justify his hate and disseminate it. Education, my friend, is not always a boon either. Like an automatic—it all depends on who's holding it."

"Education is always a boon," Maxim said with resolute conviction.

"Oh, no. I'd prefer it if all the Hontians were uneducated. Then at least we could live normal, human lives without expecting a nuclear strike all the time. We'd soon crush them."

"Yes," Mak said in a strange tone of voice. "We know how to crush people. We've got no shortage of cruelty, and that's a fact."

"There you go, talking like a kid again. We're not cruel, it's the times that are cruel. We'd be glad to make do with just persuasion—it would cost us less, and there'd be no bloodshed. But what would you have us do? If there's no way to change their minds—"

"So they're already convinced, then?" Mak interrupted him. "So they're convinced? And if a knowledgeable man is convinced that he's right, what does Hontian money have to do with it?"

Gai was fed up. As a last resort, he was on the point of throwing in a quotation from the Codex of the Fathers to put an end to this stupid, interminable quarrel, but at that very moment Mak interrupted himself with an impatient gesture and shouted, "Rada! No more sleeping! The Guards are famished and pining for some female company!"

Gai was absolutely amazed to hear Rada's voice from behind the screen. "I've been awake for ages already. You gentlemen Guards have been screaming and shouting as if you were on the parade ground."

"Why are you at home?" Gai snapped.

"I was given notice," she explained. "Mama Tei has closed down her place—she came into an inheritance and she's moving to the country. But she's already recommended me for a good job . . . Mak, why are your things thrown all over the place? Put them in the wardrobe. Boys, I asked you not to come into the room in your boots! Where are your boots, Gai? . . . Set the table, we're going to have lunch now . . . Mak, you've lost weight. What are they doing to you in there?"

"Come on, come on!" said Gai. "No more talking in the ranks! Bring in the lunch."

She stuck her tongue out at him and walked out. Gai glanced at Mak. Mak was watching Rada go with the usual good-natured expression on his face.

"A fine girl, right?" Gai asked, and then took fright when Mak's face suddenly turned to stone.

"Listen," said Mak. "You can do anything. Even use torture, I suppose. All of you are in a better position to judge. But shooting women . . . torturing women . . ." He grabbed his boots and walked out of the room.

Gai cleared his throat, scratched the back of his head hard with both hands, and started setting the table. This entire conversation had left a bad taste in his mouth. A strange, schizophrenic kind of feeling. Of course, Mak was still green and not really of this world. But somehow, amazingly, he had done it again. And that was just it—when it came to logic, he was incredible. Like just now he was spouting nonsense, but how logically he had it all laid out! Basically, Gai was obliged to admit that if not for this conversation, he himself would probably never have arrived at what was essentially a very simple idea: the most important thing about degenerates is that they're degenerates. Take that characteristic away, and all the other accusations against them— treason, cannibalism, and all the rest—are all reduced to drivel. Yes, the whole point is that they're degenerates and they hate everything normal. That's enough, and there's no need for any Hontian gold . . . And the Hontians, are they degenerates as well, then? They don't tell us that. But if they're not degenerates, then our degenerates ought to hate them like they hate us . . . Ah, massaraksh! Damn this logic to hell!

When Mak came back, Gai pounced on him: "How did you know Rada was home?"

"What do you mean, how? It was just obvious."

"But if it was obvious to you, massaraksh, why didn't you warn me? And why, massaraksh, do you go blabbing about things in front of outsiders? Thirty-three massarakshes . . ."

Mak blew his top too. "Who's an outsider here, massaraksh? Rada? Why, all of you and your cornet are more outsiders to me than Rada is."

"Massaraksh! What does it say in the regulations about official secrets?"

"Massaraksh and massaraksh! What are you hassling me for? I didn't know that you didn't know she was home! I thought you were kidding me! And anyway . . . what official secrets are we talking about here?"

"Everything that concerns service activity."

"You can all go to hell with your service activity that has to be hidden from your own sister! And from absolutely any-body at all, massaraksh! You've heaped every corner so high with secrets, there's no room left to breathe—you can't even open your mouth!"

"And now you're shouting at me too! I'm trying to teach you, you fool, and you're yelling at me!"

But Mak had already stopped being angry. Suddenly he was right up close, and before Gai could even stir a muscle, strong arms crushed his sides, the room swung around in front of his eyes, and the ceiling came hurtling toward him. Gai gave a stran-gled gasp, and Mak, carefully carrying Gai above his head with his arms fully extended, walked over to the window and said, "Right, where shall we put you and all your secrets? Want to go out the window?"

"What stupid sort of joke is this, massaraksh?" Gai yelled, frantically waving his arms around in search of support.

"You don't want to go out the window? All right, then, stay here."

Gai was carried to the screen and dumped onto Rada's bed. He sat up, pulled down his hitched-up pajama jacket, and mut-tered, "Damn giant muscleman . . ." He wasn't angry any longer either. And there wasn't anybody to be angry with, except maybe the degenerates.

They started setting the table, and then Rada arrived with a saucepan of soup, followed by Uncle Kaan with his beloved flask—which, so he assured them, was the only thing that saved him from catching a cold and various other geriatric ailments. They sat down and started on the soup. Uncle downed a shot, sniffed in air through his nose, and began telling them about his enemy, his colleague Shapshu, who had written another article about the function of some bone or other in some ancient lizard or other, an article that was founded on nothing but stupidity from start to finish, and designed for stupid fools . . .

For Uncle Kaan, all the people around him were fools. His colleagues in his department were fools, some diligent and some indolent. The assistants were all born fools, who ought to be up in the mountains tending animals, and even then, if the truth be told, it wasn't certain that they could manage that. As for the students, all the young people nowadays seemed to have been replaced by changelings, and apart from that, the ones who became students were the stupidest of all, the ones that a judicious entrepreneur wouldn't even let near his machine tools and a knowledgeable officer would refuse to take as soldiers. And so the fate of the science of fossil animals had already been determined.

Gai didn't really regret that very greatly. To hell with the fossils, he had other things to think about, and in general he didn't understand what anybody could ever need this science for. But Rada loved her uncle very much and always supported his expressions of horror at the stupidity of his colleague Shapshu and his grief that the university authorities wouldn't approve the funding required for expeditions.

Today, however, the conversation took a different turn. Rada, who had heard everything, massaraksh, behind her screen, asked her uncle in what way degenerates were different from ordinary people. Gai gave Mak a menacing look and suggested that instead of spoiling her near and dear ones' appetites, she should read the literature. However, Uncle Kaan declared that the literature was written only for the absolute stupidest of fools, and the people in the Department of Public Education imagined everybody else to be the same kind of ignoramuses as they were. But the question of the degenerates was by no means as simple and by no means as trivial as they tried to make it appear in order to mold public opinion in a specific manner, and he said they could discuss this here either like civilized individuals or like their courageous but—unfortunately!—poorly educated officers in the barracks. Mak suggested discussing like civilized individuals for a change.

Uncle Kaan downed another shot and started expounding the theory that was current in scientific circles about the degenerates being nothing less than a new biological species that had appeared on the face of the World as a result of exposure to radiation. The degenerates were undoubtedly dangerous, but not as a social and political phenomenon; the degenerates were biologically dangerous, for they were not waging their struggle against any single nationality, they were simultaneously waging it against all peoples, nationalities, and races. They were fighting for their place in this world, for the survival of their species, and that struggle was not dependent on any social conditions, and it would only end when either the last human being or the last degenerate mutant departed from the arena of biological history.

"Hontian gold—gibberish!" yelled the raging professor. "Sabotage of the ADT system—nonsense! Look to the South, dear gentlemen! To the South! Beyond the Blue Serpent! That's where the real danger is coming from! That's where the monsters in human form will multiply, that's the place from which their columns will advance to trample us underfoot and wipe us off the face of the World. You're a blind man, Gai. And your commanders are blind men. You don't understand the truly great destiny of our country and the historically heroic task of the Unknown Fathers! To save humankind! Not just one nation or other, not just our mothers and children, but the whole of humankind!"

Gai got angry and said he wasn't much concerned about the fate of humankind. He didn't believe in all these armchair ravings. And if he was told there was a chance of setting the wild degenerates on Hontia, bypassing his own country, he would dedicate his entire life to that. The professor flew into a rage and called him a blind fool again. He said that the Unknown Fathers were the most heroic of heroes—that the battle they had to wage was truly against the odds if the only foot soldiers they had at their disposal were as pathetic and blind as Gai. Gai decided not to argue with him. His uncle didn't have a clue about politics, and in some ways he was an animal fossil himself.

Mak tried to intervene and started telling them about the degenerate who had fought against the authorities before the war, but Gai forestalled this feeble impulse to disclose official service secrets by telling Rada to serve the main course. And he told Mak to turn on the television. "Too many conversations today," he said. "Let the soldier home on leave get a bit of rest."

But Gai's imagination had been stimulated, and they were showing some kind of nonsense on the television, so he gave in and started telling stories about the wild degenerates. He knew a thing or two about them—God be praised, hadn't he fought against them for three years rather than sitting it out in the rear like certain philosophers? Rada felt offended for the old man and called Gai a boaster, but for some reason her uncle and Mak took Gai's side and asked him to continue. Only Gai declared that he wouldn't say another word. In the first place, he was actually feeling rather offended himself, and in the second place, after rummaging around in his memory, he couldn't find anything in there that would have refuted the old drunkard's fabrications. The southern degenerates really were hellish beings, and absolutely merciless. Maybe their kind could exterminate the whole of humankind without a second thought, and perhaps even take pleasure in it. But then he suddenly recalled what Zef, the master sergeant of the 134th Unit, had once told him. Ginger-haired Zef had said that the degenerates were constantly getting more active because the radioactive desert was advancing on them from the south, and the poor wretches had nowhere to go—they had no choice but to try fighting their way north into regions where there was no radiation.

"Who told you that?" his uncle asked scornfully. "What block-head could ever get such a primitive idea into his head?" Gai looked at him with a gloating expression and gravely replied, "That is the opinion of a certain Allu Zef, an Imperial Prize winner and our foremost psychiatrist."

"And where did you meet him?" Gai's uncle asked even more contemptuously. "Not in the company mess, was it?"

In the heat of the moment, Gai was about to say where he had met Zef, but he bit his tongue, put on an important expression, and started demonstratively listening to the television announcer, who was reading out the weather forecast.

And at that moment, massaraksh, Mak butted into the con-versation again. "I am prepared to acknowledge," he said, "that the monsters in the South are some new breed of humans, but what do they have in common with the property owner Renadu, for instance? Renadu is also considered a degenerate, only he clearly doesn't belong to any new breed. In fact, to be quite frank, he belongs to a very old breed of people."

Gai had never thought about this point, so he was very glad when his uncle jumped in to answer the question. Calling Mak a clodhopping dolt, Kaan started explaining that the secret degener-ates, otherwise known as urban degenerates, were nothing other than surviving remnants of the new breed that had been almost completely exterminated in our central region while they were still in the cradle. "I can still remember all the horrors: they were killed at birth, sometimes together with their mothers. The only ones who survived were those in whom their new species characteristics were not manifested in any external form." Uncle Kaan downed a fifth shot, then went on a rampage, setting out in front of his audience a precise plan for the universal medi-cal screening of the entire population, which would have to be carried out sooner or later, and preferably sooner rather than later. And no legal degenerates! No tolerance! The weeds had to be mercilessly pulled out by the roots!

On that note lunch came to an end. Rada started washing the dishes, and her uncle, without waiting for any objections, put the stopper in his flask and carried it off to his room, muttering that he was going to write a reply to that fool Shapshu. But for some reason, he happened to take the shot glass with him too. Gai watched him go, looking at his shabby, threadbare jacket, at his old, patched trousers, at his darned socks and darned slippers, and he felt sorry for the old man. That cursed war! His uncle used to own this entire apartment, he had a wife and a son and a servant, and there was luxurious tableware, plenty of money, and even an estate somewhere, but now . . . Just a dusty study crammed with books, which was also his bedroom and all his other rooms as well; shabby clothes, loneliness, and obscurity. Yes.

Gai moved the only armchair up to the television, stretched out his legs, and started drowsily gazing at the screen. Mak sat beside him for a while, then instantly and silently, as only he was capable of doing, disappeared and turned up in a different corner. He rummaged in Gai's little library for a while, selected some kind of textbook, and started leafing through it, leaning his shoulder against the wardrobe. Rada cleared the table, sat down beside Gai, and started knitting, occasionally glancing at the screen. The home was filled with peace, quiet, and contentment. Gai dozed off.

He dreamed about some kind of rubbish: he captured two degenerates in some kind of iron tunnel, started interrogating them, and suddenly discovered that one of the degenerates was Mak. The other degenerate, smiling gently and kindly, said to Gai, "You were mistaken all the time. Your place is with us, and the cornet is simply a professional killer, without any patriotism, without any real loyalty—he simply likes killing, the way you like shrimp soup." Gai suddenly felt a suffocating doubt. He sensed that he was on the brink of completely understanding everything through and through; just one more second and not even a single question would be left. But this unfamiliar condition was so agonizing that his heart stopped beating and he woke up.

Mak and Rada were talking in quiet voices about some nonsense or other—about swimming in the sea, about sand and seashells . . . He didn't listen to them. A thought had suddenly occurred to him: Could he really be capable of doubts of any kind, of hesitation or uncertainty? But he had doubted in his sleep, hadn't he? Did that mean he would have doubts in the same situation when he was awake? He tried for a while to recall all the details of his dream, but the dream slipped away from him, like wet soap skidding out of wet hands, blurring until eventually it became completely implausible, and Gai decided in relief that it was all a load of drivel. And when Rada noticed that he wasn't sleeping and asked what he thought was better, the sea or a river, he replied in soldierly fashion, in the style of good old Doga, "The best thing of all is a good bathhouse."

The program showing on television was *Patterns*. They were bored. Gai suggested having a beer. Rada went to the kitchen and brought two bottles from the refrigerator. Over the beers they talked about this and that, and somehow in passing it emerged that Mak had mastered the textbook on geopolitics in the last half hour. Rada was delighted. Gai didn't believe it. He said half an hour was enough time to leaf through the textbook, perhaps even to read it, but only mechanically, without any understanding. Mak demanded an examination. Gai demanded the textbook. A wager was struck: the loser would have to go to Uncle Kaan and declare to him that his colleague Shapshu was an intelligent man and an excellent scientist.

Gai opened the textbook at random, found the test questions at the end of a chapter, and asked, "What is it that makes our state's expansion to the north a morally noble endeavor?" Mak replied in his own words, but very close to the text, and added that in his view moral nobility had nothing at all to do with it; as he understood things, it was all a matter of the aggressive stance

of the Hontian and Pandeian regimes, and in general this section
of the textbook contradicted the basic thesis of the first chapter
on the sovereignty of each and every nation. Gai scratched the
back of his head with both hands, turned over a few pages, and
asked, "What is the average harvest of cereals in the northwestern
regions?" Mak laughed and said there was no data on the northwestern regions. The attempt to trick him had failed, and Rada
delightedly stuck her tongue out at Gai. "Then what is the population pressure per unit area in the estuary of the Blue Serpent
River?" Mak gave the figure, also giving the margin of error,
and took the opportunity to add that he thought the concept
of population pressure was rather vague. In any case, he didn't
understand why it had been introduced. Gai started explaining to
him that population pressure was a measure of aggressiveness,
but at that point Rada intervened. She said that Gai was twisting
things and trying to back out of the rest of the exam because he
realized it was looking bad for him.

Gai absolutely did not want to go and speak to Uncle Kaan,
so he started bickering to drag things out. Mak listened to him for
a while, then suddenly announced that under no circumstances
should Rada go back to working as a waitress; she needed to
study, he said. Gai, delighted by the change of subject, exclaimed
that he had told her the same thing a thousand times, and had
already suggested that she should apply to the Women's Guards
Corps, where they would make a really useful person out of her.
Mak only shook his head, and Rada, as she had always done
before, expressed her opinion of the Women's Guards Corps in
highly disrespectful terms

Gai didn't try to argue. He put down the textbook, reached
into the wardrobe, took out a guitar, and started tuning it. Rada
and Mak immediately moved the table aside and stood facing
each other, ready to roar out *"Yes-yes, no-no."* And Gai gave
them *"Yes-yes, no-no,"* tapping out the rhythm and strumming so
that the notes chimed out. He watched them dance and thought
what a splendid couple they made, only they had nowhere to

live, and if they got married, he would have to move out completely into the barracks. Well, what of it? Plenty of corporals
lived in the barracks . . . Only, then again, Mak wasn't giving
any signs of planning to get married. He treated her more like a
friend, only with more tenderness and respect, but all the signs
were that Rada had really fallen for him. Oh, just look at the
way her eyes flash. And how could she possibly not fall for a
young guy like that? Even that old hag Madam Go acts the same
way, and she's well past sixty; when Mak walks along the corridor, she opens her door, sticks her skull out, and grins. But
then, damn it all, the entire building loves Mak, even the guys
in the section love him, only the cornet takes a strange sort of
attitude toward him—but even the cornet doesn't deny that the
guy's a real ball of fire.

The couple danced until they were ready to drop. Then Mak
took the guitar from Gai, retuned it in his own outlandish manner, and started singing his strange Highlander songs. Thousands
of songs, and not a single one that Gai knew. Something new
every time. And the strangest thing of all was that Gai didn't
understand a single word, but when he listened, he felt like crying, or he laughed until he almost split his sides.

Rada had already memorized some of the songs, and now
she tried to sing along. She was especially fond of a funny song
(Mak had translated it) about a girl who is sitting on a mountain
and waiting for her boyfriend, but her boyfriend just can't get to
her—first one thing stops him, and then another . . . Through the
sounds of the guitar and the singing, they didn't hear the front
doorbell ring. There was just a loud knock, and Cornet Chachu's
orderly lumbered into the room.

"Mr. Corporal, sir, permission to speak!" he barked out,
squinting sideways at Rada.

Mak stopped playing. Gai said, "Permission granted."

"The cornet has ordered you and Candidate Sim to report
immediately to the company office. The car is waiting downstairs."

Gai jumped to his feet. "Off you go," he said. "Wait in the car, we'll be down immediately. "Quick, get dressed," he said to Maxim.

Rada took the guitar in her arms, as if it were a child, and stood at the window, turned away from them.

Gai and Mak hastily got dressed. "What do you think this is about?" asked Mak.

"How should I know?" Gai growled. "Maybe it'll be an alarm drill."

"I don't like this," said Mak.

Gai looked at him and switched on the radio, just to make sure. They were broadcasting *Businesswomen's Small Talk*.

After they had gotten dressed and tightened their belts, Gai said, "Rada, we're off, then."

"Go," said Rada, without turning around.

"Let's go, Mak," said Gai, tugging his beret down on his head.

"Give me a call," said Rada. "If you're delayed, be sure to call." But she still didn't turn around.

The orderly obligingly opened the car door for Gai. They got in and drove off. The business was obviously urgent; the driver drove hard and fast, with the siren on, in the reserve lane. Gai rather regretfully thought that now their little party, and a fine, cozy, carefree evening at home, had been ruined. But such was the life of a guardsman. Now they would tell him, *You're going to get into this tank and you're going to fire*, straight after the bottle of beer, after his cozy pajamas, after the jolly songs to the strains of the guitar. Such was the glorious life of a guardsman, the best of all possible lives. And we don't need any girlfriends or wives. And Mak's right for not looking to marry Rada, although I feel sorry for my sweet sister, of course . . . Never mind, she'll wait. If she loves him, she'll wait.

They turned onto the parade ground and braked to a halt at the entrance to the barracks building. Gai jumped out and ran up the steps. He stopped outside the door of the office, checked the position of his beret and his buckles, cast a quick glance over

Mak, fastened Mak's collar button—massaraksh, that thing was always unfastened!—and knocked.

"Come in!" the familiar voice croaked. Gai walked inside and reported in. Cornet Chachu was sitting at his desk, wearing a wool cape and peaked cap. He was smoking and drinking coffee, and the shell casing in front of him was full of cigarette butts. Lying next to it on the desk were two automatic rifles.

The cornet slowly got to his feet, leaned heavily on the desk with both hands, and started to speak, staring fixedly at Mak. "Candidate Sim. You have shown yourself to be an outstanding soldier and a loyal comrade in arms. I have petitioned the brigade commander for your early promotion to the status of an active private in the Battle Guards. You have passed the test of fire quite satisfactorily. There remains only the final test—the test of blood."

Gai's heart leaped in joy. He hadn't expected it to happen so soon. Good for you, Cornet! That's an old war dog for you! What a fool I was to think he was scheming against Mak . . . Gai looked at Mak, and his joy dwindled. Mak's face was completely wooden and his eyes were goggling—which was all correct according to the rules, but just at this moment he didn't need to adhere so strictly to all the rules and regulations.

"I am handing you an order, Candidate Sim," the cornet continued, holding a sheet of paper out to Mak. "This is the first written order addressed to you in person. I hope it will not be the last. Read it and sign it."

Mak took the order and ran his eyes over it. Gai's heart leaped again, only this time not in joy but with a strange, oppressive sense of foreboding. Mak's face remained as motionless as ever, and everything seemed to be in order, but he hesitated slightly before taking the pen and signing his name. The cornet examined the signature and put the sheet of paper in his map-case.

"Corporal Gaal," he said, taking a sealed envelope off the desk. "Go to the guardhouse and bring the condemned prisoners. Take a rifle . . . no, this one, at the edge."

Gai took the envelope, hung the rifle over his shoulder, made an about-face, and walked toward the door. He had time to hear the cornet say to Mak, "It's all right, Candidate, don't get cold feet. It's only frightening the first time around . . ." Gai set off at a run across the parade ground toward the building of the brigade jail, handed the envelope to the officer of the guard, signed where he had to, and was given the necessary receipts, and the condemned prisoners were led out to him. They were two of the conspirators he had seen recently: the fat man whose fingers Maxim had dislocated, and the woman. Massaraksh, this was the last thing they needed! The woman would be too much of a shock . . . This wasn't for Mak.

Gai led the prisoners out onto the parade ground and herded them toward the barracks building. The man plodded along, step after step, all the while cradling his arm, and the woman walked ramrod straight, with her hands thrust deep into the pockets of her little jacket, not seeming to see or hear anything. Massaraksh, just why exactly wasn't she for Mak? What the hell? This woman was exactly the same kind of low snake as the man. What right did she have to any special privileges? And why, massaraksh, did any special privileges have to be granted to Candidate Sim? Let him get used to it, massaraksh and massaraksh.

The cornet and Mak were already in the truck. The cornet was at the wheel, and Mak was in the backseat, with his rifle between his legs. Gai opened the door and the condemned prisoners got in. "On the floor!" Gai commanded. They obediently sat down on the iron floor, and Gai sat on the seat facing Mak. He tried to catch Mak's eye, but Mak was looking at the condemned prisoners. No, he was looking at that woman, huddled on the floor with her arms around her knees. Without looking around, the cornet asked, "Ready?" and the truck set off.

They didn't talk along the way. The cornet drove the truck insanely fast—he obviously wanted to get it all over with before twilight set in, and what point was there in dragging it out anyway? Mak kept looking at the woman as if he was trying to catch her eye, and Gai kept trying to catch Mak's eye. The condemned pair clutched at each other and squirmed about on the floor; the fat man tried to talk to the woman, but Gai shouted at him. The truck hurtled out of the city, passed through the southern gate, and immediately turned onto an abandoned cart track, a very familiar cart track for Gai, leading to the Pink Caves. The truck bounced on all four wheels, there was nothing to hold on to, and Mak didn't want to raise his eyes—and there were the semi-corpses, grabbing at Gai's knees all the time, trying to escape from the merciless jolting. Eventually Gai's patience ran out and he jabbed the fat man under the ribs with his boot, but that didn't do any good; the fat man kept grabbing at his knees anyway. The cornet turned the wheel again, braked sharply, and the truck slowly and cautiously drove down into a quarry. The cornet turned off the engine and commanded, "Get out!"

It was already about eighteen hundred hours, a light evening mist was gathering in the quarry, and the weathered stone walls shimmered pink. Marble had once been quarried here, but who needed it now, that marble?

The business was approaching its conclusion. Mak was still conducting himself like an ideal soldier: not a single superfluous movement, an indifferently wooden expression, eyes trained on his superior in anticipation of a command. The fat man was conducting himself well, with dignity. They clearly wouldn't have any trouble with him. But as the end approached, the woman had fallen apart. She kept convulsively clenching her fists, pressing them against her chest, and lowering them again, and Gai decided there would be hysterics, but he didn't think they would have to lug her to the execution site in their arms.

The cornet lit up a cigarette, looked at the sky, and said to Mak, "Take them along this path. When you reach the caves, you'll see for yourself where to stand them. When you're done, be sure to check and if necessary give them a finishing shot. Do you know what a finishing shot is?"

"Yessir."

"Don't lie, you don't know. It's a shot to the head. Go ahead, Candidate. When you come back, you'll be a genuine private."

The woman suddenly spoke: "If there is at least one human being among you . . . let my mother know. . . Utki Village, house number two . . . it's close by here . . . Her name is—"

"Don't debase yourself," the corpulent man said in a deep voice.

"Her name is Illy Tader—"

"Don't debase yourself," the corpulent man repeated, raising his voice, and the cornet jabbed a fist into his face, without even bothering to take a swing. The corpulent man fell silent, clutching at his cheek, and cast a look filled with hate at the cornet.

"Go ahead, Candidate," the cornet repeated.

Mak turned to the condemned prisoners and gestured with his automatic rifle. The condemned pair set off along the path. The woman looked back and shouted once again. "Utki Village, house two, Illy Tader!"

Holding his rifle out in front of him, Mak slowly walked along behind them. The cornet swung the door of the truck open, sat sideways on the driver's seat, stretched out his legs, and said, "Right, now we'll wait for a quarter of an hour."

"Yes, sir, Mr. Cornet, sir," Gai replied mechanically. He watched Mak walking away and carried on watching until the entire group was hidden from sight behind a pink outcrop of rock. We'll have to buy some vodka on the way back, he thought. Let him get drunk. It helps some men.

"You may smoke, Corporal," said the cornet.

"Thank you, Mr. Cornet, but I don't smoke."

The cornet spat a long way through his teeth. "Are you not afraid of being disappointed in your friend?"

"No indeed, sir," Gai said indecisively. "Although, with your permission, I'm very sorry that he got the woman. He's a Highlander, and for them—"

"He's no more a Highlander that you are or I am," said the cornet. "And this isn't a question of women . . . However, let's wait and see. What were you doing when you were summoned?"

"Singing together, Mr. Cornet."

"And what were you singing?"

"Highlanders' songs, Mr. Cornet. He knows an awful lot of songs."

The cornet got out of the truck and started walking backward and forward on the path. He didn't talk anymore, but after about ten minutes he started whistling the Guards' march. Gai kept waiting for the sound of shots, but no shots came, and he started feeling anxious. He didn't know himself why he felt anxious. It was unconceivable for anyone to get away from Mak. And disarming him was even more inconceivable. But then why didn't he fire? Perhaps he had taken them farther than the usual place? The smell there was very strong—the grave diggers didn't bury the bodies very deep—and Mak's sense of smell was far too keen. He might walk several extra miles out of sheer squeamishness.

"*Weeell* now . . ." said the cornet, halting. "That's it then, Corporal Gaal. I'm afraid we won't be seeing your little friend back here. And I'm afraid today's the last day we'll be calling you Corporal."

Gai looked at him in amazement, and the cornet chuckled.

"Well, what are you looking at? Why are you gawking like a pig at ham? Your friend has run off, deserted—he's a coward and a traitor. Is that clear, Private Gaal?"

Gai was dumbfounded. And not so much by what the cornet had said as by his tone of voice. The cornet was elated; he looked like a man who had just won a large bet. Gai automatically glanced into the depths of the quarry and suddenly saw Mak: he was coming back alone, carrying his automatic rifle by its strap.

"Massaraksh!" the cornet wheezed. He had seen Mak too, and he looked totally stupefied.

They didn't speak anymore, they just watched as Mak drew closer, walking unhurriedly and stepping lightly over the crushed stone. They watched his calm, good-natured face with the strange eyes, and Gai's head was filled with total confusion: There weren't any shots, were there? But surely he couldn't have strangled them, or beaten them to death with his rifle butt. Mak kill a woman like that? No, that's rubbish . . . But there weren't any shots!

Five steps away from them Mak stopped, looked into the cornet's face, and flung the automatic down at his feet. "Good-bye, Mr. Cornet," he said. "I let those poor, unfortunate people go, and now I want to go myself. Here's your weapon, here's your clothing . . ." Mak turned toward Gai as he unfastened his belt and told him, "Gai, this is a dirty business. They tricked us, Gai."

He took off his boots and coverall and rolled everything up into a bundle, leaving himself standing there as Gai saw him for the first time on the southern border—almost naked and now without even any footwear, in nothing but his silvery under-shorts. He walked over to the truck and put the bundle on the radiator. Gai was horrified. He looked at the cornet and felt even more horrified.

"Mr. Cornet!" he shouted out. "Don't! He's gone mad! It's another—"

"Candidate Sim," the cornet croaked, holding his hand on his holster. "Get into the truck immediately! You're under arrest."

"No," said Mak. "You just think I'm under arrest. I'm free. And I've come for Gai. Come on, Gai, let's go! He duped you. These are sordid people. I had some doubts before, but now I'm certain. Let's go."

Gai shook his head. He wanted to say something, to explain something, but he didn't have any time, and he didn't have any words.

The cornet took out his revolver. "Candidate Sim! Into the car!" he croaked.

"Are you coming?" Mak asked.

Gai shook his head again. He looked at the pistol in the cornet's hand, and there was only one thought in his head, and he knew only one thing: Mak was going to be killed now. And he didn't understand what he ought to do.

"All right," said Mak. "I'll find you. I'll find out everything and I'll find you. This isn't the place for you . . . Kiss Rada for me, I'll be seeing you."

He turned and walked over the crushed stone in his bare feet, with the same light stride as when he was in his boots, and Gai, shuddering as if he had a fever, mutely watched Mak's triangular back and waited for a shot and a little black hole under Mak's left shoulder blade.

"Candidate Sim," the cornet said, without raising his voice, "I order you to come back. I'll shoot."

Mak stopped and turned back toward him again. "Shoot?" he said. "At me? For what? But then, that's not important . . . Give the pistol to me."

The cornet held the pistol beside his hip with the barrel aimed at Mak. "I'm counting to three," he said. "Get into the car, Candidate. One!"

"Come on now, give me the pistol," said Mak, reaching out his hand and moving toward the cornet.

"Two!" said the cornet.

"Don't!" shouted Gai.

The cornet fired. Mak was already close and Gai saw the bullet hit his shoulder, making Mak stagger, as if he had run into an obstacle.

"You stupid fool," said Mak. "Give me that gun, you malicious, stupid fool . . ."

He didn't stop, he just kept on walking toward the cornet, holding out his hand for the gun, and blood suddenly spurted out of the little hole in his shoulder. The cornet made a strange screeching sound and backed away, firing three very rapid rounds into that broad, brown chest. Mak was flung backward; he fell on his back but immediately jumped up, then fell down again, and then sat up, and the cornet, crouching down in his state of stress, fired another three bullets into him. Mak tumbled over onto his stomach and lay still.

Everything started blurring and swaying in front of Gai's eyes, and he lowered himself onto the running board of the truck. His legs refused to hold him up. His ears were still filled with the repulsive crunching of flesh as the bullets entered the body of this strange man whom he loved. Then he recovered his senses, but he kept sitting there for a while, afraid to risk getting to his feet.

Mak's brown body lay there among the white and pink rocks, itself as motionless as a rock. The cornet was standing in the same spot, holding his pistol at the ready as he greedily drew in the smoke of a cigarette. He didn't look at Gai. Then he finished smoking his cigarette right down to the end, burning his lips, threw away the stub, and took two steps toward the dead man. But the second step was a very short one, and Mr. Cornet Chachu couldn't bring himself to move in really close. He fired the finishing shot from a distance of ten paces, and he missed. Gai saw the stone dust spurt up right beside Mak's head.

"Massaraksh," the cornet hissed, and started stuffing his pistol into its holster. It took him a long time to stuff it in, and then he simply couldn't button the holster. After that he walked over to Gai, grabbed hold of the chest of Gai's uniform with his mutilated hand, and jerked Gai up onto his feet. Breathing loudly into his face, and drawling his words like a drunk, the cornet said, "All right, you will remain a corporal. But there's no place for you in the Guards. You will write a request to be transferred to the army. Get in the truck."

"THERE'S A BAD KIND OF SMELL HERE . . ."

"There's a bad kind of smell here," said Dad.

"Really?" asked Father-in-Law. "I can't smell anything."

"It stinks, it stinks," Stepfather peevishly grouched. "Some kind of rotten meat. Like at a garbage dump . . ."

"The walls must have rotted," Dad decided.

"Yesterday I saw a new tank," said Brother-in-Law. "The Vampire. Impeccable hermetic sealing, thermal barrier good for up to a thousand degrees . . ."

"*They probably went rotten in the late emperor's time,*" said Dad, "*And there hasn't been any refurbishment work since the coup . . .*"

"*Did you approve it?*" Stepbrother asked Brother-in-Law.

"*Yes,*" said Brother-in-Law.

"*So when does it go into mass production?*" asked Stepbrother.

"*It already has,*" said Father-in-Law. "*Ten units a day.*"

"*With these tanks of yours we'll all be left with no pants soon,*" Stepfather grumped.

"*Better no pants than no medals,*" Brother-in-Law objected.

"*You used to be a colonel,*" Stepfather cantankerously told him, "*and you haven't changed. Always wanting to play with tanks . . .*"

"*My tooth's nagging at me,*" Dad pensively complained. "*Wanderer, is it really so difficult to invent a painless way of fixing teeth?*"

"*I could think about it,*" said Wanderer.

"*You'd better think about heavy weapons systems,*" Stepbrother angrily told him.

"*I can think about heavy weapons systems too,*" said Wanderer.

"*Let's not talk about heavy weapons systems today,*" Dad suggested. "*Let's just say this isn't the time.*"

"*Well, in my opinion, it's a very good time,*" objected Stepbrother. "*The Pandeians have thrown another division at the Hontian border.*"

"*What does that have to do with you?*" Stepfather morosely inquired.

"*Plenty,*" replied Stepbrother. "*I made calculations for the following scenario: the Pandeians intervene in the Hontians' mess, quickly put their own man in there, and we face a united front—fifty million against our forty.*"

"*I'd give big money to have them intervene in the Hontians' mess,*" said Stepfather. "*You're the one who always imagines any mess is a mess of pottage, so it can simply be eaten . . . But what I say is, anyone who touches Hontia has already lost.*"

"*That depends on how they touch it,*" Father-in-Law said in a quiet voice. "*If it's done delicately, with small forces and without getting bogged down—just a light touch and then spring back as soon as they stop their quarreling . . . and at the same time, before the Pandeians can manage—*"

"In the final analysis, what do we want?" asked Brother-in-Law. "It's either the Hontians united, without that civil mess of theirs, or Hontians who are ours, or Hontians who are dead . . . In any case we can't dispense with an invasion. Let's agree on an invasion, and after that it's a matter of the details. There's a plan ready for every alternative."

"You absolutely have to throw us in there without any pants," said Stepfather. "You don't care if there are no pants, just as long as there are medals . . . What do you want a united Hontia for, if we can have a disunited Pandeia?"

"A fit of detective novel raving," Stepbrother remarked to nobody in particular.

"It's not funny," said Stepfather. "I'm not suggesting any unreal alternatives. If I say something, I have good grounds for it."

"You can hardly have any good grounds," Father-in-Law gently said. "It's just that you're seduced by the cheapness of a solution, and I understand you there—it's just that the northern problem can't be solved with small resources. You can't get the job done with putsches or coups there. The Stepfather who came before you divided the Hontians, and now we have to unite them again . . . Putsches are all well and good, but that way you can end up with a revolution. After all, things don't work the same way there as they do here."

"And why don't you say anything, Egghead?" asked Dad. "You are our egghead, after all."

"When fathers talk, prudent children should hold their tongues," Egghead replied with a smile.

"Come on, speak, speak, damn you."

"I'm not a politician," said Egghead. They all laughed. Brother-in-Law actually choked. "Honestly, gentlemen, there's nothing funny about this . . . I really am only a narrow specialist. And as such, I can only inform you that, according to my data, the mood of the army officers is in favor of war."

"So that's how it is?" said Dad, giving him an intent look. "And you're inclined the same way?"

"I'm sorry, Dad," Egghead passionately exclaimed. "But in my view now is an expedient moment for an invasion: the reequipping of the army is being concluded."

"All right, all right," Dad good-naturedly said. "I'll have a talk with you about that later."

"There's no need to have a talk with him later," Father-in-Law objected. "We're all on the same team here, and a specialist is obliged to express his opinion. That's what we keep him for."

"By the way, on the subject of specialists," said Dad, "why don't I see Twitcher here?"

"Twitcher is inspecting the mountain defensive belt," said Brother-in-Law. "But we know his opinion anyway. He worries about the army, as if it were his own army . . ."

"Yes," said Dad. "The mountains are serious business. Stepbrother, was it you who told me they'd found a Highlander spy in the Guards? Yes, dear gentlemen, the North is all well and good, but there are mountains looming in the east, and beyond the mountains is the ocean . . . We'll cope with the North one way or another . . . You want to fight a war, well, we can fight one. Although . . . How long can we last, Wanderer?"

"About ten days," said Wanderer.

"Well then, we can fight for five or six . . ."

"The plan of deep invasion," said Brother-in-Law, "envisages the rout of Hontia in eight days."

"A good plan," Dad approvingly remarked. "All right, then that's what we'll decide on . . . You seem to be opposed, Wanderer?"

"It's none of my business," said Wanderer.

"All right," said Dad, "so be against it . . . Well then, Stepfather, shall we join the majority?"

"Ah," Stepfather said in disgust. "Do what you want . . . He's frightened of a revolution . . ."

"Dad!" Father-in-Law triumphantly exclaimed. "I knew you'd be with us!"

"But of course!" said Dad. "Where would I be without you? I recall, I used to have some mines in the Governorate General of Hontia . . . copper mines . . . I wonder how they're doing now? . . . Yes, Egghead! And we'll probably have to organize public opinion too, won't we? You've probably already come up with something, haven't you? You are our egghead after all."

"Of course, Dad," said Egghead. "Everything's ready."

"Some kind of assassination attempt? Or an attack on the towers? You go off right now and prepare the materials for me before nightfall, and we'll discuss the time frame here . . ."

When the door closed behind Egghead, Dad said, "Was there something you wanted to tell us about Blister, Wanderer?"

PART III

THE TERRORIST

9

His guide quietly said "Wait here" and walked away, disappearing among the bushes behind the trees. Maxim sat down on a tree stump in the center of the clearing, thrust his hands deep into the pockets of his canvas trousers, and started waiting. The forest was old and untended, stifled by dense underbrush, and the ancient, wizened tree trunks exuded an odor of dead, decaying wood. The air was damp. Maxim shivered; he was feeling nauseous and wanted to sit in the sunshine for a while to warm up his shoulder. There was someone in the bushes nearby, but Maxim took no notice—he had been followed all the way from the village, and he had nothing against that. It would have been strange if they immediately trusted him.

Off to one side a little girl came out into the clearing, wearing a huge, patched blouse and carrying a basket in one hand. She fixed Maxim with an intent stare and kept her eyes on him as she walked past, stumbling and getting her feet tangled in the grass. Some kind of small animal like a squirrel streaked through the bushes, flew up a tree, glanced down, took fright, and disappeared. It was quiet here, with only the irregular throbbing of an engine somewhere in the distance—a machine was cutting reeds at a lake.

The man in the bushes didn't go away—Maxim could feel his baleful stare boring into his back. It was unpleasant, but Maxim had to get used to it. Things would always be like this now. The inhabited island had ganged up on him; first it had shot at him, and now it was trailing him, and it didn't trust him. Maxim fell into a doze. Recently he had started frequently dozing off at the most inappropriate moments—falling asleep, waking up, and falling asleep again. He didn't try to resist this; it was what his body wanted, and his body knew best. It would pass; all he needed to do was not fight against it.

He heard the rustling of footsteps, and the guide said "Follow me." Maxim got up without taking his hands out of his pockets and set off after the guide, looking down at his feet in their soft, wet boots. They went deeper into the forest and started walking in circles and complicated loops, gradually moving closer to a dwelling of some kind, which was actually very close to the clearing in a straight line. Then the guide, deciding that he had confused Maxim enough, set off directly toward their goal through the scrub and wind-fallen trees. Being a town man, he made such a loud racket, with so much rustling, that Maxim couldn't even hear the footsteps of the man creeping along behind them any longer.

When the wind-fallen trees came to an end, beyond them Maxim saw a small clearing and a lopsided log house with boarded-up windows. The clearing was overgrown with tall grass, but Maxim could see that people had walked here—both very recently and a long time ago. They had walked cautiously, trying to approach the house by a different route every time. The guide opened a squeaky door, and they walked into a dark, musty vestibule. The man who was following them remained outside. The guide heaved open the trapdoor of the cellar and said, "Go down there, and be careful." He couldn't see very well in the dark. Maxim walked down the wooden stairs.

The cellar was warm and dry, and there were people it, sitting around a wooden table and goggling with amusing expressions as they tried to scrutinize Maxim. The fumes of a newly extinguished candle hung in the air. They obviously didn't want Maxim to see their faces. He only recognized two of them: the woman Ordi, old Illy Tader's daughter, and fat Memo Gramenu, sitting right beside the stairs with a machine gun across his knees. The trapdoor crashed shut above them and someone said, "Who are you? Tell us about yourself."

"Can I sit down?" Maxim asked.

"Yes, of course. Come this way, toward my voice. You'll run up against a bench."

Maxim sat down at the table and ran his glance over the people there. Apart from him, there were four people at the table. In the darkness they looked gray and flat, like an old-fashioned photograph. Ordi was sitting on Maxim's right, but all the talking was done by a thickset, broad-shouldered man sitting opposite Maxim. He looked unpleasantly like Cornet Chachu.

"Tell us," he repeated.

Maxim sighed. He really didn't want to begin this introduction to new acquaintances by lying, but there was nothing to be done about it. "I don't know my past," he said. "They say that I'm a Highlander. Maybe so. I don't remember . . . My name is Maxim, and my surname is Kammerer. In the Guards they called me Mak Sim. My memory of myself begins from the moment when I was arrested in the forest near the Blue Serpent . . ."

That was the end of the lying, and after that things went more easily. He told his story, trying to be brief and at the same time not to omit anything that seemed important to him.

" . . . I led them as far as I could into the quarry, told them to run for it, and walked back without hurrying. Then the cornet shot me. That night I came around, clambered out of the quarry, and soon I came across a pasture. During the day I hid in the bushes, and at night I snuck up to the cows and drank their milk. After a few days I started feeling better. I got some old rags from the cowherds, made my way to Utki Village, and found Illy Tader there. You know all the rest."

Nobody said anything for a while. Then a rustic-looking man, with long hair down to his shoulders, said, "I don't understand how it is that he doesn't remember his past life. I don't think that happens. Let's hear what Doc thinks."

"It does happen," Doc tersely said. He was a thin, exhausted-looking man, twirling a pipe in his hands. He obviously wanted very badly to smoke.

"Why didn't you run off with the condemned prisoners?" the broad-shouldered man asked.

"I'd left Gai there," Maxim said. "I was hoping Gai would go with me." He fell silent, recalling Gai's pale face and confused expression, and the cornet's terrible eyes, and the searing jolts in his chest and belly, and the sensation of helplessness and resentment. "It was stupid, of course," he said. "But I didn't understand that then."

"Did you take part in operations?" corpulent Memo asked behind Maxim's back.

"I've already told you."

"Tell us again!"

"I took part in only one operation, when Ketshef, Ordi, you, and two others, who didn't give their names, were arrested. One of them had an artificial hand—he was a professional revolutionary."

"How do you explain your cornet's haste? After all, before a candidate is allowed to take the test of blood, he is supposed to take part in at least three operations."

"I don't know. All I do know is that he didn't trust me. But I don't understand why he sent me to execute—"

"And exactly why did he shoot you?"

"I think he was frightened. I wanted to take his pistol from him."

"I don't understand," said the man with long hair. "All right, so he didn't trust you. All right, so he sent you to execute the prisoners as a check—"

"Wait, Forester," said Memo. "This is all just talk, empty words. Doc, if I were you, I'd examine him. Somehow I don't believe all this business about the cornet."

"I can't examine him in the dark," Doc irritably snapped.

"Then let's have some light," Maxim advised him. "I can see you anyway."

A sudden silence fell.

"What do you mean, you can see us?" the broad-shouldered man asked.

Maxim shrugged. "I just can," he said.

"What rubbish," said Memo. "OK, so what am I doing now, if you can see?"

Maxim looked around. "You're pointing your submachine gun at me—that is, you think you are, but actually it's pointing at Doc. You're Memo Gramenu, I know you. You have a scratch on your right cheek that wasn't there before."

"Nyctalopia," Doc growled. "So yes, let's have some light. It's stupid. He can see us, but we can't see him." He groped about in front of himself for a box of matches and started striking one match after another. They kept breaking.

"Allow me . . ." Maxim reached out his hand, took the matches from Doc, and lit the candle.

They all squeezed their eyes shut and put their hands over them. Doc immediately lit up his pipe. "Get undressed," he said through the pipe's crackling.

Maxim pulled his canvas shirt off over his head. They all stared at his chest. Doc clambered out from behind the table, walked up to Maxim, and started turning him this way and that, palpitating him with firm, cold fingers.

The room was quiet. Then the long-haired man said with a regretful air, "A good-looking boy. My son was . . . good-looking too . . ."

When no one replied, he cumbersomely got up and rummaged in the corner of the room, pulling out a large bottle bound in woven straw and putting it on the table. Then he set out three mugs. "We can take turns," he explained. "If anybody wants a bite to eat, there's cheese to be had. And onions—"

"Wait, Forester," the broad-shouldered man said in annoyance. "Move the bottle out of the way, I can't see anything . . . Well then, Doc?"

Doc ran his cold fingers over Maxim's body one more time, wreathed himself in smoke, and sat back down in his place. "Pour me one, Forester," he said. "Cases like this deserve a toast . . . Get dressed," he said to Maxim. "And stop smiling like a fresh rose in spring. I shall have to ask you a few questions."

Maxim got dressed.

Doc took a sip from his mug, made a wry face, and asked, "When did you say you were shot?"

"Forty-seven days ago."

"And what did you say you were shot with?"

"A pistol. An army pistol."

Doc took another sip, made a wry face again, then turned to the broad-shouldered man and said, "I'd stake my life on the fact that this young fellow really was shot with an army pistol, and at very close range, only not forty-seven days ago, but at least a hundred and forty-seven . . . Where are the bullets?" he abruptly asked Maxim.

"They came out, and I threw them away."

"Listen, whatever your name is . . . Mak! You're lying. Confess now—who did this for you?"

Maxim bit on his lip. "I'm telling the truth. You simply don't know how quickly our wounds heal. I'm not lying." He paused for a moment. "Anyway, you can easily check what I say. Cut my arm. If it's not a deep cut, I'll heal it up in ten or fifteen minutes."

"That's true," said Ordi, only now speaking for the first time. "I've seen it myself. He was peeling potatoes and cut his finger. Half an hour later there was only a white scar left, and the next day there was nothing at all. I think he really is a Highlander. Gel told me about the ancient Highland medicine—they know how to charm away their wounds."

"Ah, Highland medicine," said Doc, wreathing himself in smoke again. "Well now, let's suppose so. Of course, a cut finger is one thing and seven bullets at point-blank range is a different matter, but let's suppose so. The fact that the wounds healed so successfully isn't the most surprising thing. What I would like an explanation for is something different. This young man has seven holes in him. And if those holes really were made by genuine pistol bullets, then at least four of them—and each one individually, note!—were fatal."

Forester gasped and prayerfully folded his hands together.

"What the hell?" exclaimed the broad-shouldered man.

"Oh, no, you must believe me," said Doc. "A bullet in the heart, a bullet in the spine, and two bullets in the liver. And on top of that, the general loss of blood. And on top of that, the inevitable sepsis. And on top of that, the absence of any traces at all of qualified medical intervention. Massaraksh, the bullet in the heart would have been enough."

"What do you have to say to that?" the broad-shouldered man asked Maxim.

"He's mistaken," Maxim said. "He described everything quite correctly, but he's mistaken. For us these wounds are not fatal. Now, if the cornet had shot me in the head . . . but he didn't . . . You see, Doc, you can't even imagine how resilient these organs are—the heart, the liver—they're simply brimming over with blood . . ."

"Well now . . ." said Doc.

"One thing is clear to me," said the broad-shouldered man said. "They wouldn't be likely to send us a botched job like this. They know that we have doctors among us."

There was a long silence. Maxim patiently waited. Would I believe it? he thought. I probably would. But I seem to be altogether too gullible for this world. Although not as gullible as I used to be. For instance, I don't like Memo. He's afraid of something all the time. Sitting here among his own people with a machine gun, he's still afraid of something. It's strange. But then, he's probably afraid of me. He's probably afraid I'll take his machine gun from him and dislocate his fingers again. Well, maybe he's right there. I won't let anybody shoot me again. It's too hideous when somebody shoots you . . . He recalled the freezing cold night in the quarry, the dead, phosphorescent sky, the cold, sticky pool that he was lying in. No, no more. I've had enough. I'd rather do the shooting myself now . . .

"I trust him," Ordi suddenly said. "What he says doesn't add up, but that's simply because he's a strange kind of man. It's not possible to make up a story like this, it would be too absurd.

If I didn't trust him and I heard a story like this, I'd just shoot him straightaway, but he just piles up one absurdity on top of another. Provocateurs are never like that, comrades . . . Perhaps he's insane. That's possible . . . But he's not a provocateur . . . I vote for him," she added after a brief pause.

"All right, Bird," said the broad-shouldered man. "Now keep quiet for a while . . . Did you go through the medical examination at the Department of Public Health?" he asked Maxim.

"Yes."

"And you were passed as able-bodied?"

"Of course."

"With no qualifications?"

"All it said on the card was simply 'Able-bodied.'"

"What do you think about the Battle Guards?"

"Now I think that they are a mindless weapon in somebody else's hands. Most likely in the hands of these celebrated Unknown Fathers. But there's still a lot that I don't understand."

"And what do you think about the Unknown Fathers?"

"I think they're the top brass of a military dictatorship. What I do know about them is very contradictory. Maybe their goals are honorable enough, but the means . . ." Maxim shook his head.

"What do you think about degenerates?"

"I think the term is inappropriate. I think you are conspirators. I only have a rather vague idea of your goals. But I like the people that I've seen for myself. They all seemed to be sincere and . . . how can I put it? . . . not anybody's dupes, acting with their eyes open."

"Right," said the broad-shouldered man. "Do you get pains?"

"In my head? No, I don't."

"Why ask him about that?" said Forester. "If he had the pains, he wouldn't be sitting here."

"That's what I'm trying to understand: Why is he sitting here?" said the broad-shouldered man. "Why did you come to us? Do you want to join in our struggle?"

Maxim shook his head. "I wouldn't put it like that. It wouldn't be true. I want to make sense of things. Right now I'm with you rather than with them, but after all, I know too little about you too."

They all exchanged glances.

"That's not the way we do things, my friend," said Forester. "Where we're concerned, it's like this: either you're with us and then here's your gun, go and fight, or else you're not one of us and then, I'm sorry . . . you understand . . . where should we shoot you, in the head, right?"

Silence fell again. Doc heaved a sigh and knocked out his pipe against the bench. "A very unusual and difficult case," he declared. "I have a suggestion. Let him ask a few questions . . . You do have questions, don't you, Mak?"

"Yes, I came here to ask them," Maxim replied.

"Ic has lots of questions," Ordi confirmed, laughing. "He pestered my mother to death with his questions. And he pestered me with them too."

"Ask away," said the broad-shouldered man. "You can answer him, Doc. And we'll listen."

"Who are the Unknown Fathers, and what do they want?" Maxim asked to begin.

They all stirred—they obviously hadn't been expecting this question.

"The Unknown Fathers," said Doc, "are an anonymous group of highly experienced schemers, the remnants of a party of putschists who survived a twenty-year struggle for power among military, financial, and political circles. They have two goals: a principal one and a fundamental one. Their principal goal is to stay in power. Their fundamental goal is to derive the maximum gratification from that power. There are some honorable individuals among them, who derive gratification from the fact that they are the people's benefactors. But for the most part they are money-grabbers, sybarites, and sadists, and they are all lovers of power . . . Are you satisfied?"

"No," said Maxim. "You have simply told me that they are tyrants. I already suspected that anyway . . . What is their economic program? Their ideology? The social base that they rely on?"

They all exchanged glances again. Forester gaped at Maxim with his mouth hanging open.

"Their economic program . . ." said Doc. "You're asking too much of us. We're not theoreticians, we're practical activists. As for what they rely on, I can tell you that. Bayonets. Ignorance. The weariness of the nation. They won't build a just society, they don't even want to think about that . . . And they don't have any economic program—they don't have anything except bayonets, they don't want anything except power. The most important thing for us is that they want to annihilate us. Quite simply, we're fighting for our lives." He started irritably stuffing his pipe.

"I didn't mean to offend anyone," said Maxim. "I'm just trying to make sense of things." He would have been glad to expound the fundamentals of the theory of historical sequentiality for Doc, but he didn't have enough words. He still had to shift to thinking in Russian sometimes as it was. "All right. But you said 'a just society.' What is that? And what do you want? What are you striving for, apart from saving your own lives? And who are you?"

Doc's pipe rustled and crackled, and its oppressive stink spread through the cellar.

"Let me," Forester suddenly put in. "Let me tell him . . . Let me try . . . You, my good sir, are too . . . I don't know how things are up in your mountains, but here people like to live. What kind of way to talk is that—'apart from saving your own lives'? Maybe I don't need anything apart from that! Isn't that enough for you? You're a fine, brave hero! You try living in a cellar when you have a house and a wife and a family, and everybody has disowned you . . . Come off it, now!"

"Wait, Forester," said the broad-shouldered man.

"No, let him wait! So high and mighty! Give him society, give him some kind of base or other—"

"Wait, my man," said Doc. "Don't be angry. You can see he doesn't understand anything . . . You see," he said to Maxim, "our movement is very heterogeneous. We don't have any unified political program, and we couldn't have one. We all kill because we are being killed. That's what has to be understood. You must understand that. We're all condemned to death; we don't have much chance of surviving. And all our politics is basically over-shadowed by biology. The most important thing is to survive. There's no time to worry about a social base. So if you've shown up with some kind of social program, you won't get anywhere with it."

"What's the basic problem?" Maxim asked.

"We are regarded as degenerates. Where the idea came from, I can't even remember anymore. But right now it's advantageous for the Unknown Fathers to hound us—it distracts the people's attention from internal problems, from the corruption of the finan-ciers, who rake in money from military contracts and building towers. If we didn't exist, the Fathers would have invented us."

"That's already something," said Maxim. "So money's at the basis of everything again. So the Unknown Fathers serve money. Who else are they shielding?"

"The Unknown Fathers don't serve anyone. They *are* money. They are *everything*. And at the same time, they're nothing, because they're anonymous, and they devour each other all the time . . . He should have talked to Wild Boar," he said to the broad-shouldered man. "They would have understood each other."

"All right, I'll talk to Wild Boar about the Fathers, but right now—"

"You can't talk to Wild Boar any longer," Memo said in a spiteful tone. "Wild Boar's been shot."

"He was the man with one hand," Ordi explained. "You should remember him."

"I do remember him," said Maxim. "But he wasn't shot. He was sentenced to hard labor."

"That's not possible," the broad-shouldered man said. "Wild Boar? Hard labor?"

"Yes," said Maxim. "Gel Ketshef, sentenced to be executed; Wild Boar, sentenced to hard labor; and another man, who didn't give his name, was taken by the man in civilian clothes. Obviously for counterintelligence."

They all fell silent again. Doc took a sip from his mug. The broad-shouldered man sat there with his head propped on his hands. Forester mournfully groaned and cast a pitying glance at Ordi, who tightly pursed her lips and looked down at the table. This was genuine grief, and only Memo in the corner was more fearful than sorrowful . . . Men like that shouldn't be trusted with machine guns, Maxim fleetingly thought. He'll shoot all of us right here.

"All right, then," said the broad-shouldered man. "Do you have any more questions?"

"I have a lot of questions," Maxim slowly replied. "But I'm afraid all of them are more or less tactless."

"Well, never mind, ask your tactless questions."

"All right, my final question. What do the antiballistic defense towers have to do with all of this? What do you have against them?"

They all laughed in a rather unpleasant manner. "What a fool," said Forester. "There he goes again—give him a social base . . ."

"They're not ADTs," said Doc. "They're our curse. They invented a kind of radiation that helped them create the concept of the degenerate. Most people—you, for instance—don't even notice this radiation, as if it doesn't even exist. But owing to certain peculiarities of their biology, an unfortunate minority suffer agonizing pains when exposed to it. Some of us—only very few— can tolerate this pain, but some can't bear it and they scream out loud, some lose consciousness, and some actually go insane and die . . . The towers aren't antiballistic defense structures—no defenses of that kind exist. They're not necessary, because neither Hontia nor Pandeia have any ballistic missiles or aircraft. They have no time for any of that; their civil war has been going on for more than three years. The towers are radiation transmitters. They're switched on twice every twenty-four hours, all across the country, and then they catch us while we're lying there helpless with pain. And in addition, there are limited-range devices in patrol vehicles, plus freestanding mobile transmitters, plus random radiation transmissions at night. There's nowhere for us to hide; there are no screens against it. We go insane, shoot ourselves, commit stupid acts in our desperation. We're dying out . . ."

Doc broke off, grabbed his mug, and drained it in a single gulp. Then he started furiously lighting his pipe, with his face twitching.

"*Yeeeah*, we had a fine life once," Forester mournfully said. "The bastards," he added after a pause.

"There's no point in telling him about it," Memo suddenly said. "He doesn't know what it's like. He has no idea what it means—waiting for the next session every day . . ."

"All right," said the broad-shouldered man. "He has no idea, so there's nothing to talk about. Bird has spoken in his favor. Who else is for or against?"

Forester opened his mouth to speak, but Ordi got her word in first. "I want to explain why I'm for him. First, I trust him. I've already said that, but perhaps that's not so important, because it only concerns me. But this man has abilities that could be useful to all of us. He can heal other people's wounds as well as his own—and far better than you, Doc, no offense intended."

"What kind of doctor am I?" asked Doc. "A mere forensic specialist . . ."

"But that's still not all," Ordi went on. "He can relieve the pain."

"How do you mean?" Forester asked.

"I don't know how he does it. He massages your temples and whispers something, and the pain passes off. It grabbed me twice at my mother's place, and both times he helped me. The first time not a lot, but even so I didn't pass out as usual. And the second time there was no pain at all."

And immediately everything changed. Just a moment ago
they had been judges, a moment ago they had thought they were
deciding if he should live or die, but now the judges had disappeared and there remained only tormented, doomed people who
suddenly felt hope. They looked at him as if they were expecting
him to immediately, this very moment, take away this nightmare
that had tormented them every minute, every day, and every
night for years on end . . . Well now, Maxim thought, at least
here I'll be needed for healing and not for killing. But somehow the idea failed to bring him any satisfaction. The towers, he
thought. How repulsive . . . Someone had to invent them. But
you'd have to be a sadist to invent them . . .

"Can you really do that?" Doc asked.

"What?"

"Relieve the pain."

"Relieve the pain . . . Yes."

"How?"

"I can't explain it to you. I don't have enough words for that,
and you don't have enough knowledge . . . Surely you must have
some medication, some kind of analgesic drugs?"

"No drugs are any help against this . . . Except perhaps a fatal
dose."

"Listen," said Maxim. "Of course I'm prepared to alleviate the
pain . . . I'll do my best. But that's not a solution. You have to look
for some kind of large-scale remedy . . . Do you have any chemists?"

"We have everyone," said the broad-shouldered man, "But
this problem can't be solved, Mak. If it could, the state prosecutor
wouldn't suffer the same torments as we do. He'd be certain to
get hold of the medication. But now before every regular transmission he gets dead drunk and soaks in a hot bath."

"The state prosecutor is a degenerate?" asked Maxim, bewildered.

"According to the rumors," said the broad-shouldered man.
"But we've gotten distracted. Have you finished, Bird? Who else
wants to speak?"

"Wait, General," said Forester. "So what do we have here? Doesn't this mean that he can help us? Can you take away my pain? . . . Why, this man is absolutely priceless, I won't let him out of this cellar! Begging your pardon, but the pains I get are absolutely unbearable . . . And maybe he'll invent some kind of powders or something? You will invent some, won't you, eh? Oh no, gentlemen and comrades, we have to take good care of this man . . ."

"So you're 'for,' then?" General asked.

"I'm so much 'for' that if anyone lays a finger on him . . ."

"Clear enough. And you, Doc?"

"I would be 'for' even without this," Doc growled, puffing on his pipe. "I have the same impression as Bird. He's not one of us yet, but he will be—it can't be any other way. He's no good to them in any case. Too intelligent."

"All right," said General. "And you, Hoof?"

"I'm 'for,'" said Memo. "He's a useful man."

"Well then," said General. "I'm 'for' as well. I'm very glad for you, Mak. You're a likable young guy, and I would have been sorry to kill you." He looked at his watch. "Let's eat," he said. "There's a transmission soon, and Mak can demonstrate his skill to us. Pour him some beer, Forester, and put some of that celebrated cheese of yours on the table. Hoof, you go and relieve Green—he hasn't eaten since morning."

10

General called the final consultation before the operation at the Castle of the Two-Headed Horse. This was the ruins of a museum outside of town that had been destroyed during the war. It was an isolated spot that the townsfolk didn't visit, because of the close proximity of a malarial swamp, and it also had a bad reputation among the local people as a hangout for thieves and bandits. Maxim arrived on foot together with Ordi. Green arrived on a motorcycle and brought Forester with him. General and Memo/Hoof were already waiting for them in an old sewage pipe that opened directly into the swamp. General was smoking and the morose Memo was frenziedly waving away the mosquitoes with an incense stick.

"Did you bring it?" he asked Forester.

"Sure I did," said Forester, tugging a tube of insect repellent out of his pocket. They all smeared themselves with it, and General opened the meeting.

Memo laid out a diagram and ran through the sequence of the operation once again. They already knew it all by heart. At one in the morning the group creeps up to the barbed wire entanglement from four sides and places the elongated demolition charges. Forester and Memo each act alone—from the north and the west, respectively. General and Ordi approach together from the east. Maxim and Green approach together from the south. The detonations take place simultaneously at precisely one in the morning, and immediately General, Green, Memo, and Forester dash through the gaps, their task being to run to the fortified bunker and attack it with grenades. As soon as the firing from the bunker stops or slackens off, Maxim and Ordi run up to the tower with magnetic mines and place them for detonation, having each first tossed another two grenades into the bunker to be on the safe side. Then they activate the detonators, collect the wounded—only the wounded!—and withdraw to the east through the forest to the road, where Tiny Tot will be waiting by a boundary marker with the motorcycle. The seriously wounded are loaded into the motorcycle; those who are lightly wounded or unhurt leave on foot. The assembly point is Forester's little house. Wait at the assembly for no more than two hours, and then leave in the usual manner. Any questions? No. That's all.

General tossed away his cigarette butt, reached inside his jacket, and took out a small bottle of yellow tablets. "Attention," he said. "By decision of HQ the plan of the operation has been slightly changed. The commencement of the operation has been moved to twenty-two hundred hours."

"Massaraksh!" said Memo. "What kind of news is this?"

"Don't interrupt," said General. "At precisely ten o'clock the evening transmission begins. Several seconds before that each one of us will take two of these tablets. After that everything follows the old plan, with one exception. Bird advances as a grenade thrower, together with me. Mak will have all the mines—he'll blow up the tower alone."

"How's that?" Forester pensively asked, examining the diagram. "I can't understand this at all. Twenty-two hundred—that's the evening session . . . I'm sorry, but once I lie down, I won't get back up, I'll just be lying flat out . . . I'm sorry, but you won't pry me back up with a stake."

"Just a moment," said General. "I repeat once again. At ten seconds to ten, everyone takes this painkiller. Do you understand, Forester? You'll take a painkiller. So by ten o'clock—"

"I know those pills," said Forester. "Two short minutes of relief, and then you get completely tied in knots . . . We know, we've tried them."

"These are new pills," General patiently said. "They act for up to five minutes. We'll have time to run up to the bunker and fling our grenades, and Mak will do the rest."

Silence fell. They were thinking. Slow-witted Forester rummaged in his hair with a scraping sound, biting on his lower lip. They could see the idea slowly getting through to him. He started rapidly blinking, left his hair in peace, and looked around at them all with a glance of realization, suddenly coming to life, and slapping himself on the knees. Forester was a marvelous, good-hearted fellow, who had been slashed and scarred from head to foot by life but still hadn't learned anything about life. He didn't need anything and he didn't want anything, except to be left in peace and allowed to go back to his family and plant beets. He had spent the war in the trenches and had been less afraid of atomic shells than he was of his own corporal, a countryman just like him, but a very cunning man, and a great villain. Now Forester had taken a great liking to Maxim and felt eternally grateful to him for healing an old fistula on his shin, and ever since that, he had believed that as long as Maxim was there, nothing bad could happen to him. For the last month Maxim had spent the night in Forester's cellar, and every time they went to bed, Forester told Maxim a story, the same story every time, but with different endings: "There was this toad that lived in a swamp, a great fool he was, so stupid nobody could even believe it, and then this fool got into the habit . . ." Maxim simply couldn't imagine Forester involved in bloody work, although he'd been told that Forester was a skillful and merciless fighter.

"The new plan has the following advantages," said General. "First, they don't expect us at that time. The advantage of surprise. Second, the previous plan was devised a long time ago, and there's a quite real danger that the enemy already knows about it. This way we get a head start on the enemy. The probability of success is increased . . ."

Green kept nodding in approval all the time. His predatory face glowed in malicious satisfaction, and his long, nimble fingers kept clenching and opening. He liked all kinds of surprises and loved anything risky. His past life was obscure. He was a thief and, apparently, a killer, a child of the dark postwar years: an orphan and a hooligan, raised by thieves, fed by thieves, and thrashed by thieves. He had served time in jail and escaped—brazenly and unexpectedly, as he did everything—and tried to go back to his thieves' gang, but times had changed, his cronies wouldn't tolerate a degenerate, and they wanted to hand him in. But he fought them off and escaped again, hiding out in villages until the late Gel Ketshef found him.

Green was a smart young guy with a lively imagination: he believed the earth was flat and the sky was solid, and precisely because of his naive ignorance, stimulated by his turbulent fantasy, he was the only person on this inhabited island who suspected that Maxim was not some kind of Highlander ("I've seen these Highlanders, I've seen all their different varieties") or some strange trick of nature ("Nature made us all the same, the ones in jail and the ones on the outside") but actually an alien from impossible places, like somewhere beyond the heavenly firmament. He had never openly spoken about this to Maxim, but he had hinted at it, and he regarded Maxim with respect bordering on obsequiousness. "You'll be our boss," he kept repeating. "And then I'll spread my wings under you . . ."

How and where exactly he intended to spread his wings remained entirely obscure, but one thing was clear: Green really loved any risky business and he couldn't stand any kind of work. And another thing that Maxim didn't like about him was his wild and barbaric cruelty. He was a genuine spotted monkey, only domesticated and trained to hunt armored wolves.

"I don't like it," Memo morosely said. "It's a reckless gamble. No preparations, no checks . . . No, I don't like it."

He never liked anything, this Memo Gramenu, nicknamed Hoof of Death. He was never satisfied with anything, and he was always afraid of something. His past was kept secret, because at first he had held an extremely high position in the underground. And then one day he had fallen into the hands of the gendarmes and survived only by a miracle—crippled by torture, he had been dragged out by his cellmates, who had set up an escape.

After that, in accordance with the laws of the underground, he had been removed from HQ general staff, although he hadn't aroused any suspicions. He had been appointed as Gel Ketshef's deputy, taken part in two attacks on towers, personally destroyed several patrol vehicles, tracked down the commander of one of the brigades of Battle Guards and shot him in person, and was known as an individual of fanatical courage and an excellent machine gunner.

He had been about to be appointed the leader of a group in a small town in the southwest, but then Gel's group had been taken. Hoof still didn't arouse any suspicions; he was even appointed the leader of the new group. But all the time he fancied that he sensed sideways glances that might not even exist but could easily have existed: in the underground they weren't fond of people who were too lucky. Memo was taciturn and fastidious; he had a thorough knowledge of the science of clandestine activity and demanded unconditional obedience of all his rules, even the most insignificant. He never discussed general matters with anyone, dealing only with the business of the group, and he made sure that the group had everything: weapons, food, money, a good network of safe houses, and even a motorcycle.

He disliked Maxim. Maxim could sense that, but he didn't know why, and he didn't want to ask; Memo wasn't the kind of person you could enjoy a frank conversation with. Perhaps it was all simply because Maxim was the only one who could sense Memo's constant fear—the others could never even have imagined that the morose Hoof of Death, who spoke on familiar, casual terms with any representative of HQ, one of the founders of the underground, and a terrorist to the marrow of his bones, could possibly be afraid of anything.

"I don't understand the HQ's reasoning," Memo went on, smearing a new dollop of insect repellent on his neck with a grimace of disgust. "I've known this plan for a dog's age. We were about to try it a hundred times, and we rejected it a hundred times, because it means almost certain death. While there's no

radiation, if things go badly, at least we still have a chance of slipping away and striking again somewhere else. This way, if just
one thing goes wrong, we're all done for."

"You're not entirely right, Hoof," Ordi objected. "We have
Mak now. If something does go wrong, he'll be able to drag us
out, and he might even manage to blow up the tower."

She was lazily smoking and looking into the distance, toward
the swamp, cool and calm, not showing any surprise, and ready
for anything. She made people feel timid, because she saw them
only as more or less efficient means of destruction. She was all
there in plain sight—there were no dark or hazy patches, either in
her past, or her present, or her future. She came from an intellectual family; her father had been killed in the war, and her mother
still worked even now as a teacher in Utki Village. Ordi herself
had worked as a teacher until she was thrown out of the school
because she was a degenerate. She went into hiding, tried to flee
to Hontia, and ran into Gel at the border as he was bringing in
weapons. He had made her into a terrorist.

At first she had worked out of purely ideological motivation—
she was fighting for a just society in which everyone was free
to think and to do whatever he wanted to do and was capable
of doing—but seven years ago the gendarmes had picked up
her trail and taken her child hostage, in an attempt to force
her to surrender and turn her husband in. HQ had forbidden
her to turn herself in, because she knew too much. She had
never heard anything more about her child and regarded him as
dead, although privately she didn't believe that, and for seven
years now she had been primarily motivated by hate. Hate
came first, followed by the substantially dimmed dream of a
just society. She had taken the loss of her husband incredibly
calmly, although she loved him very much. Probably she had
simply become accustomed, long before his arrest, to the idea
that you shouldn't cling too tightly to anything in this world.
And now, like Gel at the trial, she was a living corpse, but a
very dangerous corpse.

"Mak's a greenhorn," Memo morosely said. "Who can guarantee that he won't lose his head when he's left on his own? It's absurd to count on it. It's absurd to abandon the old, well-thought-through plan, just because we now have the greenhorn Mak. As I've already said, this is a reckless gamble."

"Ah, come off it, boss," said Green. "That's what our work's like. If you ask me, old plan or new plan—it's all just a reckless gamble. How could it be anything else? You can't do it without any risk, and with these pills, there's less risk. They'll go crazy down there under the tower when we pounce on them at ten o'clock. At ten o'clock they're probably drinking vodka and singing songs, and we'll pounce on them, and maybe their rifles aren't even loaded and they're all sprawled around drunk . . . No, I like it. Right, Mak?"

"And I, you know, like it too," said Forester. "The way I reckon it is, if this plan surprises me, it'll absolutely amaze the Battle Guards. Green's right when he says they'll go crazy . . . Anyway, we'll get an extra five minutes without agony, and after that we'll see . . . If Mak brings down the tower, everything will be fine altogether . . . Oh, won't it be fine!" he suddenly exclaimed, as if struck by a new idea. "No one before us has ever brought down a tower, have they? They've only bragged about doing it, but we'll be the first . . . And then, while they're fixing this tower up again—think how long it'll take! We can live like human beings for a month at least . . . without these rotten, lousy fits . . ."

"I'm afraid you have misunderstood me, Hoof," said General. "Nothing in the plan changes. We simply make our attack unexpectedly, strengthening it by using Bird and somewhat changing the procedure of withdrawal."

"And if you're afraid Mak won't be able to drag us all out," Ordi said in the same lazy voice, still gazing at the swamp, "don't forget that he'll only have to drag out one, or two of us at the most, and he's a strong boy."

"Yes," said General, looking at her. "That's true . . ."

General was in love with Ordi. No one saw it apart from Maxim, but Maxim could tell that it was an old, hopeless love, which had begun when Gel was alive, and had now become even more hopeless, if that was possible.

General wasn't a general. Before the war he had been a worker on an assembly line, then he had ended up in a training college for junior officers and fought in the war as a corporal, finishing it as a cornet. He knew Cornet Chachu very well and had scores to settle with him (following disturbances in a certain regiment immediately after the war). General had been hunting Chachu without any success for a long time. He was a member of underground HQ staff but often took part in practical operations, being a good soldier and a knowledgeable commander. He liked working in the underground, although he didn't have any real idea of what would happen after the victory was won.

But then, he didn't really believe in the victory. As a born soldier, he easily adapted to any circumstances and never tried to think more than ten to twelve days ahead. He didn't have any ideas of his own—he had picked up a few things from the one-handed man and borrowed a few things from Ketshef, and a few things had been planted in his mind at HQ, but the most important things still remained what had been hammered into his head at the junior officers' college. So when he theorized, he produced a strange mixture of ideas: the power of the rich has to be overthrown (that was from one-handed Wild Boar, who was evidently something like a socialist or communist); engineers and technicians should be put in charge of the state (that came from Ketshef); cities should be razed to the ground and we should live in harmony with nature (some bucolic philosopher at HQ); and all of this could only be achieved by absolute obedience to the orders of senior commanders and a bit less idle chatter on abstract subjects.

Maxim had clashed with him twice. It was absolutely impossible to understand what point there was in demolishing the towers, losing brave comrades and wasting time, funds, and weapons in the process, if a tower would be restored anyway and everything would carry on as it had been before, except that the population of the local villages would be convinced by the evidence of their own eyes what heinous devils these degenerates were. General had not been able to give Maxim an adequate justification for sabotage activity. Either he was hiding something or he himself didn't understand what it was needed for, but he had repeated the same thing over and over every time: orders are not subject to discussion, every attack on a tower is a blow struck at the enemy, people must not be prevented from becoming actively engaged, otherwise their hate will fester inside them and they will have nothing at all to live for . . .

"We need to look for the center!" Maxim had insisted. "We need to strike directly at the center, with all our forces at once! What kind of heads do they have in this HQ of yours if they don't understand a simple thing like that?"

"HQ knows what it's doing," General had gravely replied, thrusting out his chin and jerking his eyebrows up high. "In our situation, discipline comes first, and let's not have any freebooting peasant anarchy. Everything in its own good time, Mak—you'll get your center, if you live that long . . ." However, he regarded Mak with respect and gladly made use of his services when the radiation attacks caught him in Forester's cellar.

"All the same, I'm against it," Memo stubbornly said. "What if they just shoot us down? What if we don't manage it in five minutes and we need six? The plan's crazy. And it always was crazy."

"It's the first time we've used demolition charges," said General, tearing his eyes away from Ordi with an effort. "But even if we take the previous means of breaking through the wire, then the fate of the operation is already decided on average after three or four minutes. If we catch them by surprise, we'll have one or even two minutes in reserve."

"Two minutes is a lot of time," said Forester. "In two minutes I'll strangle all of them in there with my bare hands. Just as long as I can get all the way there."

"Getting there . . . *yeeaah*," Green drawled in a strange, balefully pensive voice.

"Don't you want to say anything, Mak?" General asked.

"I've already said what I think," said Maxim. "The new plan's better than the old one, but it's still bad. Let me do it all myself. Take the risk."

"We won't talk about that," General replied in annoyance. "There's no more to be said. Do you have any practical comments?"

"No," said Maxim. He already regretted having brought up the subject again.

"Where did the new tablets come from?" Memo suddenly asked.

"They're the old tablets," said General. "Mak managed to improve them a bit."

"Ah, Mak . . . So this is his idea?"

Hoof said it in a tone of voice that made everyone feel awkward. The words could be understood like this: *A greenhorn, not really one of us, and a crossover from the other side—so doesn't the whole business have the whiff of an ambush? There have been cases like that . . .*

"No," General abruptly snapped. "It's HQ's idea. So kindly comply, Hoof."

"I am complying," Memo said with a shrug. "I'm against it, but I'm complying anyway. What else can I do?"

Maxim sadly looked at them all sitting there in front of him, all very different from each other. In ordinary circumstances, the idea of gathering together would never even have occurred to them: a former farmer, a former criminal, a former teacher . . . They had only one thing in common: they had been declared enemies of society, for some idiotic reason they were detested by everybody, and the entire, immense state apparatus of oppression was directed against them.

What they were about to do was senseless; in just a few hours' time, most of them would be dead, but nothing in the world would change, and nothing would change for those who were left alive. In the best case they would have a brief respite from their hellish torments, but they would be lacerated with wounds and exhausted by fleeing from pursuit, they would be hunted with dogs, they would have to lie low in foul-smelling burrows, and then everything would start all over again. Making common cause with them was stupid, but abandoning them would be a shabby trick, so he had to choose the stupid option. And maybe no other way was possible here, with them, and if he wanted to get something done, he would have to put up with the stupidity and the pointless bloodshed, or just maybe he would have to go through with the shabby trick. A pitiful individual . . . a stupid individual . . . a shabby individual . . . But what else could you expect from a human being in a pitiful, stupid, shabby world like this?

He just had to remember that stupidity was a consequence of powerlessness, and powerlessness derived from ignorance, from not knowing the true path . . . But surely it wasn't possible that no true path could be found among a thousand paths? I've already followed one path, thought Maxim, and it was a false path. Now I have to follow this one to the end, even though I can already see that it's a false path too. And maybe I'm fated to follow even more false paths and find myself in dead ends. But who am I trying to justify myself to? he thought. And what for? I like them, I can help them, and for today that's all I need to know.

"We'll split up now," said General. "Hoof goes with Forester, Mak goes with Green, and I go with Bird. Rendezvous at nine o'clock on the dot at the boundary marker. Only make your way through the forest, no roads. The pairs must not split up. Each person is responsible for the other. Off you go now. Memo and Forester leave first." He gathered up all the cigarette butts onto a sheet of paper, folded it up, and put it in his pocket.

Forester rubbed his knees. "My bones are aching," he announced. "That means a spot of rain. It's going to be a good night, dark . . ."

11

They had to crawl from the edge of the forest to the wire. Green crawled in front, dragging the pole with the demolition charge on it and swearing under his breath at the prickles jabbing into his skin. Maxim crawled after him, clutching a sack of magnetic mines. The sky was veiled in dark clouds, and it was drizzling. The grass was wet, so they got soaked through in the first few minutes, and they couldn't see anything through the rain. Green crawled along by the line of the compass, without deviating even once—he was an experienced man, all right. Then Maxim caught an acrid odor of wet rust and saw three rows of barbed wire, and beyond the wire was the vague latticework bulk of the tower. When he raised his head he could make out a squat structure with rectangular outlines at its base; that was the fortified bunker, and there were three battle guards with a machine gun inside it. Indistinct voices reached him through the rustling of the rain, and then a candle was lit inside, and a weak yellow light illuminated the long embrasure.

Still cursing under his breath, Green shoved his pole in under the wire. "All set," he whispered. "Crawl away." They crawled about ten steps away and started waiting. Green clutched the detonator lead in his hand and looked at the glowing hands of his watch. He was shaking. Maxim could hear his teeth chattering and his constrained breathing. Maxim was shaking too. He stuck his hand into the bag and touched the mines—they felt rough and cold. The rain grew stronger, and now its rustling drowned out all other sounds. Green got up on all fours. He kept whispering something all the time, either praying or cursing.

"Right, you bastards!" he suddenly said in a loud voice, making an abrupt movement with his right hand. A piston clicked and there was a hissing sound, up ahead of them a sheet of red flame erupted from under the ground, and another broad sheet soared up far away on their left. They felt a sudden blow on their ears, and then hot, wet earth, clumps of decaying grass, and red-hot pieces of something came showering down. Green went hurtling forward, shouting out in a strange voice, and suddenly everything turned as bright as day, even brighter than day, blindingly bright. Maxim squeezed his eyes shut, feeling himself turn cold inside, and a thought briefly flitted through his mind—Everything's lost—but there weren't any shots, the silence continued, and he couldn't hear anything except for rustling and hissing.

When Maxim opened his eyes, through the blinding light he could make out the gray bunker, a wide gap in the wire, and figures looking very small and isolated in the huge empty space around the tower—they were running as fast as they could toward the bunker, running silently, without speaking, stumbling and falling, jumping up again and running. Then Maxim heard a pitiful moan, and he saw Green, who wasn't running anywhere but sitting on the ground just beyond the wire, swaying to and fro with his head clutched in his hands. Maxim dashed over to him, tore his hands away from his face, and saw his rolled-back eyes and bubbles of saliva on his lips . . . But there still weren't any shots; an eternity had gone by, and the bunker still remained silent. Then suddenly the familiar battle march thundered out.

Maxim flung the bungling blockhead onto his back and fumbled in his own pocket with one hand, feeling glad that General was so cagey, he had given Maxim some extra pain pills just to be on the safe side. He forced open Green's mouth, which was locked shut by cramp, and thrust the pills deep into the black hole of his wheezing throat. Then he grabbed Green's rifle and swung around, looking to see where the light was coming from and why there was so much of it—there shouldn't be so much light . . .

There still weren't any shots, and the isolated figures were still running. One of them was already very close to the bunker, another was a little way behind, and a third, running from the right, suddenly fell, moving at full speed, and went tumbling head over heels. *"When Guards appear upon the battle scene . . ."* they roared in the bunker, while the light continued to beat down from a height of about ten yards—probably from the tower, which was impossible to make out now. Maxim could see five or six blinding blue-white disks; he flung up the automatic rifle and squeezed the trigger, and the homemade weapon, small, awkward, and unfamiliar, jerked hard in his hands. As if in reply, red flashes glinted in the embrasure of the bunker, and the rifle was suddenly torn out of his hands. Maxim still hadn't hit a single one of the blinding disks, and now Green had grabbed the rifle; he set off, rushing forward, and immediately fell, stumbling on level ground.

Then Maxim lay down and crawled back to his bag. Behind him automatics frantically crackled, a machine gun roared with a terrifying, hollow sound, and then—at long last!—a grenade burst, then another, and then two together, and the machine gun fell silent. Now there were only automatics chattering, and then came the bursts of more explosions, and then someone shrieked in an inhuman voice and it went quiet. Maxim grabbed the bag and ran. Smoke was rising in a column above the bunker; the air smelled of burning and gunpowder. And everything all around it was bright and empty, with only a black, hunched-over figure groping his way along right beside the bunker, clinging to the wall. The figure reached the embrasure, tossed something into it, and dropped to the ground. The embrasure suddenly lit up with red light, Maxim heard a popping sound, and everything went quiet again . . .

Maxim stumbled and almost fell. A few steps farther on he stumbled again, and then he noticed that there were little stakes jutting up out of the ground—short, thick stakes hidden in the grass. So that's it . . . That how things are here . . . If General had sent me in alone, I'd have immediately smashed both my legs, and now I'd be lying there, stretched out dead on these repulsive little stakes . . . You boaster . . . You stupid ignoramus . . . The tower was really close now. He ran, looking down at his feet; he was alone, and he didn't want to think about the others.

He ran up to a huge iron support and dropped the bag. He badly wanted to slap a heavy, rough pancake onto the wet iron immediately, but there was still the bunker . . . The iron door was ajar, with lazy tongues of flames flicking out of it, and a guardsman was lying on the steps—it was all over there. Maxim set off around the bunker and found General, who was sitting slumped against the concrete wall. His eyes were blank, and Maxim realized that the tablets had already stopped working. He looked around, picked General up in his arms, and carried him away from the tower. About twenty paces away Ordi was lying in the grass with a grenade in her hand. She was lying facedown, but Maxim immediately realized that she was dead. He started looking farther and found Forester, also dead. And Green had been killed too—there was no one for him to leave General with.

He walked across the open space, casting multiple black shadows, stunned by all these deaths even though a minute earlier he had thought he was prepared for them, feeling an impatient urge to go back and blow up the tower in order to finish what they had begun, but first he had to see how Hoof was. He found Memo right beside the wire. He was wounded, and had probably tried to crawl away toward the wire before he collapsed, unconscious. Maxim put General beside him and started running toward the tower again. It was strange to think that now he could cross these miserable two hundred yards without being afraid of anything.

He started attaching the mines to the supports, two on each one to make sure. He hurried, although there was plenty of time—but General was losing blood, and Memo was losing blood, and somewhere trucks carrying Battle Guards were already hurtling along the highway, and Gai had been roused from his bed by the alarm, and now he was jarring over the cobblestones beside Pandi, and in the nearby villages the people had already woken up; the men were grabbing guns and axes, the children were crying, and the women were cursing the bloodthirsty spies who robbed them of their sleep and their peace. Maxim could feel the drizzly darkness all around him with every pore of his skin, sense it slowly stirring, coming to life, becoming menacing and dangerous . . .

The detonators were set for five minutes' delay; he activated them all, one by one, and ran back, toward General and Memo. Something was bothering him; he stopped, looked around, and realized what it was: Ordi. He ran back to her, looking down at his feet in order not to stumble, lifted the light body up onto his shoulder, and started running again, looking down at his feet—toward the wire, toward the gray gap where General and Memo were suffering agony, but they wouldn't have to suffer much longer now. He stopped beside them and turned back toward the tower.

And then the underground terrorists' nonsensical dream came true. Rapidly, one after another, the mines detonated, the base of the tower was enveloped in smoke, and then the blinding lights went out, everything went pitch black, and the darkness was filled with scraping and rumbling, the earth shook and bounced with a metallic clang, and then it shook again.

Maxim looked at his watch. It was seventeen minutes past ten. His eyes had adjusted to the darkness, he could see the ripped-apart wire again, and he could see the tower. It was lying to one side of the bunker, in which everything was still burning, and its supports, mangled and twisted by the explosions, were haphazardly jutting out.

"Who's there?" wheezed General, starting to stir.

"It's me," said Maxim. He leaned down. "'It's time to leave. Where are you hit? Can you walk?"

"Wait," said General. "What about the tower?"

"The tower's finished," said Maxim. Ordi was lying over his shoulder, and he didn't know how to tell General about her.

"I can't believe it," said General, sitting up. "Massaraksh! Is it really true?" he laughed and lay down again. "Listen, Mak, I can't gather my wits . . . What time is it?"

"Ten twenty."

"So everything was right! We took it out . . . Well done, Mak. Wait, who's this here beside me?"

"Hoof," said Mak.

"He's breathing," said General. "Wait, who else is still alive? Who's that you have there?"

"It's Ordi," said Maxim, struggling to force the words out.

General said nothing for a few seconds. "Ordi," he hesitantly repeated, and got up, staggering on his feet. "Ordi," he repeated again, and laid his palm on her cheek.

They both said nothing for a while. Then Memo asked in a hoarse voice, "What time is it?"

"Ten twenty-two," said Maxim.

"Where are we?" Memo asked.

"We have to go," said Maxim.

General turned around and set off through the gap in the wire, staggering very badly. Then Maxim leaned down, threw corpulent Memo across his other shoulder, and set off after General. He caught up with him, and General stopped.

"Only the wounded," he said.

"I can get her there," said Maxim.

"Follow orders," said General. "Only the wounded."

He reached out his hands and, groaning with pain, lifted Ordi's body off Maxim's shoulder. He couldn't hold her up and immediately put her down on the ground.

"Only the wounded," he said in a strange voice. "On the double . . . march!"

"Where are we?" asked Memo. "Who's here? Where are we?"

"Hold on to my belt," Maxim told General, and started running.

Memo shrieked and went limp. His head dangled, his arms dangled, and his legs pounded against Maxim's back. General ran close on Maxim's heels, breathing loudly and hoarsely and holding on to his belt.

They ran into the forest and wet branches lashed at Maxim's face. He dodged away from trees that came dashing toward him and jumped over tree stumps that leaped up in front of him. It was harder than he had expected—he was no longer the same man, and the air here wasn't right, and in general nothing here was right, everything was wrong and nonsensical.

They left broken bushes and a trail of blood behind them, and the roads had been cordoned off long ago, the dogs were straining at their leashes, and Cornet Chachu, with his pistol in his hand, was croaking commands as he ran pigeon-toed across the asphalt, soared over the roadside ditch, and was the first to dive into the forest. They left the idiotic toppled tower and the burned battle guards behind them, together with three dead comrades, already stiff. And here he had two badly wounded, half-dead men with almost no chance of making it—and all for the sake of one tower, one idiotic, pointless, dirty, rusty tower, one of thousands exactly the same . . . I'll never let anyone do anything so stupid again. *No, I'll say. I've already seen that.* All that blood, and all for a heap of useless, rusty iron; one young, stupid life for rusty iron; and one old, stupid life for the pitiful hope of living like other people at least for a few days; and one love shot down, not even for iron, and not even for hope. *If you simply want to survive, I'll say, then why do you die, die so cheaply?* Massaraksh, I won't allow them to die, I'll get them to live, they'll learn how to live! What a block-head—how could I do it, how could I let them do it?

He darted out headlong onto the country road, holding Memo on his shoulder and dragging General along under his arm. Tiny Tot, soaking wet and smelling of sweat and fear, was already running toward him from the boundary marker.

"Is this everyone?" he asked in horror, and Maxim felt grateful to him for that horror.

They dragged the wounded men to the motorcycle, squeezed Memo into the sidecar, and sat General on the rear saddle; Tiny Tot lashed General to him with his belt. The forest was still quiet, but Maxim knew that didn't mean anything.

"Get going," he said. "Don't stop, just break through."

"I know," said Tiny Tot. "What about you?"

"I'll try to distract them. Don't worry, I'll get away."

"Some chance . . ." Tiny Tot said in an anguished voice, and jerked the starter; the motorcycle sputtered to life. "Did you blow up the tower at least?" he shouted.

"Yes," Maxim said, and Tiny Tot went racing away.

Left alone, Maxim stood there without moving for a few seconds, then dashed back into the forest. At the first clearing he came across, he tore off his jacket and flung it into the bushes. Then he ran back to the road and ran along it for a while as fast as he could go in the direction of the town, stopped, unclipped the grenades off his belt, scattered them across the road, and started scrambling through the bushes on the other side, trying to break as many branches as possible. He dropped his handkerchief behind the bushes, and only then ran off through the forest, shifting into the smooth, rhythmical hunting stride in which he would have to cover five or ten miles.

He ran without thinking about anything, except for making sure that he didn't deviate too much from a southwesterly direction, and carefully choosing where he set down his feet. He crossed roads twice—the first was a deserted country road, and the second was the Resort Highway, which was also empty, but he heard dogs there for the first time. He couldn't tell what kind of dogs they were, but to be on the safe side he gave them a very wide berth, and an hour and a half later found himself among the freight sheds of the city's rail yard.

Here there were lights shining, steam locomotives mournfully whistling, and people darting about. Here probably nobody knew anything, but he couldn't run any more—he might be taken for a thief. He switched to a walk, and when a heavy freight train ponderously rumbled by on its way into the city, he leaped up onto the first flatcar carrying a load of sand, lay down, and rode like that all the way to the concrete plant, where he jumped down, dusted off the sand, lightly smeared his hands with heavy fuel oil, and started thinking about what to do next.

There was no point in making his way to Forester's place, and that was the only safe house in the vicinity. He could try spending the night in Utki Village, but that was dangerous—that address was known to Cornet Chachu—and apart from that, Maxim was afraid even to think of showing up at old Illy's house and telling her that her daughter was dead. He had nowhere to go.

He went into a decrepit little night tavern for workers, ate a few sausages, drank some beer, and dozed for a while, slumped against the wall. Everybody here was as dirty and tired as he was; they were workers who had finished their shift and missed the last streetcar. He dreamed about Rada, and in his dream he thought that Gai was probably in the dragnet right now, and that was good. But Rada loved him and she would take him in, let him change his clothes and get washed; his civilian suit should still be there, the same one that Fank had given him . . . and in the morning he could leave and go east, to where the second safe house he knew was located . . . He woke up, paid his bill, and walked out.

It was only a short walk and not dangerous. There was nobody on the streets, and the only person he encountered was the janitor right there at the house. He was sitting on his stool in the entrance passage and sleeping. Maxim cautiously walked past him, went up the stairs, and rang the way he always used to ring. At first it was quiet on the other side of the door, then something scraped, he heard steps, and the door slightly opened. He saw Rada.

The only reason she didn't cry out was that she choked and squeezed her mouth shut with her hand. Maxim took her in his arms and kissed her on the forehead; he felt as if he had come back home, to a place where they had long ago stopped expecting him. He closed the door behind him, they quietly walked through into the room, and Rada suddenly started crying. Everything in the room was still the same as before, except that his camp cot was gone, and Gai was sitting up on the sofa bed in his nightshirt, gaping wide-eyed at Maxim with an expression of wild amazement. Several seconds went by like that, with Maxim and Gai looking at each other, and Rada crying.

"Massaraksh," Gai eventually said in a helpless voice. "You're alive? You're not dead?"

"Hello, old buddy," said Maxim. "It's a pity you're home. I didn't want to land you in trouble. If you tell me to, I'll leave straightaway."

At that Rada took a tight grip on his arm. "You're not going anywhere!" she said in a throttled voice. "Not for anything! You're not going . . . Just let him try . . . Then I'll go too . . . I won't care . . ."

Gai flung off his blanket, lowered his feet down off the sofa-bed, and walked up to Maxim. He touched Maxim on the shoulders and the arms, getting engine oil smeared on his hands, then rubbed his forehead and smeared that too. "I don't understand a thing," he said in a plaintive voice. "You're alive . . . Where have you come from? Rada, stop bawling . . . You're not wounded? You look terrible . . . And there's blood here . . ."

"It's not mine," said Maxim.

"I don't understand a thing," Gai repeated. "Listen, you're alive! Rada, heat up some water. Wake up that old fogy, tell him to give us some vodka—"

"Quiet," said Maxim. "Don't make a noise, they're hunting me!"

"Who? What for? What nonsense . . . Rada, let him get changed! . . . Mak, sit down, sit down . . . or maybe you want to lie down? How did this happen? Why are you still alive?"

Maxim cautiously sat down on the edge of the bed, put his hands on his knees to avoid smearing oil on anything, and looked at these two people. Looking at them for the last time as his friends, and even feeling a strange kind of curiosity about what would happen next, he said, "I'm a state criminal now, folks. I've just blown up a tower."

He wasn't surprised that they immediately understood him and instantly realized what kind of tower he meant, without having to ask. Rada only clenched her hands together, without taking her eyes off him. Gai grunted and scratched his head with both hands in the ancestral family gesture, looked away, and said in an irked voice, "You blockhead. So you decided to take revenge . . . Take revenge on whom? Ah, you, you're the same crazy weirdo you always were. A little kid . . . OK, you didn't say anything, and we didn't hear anything . . . I don't want to hear anything. Rada, go and heat up some water. And don't make any noise in there, don't wake people up . . . Take your clothes off," he told Maxim in a severe voice. "You're as filthy as hell, where on earth did you get to?"

Maxim got up and started getting undressed. He took off his dirty, wet shirt (Gai gave a loud gulp when he saw the scars from the bullets) and tugged off his repulsively filthy boots and trousers with an air of disgust. All his clothes were covered in black blotches, and Maxim felt relieved to be free of them.

"Well, that's great," he said, and sat down again. "Thanks, Gai. I won't stay long, only until the morning, and then I'll go."

"Did the janitor see you?" Gai morosely asked.

"He was sleeping."

"Sleeping . . ." Gai dubiously repeated. "You know, he . . . Well, of course, maybe he was sleeping. He does sleep sometimes."

"Why are you home?" Maxim asked.

"I'm on leave."

"What kind of leave could you be on?" asked Maxim. "The entire corps of guards is probably out in the country right now . . ."

"But I'm not a guardsman any longer," Gai said with a crooked grin. "They threw me out of the Guards, Mak. I'm just a simple army corporal now—I teach peasant hicks which leg is the right one and which is the left one. Once I've taught them, off they go to the Hontian border, into the trenches . . . That's how things are with me now, Mak."

"Is that because of me?" Maxim asked in a quiet voice.

"Well, what can I say? Basically, yes."

They looked at each other, and Gai turned his eyes away. Maxim suddenly thought that if Gai turned him in, he would probably get back into the Guards and his correspondence school for officers, and he also thought that only two months ago a thought like that couldn't possibly have occurred to him. He suddenly had a bad feeling and wanted to leave immediately, this very moment, but at that point Rada came back and summoned him to the bathroom. While he was getting washed up, she prepared something to eat and warmed up some tea. Gai sat in the same place with his cheeks propped on his fists and a melancholy expression on his face. He didn't ask any questions—no doubt he was afraid of hearing something terrible, something so bad that it would rupture his last line of defense and sever the final threads that still connected him to Maxim. And Rada didn't ask any questions either; no doubt she simply wasn't interested in questions. She never took her eyes off Maxim or let go of his hands, and occasionally sobbed—she was afraid that he would suddenly disappear, this man she loved. Disappear and never appear again. And then, because there wasn't much time left, Maxim pushed away his unfinished cup of tea and started telling them everything himself.

About how he had been helped by the mother of a state criminal; about how he had met degenerates; about who they—the degenerates—really were, why they were degenerates and what the towers were, what a diabolical, abominable invention the towers were. About what had happened that night, how people had run at a machine gun and died one after another, about how that odious heap of wet iron had collapsed, and how he had carried a dead woman, whose child had been taken away, and whose husband had been killed . . .

Rada avidly listened, and Gai eventually became interested too. He even started asking questions—malicious and spiteful questions, stupid and cruel questions, and Maxim realized that he didn't believe anything, that the very idea of the Unknown Fathers' perfidy simply slid off his mind, like water off grease, that he didn't like listening to all of this and was struggling to hold himself back and not interrupt Maxim. And when Maxim had finished his story, he said with a dark chuckle, "Well, they certainly wound you around their little finger!"

Maxim looked at Rada, but she turned her eyes away, biting on her lip, and indecisively said, "I don't know . . . Of course, maybe there was one tower like that. You come across villains even in the city council . . . and the Fathers simply don't know about it . . . Nobody tells them about it, and they don't know . . . You must understand, Mak, it simply can't be the way you tell it . . . Those are ballistic defense towers, you know . . ."

She spoke in a quiet, swooning voice, obviously trying not to offend him, beseechingly glancing into his eyes and stroking his shoulder, but Gai suddenly flew into a rage and started saying that all of this was stupid, that Maxim simply had no idea how many of those towers there were right across the country, how many of them were built every year and every day, and how, he asked, could such vast billions possibly be spent in our poor state, simply in order to cause trouble twice a day for a pitiful little group of degenerates, who in and of themselves amounted to nothing, a mere drop in the ocean of the people . . . "And so much money is spent simply on guarding them," he added after a pause.

"I've thought about that," said Maxim. "Probably everything really isn't all that simple. But Hontian money has nothing to do with it . . . And then, I saw it for myself: as soon as the tower collapsed, they all started feeling better. And as for antiballistic defense . . . You have to understand, Gai, that there are simply too many towers for defense against attack from the air. Nowhere near as many as that are needed to close off airspace . . . And then, why have ADTs on the southern border? Do the wild degenerates really have ballistic weapons?"

"There are plenty of things down there," Gai waspishly said. "You don't know anything, and you believe everything. I'm sorry, Mak, but if you weren't you . . . We're all too trusting," he added in a bitter tone of voice.

Maxim didn't want to argue anymore, or to speak about this subject at all. He started asking how life was treating them, where

Rada was working, why she hadn't gone to study, how their uncle was, and the neighbors . . . Rada livened up and started telling him, then she checked herself, collected the dirty dishes, and went out to the kitchen. Gai briskly scratched his head with both hands, frowned at the dark window, made his mind up, and launched into a serious man-to-man conversation.

"We love you," he said. "I love you, and Rada loves you, although you're an unsettled kind of man, and because of you everything has gone kind of awry for us. But the real problem is this. Rada doesn't just simply love you, not like that, you understand . . . but, how can I put it . . . basically, you understand, she's really devoted to you, she spent all this time crying, and for the first week she was actually ill. She's a good girl and a good homemaker, lots of men admire her, and that's not surprising . . . I don't know how you feel about her, but what would I advise you to do? Give up all this nonsense. It's not for you, you're out of your depth, they'll get you embroiled, you'll get killed yourself, and you'll spoil the lives of many innocent people—that doesn't make any sense. You just go back up into your mountains and find your own people. You won't find the place with your head, but your heart will tell you where your homeland is . . . Nobody will look for you there, you'll settle down, rebuild your life, then come back and collect Rada, and you'll both be happy there. Or maybe, by that time we'll be finished with the Hontians, peace will come at last, and we'll start living like normal people."

Maxim listened to him and thought that if he really were a Highlander, that was probably what he would do: I'd go back to my homeland and live a quiet life there with a young wife, forget about all these horrors and all the complexities . . . No, I wouldn't forget, I'd organize defenses so the Fathers' bureaucrats wouldn't stick their noses in there, and if the Guards showed up there, I'd fight to the last on the threshold of my own home . . . Only I'm not a Highlander. I have no business up in the mountains—my business is down here, I don't intend to put up with all of this . . . And Rada? Well, if Rada really does love me, then she'll understand, she'll have to understand . . . I don't want to think about that now, I don't want to love, this is not the time for me to love . . .

He started thinking and didn't immediately realize that something had changed inside the building. Someone was walking along the corridor, someone was whispering on the other side of the wall, and suddenly someone started bustling about in the corridor. Rada desperately cried out "Mak!" and immediately fell silent, as if someone had squeezed her mouth shut. He stood up and dashed to the window, but the door swung open and Rada appeared in the doorway, with her face completely drained of blood. He caught the familiar odor of the Guards' barracks, and metal-tipped boots started clattering, no longer trying to conceal their presence. Rada was shoved into the room and men in black coveralls came pouring in after her. Pandi aimed an automatic rifle at Maxim with a bestial expression on his face, and Cornet Chachu, as cunning as ever, and as clever as ever, stood beside Rada, with his pistol jammed against her side.

"Stay where you are!" he shouted. "If you move a single muscle, I'll shoot!"

Maxim froze. There was nothing he could do; he needed at least two seconds, maybe one and a half, but this killer only needed one.

"Hands up!" the cornet croaked. "Corporal, handcuffs! And ankle cuffs! Move it, massaraksh!"

Pandi, whom Maxim had repeatedly thrown over his head in training, approached with great caution, unclipping a heavy chain from his belt. The bestial expression on his face had been replaced by an expression of concern. "Watch yourself, now," he told Maxim. "If anything happens, Mr. Cornet will . . . you know . . . blow her away . . . this love of yours . . ."

He clicked the steel bracelets onto Maxim's wrists, then squatted down and shackled his legs together. Maxim smiled to himself. He knew what he was going to do next. But he had underestimated the cornet. The cornet didn't let Rada go. They all went down the stairs together, they all got into the truck together, and the cornet didn't lower his pistol for a second. Then Gai was shoved into the truck with his hands shackled.

Dawn was still a long way off, it was still drizzling, and the blurred lights barely even lit up the wet street. The guardsmen took their seats on the benches in the back of the truck, the huge, wet dogs silently tried to break free of their leashes, and when they were reined back, they yawned and whimpered. And in the entranceway, the janitor was standing, leaning against the doorpost, with his hands clasped on his stomach. He was dozing.

12

The state prosecutor leaned back in his chair, popped a few dried berries into his mouth, chewed for a while, and took a sip of medicinal water. Squeezing his eyes firmly shut and pressing his fingertips against his weary eyes, he listened. For many hundreds of yards all around, everything was good. The building of the Palace of Justice was empty, the night rain was monotonously drumming on the windows, he couldn't even hear any sirens or squealing brakes, and the elevators weren't clanging and humming. There was nobody here except for his night secretary in the reception area, where he was languishing as quiet as a mouse behind the tall door, awaiting instructions. The prosecutor slowly unsealed his eyes and glanced through the drifting blotches of color at the chair for visitors, made to a special design. I should take that chair with me. And I should take the desk too—I've grown accustomed to it . . .

But I'll probably feel sorry to leave here anyway, won't I? I've warmed this seat so thoroughly over the last ten years . . . And why should I leave? A man is a strange piece of work: if he's facing a flight of steps, he simply has to scramble right up to the very top. Up at the very top it's cold, the drafts blowing up there are very detrimental to one's health, a fall from that height is fatal, the steps are slippery and dangerous, and you know all that perfectly well, but you still clamber up anyway. You clamber up in defiance of any and all advice, clamber up in defiance of your enemies' opposition, clamber up in defiance of your own instincts, common sense, and apprehensions—you clamber higher, higher, higher . . . Anyone who doesn't clamber higher goes tumbling down, it's true. But anyone who clambers right up to the top tumbles down anyway . . .

The chirping of the internal phone interrupted his thoughts. He picked up the receiver and, wincing in annoyance, said, "What is it? I'm busy."

"Your Excellency," said the secretary, his voice sighing like a gentle breeze, "a person giving his name as Wanderer, calling on the gray line, insists on speaking with you."

"Wanderer?" The prosecutor livened up. "Put him through."

There was a click in the earpiece of the receiver and the secretary sighed, "His Excellency is on the line."

Following another click, a familiar, self-assured voice spoke in Pandeian. "Egghead? Hello. Are you very busy?"

"Not to you."

"I have to talk to you."

"When?"

"Right now, if possible."

"I am at your disposal," said the prosecutor. "Come."

"I'll be there in ten or fifteen minutes. Expect me then."

The prosecutor put down the receiver and sat completely still for a while, plucking at his lower lip. So he's shown up, the old darling. And once again completely out of the blue. Massaraksh, the amount of money I've blown on that man, probably more than on all the rest, taken together, but I still only know the same as all the rest, taken individually. A dangerous character. Unpredictable. He has spoiled my mood . . .

The prosecutor cast an angry glance at the documents laid out across the desk, casually raked them into a heap, and stuffed them into the drawer. Just how long has he been gone? Yes, two months. The same as usual. He disappears, destination unknown, no information for two months, and then—he just pops up, like a jack-in-the-box . . . No, something will have to be done about this jack. It's not possible to work like this . . .

Well, all right, what does he want from me? What has actually happened during these two months? Dodger got eaten . . . He's not likely to be interested in that. He despised Dodger. But then, he despises everybody . . . There hasn't been anything concerning his outfit, and he wouldn't come to see me about trivial nonsense like that—he would go straight to Dad or Father-in-Law . . . Perhaps he has sniffed out something curious and wants to form an alliance? God grant, I hope that's it—only if I were him, I wouldn't enter into an alliance with anyone . . . Perhaps it's the trial? But no, what does the trial have to do with anything . . .

Ah, what point is there in guessing? We'd better just take the requisite measures. He pulled out a secret drawer and switched on all the phonographs and hidden cameras. We'll preserve this scene for posterity.

Well, where are you, Wanderer? In his agitation he broke into a sweat and started violently trembling. To calm himself down, he tossed a few more berries into his mouth, chewed for a moment, closed his eyes, and started counting. When he had counted to seven hundred, the door opened and, waving aside the secretary, *he* walked into the office—that lanky spindle-legs, that bleak humorist, that hope of the Fathers, hated and adored, dangling by a thread from second to second and never falling; scraggy and stoop-shouldered, with round, green eyes and large, protruding ears, wearing his perpetual, ludicrous anorak reaching down to his knees; as bald as a baby's bottom, a sorcerer, power broker, and devourer of billions . . .

The prosecutor stood up to greet him. With this man there was no need to pretend and speak in constrained words. "Greetings, Wanderer," he said. "Have you come to boast?"

"About what?" Wanderer asked, collapsing into the familiar chair and raising his knees incongruously high. "Massaraksh, I forget about this damned contraption every time. When are you going to stop deriding your visitors?"

"A visitor should feel awkward," the prosecutor declared in an edifying tone of voice. "A visitor should be ludicrous, otherwise what enjoyment will I get from him? Here I am looking at you now, and I feel quite jolly."

"Yes, I know you're a jolly fellow," said Wanderer. "Only your sense of humor is very unsubtle . . . And, by the way, you may sit."

The prosecutor realized that he was still standing. As usual, Wanderer had been quick to even the score. The prosecutor sat as comfortably as he could manage and took a sip of his curative swill. "So?" he asked.

"You have in your clutches," his visitor said, "a man whom I very much want. A certain Mak Sim. You put him away him for reeducation, remember?"

"No," the prosecutor sincerely replied, feeling a certain degree of disappointment. "When did I put him away? In connection with what case?"

"Only just recently. In connection with the blown-up tower case."

"Ah, I remember . . . Well, what of it?"

"That's all," said Wanderer. "I need him."

"Hang on," the prosecutor said in annoyance. "I didn't conduct the trial. I can't possibly remember every convicted offender."

"I thought the people in the department were all yours."

"There was only one of mine—all the rest were genuine . . . What did you say he was called?"

"Mak Sim."

"Mak Sim," the prosecutor repeated. "Ah, that Highlander spy . . . I remember. There was some strange kind of business with him—he was shot, but unsuccessfully."

"Yes, it appears so."

"Some kind of exceptional strongman. Yes, something was reported to me. But what do you need him for?"

"He's a mutant," said Wanderer. "He has very curious mentograms, and I need him for my work."

"Are you going to have him dissected?"

"Possibly. My people spotted him a long time ago, when he was still being exploited in the Special Studio, but then he gave us the slip."

Feeling monumentally disappointed, the prosecutor stuffed his mouth with berries. "OK," he said, feebly chewing. "So how are things going with you?"

"As always, wonderful," Wanderer replied. "And with you too, I've heard. You finally undermined Twitcher after all. Congratulations . . . So when will I receive my Mak?"

"Well, I'll send the dispatch tomorrow. He'll be delivered in five or seven days."

"Surely not for free?" Wanderer said.

"As a favor," said the prosecutor. "But what can you offer me?"

"The very first protective tin hat."

The prosecutor chuckled. "And the World Light into the bargain," he said. "But anyway, bear in mind that I don't want the first tin hat. I want the only one . . . And incidentally, is it true that your gang has been commissioned to develop a directional radiation unit?"

"It might be."

"But listen, what the hell do we need it for? Don't we have enough troubles already? Couldn't you just clamp down on this work?"

Wanderer bared his teeth. "Are you afraid, Egghead?" he asked.

"Yes, I am," said the prosecutor. "And aren't you afraid? Or did you, perhaps, imagine that the love between you and Brother-in-Law is forever? He'll zap you with your own radiation unit . . . As sure as I'm sitting here."

Wanderer bared his teeth again. "You've convinced me," he said. "That's agreed, then. "I'm going to see Dad now. Is there anything you'd like me to pass on?"

"Dad's angry with me," said the prosecutor. "And I find that damned unpleasant."

"All right," said Wanderer. "That's what I'll tell him."

"Joking aside," said the prosecutor, "if you could just put in a little word . . ."

"Well, you are our Egghead," Wanderer said in Dad's voice. "I'll give it a try."

"Is he, at least, happy with the trial?"

"How should I know? I've only just arrived."

"Well then, find out . . . And concerning your . . . what did you say his name was? Let me make a note of it . . ."

"Mak Sim."

"Right . . . I'll write concerning him tomorrow."

"Keep well," Wanderer said, and walked out.

The prosecutor sullenly watched him go. Yes, I can only envy him. What a position he holds. The only one that our defense depends on. It's too late now for regrets, but perhaps I ought to have cozied up to him. But how could I cozy up to him? There's nothing he needs; he's the most important one anyway, we're all dependent on him, we all swear by him . . . Ah, if I could simply grab a man like that by the throat—wouldn't that be just wonderful! If only there was at least something he needed! But it's always just *Here you are, then* with him . . . He wants an educatee, some kind of rare jewel . . . *He has interesting mentograms, don't you know* . . . But actually this educatee is a Highlander, and just recently Dad has been talking a lot about the mountains . . . Perhaps it's worthwhile paying some attention to this . . . No matter how the war turns out, Dad is still Dad . . . Massaraksh, it's impossible to do any more work today anyway . . .

He spoke into the microphone. "Koch, what do you have on the convict Sim?" He suddenly remembered something. "I think you put together some kind of dossier about him . . ."

"Yes indeed, Your Excellency," the secretary sighed like a breeze. "I had the honor to draw Your Excellency's attention to—"

"Let me have it. And bring me some water."

He put down the receiver and the night secretary instantly appeared in the doorway, as intangible as a shadow. A thick document folder appeared on the desk; there was a quiet tinkling, a glugging of water, and a full glass appeared beside the folder. The prosecutor took a sip as he scrutinized its cover.

"An abstract of the case of Mak Sim (Maxim Kammerer). Prepared by Administrative Aide Koch." Holy cow, this is one thick abstract . . . He opened the folder and took out the first sheaf of paper.

"The testimony of Cornet To'ot" . . . "The testimony of the accused Gaal" . . . sketch maps of some border region in the South . . . "He was not wearing any other clothing. His speech seemed articulate to me but was absolutely incomprehensible. An attempt to speak to him in Hontian produced no response . . ." Oh, these border cornets! A Hontian spy on the southern border . . . "The drawings made by the prisoner appeared quite surprisingly skillful to me . . ." Well, there are plenty of surprising things in the South. Unfortunately. And the circumstances of this Sim's appearance don't stand out too distinctly against the general background of various other southern circumstances. Although, of course . . . But let's take a look.

The prosecutor set that sheet of paper aside, selected two of the larger berries, popped them into his mouth, and picked up the next sheet. "The conclusions of an expert commission, consisting of staff members of the Institute of Fabrics and Clothing . . . We, the undersigned . . ." hmm . . . right . . . right . . . "have investigated with all the laboratory methods available to us the item of clothing sent to us from the Department of Justice . . ." more gibberish of some kind . . .

and have come to the following conclusion:

1. The aforementioned item of clothing is a pair of short pants of size number 4B, suitable to be worn by both men and women.
2. The cut of the pants cannot be correlated with any known standard and cannot actually be referred to as a cut, since the pants are not sewn together but manufactured by some process unknown to us.
3. The pants are manufactured out of a soft, porous fabric of a silvery color, which cannot actually be called a fabric, since even microscopic investigation failed to identify any structure in it. This material is noncombustible, nonwettable, and possesses very great tensile strength. Chemical analysis . . .

A strange pair of pants. So am I supposed to understand that these are his pants . . . The prosecutor took a finely sharpened pencil and wrote in the margin: "Secretary. Why do you not provide explanatory notes? Whose pants are they? Where did the pants come from?" Right . . .

And the conclusions? Formulas . . . Yet more formulas . . . Massaraksh, more formulas . . . Aha! " . . . a technology that is not known in our country or in any other civilized states (according to prewar data)."

The prosecutor set the conclusion aside. Well, pants . . . So OK. Pants are pants . . . What comes next? "Certificate of medical examination." Interesting. What, that's his blood pressure? Oho, those are some lungs! And what on earth is this? Signs of four fatal wounds . . . Now this is sheer mysticism. Aha . . . "See the testimony of the witness Chachu and the accused Gaal." Seven bullets—well, well. Hmm . . . And there are certain divergences: Chachu testifies that he fired his gun for purposes of self-defense when in danger of being killed, but this Gaal claims that Chachu fired because Sim wanted to take his pistol from him. Well, that's no concern of mine . . . Two bullets into the liver—that's too many for any normal man . . . *Riiight*, he can bend a coin into a tube . . . He can run with a man on his shoulders . . . Aha, I read that before. I remember now—at that point I thought that this was an extremely large and healthy young man, and they are usually stupid. And I didn't read any more . . .

But what's this? Aah, an old friend:

Extract from a report by Agent No. 711 . . . He can see quite clearly on a rainy night (he can even read) and in total darkness (he can distinguish objects and see facial expressions at a distance of up to ten yards) . . . Possesses an extremely keen sense of smell and taste—he distinguished members of the group by smell at a distance of up to fifty yards. For a wager, he identified various drinks in tightly sealed vessels . . . He can find his bearings in relation to the cardinal directions without a compass . . . He can determine the time with great accuracy without a watch . . . The following incident occurred: a fish had been bought and boiled, but he forbade us to eat it, asserting that it was radioactive. On being checked with a radiometer, the fish did indeed prove to be radioactive. I draw your attention to the fact that he himself ate the fish, saying that it was not dangerous for him, and indeed he suffered no harm, although the level of radiation was more than three times higher than the safety limit (almost 77 units) . . .

The prosecutor leaned back in his chair. No, this really is too much. Perhaps he is actually immortal for good measure. Yes, Wanderer ought to find all of this interesting. Let us see what comes next.

Here's a serious document. "Conclusion of a Special Commission of the Department of Public Health. Subject: Mak Sim. No reaction to white radiation. No counterindications to his serving in the special forces." Aha . . . That was when he was enlisting in the Guards. White radiation, massaraksh . . . the bloody butchers, the sons of bitches . . . And this is their evaluation for purposes of the investigation . . .

On being tested with white radiation at various different intensities, up to and including the maximum level, he failed to display any reaction. His reaction to A-radiation was zero level in both senses. His reaction to B-radiation was zero level. NOTE: We consider it our duty to state that the subject (Mak Sim, approximately 20 years of age) represents a danger in view of possible genetic consequences. Complete sterilization or elimination is recommended . . .

Oho! These guys don't mess around. Who is it they have there now? Ah, it's Amateur. Yes, no joker, no joker, that's for sure. I recall that Colt the Joker used to tell an excellent joke about that . . . massaraksh, I can't remember it . . . But anyway, there's nobody here. Now we'll eat a little berry, wash it down with a bit of water . . . filthy swill, but they say it helps . . . OK, what comes next?

Oho, so he's already been there too! Let's see now . . . Zero-level reaction again, probably . . .

> When subjected to augmented methods of interrogation, the suspect Sim did not provide any testimony. In accordance with paragraph 12 concerning the noninfliction of visible physical harm on suspects who are due to appear at a public court hearing, only the following methods were applied:
> A. Acu-surgery, including at the deepest level, with penetration of nerve ganglia (a paradoxical reaction, with the stimulated subject falling asleep).
> B. Chemical processing of the nerve ganglia with alkaloids and alkalis (a similar reaction).
> C. Light chamber (no reaction; the stimulated subject was surprised).
> D. Steam thermal chamber (weight loss without any unpleasant sensations). After this last investigation the use of augmented methods had to be discontinued.

Brrrrr . . . What a horrific document.

Yes, Wanderer is right—this man is some kind of mutant. Normal people can't do things like that . . . Yes, I have heard that mutations can have positive outcomes, if only rarely . . . That explains everything . . . apart from the pants, that is. As far as I know, pants don't mutate . . .

He picked up the next sheet of paper. It wasn't interesting: the testimony of the director of the Special Studio at the Directorate of Television and Radio Broadcasting. An idiotic institution. They record the ravings of various psychos for the amusement of their distinguished audience. As I recall, this studio was thought up by Kalu the Swindler, who was a bit of a wackadoodle himself . . . Well, well, so the studio has survived! Swindler's long gone, but his batty studio is flourishing . . . From the director's testimony, it appears that Sim was an exemplary subject, and it would be most desirable to have him back again . . .

Stop, stop, stop! Transferred to the authority of the Department of Special Research in accordance with warrant number such and such on such and such a date . . . And there it is, the warrant, and it's signed by Fank . . . The prosecutor sensed a faint dawning of enlightenment. Fank . . . You've been up to something here, Wanderer.

No, let us not be hasty with our conclusions. He counted to thirty to calm himself down and picked up the next sheet of paper—or, in fact, a rather thick sheaf of sheets: "Abstract from a report of the Special Ethnolinguistic Commission concerning verification of the presumed Highland origins of M. Sim."

He began absentmindedly reading, still thinking about Fank and Wanderer, but then, to his own surprise, he became interested. This was a curious investigation that linked together and discussed all the denunciations, evidence, and witness testimony that had any bearing on the matter of Mak Sim's origins: anthropological, ethnographic, and linguistic data and their analysis, the conclusions from studying the suspect's phonograms and mentograms and his own drawings. The whole thing read like a novel, although the conclusions were extremely meager and cautious. The commission did not assign M. Sim to any of the known ethnic groups living on the continent. (The report cited the special opinion of the well-known paleoanthropologist Shapshu, stating that he discerned a great degree of similarity between the skull of the suspect and the fossil skull of so-called Ancient Man, who had lived on the Archipelago more than a hundred thousand years ago, but the two were not identical.) The commission confirmed the complete psychological normality of the suspect at the present moment, but conceded that in the recent past he could have suffered from one form or another of amnesia, conjointly with the comprehensive displacement of his true memory by a false one.

The commission had conducted an analysis of the phonograms preserved in the archive of the Special Studio and had reached the conclusion that the language in which the suspect spoke at that time could not be assigned to any of the groups of known languages living or dead. For this reason the commission conceded the possibility that this language could be a product of the suspect's imagination (a so-called fish language), especially since at the present time he himself claimed that he no longer remembered that language. "The commission abstains from any definite conclusions, but is inclined to assume that in the person of M. Sim we are dealing with a mutant of some previously unknown type . . ."

Good ideas occur to great minds at the same moment, the prosecutor enviously thought, and quickly leafed through the "Special Opinion of Commission Member Professor Porrum-ovarrui." The professor, himself a Highlander, recalled the existence deep in the mountains of the semilegendary land of Zartak, inhabited by the Birdcatcher tribe, which to this day had still not been subjected to ethnographical study, and to which the civilized Highlanders attributed magical knowledge and the ability to fly through the air without any mechanical devices. "According to existing accounts, Birdcatchers are extremely large and tall, possess immense physical strength and stamina, and also have golden-brown skin. All of this coincides quite remarkably with the physical characteristics of the suspect . . ."

The prosecutor toyed with his pencil above Professor Porru- . . . etc., then put the pencil down and said in a loud voice, "This opinion would probably account for the pants too. Those incombustible pants . . ."

He ate a berry and glanced over the next sheet of paper. "An abstract from the stenographic record of the trial." Hmm . . . So what's this?

STATE COUNSEL: You will not deny that you are an educated individual?

ACCUSED: I do have an education, but I have a poor grasp of history, sociology, and economics.

STATE COUNSEL: Do not be overmodest. Are you familiar with this book?

ACCUSED: Yes.

STATE COUNSEL: Have you read it?

ACCUSED: Naturally.

STATE COUNSEL: For what purpose did you, while under arrest, take up the reading of a monograph entitled *Tensor Calculus and Contemporary Physics*?

ACCUSED: I don't understand . . . For my own enjoyment . . . In order to amuse myself, if you like . . . It contains some very amusing pages.

STATE COUNSEL: I think it must be clear to the court that only a highly educated individual would read such a specialized research work for amusement and his own pleasure . . .

What kind of nonsense is this? Why am I being fobbed off with this? What comes next? Massaraksh, the trial again.

DEFENSE COUNSEL: Are you aware of the extent to which the Unknown Fathers finance efforts to solve the problem of juvenile criminality?

ACCUSED: I don't entirely understand you. What is juvenile criminality? Crimes against children?

DEFENSE COUNSEL: No. Crimes committed by children

ACCUSED: I don't understand. Children cannot commit crimes . . .

Hmmm, amusing . . . But what's this at the end?

DEFENSE COUNSEL: I hope I have succeeded in demonstrating to the court the naïveté of my client, which amounts to worldly imbecility. My client acted against the state without having the slightest idea of what it is. He is not familiar with the concepts of juvenile criminality, philanthropy, and social welfare assistance . . .

The prosecutor smiled and put the piece of paper down. I get it. Indeed, a strange combination: math and physics for his pleasure, but he doesn't know elementary things. Just like an eccentric professor in some trashy novel.

The prosecutor glanced through a few more pages. I don't understand, Mak, why you cling to this little female . . . What was her name? . . . Rada Gaal. You don't have an intimate relationship with her, you don't owe her anything, the idiotic state counsel doesn't have the slightest grounds for tying her in with the underground . . . But the impression is given that, by keeping her in their sights, they can make you do absolutely anything. A very useful quality—for us, but a very inconvenient one for you . . .

Riiight—basically all this evidence comes down to the fact that you, my brother, are a slave to your word and an inflexible individual in general. You didn't make the grade as a political activist. And you're not really interested anyway . . .

Hmmm, photographs . . . So that's what you're like. A likable face—very, very likable . . . Rather strange eyes . . . Where was it they photographed you? At the trial? . . . Just look at you: cheerful, clear-eyed, in such a relaxed pose. Where did they teach you to sit so elegantly and in general to carry yourself like that? The bench for the accused is something like my visitors' chair— impossible to sit on in a relaxed pose. A curious individual, most curious . . . But then, that's all trivia. That's not the point.

The prosecutor crept out from behind his desk and started striding around his office. Something was sweetly tickling his brain, something was inciting him, egging him on . . . I found something in this folder . . . something important, something extremely important . . . Fank? Yes, that's important, because Wanderer only uses his Fank for the very important cases, the most important ones. But Fank is only the confirmation. What's the most important thing? The pants . . . humbug . . . Ah! Yes, yes, yes. It isn't in the folder.

He picked up the phone. "Koch, what was that about an attack on a convoy?"

"Fourteen days ago," the secretary immediately sighed gently, as if he were reading a text prepared in advance, "at eighteen hundred hours and thirty-three minutes, an armed assault was carried out on police vehicles transferring the suspects in cases 6981–84 from the courthouse to the municipal jail. The assault was beaten off, and during the exchange of fire one of the attackers was seriously wounded and died without regaining consciousness. The body was not identified. The investigation into the attack was discontinued."

"Who did it?"

"That was not determined."

"Meaning . . ."

"The official underground had nothing to do with it."

"Your observations?"

"It is possible that the attack was carried out by members of the left wing of the underground, attempting to free the accused Dek Pottu, a.k.a. General. Dek Pottu is a high-level, experienced HQ staff officer, known to have close ties with the left wing—"

The prosecutor dropped the receiver. Well then, it could all really be so. And it could all not be so. Right, let's skim through it again. Southern border, idiotic cornet . . . Pants . . . Runs with a man on his shoulders . . . Radioactive fish, 77 units . . . Reaction to A-radiation . . . Chemo-processing of nerve ganglia . . . Stop! Reaction to A-radiation. "His reaction to A-radiation was zero level in both senses." The prosecutor pressed his open palm against his pounding heart. *Zero in both senses!*

He grabbed the receiver again. "Koch! Immediately prepare a special courier with an armed escort. And a private railcar to the south . . . No! My electromotive . . . Massaraksh!" He hastily thrust his hand into the desk drawer and turned off all the recording devices. "Get on with it!"

Still pressing his left hand to his heart, he took a personal dispatch form out of a writing case and started rapidly but legibly inscribing:

National importance. Top secret. To the Commandant-General of the Special Southern District. For urgent and rigorous implementation, on your strictly personal responsibility. Immediately transfer into the custody of the bearer of this dispatch the educatee Mak Sim, case no. 6983. From the moment of such transfer the educatee Mak Sim is to be regarded as having disappeared without a trace, concerning which the pertinent documents shall be kept in the archives.
—State Prosecutor

He grabbed another form:

Instruction. I herewith order all officials of the military, civil, and railroad administrations to provide assistance under the category EXTRA to the bearer of this instruction, a special courier of the state prosecutor's office, and also to his accompanying escort.
—State Prosecutor

Then he finished his glass of water, poured himself some more, and started writing on a third form, but this time slowly, pondering every word: "Dear Wanderer! Things have turned out rather stupidly. It has only just come to light that the subject in which you are interested has disappeared without a trace, as quite often happens in the southern jungles . . ."

PART IV

THE
CONVICT

13

His first shot shattered one of its caterpillar tracks, and for the first time in more than twenty years, it abandoned its well-worn rut, in the process wrenching up chunks of concrete, then smashed its way into the thickets of the forest and began slowly slewing around on the spot, crunching heavily through the bushes with its broad forehead and brushing aside the shuddering tree trunks. When it displayed its immense, dirty stern with a sheet of iron dangling on rusty rivets, Zef fired neatly and precisely so that he wouldn't—God forbid!—hit the atomic boiler, sending a blast charge deep into the engine, into the muscles, sinews, and nerve ganglia, and it gasped in an iron voice, belched a cloud of incandescent smoke from out of its articulated joints, and stopped forever. But *something* carried on living in its vile, armored belly. Some nerves or other that had survived continued to transmit meaningless signals; emergency response systems kept switching on and immediately switching off, hissing and spitting out foam. That *something* continued flaccidly palpitating, feebly scrabbling with its surviving caterpillar track, and up on top of the dying dragon the peeling latticework barrel of its rocket launcher continued rising up and sinking back down in meaningless menace, like the abdomen of a splatted wasp.

Zef watched this death agony for a few seconds, then turned and walked into the forest, dragging the grenade launcher along by its strap, and Maxim and Wild Boar set off after him. When they emerged into a quiet clearing that Zef must have spotted earlier on the way here, they all collapsed into the grass. "Let's have a smoke," said Zef.

He made a roll-up for the one-handed man, gave him a light, and lit up himself. Maxim lay there with his chin propped on his hands, still watching through the sparse trees as the iron dragon died, pitifully jangling some final gear-wheels or other, and whistling as it released jets of radioactive steam from its lacerated innards.

"That's the way—that's the only way," Zef said in a patronizing tone of voice. "And if you do it any other way, I'll box your ears."

"Why?" asked Maxim. "I wanted to stop it."

"Because," Zef replied, "the grenade could ricochet into the rocket, and then we'd be dead meat."

"I was aiming at the caterpillar tread," said Maxim.

"But you have to aim at its butt," said Zef. He stretched. "And in general, while you're still a greenhorn, don't go sticking your nose anywhere first. Not unless I ask you to. You got that?"

"Yes," said Maxim. He wasn't interested in all these subtle points of Zef's. And he wasn't really very interested in Zef himself. He was interested in Wild Boar. But as always, Wild Boar remained indifferently silent, resting his artificial hand on the scruffy housing of the mine detector. Everything was the same as it always was. And nothing was the way Mak would have liked it to be.

When the newly arrived educatees were lined up in front of the bunkhouses a week earlier, Zef had walked straight up to Maxim and taken him into his 134th Sappers' Unit. Maxim had been delighted. He immediately recognized that massive, fiery-red beard and the square, stocky figure, and it gave him a good feeling to have been recognized in that stifling crowd of check coveralls, in which nobody gave a damn for anybody else and nobody was even interested in anybody else. In addition, Maxim had every reason to suppose that Zef—the formerly famous psychiatrist Allu Zef, an educated, cultured individual, and a total contrast with the semicriminal riffraff crammed into the convict car—was here because of his politics and was connected in some way with the underground. And when Zef led him into the bunkhouse and pointed to a place on the bunks beside one-handed Wild Boar, Maxim thought that his fate here had definitely been decided.

Very soon, however, he realized he had been wrong. Wild Boar didn't want to make conversation. After listening to Maxim's hastily whispered story about what had happened to his group, the demolition of the tower, and the trial, he mumbled through a yawn, "Stranger things than that happen," and lay down, turning his face away. Maxim felt cheated. And then Zef clambered up onto the bunks. "I've just gobbled a real gutful," he informed Maxim, burping loudly with his stomach gurgling, and then attempted, in a crude, pushy style, to drag all the names and meeting places out of Maxim. Maybe he had once been a famous scientist, an educated and cultured individual. Maybe—and even probably—he used to have some kind of connection with the underground. But at that moment he produced the impression of a run-of-the-mill stooge with an overstuffed gut who, for want of anything else to do, had decided to work on a stupid greenhorn before turning in. Maxim only managed to shake him off with a serious effort. After Zef suddenly started snoring and snorting in a satisfied, well-fed tone, Maxim lay there for a long time, unable to sleep, recalling how many times he had been deceived by people and circumstances here.

His nerves were at the breaking point. He recalled the hideous, fraudulent trial, thoroughly rehearsed in advance, arranged in detail even before the group had received the order to attack the tower, and the written denunciations of some bastard who knew everything about the group and maybe was even a member of the group, and the movie that was shot from the tower during the attack, and his own feeling of shame when he recognized himself on the screen, blazing away with his automatic rifle at those spotlights—no, at those movie floodlights illuminating the set for that appalling production . . . It was repulsively stifling in the hermetically sealed bunkhouse, the parasites were biting, the educatees were deliriously raving, and down in the farthest corner the privileged inmates were playing a passionate game of cards by the light of an improvised candle, abusing each other in harsh, vehement voices.

And the next day even the forest deceived Maxim. He couldn't take a single step there without running into iron: dead, rusted-through iron; iron that was just lying in wait, ready to kill at any moment; iron that was furtively stirring, taking aim; iron that was moving, blindly and senselessly plowing up the remains of the roads. The earth and the grass gave off a smell of rust, radioactive pools had accumulated at the bottoms of gullies, the birds didn't sing but hoarsely lamented, as if bewailing their death agony, there weren't any animals, and there wasn't even any sylvan repose—on their right and on their left explosions erupted and rumbled, grayish-blue fumes swirled and eddied among the branches, and gusts of wind brought the harsh roaring of exhausted engines . . .

And so it went on, day and night, night and day. In the daytime they went out into the forest, which wasn't a forest but an old fortified area. It was literally crawling with automated combat devices—self-propelled guns, rockets on caterpillar tracks, flamethrowers, and gas projectors—all of which still hadn't died yet after more than twenty years. It was still living its own unnecessary mechanical life, still taking aim, vectoring in, and belching forth lead, fire, and death, and all of it had to be strangled, blown up, and killed in order to clear a corridor for the construction of more radiation towers. At night Wild Boar remained as taciturn as ever, while Zef pestered Maxim with questions again and again, switching approaches between stupidly forthright and incredibly subtle and cunning. And there was the coarse food, and the educatees' strange songs, and the Guards beating someone's face in, and twice a day everyone in the bunkhouses and the forest writhed in agony from the radiation attacks, and hanged fugitives dangled in the wind . . . Day and night . . . day and night . . .

"Why did you want to stop it?" Wild Boar suddenly asked.

Maxim hastily sat down. This was the first question the one-handed man had asked him. "I wanted to take a look at how it was made."

"Did you want to escape?"

"No, not that. But it's a tank, after all, a battle machine . . ."

"What would you want with a tank?" Wild Boar asked. He spoke as if the red-haired stooge weren't there.

"I don't know," said Maxim. "I still need to think about that. Are there a lot of them here?"

"Yes, a lot," the red-haired stooge butted in. "There are lots of tanks here, and there have always been lots of fools here too." He yawned. "The number of times it's been tried already. They climb in, rummage around and rummage around, and then give up. And there was one fool—someone like you—who simply blew himself up."

"Don't worry, I wouldn't have blown myself up," Maxim coolly said. "It's not a complicated mechanism."

"But still, what would you want with it?" the one-handed man asked. He was smoking, lying on his back, holding the roll-up in his artificial fingers. "Let's suppose you get it going. Then what?"

"A break-out across the bridge," Zef chuckled.

"And why not?" asked Maxim. He had no idea at all how to behave. This redheaded character didn't seem to be a stooge after all. Massaraksh, why were they suddenly pestering him like this?

"You'd never get as far the bridge," said the one-handed man. "They'd gun you down thirty-three times over. And even if you did reach it, you'd see that the bridge has been demolished."

"How about across the bottom of the river?"

"The river's radioactive," Zef said, and spat. "If it were a decent sort of river, now, you wouldn't need any tanks. Just swim across it anywhere at all—the banks aren't guarded." He spat again. "But in that case, they would be guarded. And, so, young man, stop kicking up dust. You're stuck here for the long term, so get used to it. Adapt and things will work out. But if you don't listen to your elders, you could even find yourself beholding the World Light this very day."

"Escaping's not difficult," said Maxim. "I could escape right now—"

"Well, aren't you something!" Zef admiringly exclaimed.

". . . and if you intend to carry on playing the conspirator . . ."
Maxim continued, pointedly addressing only Wild Boar, but Zef
interrupted him again.

"I intend to fulfill the daily norm," he declared, getting up.
"Otherwise they won't let us feed our faces today. Let's go!"

He walked off ahead, striding between the trees with a waddling gait, and Maxim asked the one-handed man, "Is he really a
political prisoner?"

The one-handed man cast a quick glance at Maxim and said,
"Come on, how can you ask that?"

They set off after Zef, trying to tread in his footsteps. Maxim
brought up the rear. "What's he in here for?"

"Crossing the street at the wrong place," the one-handed man
said, and once again Maxim's desire to talk evaporated.

Before they had gone even a hundred paces, Zef gave the
command "Halt!" and work began. "Get down!" Zef roared. He
flung himself down flat on the ground, and the thick tree ahead
of them revolved with a long screech, thrust a long, slim gun barrel out from inside itself, wiggled it from side to side as if taking
aim, and started droning; there was a click, and a little puff of
yellow smoke lazily crept out of the black muzzle. "It's defunct,"
Zef said in a brisk tone, and got up first, dusting off his trousers.
They blew up the gun tree.

After that there was a minefield, then a hill with a machine
gun trap, which wasn't defunct and kept them pinned down on
the ground for a long time, setting the forest ringing with its
roaring. Then they ended up in a genuine jungle of barbed wire
and barely managed to scramble through it, and when they finally
did get through it, something opened fire on them from above,
and everything on all sides started exploding and burning. Maxim
couldn't understand a thing, the one-handed man calmly lay there
facedown, and Zef fired his grenade launcher up into the sky and
suddenly yelled, "Follow me, move it!" They ran, and flames
suddenly flared up where they had just been. Zef swore terrible
oaths and the one-handed man laughed. Then they clambered

into a dense thicket, but suddenly something started whistling and wheezing, and clouds of greenish gas with a repulsive smell started billowing down through the branches, and again they had to run, scrambling through the bushes, and Zef swore again, and the one-handed man agonizingly vomited . . .

Zef eventually got tired and announced a break. They lit a campfire, and Maxim, as the junior comrade, prepared to cook lunch by boiling up soup out of canned food in the old, familiar cooking pot. Zef and the one-handed man, both grubby and tattered, lay right there beside him, smoking. Wild Boar looked worn out; he was already old and found all of this harder going than the others.

"The mind boggles," said Maxim. "How did we manage to lose a war with so much weaponry per square yard?"

"What makes you think we lost?" Zef lazily asked.

"Well, we didn't win," said Maxim. "Victors don't live like this."

"In modern war there are no victors," the one-handed man remarked. "You're right, of course. We did lose the war. Everybody lost this war. Only the Unknown Fathers won it."

"The Unknown Fathers have it tough too," said Maxim, stirring the soup.

"Yes," Zef said in a serious voice. "Sleepless nights and agonized pondering on the fate and fortunes of their people . . . Weary and benign, all-seeing and all-understanding . . . Massaraksh, it's a long time since I read any newspapers, I've forgotten what comes next . . ."

"Faithful and benign," the one-handed man corrected him. "Totally dedicated to progress and the struggle against chaos."

"I've grown unused to words like that," said Zef. "Around here, there's more of 'lousy mug' and 'ugly snout' . . . Hey, kid, whatever your name is . . ."

"Maxim."

"Yes, right . . . You keep stirring, Mak, keep stirring. If it burns, you're in trouble!"

Maxim kept stirring. And then Zef announced that it was time, he couldn't bear to wait any longer. They ate the soup in complete silence.

Maxim could sense that something had changed, something would be said today. But after lunch the one-handed man lay down again and started looking up at the sky, and Zef muttered unintelligibly as he took the pot and started mopping the bottom of it with a thick crust of bread. "I feel like shooting something . . ." he muttered. "I want to really gorge myself, it's like I haven't eaten at all . . . just aggravated my appetite . . ." Feeling awkward, Maxim tried to strike up a conversation about the hunting in these parts, but no one backed him up. The one-handed man lay with his eyes closed and seemed to be sleeping. After hearing out Maxim's comments, Zef merely growled, "What kind of hunting can there be here? Everything's polluted, radioactive," and he also collapsed onto his back.

Maxim sighed, took the cooking pot, and plodded toward a stream that he could hear somewhere close by. The water in the stream was clear; it looked so pure and delectable, it made Maxim really want to take a drink, and he scooped up a handful. Unfortunately, he realized he definitely couldn't wash the cooking pot here, and it would be a bad idea to drink the water too—the stream was distinctly radioactive. Maxim squatted down, placed the cooking pot beside him, and started pondering.

First he thought about Rada for some reason, about how she always washed the dishes after a meal and wouldn't let him help, on the absurd excuse that it was a woman's job. He remembered that she loved him and felt proud, because no woman had ever loved him before. He wanted very badly to see Rada, and then immediately, with supreme inconsistency, thought what a good thing it was that she wasn't here. This was no place for even the most obnoxious of men; they ought to herd a thousand cyberjanitors in here. Or maybe just atomize all these forests with everything in them and cultivate new, cheerful ones—or even gloomy ones, but pure with the gloominess of nature.

Then he remembered that he had been banished here in per-
petuity, and felt amazed by the naïveté of those who had banished
him without making him promise anything, who had imagined
that he would voluntarily live here and even help them set up a
line of radiation towers through these forests. In the convict car
they had told him that the forests stretched southward for hundreds of miles, and the war technology was still there, even in the
desert . . . Ah no, I'm not going to hang around here. Massaraksh,
only yesterday I was knocking these towers down, and today
I'm supposed to clear the sites for them? I've had enough of this
nonsense.

Wild Boar doesn't trust me. He trusts Zef but not me. And
I don't trust Zef, but apparently I'm wrong about that. Probably I
seem as suspiciously nosy to Wild Boar as Zef seems to me . . . Well,
OK, Wild Boar doesn't trust me, so I'm on my own again. Of
course, I could hope to run into General or Hoof, only that's just
too unlikely; they say there are more than a million educatees
here, and this is a vast region. No, no, there's no point in hoping to
meet anyone like that . . . Of course, I could try to cobble together
a group of strangers, but—massaraksh—I have to be honest with
myself: I'm not suited to that. I'm not suited to that just yet, that
is. I'm too trusting . . .

But hang on, let's define the goal first. What do I want? He
spent several minutes clarifying his goal. It turned out as follows:
Overthrow the Unknown Fathers. If they're military men, let
them serve in the army, and if they're financial experts, let them
deal with financial matters, whatever that might mean. Establish
a democratic government—he had a more or less clear idea of
what a democratic government was, and he was even aware that
a republic would be bourgeois democratic at first. It wouldn't
solve all the problems, but it would at least make it possible to
put an end to lawlessness and eliminate the senseless expenditure
on the towers and preparations for war.

However, he honestly admitted that he only had a clear idea
of the first point of his program: the overthrow of tyranny. His

thoughts were pretty vague on what came after that. And what was more, he wasn't even certain that the broad masses of the people would actually support his idea of overthrowing authority. The Unknown Fathers were absolutely obvious liars and scoundrels, but for some reason they enjoyed unchallenged popularity with the people.

OK, he decided, let's not look so far ahead. Let's stick with the first point and take a look at what stands between me and the fat necks of the Unknown Fathers. In the first place, the armed forces—the excellently trained Guards and the army, about which all I know is that my Gai is serving in a penal company (what a strange expression!) somewhere or other. In the second place—and this is more substantial—the actual anonymity of the Unknown Fathers. Who are they? Where do I look for them? Where do they come from, where do they reside, how do they become Unknown Fathers? He tried to recall how things had been on Earth in the age of revolutions and dictatorships . . . . Massaraksh, all I remember are the main dates, the most important names, the most basic alignment of forces—but I need details, analogies, precedents . . . Take fascism, for instance—what were things like then? I remember how horrible it was reading about it and hearing about it. That Himmler was some repulsive kind of bloodsucking spider . . . But hang on, that means it wasn't an anonymous government . . . *Yeeeah*, I don't remember much. But it was so long ago, wasn't it, and it was so abhorrent, and who could have known that I'd end up in a mess like this?

They ought to send the guys from Galactic Security or the Institute of Experimental History here—they'd figure out what's what soon enough. Maybe I should try to construct a transmitter? He sadly laughed, remembering that he had already thought about building a transmitter here—and right here in this very area, somewhere not far away . . . No, I'll obviously have to rely on nobody but myself. OK. There's only one weapon against an army: another army. And the weapon against anonymity and mystery is intelligence work. It all turns out to be very simple . . .

In any case, I have to get away from here. Of course, I'll try to get some kind of group together, but if that doesn't work out, I'll go on my own . . . And a tank is a definite must. The weapons here are worth a hundred armies. They're a bit battered after twenty years, it's true, and they're automated, but I'll just have to try to adapt them . . . Does Wild Boar really still not trust me? he thought, almost in despair, grabbed the cooking pot, and ran back to the campfire.

Zef and Wild Boar weren't sleeping, they were lying with their heads together, quietly but passionately arguing about something. Catching sight of Maxim, Zef hastily said "That's enough!" and got to his feet. Jerking up his ginger beard and glaring wide-eyed, he yelled, "Where did you get to, massaraksh! Who gave you permission to leave? We have to work, or they won't give us any chow, thirty-three massarakshes!"

At that point Maxim blew his top. "You go to hell, Zef! Can't you think about anything else except gorging on chow? That's all I've heard from you all day long: gorge, gorge, gorge! You can gorge on my canned stuff, if it tortures you so badly!"

He flung the cooking pot down on the ground, grabbed his backpack, and started threading his arms though the straps. Zef, who had crouched down in the face of this acoustic onslaught, gazed at Maxim with a stunned expression, his mouth gaping like a black hole in his fiery ginger beard. Then the mouth snapped shut with a gurgling, snorting sound, and Zef started roaring with laughter, setting the forest ringing. The one-handed man joined in, although his laughter could only be seen, not heard. Maxim couldn't help himself, and he started laughing too, rather awkwardly. He felt embarrassed at his own rudeness.

"Massaraksh," Zef eventually wheezed. "You got some voice! . . . Yes, my old buddy," he said, turning to Wild Boar, "just you remember what I said. And by the way, I just said 'That's enough' . . . Get up!" he yelled. "And move it, if you want to . . . hmm . . . gorge yourselves this evening."

And that was all. They yelled a bit, laughed a bit, turned serious, and set off again—to risk their lives in the names of the Unknown Fathers. Maxim furiously disarmed mines, smashed twin-barreled machine guns out of their nests, and unscrewed the warheads of surface-to-air missiles jutting out of their open hatches. Once again there was fire, stench, hissing jets of tear gas, and the repulsive odor of the decomposing corpses of animals shot by the automatons. They all got even dirtier, even angrier, even more ragged and tattered, and Zef wheezed to Maxim, "Move it, move it! If you want to gorge yourself, move it!"—and one-handed Wild Boar was finally exhausted and could barely drag himself along far behind them, leaning on his mine detector as if it were a staff . . .

In the course of those hours Maxim grew thoroughly sick and tired of Zef, and he was actually glad when his ginger-bearded companion suddenly bellowed and disappeared under the ground with a bump. Wiping the sweat off his dirty forehead with his dirty sleeve, Maxim unhurriedly walked over and stopped at the edge of a dark, narrow crevice hidden in the grass. The crevice was deep and pitch black, with a chilly, damp draft blowing up out of it; he couldn't see anything, and all he could hear was a kind of crunching, fluttering sound, as well as unintelligible swearing. Wild Boar limped up, glanced into the crevice, and asked Maxim, "Is he in there? What's he doing in there?"

"Zef!" Maxim called, leaning down. "Are you down there, Zef?"

A rumbling reply surfaced out of the crevice. "Come down here! Jump, it's soft."

Maxim looked at the one-handed man, who shook his head. "That's not for me," he said. "You jump, and I'll lower a rope down to you afterward."

"Who's there!" Zef suddenly roared down below them. "I'll fire, massaraksh!"

Maxim lowered his legs into the crevice, pushed off, and jumped. Almost immediately he sank up to his knees in some kind of crumbly mass and sat down. Zef was somewhere close by. Maxim closed his eyes and sat there for a few seconds, getting used to the darkness.

"Come this way, Mak, there's someone here," Zef boomed. "Boar!" he shouted. "Jump!" Wild Boar replied that he was dog tired and would be quite happy sitting up on top for a while.

"Suit yourself," said Zef. "But I think this is the Fortress. You'll regret it later."

The one-handed man replied in a feeble, indistinct voice; apparently he was feeling nauseous again, and he had no interest in any Fortress. Maxim opened his eyes and looked around. He was sitting on a heap of earth in the middle of a long corridor with rough concrete walls. The gap in the ceiling was either a ventilation duct or a shell hole. Zef was standing about twenty steps away and also looking around, shining his flashlight.

"What is this place?" asked Maxim.

"How would I know? Maybe some kind of hideaway. Or maybe it really is the Fortress. Do you know what the Fortress is?"

"No," said Maxim, and started clambering down off the heap of earth.

"You don't know . . ." Zef absentmindedly said. He was still looking around, running the beam of his flashlight over the walls. "Then what do you know? Massaraksh," he said. "Someone was here just now."

"A human being?" asked Maxim.

"I don't know," Zef replied. "He crept along the wall and disappeared . . . And the Fortress, my friend, is the kind of thing that could allow us to finish all our work in a single day . . . Aha, tracks . . ."

He squatted down. Maxim squatted beside him and saw a line of imprints in the dust along the bottom of the wall. "Strange tracks," he said.

"Yes, my friend," said Zef, looking around. "I've never seen any tracks like these before."

"As if someone walked by on his fists," said Maxim. He clenched one fist and made an imprint beside the tracks.

"Looks like it," Zef respectfully admitted. He shone the flashlight into the depths of the corridor. Something in there feebly glimmered, reflecting the light—either a bend or a dead end. "Should we go and take a look?" he asked.

"Quiet," said Maxim. "Don't talk and don't move."

The underground vault was damp and silent, but the corridor wasn't completely empty of life. Someone was there, up ahead—although Maxim couldn't make out exactly where or how far away—standing there, pressing himself against the wall, someone small, with a faint, unfamiliar smell, observing them and displeased by their presence. The creature was something entirely unfamiliar, and its intentions were unfathomable.

"Do we really have to go that way?" asked Maxim.

"I'd like to," said Zef.

"What for?"

"We ought to take a look—maybe it is the Fortress after all . . . If we found the Fortress, my friend, then everything would suddenly be different. I don't believe in the Fortress, but since they talk about it, who knows . . . Maybe not all of them are lying."

"There's someone there," said Maxim. "I can't figure out who."

"Yes? Hmm . . . If this is the Fortress, the legend has it that either the remains of the garrison live here . . . you know, they're still sitting in here, not knowing that the war is over—you know, at the very height of the war they declared themselves neutral, locked themselves in, and promised to blow up the entire continent if anyone came in after them . . ."

"And can they?"

"If this is the Fortress, they can do anything . . . *Yeeeah*, up on the surface there are explosions and shooting all the time. They could easily believe the war hasn't ended yet . . . Some prince or duke was in command here—it would be good if we could meet with him and have a talk."

Maxim intently listened. "No," he confidently said. "That isn't any prince or duke. It's some kind of animal or something . . . No, not an animal . . . Or . . ."

"What do you mean, 'or'?"

"You said, either the remains of the garrison, or . . ."

"Aah . . . That's just nonsense, old wives' tales . . . Let's go and take a look."

Zef loaded the grenade launcher, held it aimed roughly ahead, and moved forward, lighting his way with the flashlight. Maxim set off beside him. They trudged along the corridor for a few minutes, then came up against a wall and turned to the right.

"You're making a lot of noise," said Maxim. "Something's going on up there, and you're wheezing so loud . . ."

"What am I supposed to do, not breathe?" asked Zef, instantly getting his back up.

"And your flashlight is bothering me," said Maxim.

"What do you mean, it's bothering you? It's dark."

"I can see in the dark," said Maxim, "but with that flashlight of yours I can't make anything out . . . Let me go ahead, and you stay here. Or we'll never find out anything."

"*Weeell*, have it your way . . ." Zef said in an atypically hesitant tone of voice.

Maxim squeezed his eyes shut again, took a rest from the unreliable light, ducked down, and set off along the wall, trying not to make any noise at all. The unknown creature was somewhere close by, and Maxim was getting closer to it with every step. The corridor was endless. Doors appeared on the right, all made of iron and all locked. A faint draft was blowing toward him. The air was damp, filled with the odor of mold, together with that unfamiliar, living, warm scent. Zef moved after Mak with noisy caution; he was feeling uneasy and afraid of falling behind. Sensing that, Maxim laughed to himself, letting himself be distracted for literally only a second, and in that second the unknown being ahead of him disappeared.

Maxim halted, perplexed. The unknown creature had just been ahead of him, very close, and then it had seemed to dissolve into the air and appear behind his back, still very close, all in a single instant.

"Zef!" Maxim called.

"Yes!" his ginger-bearded companion responded in an echoing voice.

Maxim imagined the unknown creature standing between them, turning its head toward the voices by turns.

"He's in between us," said Maxim. "Don't even think of shooting."

"OK," Zef said after a pause. "I can't see a damn thing," he declared. "What does he look like?"

"I don't know," replied Maxim. "Something soft."

"An animal?"

"It doesn't seem like it," said Maxim.

"You said you could see in the dark."

"I don't see with my eyes," said Maxim. "Be quiet."

"Not with his eyes . . ." Zef growled, and fell silent.

The unknown creature stood there for a while, crossed the corridor, disappeared, and after a while appeared ahead of Maxim again. He's curious too, thought Maxim. He tried hard to rouse a sense of fellow feeling in himself for this creature, but something prevented him—probably the unpleasant combination of a non-animal intellect with a semi-animal appearance. He moved forward again. The unknown creature retreated, maintaining a constant distance.

"How are things?" asked Zef.

"Still the same," replied Maxim, "Maybe he's leading us somewhere, or luring us."

"Will we be able to deal with him?"

"He's not planning to attack," said Maxim. "He's feeling curious too."

He stopped talking, because the unknown creature had disappeared again, and Maxim immediately sensed that the corridor had come to an end. There was a large space around him. It was too dark here, though, and Maxim could see almost nothing, although he could sense the presence of metal and glass, there was a smell of rust, and there was high-voltage current somewhere in the space. Maxim stood there without moving for a few seconds and then, having determined where the switch was, reached his hand out to it, but then the unknown creature appeared again. And not alone. There was another one with him, similar but not exactly the same. They were standing by the same wall as Maxim, and he could hear their rapid, damp breathing. He froze, hoping that they would move closer, but they didn't approach, and then, constricting his pupils as hard as he could, he pressed the switch.

Obviously there was something wrong with the circuit—the lamps flashed on for only a split second, a circuit breaker blew somewhere with a sharp crack, and the light went out again, but Maxim had time to see that the unknown creatures were small, each about the size of a large dog, and they stood on all fours, were covered with dark fur, and had large, heavy heads. Maxim didn't get a chance to examine their eyes. The creatures immediately disappeared, as if they had never been there.

"How are things up there?" Zef asked in alarm. "What was that flash?"

"I turned the lights on," Maxim replied. "Come here."

"But where's that creature? Did you see him?"

"Only for an instant. They look like animals after all. Like dogs with big heads . . ."

Shimmers of light from the flashlight started flickering across the walls. Zef spoke as he walked. "Ah, dogs . . . I know dogs like that live in the forest. I've never seen them alive, though, but I've seen plenty that had been shot . . ."

"No," Maxim said with a doubtful air. "They aren't animals, all the same."

"Animals, they're animals," said Zef. His voice echoed hollowly under the high vault. "We needn't have gotten freaked out. I almost started thinking they were ghouls . . . Massaraksh! But this *is* the Fortress!"

He stopped in the middle of the space, running the beam of the flashlight over the walls, over the rows of dials, over the switchboards. Glass, nickel, and discolored plastic glinted. "Well, congratulations, Mak. We found it after all. I was wrong not to believe in it . . . And what's all this? Aha . . . It's an electronic brain, and it's all live, the power's on. Ah, damn it, if we could just get Blacksmith in here . . . Listen. Do you understand anything at all about this?"

"About what exactly?" asked Maxim, moving closer.

"About all these mechanisms . . . This is the control room. If we can figure it out—the entire region is ours for the taking! All that technology on the surface is controlled from here! Ah, if we could just figure it out, massaraksh!"

Maxim took the flashlight from him and set it down so that the light dispersed through the space, and looked around. Dust was lying everywhere, and it had been lying there for years: on the desk in the corner, on the spread-out sheets of decayed paper. There was a plate, stained with something black, with a fork beside it. Maxim walked along the consoles, touched the sliding gauges, and tried to switch on an electronic device—and was left holding the handle in his fingers.

"Hardly," he eventually said. "It's not very likely that anything special could be controlled from here. In the first place, everything here is too simple. Most likely this is either an observation station or one of the control substations—everything here has some kind of auxiliary function—and it's a weak machine, not big enough to control even ten tanks . . . And then, everything here has decayed, just touch anything and it falls apart. There's electric current, but the voltage is lower than it should be; the atomic boiler's probably completely decrepit. No, Zef, all this isn't as simple as it seems to you."

Suddenly he noticed two long, slim pipes protruding from the wall, connected by a rubber eye mask. Pulling up an aluminum chair, he sat down and stuck his face into the mask. To his surprise, the optics turned out to be in excellent condition, but he was even more surprised by what he saw. His field of view was filled by an entirely unfamiliar landscape: a whitish-yellow

desert, sand dunes, the skeleton of some kind of metal structure . . . A strong wind was blowing there, rivulets of sand were
running across the dunes, and the murky horizon was curved up
like a bowl.

"Take a look," he told Zef. "Where is that?"

Zef leaned his grenade launcher against a control console,
walked over, and looked. "Strange," he said after a moment's
pause. "That's the desert. And that, my friend, is about two hundred fifty miles away from us . . ." He moved back from the eye-
piece and looked up at Maxim. "All the work they put into all
this, the bastards . . . And what's the point of it? The wind sweeps
across the sands down there now, but what a land that used to be!
They used to take me to a resort there as a kid before the war . . ."

He got up. "Let's get the hell out of here," he said in a bitter
voice, and picked up the flashlight. "The two of us won't figure
out anything here. We'll have to wait until they grab Blacksmith
and put him away . . . Only they won't put him away, they'll
probably shoot him . . . Well, shall we go?"

"Yes," said Maxim. He was examining some strange tracks
on the floor. "This here interests me a lot more," he declared.

"Don't waste your time," said Zef. "All sorts of animals must
run around in here." He slung his grenade launcher behind his
shoulder and set off toward the exit from the hall. Maxim followed him, looking back at the tracks.

"I want some grub," said Zef.

As they walked along the corridor. Maxim suggested breaking in one of the doors, but Zef's opinion was that it would be
pointless. "This business has to be handled seriously," he said.
"What's the point of us wasting time here? We still haven't ful-
filled the norm, and we need to come here with someone who's
well informed . . ."

"If I were you," Maxim remarked, "I wouldn't hope for too
much from this Fortress of yours. In the first place, everything
here has rotted, and in the second place, it's already occupied."

"Who by? Ah, you mean the dogs again? You're just like the others, they harp on about ghouls, and you—"

Zef stopped. A guttural whooping sound hurtled along the corridor, reverberating off the walls in multiple echoes, and fell silent. And immediately, from somewhere far away, a voice exactly like it responded. These sounds were very familiar, but Maxim simply couldn't recall where he'd heard them.

"So that's who calls at night!" said Zef. "And we thought they were birds."

"A strange call," said Maxim.

"I don't know about strange," Zef objected. "But it's pretty scary all right. When they start yelling all the way across the forest at night, it sends your heart right down into your boots. They tell lots of stories about those calls. There was one jailbird, he used to boast about knowing that language of theirs. He used to translate it."

"And what did he translate?" asked Maxim.

"Ah, garbage. That's no kind of language . . ."

"And where is this jailbird?"

"He got eaten," said Zef. "He was one of the builders, his gang lost its way in the forest, the guys got hungry, and you know the way it goes . . ."

They turned left, and up ahead in the distance they saw a pale, hazy light-colored patch. Zef switched off the flashlight and put it away in his pocket. He was walking in front now, and when he abruptly halted, Maxim almost ran into him.

"Massaraksh," Zef muttered.

Lying across the floor of the corridor was a human skeleton.

Zef took the grenade launcher off his shoulder and looked around. "That wasn't here before," he muttered.

"No," said Maxim. "It's just been put there."

In the underground depths behind them an entire chorus of lingering, guttural howls suddenly burst out. The howls mingled with their own echo, making it seem like a thousand throats were all howling in chorus, as if they were chanting a strange word with four syllables. Maxim could sense scorn, defiance, and mockery. Then the chorus fell silent as abruptly as it had begun.

Zef noisily drew in his breath and lowered the grenade launcher. Maxim looked at the skeleton again. "I think this is a hint," he said.

"I think so too," Zef muttered. "Let's go quick."

They quickly reached the break in the ceiling, clambered onto the heap of earth, and saw Boar's alarmed face above them. He was lying with his chest on the edge of the break, dangling a rope with a loop on it.

"What happened down there?" he asked. "Was that you screaming?"

"We'll tell you in a minute," said Zef. "Have you anchored the rope?"

They clambered up. Zef rolled cigarettes for himself and the one-handed man, lit up, and said nothing for a while, apparently trying to piece together some kind of opinion about what had happened.

"OK," he said at last. "In brief, this is what happened. This is the Fortress. There are control panels in there, a brain and all the rest of it. It's all in a sorry state, but there is power, and we'll make good use of it, we just have to find people who know about these things . . . And then . . ." He dragged on his cigarette, opened his mouth wide, and released a cloud of smoke, exactly like a broken gas projector. "And then . . . It looks like dogs live there. Remember I told you about them? Those dogs with heads like a bear's. It was them screaming . . . but, if you think about it, maybe it wasn't them, because, you see . . . how can I put it? . . . while Mak and I were wandering about down there, somebody laid out a human skeleton in the corridor. And that's all."

The one-handed man looked at him, and then at Maxim. "Mutants?" he asked.

"Possibly," said Zef. "I didn't see anyone at all, but Mak says he saw dogs . . . only not with his eyes. How did you see them down there, Mak?"

"I saw them with my eyes as well," said Maxim. "And, by the way, I'd like to add that there was nobody else there apart from what you're calling dogs. I would have known. And these dogs of yours aren't what you think. They're not animals."

Wild Boar didn't say anything. He got to his feet, coiled up the rope, hung it on his belt, and sat down beside Zef again.

"Damned if I know," Zef muttered. "Maybe they aren't animals . . . Anything's possible here. In this South of ours . . ."

"Or maybe those dogs are mutants after all?" Maxim asked.

"No," said Zef. "Mutants are simply very ugly people. And the children of perfectly ordinary people. Mutants. Do you know what that means?"

"I do," said Maxim. "But the entire question is how far a mutation can go."

They all said nothing for a while, pondering. Then Zef said, "Well, if you're so well educated, there's no point in idle chatter. Let's move on!" He got to his feet. "We don't have much left to do, but time's pressing. And I want to gorge myself. . ."—he winked at Maxim—" . . . the desire's downright pathological. Do you know what 'pathological' means?"

Maxim said he did, and they set off.

There was still the southwestern quarter of the quadrant to clear, but they didn't try to clear anything. At some point in the past, something very powerful must have exploded here. All that remained of the old forest were half-rotten felled trunks and scorched stumps, looking as if they had been sheared off by a razor, and sparse young growth was already springing up on the site of the old forest. The soil was charred black and spiked with powdered rust. No kind of technology could have survived an attack like that, and Maxim realized that Zef had not brought them here to work.

A shaggy-looking man in a dirty convict's coverall clambered out of the undergrowth, coming toward them. Maxim recognized him: he was the first indigenous inhabitant that he had encountered, Zef's old partner, the vessel of universal despondency.

"Wait," said Wild Boar, "I'll have a word with him."

Zef told Maxim to sit down where he was standing, then sat down himself and started rewinding his foot-cloths, whistling into his beard a sentimental criminal's song: *"I'm a wild boy, known throughout the neighborhood."* Wild Boar walked over to the vessel of despondency and they moved away behind the bushes and started talking in a whisper. Maxim could hear them perfectly well, but he couldn't understand anything, because they were speaking some kind of argot, and the only word he could recognize was "mail," repeated several times.

Soon he stopped listening. He was feeling exhausted and dirty. Today there had been too much senseless work and senseless nervous stress, today he had breathed all sorts of garbage and been exposed to too many roentgens. And yet again in the course of the entire day nothing really genuine had been done, nothing truly necessary, and he really didn't want to go back to the bunkhouse.

Then the vessel of despondency disappeared and Wild Boar came back, sat down in front of Maxim, and said, "OK, let's talk."

"Is everything in order?" Zef asked.

"Yes," said Wild Boar.

"I told you," said Zef, examining his foot cloth against the light. "I've got a nose for his kind."

"Well now, Mak," said Wild Boar. "We've checked you out, as far as that's possible in our situation. General vouches for you. Starting from today, you'll be under my command."

"I'm very glad to hear it," Maxim said with a crooked smile. He felt like saying, *Only General hasn't vouched for you to me, has he?* but he only added, "I'm listening."

"General tells us that that you're not afraid of radiation and you're not afraid of the radiation towers. Is that true?"

"Yes."

"So you can swim across the Blue Serpent any time you like and it won't do you any harm?"

"I already told you I could escape from here right now."

"We don't want you to escape . . . And as far as I understand, you're not afraid of the patrol machines either?"

"You mean the mobile radiation devices? No, I'm not afraid of them."

"Very good," said Wild Boar. "Then your task for the immediate future is completely defined. You'll be a messenger. When I order you to, you'll swim across the river and send the telegrams I give you from the nearest post office. Is that clear?"

"That's clear," Maxim said slowly. "But there's something else that isn't clear . . ."

Wild Boar looked at him without blinking—a lean, sinewy, disfigured old man, a cool and merciless fighter, a warrior for forty years, maybe even a warrior since he was in diapers, a terrifying and exultant product of a world in which the value of human life is equal to zero, knowing nothing except fighting, rejecting everything except the fight—and in his keenly narrowed eyes Maxim read his own fate for the next few years as clearly as in a book.

"Yes?" asked Wild Boar.

"Let's agree straightaway," Maxim firmly said. "I don't want to act blindly. I don't intend to do work that, in my view, is absurd and unnecessary."

"For instance?" asked Wild Boar.

"I know what discipline is. And I know that without discipline all our work is completely worthless. But I believe that discipline must be rational, and a subordinate must be certain that an order is rational. You are ordering me to be a messenger. I'm willing to be a messenger. I'm good for more than that, but if it's necessary, I'll be a messenger. Only I have to know that the telegrams I send will not facilitate the senseless death of people who are wretched enough already—"

Zef jerked up his massive beard, but Wild Boar and Maxim stopped him with identical gestures.

"I was ordered to blow up a tower," Maxim continued. "Nobody explained to me why it was necessary. I could see it was a stupid, disastrous idea, but I carried out the order. I lost three comrades, and then it turned out that the whole thing was a trap, set by the state prosecutor's office. And I say: no more! I don't intend to attack the towers anymore. And what's more, I intend to impede operations of that kind in every way I can."

"Why, you fool!" said Zef. "You snot-nosed kid."

"Why?" asked Maxim.

"Wait, Zef," said Wild Boar, still keeping his eyes fixed on Maxim. "In other words, Mak, you want to know all of HQ's plans?"

"Yes," said Maxim. "I don't want to work blindly."

"Well, brother, you've got some nerve," Zef declared. "I don't even know the words to describe the kind of brass balls you've got! Listen, Boar, I like him. *Yeeeah*, I've got a keen eye all right . . ."

"You're demanding too much trust," Wild Boar said in a cold voice. "Trust like that has to be earned in rank-and-file work."

"And does rank-and-file work consist of knocking down those idiotic towers?" asked Maxim. "Of course, I've only been in the underground for a few months, but in all that time the only thing I've heard is towers, towers, towers . . . But I don't want to knock down towers—it's senseless! I want to fight against tyranny, against hunger, ruin, corruption, and lies . . . against the system of falsehood and not against the system of towers. Of course, I understand that the towers cause you torment, sheer physical torment . . . But even the action you take against the towers is pretty foolish. It's absolutely obvious that the towers are only relay stations, so you have to strike at the Center, and not pick them off one by one."

Wild Boar and Zef started speaking simultaneously. "How do you know about the Center?" asked Wild Boar.

"And where are you going to find this Center of yours?" asked Zef.

"The fact that a Center must exist is obvious to any even slightly competent engineer," Maxim said with a condescending

air. "And how we can find the Center is the task we should be
working on. Not running at machine guns, not pointlessly wasting peoples' lives, but searching for the Center."

"In the first place, we know all that without you," said Zef,
seething. "And in the second place, massaraksh, nobody has died
for nothing. It should be obvious to any even slightly competent
engineer, you snot-nosed twerp, that by bringing down a number of towers, we disrupt the relay system, and we can liberate
an entire region! For that, we have to be able to knock down
towers. And we're learning to do that, do you understand that
or not? And if you ever again, massaraksh, say that our guys are
dying in vain—"

"Wait," said Maxim. "Put your hands down. Liberate a region?
So OK, and then what?"

"Every snot-nose comes here and tells us we're dying in vain,"
said Zef.

"And then what?" Maxim insistently repeated. "The Guards
ship in mobile radiation devices and you're done for?"

"Damn it all!" said Zef. "In that time the population of the
region will come over to our side, and it won't be that easy for
them to stick their noses in. A dozen so-called degenerates is one
thing, but ten thousand enraged peasants is another—"

"Zef, Zef!" Wild Boar admonished him.

Zef gestured at him impatiently. "Ten thousand enraged peasants who have realized, and now will never forget, that they were
shamelessly duped for twenty years."

Wild Boar despairingly gestured and turned away.

"Wait, wait," said Maxim. "What are you saying? Why the
hell should they suddenly realize that? Why, they'll tear you to
pieces. They think the towers are for antiballistic defense . . ."

"And what do you think?" Zef asked, chuckling strangely.

"Well, I know," said Maxim. "They told me."

"Who did?"

"Doc . . . and General . . . Why, is it a secret?"

"Maybe that's enough on this subject?" Wild Boar said in a quiet voice.

"Why is that enough?" Zef objected in an equally quiet voice, and in a very cultured manner. "Why exactly is that enough, Boar? You know what I think about this. You know why I stay here and why I'll be here until my dying day. And I know what you think about this subject. So then why is that enough? We both believe that this should be shouted from all the rooftops. But when it comes to doing anything about it, we suddenly remember our underground discipline and go on meekly playing into the hands of all those leaderist types, liberals and enlighteners, all those failed Fathers . . . And now we have this boy right here in front of us. You can see what he's like. Why on earth aren't guys like him allowed to know?"

"Maybe it's precisely guys like him who shouldn't be allowed to know," Wild Boar replied, still in the same quiet voice.

Maxim shifted his gaze back and forth, from one of them to the other. He was puzzled; they had suddenly become almost unrecognizable. They had somehow wilted, and Maxim could no longer sense in Wild Boar the steely core on which so many prosecutor's offices and field courts had broken their teeth, and Zef's harum-scarum vulgarity had evaporated. A strange melancholy had broken through, a strange, previously concealed feeling of despair, resentment, and resignation—as if they had both remembered something they ought to have forgotten and had honestly tried to forget.

"I'm going to tell him," said Zef. He wasn't asking for permission or advice, he was simply stating his intention. Wild Boar said nothing, and Zef started telling Maxim the facts.

What he told Maxim was horrendous. It was horrendous in its own right, and it was horrendous because it left no more room for any doubts. All the time Zef was speaking—quietly, calmly, in correct, cultured language, and politely remaining silent when Wild Boar interpolated brief phrases—Maxim kept trying to identify some rent in the fabric of this new system of the world, but all his efforts were in vain. The picture that emerged was tidy, primitive, and hopelessly logical; it explained each of the facts known to Maxim, without leaving a single one unexplained. It was the greatest and the most terrible discovery of all the discoveries that Maxim had made on his inhabited island.

The radiation from the towers was not directed at the degenerates. It affected the nervous system of every human being on this planet. The physiological mechanism of this influence was not known, but the essential effect was that the brain of any individual exposed to the radiation lost its ability to critically analyze reality. A thinking individual was transformed into a believing individual—moreover, into an individual who believed frenziedly and fanatically, in defiance of the obvious reality in front of his very eyes. When an individual was in the field of radiation, the most elementary means could be used to instill absolutely any belief at all into him; he accepted whatever was instilled as the single, bright, and unique truth, and was willing to live for it, suffer for it, and die for it.

And the field was always there. Unnoticed, omnipresent, allpermeating. It constantly emanated from the gigantic network of towers that enmeshed the country. Like a gigantic vacuum cleaner, it sucked out of tens of millions of souls the very slightest doubt about what was proclaimed by the newspapers, pamphlets, radio, and television, about what was repeated over and over by teachers in schools and officers in barracks, about what glittered in neon signs across the streets and was pronounced from the pulpits of the churches. The Unknown Fathers directed the will and energy of the masses of millions in whatever direction they saw fit. They could and did compel the masses to adore them; they could and did incite unquenchable hatred for external and internal enemies; if they wished, they could direct millions to face artillery guns and machine guns, and the millions would go to die, exulting; they could make millions kill each other in the name of absolutely anything at all; if they conceived such a caprice, they could incite a mass epidemic of suicides . . . They could do anything.

And twice a day, at ten in the morning and ten in the evening, the gigantic vacuum cleaner was turned up to full power, and for half an hour people simply ceased to be people. All the hidden tensions that had accumulated in their subconscious as a result of the disparity between what had been instilled in them and what was real were released in an ecstatic paroxysm of obsequious servility and adulation. These radiation attacks totally suppressed all natural introspection and instinctive responses, replacing them with a monstrous complex of veneration and duty to the Unknown Fathers. In this condition a person exposed to the radiation completely lost the ability to think rationally and simply acted like a robot that had received a command.

Any danger for the Fathers could only come from those individuals who, owing to certain physiological peculiarities, were not susceptible to suggestion. They were called degenerates. The constant field of radiation had no effect on them at all, and the intense radiation attacks simply inflicted intolerable pain on them. There were relatively few degenerates, about 1 percent or so of the population, but they were the only people who were awake in this kingdom of sleepwalkers. Only they retained the ability to assess a situation soberly and to perceive the world as it was, to act on the world, to change it and control it.

And the most heinous thing of all was that they provided society with the ruling elite that were called the Unknown Fathers. All the Unknown Fathers were degenerates, but by no means were all degenerates Unknown Fathers. And those who had failed to join this elite, or did not wish to join this elite, or did not know that this elite existed—an elite of power-hungry degenerates, revolutionary degenerates, and philistine degenerates—were declared enemies of mankind and dealt with accordingly.

Maxim was overwhelmed by a despair as great as if he had suddenly discovered that his inhabited island was actually populated not by human beings but by puppets. There was nothing left for him to hope for. Zef's plan to seize control of a sizable region now seemed like plain adventurism to Maxim. He was faced with an immense machine, too simple to evolve and too immense for him to hope that he could destroy it with small forces. There was no force in the country capable of liberating an immense nation that had no idea it wasn't free, a nation that had fallen out of history, to use an expression of Wild Boar's. This machine was invulnerable from the inside. It was proof against any minor disturbances. If it was partially destroyed, it immediately restored itself. When it was irritated, it immediately and unambiguously reacted to the irritant, entirely disregarding the fate of its own individual elements.

The only remaining hope lay in the thought that the machine had a Center, a control panel, a brain. This Center could theoretically be destroyed, and then the machine would halt in a state of unstable equilibrium, and a moment would come when it would be possible to try switching this world onto a different set of tracks, setting it back on the rails of history. But the location of the Center was an absolute secret, and who would destroy it?

This was no simple attack on a tower. It was an operation that would require immense resources and, first and foremost, an army of people who were not affected by the radiation. It would require either people who were not susceptible to the radiation or some simple, readily obtainable means of protection from it. Neither of these things existed, and they could not even be expected to appear in the future. The hundreds of thousands of degenerates were fragmented, disunited, and persecuted. Many of them actually belonged to the category of so-called legals, but even if they could be united and armed, the Unknown Fathers would immediately annihilate this little army by sending mobile radiation units, set to maximum power, to confront them.

Zef had stopped talking long ago, but Maxim kept sitting there, dejectedly scrabbling at the black, dry earth with a twig. Then Zef coughed and awkwardly said, "Yes, my friend. That's the way things really are." He seemed to already regret having told Maxim the way things really were.

"What are you hoping for?" Maxim asked.

Neither Zef nor Wild Boar said anything.

Maxim raised his head, saw their faces and murmured, "I'm sorry . . . I . . . It's all so . . . I'm sorry."

"We have to fight," Wild Boar declared in a flat voice. "We are fighting, and we'll keep on fighting. Zef has told you one of HQ's strategies. There are others, equally vulnerable to criticism, that have never been tried in practice. You have to understand that everything we have right now is still in its formative stage. You can't develop a mature theory of struggle starting from scratch in just twenty-odd years."

"Tell me," Maxim said slowly, "this radiation . . . Does it affect all the races of your world in the same way?"

Wild Boar and Zef exchanged glances. "I don't understand," said Wild Boar.

"What I'm thinking of is this: Is there any nation here in which you could find at least several thousand individuals like me?"

"It's not likely," said Zef. "Except among those . . . those mutants. Massaraksh, don't be offended, Mak, but after all, you're obviously a mutant . . . An advantageous mutation, one chance in a million . . ."

"I'm not offended," said Maxim. "So, the mutants. That means down there, farther south?"

"Yes," said Wild Boar. He was gazing at Maxim intently.

"And what's actually down there, to the south?" Maxim asked.

"Forest, then desert," Wild Boar replied.

"And mutants?"

"Yes. Half animals. Insane savages . . . Listen, Mak, drop this idea."

"Have you ever seen them?"

"I've only seen dead ones," said Wild Boar. "They sometimes catch them in the forest, and then they hang them in front of the bunkhouses to improve morale."

"But what for?"

"What for?" Zef roared. "You fool! They're wild beasts! They're incurable, and more dangerous than any animals! I've seen some of them—you've never seen anything like it, even in your dreams."

"Then why are they running towers down there?" asked Maxim. "Do they want to tame them?"

"Drop it, Mak," Wild Boar said again. "It's hopeless. They hate us . . . But then, do what you think is best. We don't hold anybody here."

There was silence for a while. And then behind them, in the distance, they heard a familiar growling sound.

Zef half rose. "A tank," he mused. "Should we go and kill it? It's not far away, quadrant eighteen . . . No, tomorrow."

Maxim made a sudden decision. "I'll deal with it. You go, I'll catch up with you."

Zef gave him a doubtful look. "Will you manage OK?" he asked. "You could blow yourself up."

"Mak," said the one-handed man. "Think!"

Zef was still looking at Maxim, then suddenly he bared his teeth in a grin. "Ah, that's what you want the tank for!" he said. "You sly young dog. *Naaah*, you can't fool me. OK. Go. I'll keep your supper for you; if you change your mind, come back and gorge on it . . . Oh, and bear in mind that lots of the self-propelled vehicles are booby-trapped, so be careful how you rummage around in there . . . Let's go, Boar. He'll catch up with us."

Wild Boar was about to say something, but Maxim had already gotten up and started striding toward the road through the forest. He didn't want any more talk. He walked quickly, without looking back, holding his grenade launcher under his arm. Now that he had made his decision, he felt relieved, and what had to be done now depended only on his own know-how and his own dexterity.

14

Early in the morning Maxim drove the tank out onto the highway and pointed its nose toward the south. He could go now, but he clambered out of the control bay, jumped down onto the smashed concrete, and sat on the edge of the roadside ditch, wiping his dirty hands with grass. The rusty hulk calmly gurgled beside him, with the pointed top of its rocket aimed up at the sky.

He had worked all night but didn't feel tired at all. The indigenous population here built things soundly, and the machine was in pretty good condition. No booby traps had been discovered, of course, but on the other hand, there *was* a manual control system. If anybody really had blown himself up in a machine like this, it could only have happened because the boiler was absolutely worn out or because he was a total technical ignoramus. True, the boiler was generating no more than 20 percent of normal power, and the undercarriage was thoroughly battered, but Maxim was content—yesterday he hadn't hoped for even this much.

It was about six o'clock in the morning and already quite bright. Usually at this time the educatees were drawn up into check-cloth columns, hastily fed, and driven out to work. Maxim's absence had already been noticed, of course, and it was quite possible that now he was listed as a fugitive and had been condemned to death. Or maybe Zef had thought up some kind of explanation—that he'd sprained his foot, been wounded, or something of that sort.

The forest had turned quiet. The "dogs," who had called to each other all night, had calmed down, and probably retreated underground, where they were giggling and rubbing their paws together as they recalled how they had frightened those bipeds yesterday . . . He ought to give some serious attention to these "dogs" later on, but right now he would have to leave them behind. He wondered if they were sensitive to the radiation or not.

Such strange creatures . . . At night, while he was rummaging in the motor, two of them had loitered nearby behind the bushes all the time, slyly observing him, and then a third had come and climbed up a tree in order to get a better view. Maxim had stuck his head out of the hatch and waved to him and then, simply for the sake of mischief, reproduced as well as he could the four-syllable word that the choir had chanted the day before. The one up on the tree became absolutely furious: his eyes vehemently glinted, the fur all over his body stood up on end, and he started shouting some kind of guttural insults. The two in the bushes were obviously shocked by this, because they immediately left and didn't come back. But the abusive one stayed up in the tree for a long time, quite unable to calm down—he hissed and spat, and pretended that he was going to attack, baring his widely spaced white fangs. He only cleared off when it was almost morning, having realized that Maxim had no intention of taking him on in a fair fight . . .

It was unlikely that these creatures were rational in the human sense, but they were fascinating, and they probably represented some kind of organized force, if they had dislodged the military garrison commanded by the prince or duke from the Fortress . . . There was so little information available here, nothing but rumors and legends . . .

It would have been good to wash up now. He was smeared all over with rust, and the boiler was leaking too; his skin was stinging from the radiation. If Zef and his one-handed comrade agreed to go along, he would have to block off the boiler with three or four slabs of metal, tear some of the armor off the flanks . . .

Far away in the forest there was a loud thud, followed by a resounding echo—the suicide-squad sappers had started their working day. Senseless, so senseless . . . There was another loud thud, and a machine gun started chattering, carrying on for a long time, before eventually falling silent. The day turned completely light, and it was bright, with a cloudless sky, as even and white as glowing milk. The concrete on the highway glittered with dew, but there was no dew around the tank—the armor radiated a noxious warmth.

Zef and Wild Boar appeared out of the bushes that had crept out onto the road, saw the tank, and started walking faster. Maxim got up and went toward them.

"You're alive!" Zef said instead of greeting him. "Just as I expected. Your gruel . . . I . . . you know, brother, there was nothing to carry it in. But I brought your bread, here, scoff it down."

"Thanks," said Maxim, taking the crusty end of a loaf.

Wild Boar stood there, leaning on his mine detector and looking at Maxim.

"Eat up and get out of here," said Zef. "They've come to collect you, brother. I reckon they want you for further investigation."

"Who?" Maxim asked, and stopped chewing.

"He didn't report to us," said Zef. "Some flunky or other covered in medals from head to toe. He bawled out the entire camp, demanding to know why you weren't there, and almost shot me . . . but I, you know, just gaped at him and reported that you'd died the death of the brave in a minefield." He walked around the tank, said "Filthy heap of garbage," sat down on the shoulder of the road, and started rolling a cigarette.

"Strange," said Maxim, pensively taking a bite of the bread. "For further investigation? What for?"

"Maybe it's Fank?" Wild Boar asked in a low voice.

"Fank? Average height, square face, peeling skin?"

"Nothing of the kind," said Zef. "A lanky great beanpole, covered in pimples, as dim-witted as they come. A guardsman."

"That's not Fank," said Maxim.

"Maybe it's on Fank's orders?" Wild Boar suggested.

Maxim shrugged and dispatched the final piece of crust into his mouth. "I don't know," he said. "I used to think that Fank had something to do with the underground, but now I just don't know what to think . . ."

"Then you'd definitely better leave," said Wild Boar. "Although, to be quite honest, I don't know what's worse—that Guards officer or the mutants . . ."

"Come on, now, let him go," said Zef. "He's not going to work as a courier for you in any case, and this way at least he might bring back some kind of information about the South . . . if they don't skin him alive down there."

"You won't go with me, of course," Maxim said in an affirmative tone of voice.

Wild Boar shook his head. "No," he said. "I wish you luck."

"Dump the rocket," Zef advised him. "Or you'll get blown up along with it . . . And remember this: There'll be two checkpoints ahead. You'll easily skip through them, only don't stop. They face south. And after that the farther you go, the worse it gets. Appalling radiation, nothing to eat, mutants, and even farther on—nothing but sand and drought."

"Thanks," said Maxim. "Good-bye." He jumped up onto a caterpillar track, swung open the hatch, and clambered into the hot semi-darkness. He had already set his hands on the levers when he remembered that he had one more question to ask.

He stuck his head out. "Listen," he said, "why is the true purpose of the towers hidden from the rank-and-file members of the underground?"

Zef grimaced and spat, and Wild Boar sadly replied, "Because most of the guys at HQ are hoping someday to seize power and use the towers in the same old way, but for different goals."

"What different goals?" Maxim morosely asked.

For a few seconds they gazed into each other's eyes. Zef turned away and started intently gluing together his roll-up with his tongue. Then Maxim said, "I hope you both survive," and turned back to the levers. The tank started rumbling and clanging, its caterpillar tracks crunched, and it trundled forward.

Driving the machine was awkward. There was no seat for the driver, and the heap of branches and grass that Maxim had flung together during the night rapidly crept apart. The visibility was appallingly bad, and he wasn't able to build up any serious speed—at twenty miles an hour something in the motor started clattering and spluttering, giving out a vile smell. But this atomic bier still coped excellently with any kind of terrain. Road or no road—that didn't matter, it simply didn't notice the bushes in the shallow ruts, and it crushed fallen trees to splinters. It easily rode right over the young trees that had sprouted through the cracked concrete, and even seemed to snort in enjoyment as it crept through the deep pits filled with stagnant water. And it maintained direction excellently—turning it was extremely hard.

The highway was fairly straight, and the control bay was dirty and stifling, so eventually Maxim set the manual controls, climbed out, and comfortably settled himself on the edge of the hatch under the latticework of the rocket launching tube. The tank kept on barging forward, as if this was its genuine course, set by its old program. There was something simple-spirited and self-satisfied about it, and Maxim, who loved machines, even slapped his hand on its armor plating to express his approval.

Life was OK. The forest crept past, back, and away on the left and the right, the engine smoothly gurgled, up here on top he could hardly even feel the radiation, the breeze was relatively clean, and it soothed his stinging skin with its pleasant coolness. Maxim raised his head and glanced at the swaying nose of the rocket. He probably really ought to dump it. Unnecessary weight. It wouldn't actually explode, of course. It had been defunct for a long time—he had inspected it during the night. But it weighed a good ten tons, so why lug something like that around? The tank kept creeping forward, and Maxim started climbing over the launch tube, looking for the attachment mechanism. He found the mechanism, but everything had rusted, so Maxim had to fiddle with it, and twice while he was fiddling the tank ran off the road into the forest at a bend and started smashing down trees, wrathfully howling, so that Maxim had to hurry back to the levers, calm the iron fool down, and lead it back out onto the highway. But eventually the mechanism worked: the rocket cumbersomely keeled over, crashed down onto the concrete, and then laboriously rolled off into the ditch. The tank gave a little skip and started moving more lightly, and then Maxim saw the first checkpoint ahead.

Two large tents and a small enclosed truck were standing at the edge of the forest, and smoke was rising from a kitchen truck. Two guardsmen, naked to the waist, were getting washed—one was rinsing off the other with a mess tin. A sentry in a black cape was standing in the middle of the highway looking at the tank, and to the right of the highway two posts jutted up, connected by a crossbeam, with something long and white dangling from it, almost touching the ground. Maxim sank down into the hatch so that his check coverall wouldn't be seen, and then put his head out. Gazing at the tank in amazement, the sentry moved over to the shoulder of the road, and then looked around in confusion at the truck. The seminaked guardsmen stopped washing themselves and also looked at the tank.

The rumbling of the caterpillar tracks drew several more men out of the tents and the truck, one of them in a uniform with an officer's braids. They were very surprised but not alarmed—the officer pointed at the tank and said something, and they all laughed. When Maxim drew level with the sentry, the sentry shouted something that was inaudible above the noise of the motor, and Maxim shouted in reply, "Everything's in order, just stay where you are." The sentry couldn't hear anything either, but a reassured expression appeared on his face. After letting the tank pass by, he walked back out into the middle of the highway and resumed his former pose. Everything had obviously gone just fine.

Maxim turned his head and got a close-up view of what was hanging from the crossbeam. He looked for a second, then quickly squatted down, squeezed his eyes shut, and grabbed hold of the levers, although there was no need for that. I shouldn't have looked, he thought. It was damned stupid to turn my head— I should just have kept going and I would never have known . . . He forced himself to open his eyes. No, he thought. I have to look. I have to get used to it. And I have to find out. It's pointless to turn away. I have no right to turn away once I've taken on this job. It was probably a mutant—death couldn't mutilate a human being like that. But what mutilates people is life. It will mutilate me too, there's no way to escape that. And I shouldn't try to resist; I have to get used to it. Maybe there are hundreds of miles of roads lined with gallows trees ahead of me . . .

When he stuck his head out of the hatch again and looked back, he could no longer see the checkpoint—there was no more checkpoint, and no solitary gallows beside the road. How good it would be now to go home . . . just set off and keep going, and there at the end of it would be his home, his mother, his father, the guys . . . arrive, wake up, wash up, and tell them his terrible dream about an inhabited island . . .

He tried to picture Earth, but he couldn't manage it. It just felt strange to think that somewhere there were clean, cheerful cities with lots of kind, intelligent people, where everybody trusted each other and there was no iron, no bad smells, no radiation, no black uniforms, no coarse, brutish faces, no terrible legends mingled with an even more terrible truth. And suddenly for the first time he thought that the same thing could have happened on Earth, and at this stage it would be just like everything around him now—ignorant, deceived, servile, and devoted. You were looking for work, he thought. Well, now look, you have a job to do—a difficult job, a dirty job, but you're not likely ever to find another one anywhere as important as this . . .

Up ahead on the highway some kind of mechanism appeared, slowly creeping along in the same direction as him—southward. It was a small tractor with caterpillar tracks, dragging along a trailer with a latticework metal beam. A man in a check coverall was sitting in the open cabin smoking a pipe; he indifferently looked at the tank, looked at Maxim, and turned away. What kind of beam is that? Maxim thought. Those contours look familiar . . . Then suddenly he realized that it was a section of a tower. I could just shove it into the ditch, he thought, and drive backward and forward over it a couple of times . . . Maxim looked around, and the tractor driver apparently didn't like the expression on his face at all; he suddenly braked and lowered one leg onto a caterpillar track, as if he was getting ready to jump. Maxim turned away.

About ten minutes later he saw the second checkpoint. It was an advance outpost with an immense army of slaves in check coveralls—or maybe they weren't slaves at all but the freest men in the country—two small temporary buildings with glittering zinc roofs, and a low artificial hill with a squat blockhouse, complete with the black slits of gun embrasures, standing on it. The first sections of a tower were already rising up above the blockhouse; motorized cranes and tractors stood around the hill, and iron beams lay scattered about. The forest had been obliterated for several hundred yards on the right and left of the highway, and men in check coveralls were puttering around here and there in the open space. Behind the two small buildings Maxim could see a long, low bunkhouse, the same as the one in the camp. In front of the bunkhouse gray rags were drying on lines. A little farther on there was a wooden pylon with a platform beside the highway; a sentry in an army uniform and deep helmet was striding around on the platform, which had a machine gun on a tripod set up on it. More soldiers were jostling about under the tower; they had the air of men exhausted by mosquitoes and boredom. All of them were smoking.

Well, I'll pass through here without any trouble too, thought Maxim. This is the edge of the world, and nobody gives a damn about anything. But he was mistaken. The soldiers stopped waving away the mosquitoes and stared at the tank. Then one of them, a skinny guy who looked very much like someone or other he knew, adjusted the helmet on his head, walked out into the middle of the highway, and raised his hand. You shouldn't have done that, Maxim regretfully thought. That won't be good for you. I've decided to drive through here, and I'm going to drive through . . . He slid down to the levers, settled himself comfortably, and put his foot on the accelerator. The soldier on the highway kept standing there with his hand raised. Now I'll step on the gas, Maxim thought, roar like blazes, and he'll jump out of the way . . . And if he doesn't jump, Maxim thought with abrupt cruelty, well—this is war, after all . . .

Then suddenly he recognized this solder. Standing there in front of him was Gai—thinner and pinched-looking, with his cheeks covered in stubble, wearing a baggy soldier's coverall. "Gai," Maxim murmured. "My old friend . . . Now how can I . . ." He took his foot off the accelerator and disengaged the clutch, and the tank slowed to a halt. Gai lowered his hand and unhurriedly walked toward it. At that point Maxim actually laughed with joy. Everything was turning out very well. He engaged the clutch again and readied himself.

"Hey!" Gai imperiously shouted, hammering on the armor plating with his rifle butt. "Who are you?"

Maxim said nothing, quietly laughing to himself.

"Is anyone in there?" A note of uncertainty had appeared in Gai's voice.

Then his metal-tipped boots clattered on the armor plating, the hatch on the left swung open, and Gai stuck his head into the cabin. When he saw Maxim, his mouth dropped open, and at that precise second Maxim grabbed hold of his coverall, jerked him toward himself, dumped him on the branches under his feet, and held him down . . . The tank roared, then gave an appalling howl and jerked forward. I'll shatter the engine, thought Maxim.

Gai jerked and started squirming around, and his helmet slipped down over his face so that he couldn't see anything—he could only blindly kick up his heels as he tried to tug his automatic out from under himself. The control bay was suddenly filled with thunderous clanging—evidently the tank's rear had been struck by fire from automatic rifles and a machine gun. It wasn't dangerous, and Maxim watched impatiently as the wall of the forest advanced, coming closer and closer . . . closer . . . and there were the first bushes . . . a check-clad figure frantically darted off the road . . . and then there was forest on all sides, and there were no more bullets clattering on the armor, and the highway ahead was open for many hundreds and hundreds of miles.

Gai finally managed to drag his automatic out from under himself, but Maxim tore off his helmet, saw his sweaty, scowling face, and laughed when the expression of fury, terror, and thirst to kill was replaced first by confusion, then amazement, and finally joy. Gai moved his lips—evidently he had exclaimed, "Massaraksh!" Maxim let go of the levers, grabbed his wet, emaciated, stubbly-faced friend, and embraced him, squeezing him close in all the fullness of his feelings, then released his grip and, holding Gai by the shoulders, said, "Gai, my great friend, I'm so glad!" Absolutely nothing at all could be heard. He glanced through the observation slit: the highway was still as straight as ever, and he set the manual controls again, clambered up on top, and dragged Gai out after him.

"Massaraksh!" said the creased and crumpled Gai. "It's you again!"

"But aren't you glad? I'm so terribly glad!" Maxim had only just realized that he had never wanted to travel to the South on his own.

"What does all of this mean?" Gai shouted. His first joy had already passed, and he was looking around in alarm.

"We're going to the South!" shouted Maxim. "I've had enough of this hospitable fatherland of yours!"

"You've escaped?"

"Yes!"

"Have you lost your mind? They gave you your life."

"What does that mean, they gave it to me? This life is mine! It belongs to me!"

It was hard to talk to each other—they had to shout—and quite unintentionally, instead of a friendly conversation, it turned into a quarrel. Maxim jumped down into the hatch and throttled back the engine. The tank started moving more slowly, but it stopped roaring and clanging so loudly.

When Maxim climbed back out, Gai was sitting there hunched over, in a determined mood. "It's my duty to take you back," he declared.

"And it's my duty to drag you out of that place," Maxim declared.

"I don't understand. You've gone completely insane. It's impossible to escape from here. You have to go back . . . Massaraksh, you can't go back either, or they'll shoot you . . . And in the South they'll eat you . . . Damn you and your insanity! Getting involved with you is like picking up a counterfeit coin—"

"Wait, stop yelling," said Maxim. "Let me explain everything to you."

"I don't want to hear it. Stop this thing!"

"Just hang on," said Maxim. "Let me tell you everything!"

But Gai didn't want to be told anything. He insisted that this illegally purloined vehicle must immediately be halted and returned to the prison zone. Maxim was called a blockhead twice, three times, and four times. The howl of "massaraksh" drowned out the noise of the motor. The situation, massaraksh, was appalling. It was hopeless, massaraksh! Up ahead, massaraksh, lay certain death. And, massaraksh, it lay behind too. Maxim had always been a blockhead and a crazy freak, massaraksh, but this stunt would probably, massaraksh, be the last he would ever pull . . .

Maxim didn't interfere. He had suddenly realized that the radiation field of the final tower obviously ended somewhere around here. Or, more probably, it had already ended—the final checkpoint had to be right on the boundary of the final tower's range . . . Let Gai have his say; on the inhabited island words don't mean anything . . . Swear away, carry on swearing as long as you like, but I'll get you out—this isn't where you belong . . . I have to start with someone, and you'll be the first. I don't want you to be a puppet, not even if you like being a puppet.

After abusing Maxim up, down, and sideways, Gai slipped in through the hatch and started fiddling around down there, trying to halt the tank. He couldn't do it, and he clambered back out, wearing his helmet now, very taciturn and intent. He was clearly intending to jump off and walk back. He was very angry. Then Maxim caught him by his pant leg, sat him down beside him, and started explaining the situation.

Maxim spoke for more than an hour, occasionally breaking off to adjust the movement of the tank at bends. He talked, and Gai listened. At first Gai tried to interrupt, attempted to jump off as they moved along, and plugged his ears with his fingers, but Maxim just carried on and on talking, repeating the same thing over and over again, explaining, hammering it home, trying to change Gai's mind. And Gai finally started listening, then he started thinking, started pining, stuck both hands in under his helmet, rapidly scratched his thick thatch of hair, and then suddenly moved on to the attack. He started interrogating Maxim about where he had found out all of this, and who could prove that it wasn't all a load of lies, and how anyone could believe all of this when it was an obvious fabrication . . . Maxim hit him with facts, and when the facts weren't enough, he swore that he was telling the truth, and when that didn't do any good, he called Gai a dunderhead and a puppet and a robot, and the tank kept on moving farther and farther south, burrowing its way deeper and deeper into the land of the mutants.

"Well, all right," Maxim eventually said in a fury. "Now, let's check all of this. According to my calculations, we left the radiation field behind a long time ago, and now it's about ten minutes to ten. What do you all do at ten o'clock?"

"Ten hundred hours is formation time," Gai morosely said.

"Exactly. You form up in neat ranks and start howling appalling, idiotic hymns and bursting a gut in your enthusiasm. Remember?"

"The enthusiasm is in our blood," Gai declared.

"They hammer the enthusiasm into your thick heads," Maxim retorted. "But OK, now we'll see just what kind of enthusiasm you've got in your blood. What time is it?"

"Seven minutes to ten," Gai morosely replied.

They traveled on in silence for a while.

"Well?" asked Maxim.

Gai looked at his watch and started singing in an uncertain voice, *"The Battle Guards advance with fearsome cries . . ."* Maxim mockingly watched him. Gai lost the thread and got the words confused.

"Stop gawking at me," he angrily said. "You're throwing me off. And anyway, what kind of enthusiasm can there be out of formation?"

"Give it up, give it up," said Maxim. "You used to yell just as loud out of formation. It was frightening to watch you and Uncle Kaan. One yelling 'The Battle Guards,' and the other droning 'Glory to the Fathers.' And then there was Rada . . . Well then, where's your enthusiasm? Where's your love for the Fathers?"

"Don't you dare," said Gai. "Don't you dare talk that way about the Fathers. Even if your story is true, it simply means that the Fathers have been deceived."

"So who deceived them?"

"*Weeell* . . . It could be anyone . . ."

"So the Fathers aren't all-powerful, then? So they don't know everything?"

"I don't want to discuss this subject," Gai declared.

He turned morose and gloomy, and hunched over; his face turned even more pinched-looking, his eyes dimmed, and his lower lip started drooping. Maxim suddenly remembered Fishta the Onion and Handsome Ketri from the convicts' car. They were drug addicts, individuals habituated to the use of especially strong narcotic substances. They suffered terrible torment without their fix—they didn't eat or drink and spent days on end sitting like that, with dead eyes and drooping lower lips. "Do you have a pain somewhere?" he asked Gai.

"No," Gai drearily replied.

"Then why are you all huddled up like that?"

"I don't know, it's just . . ." Gai tugged on his collar and feebly turned his neck. "I'll lie down for a while, OK?"

Without waiting for Maxim to answer, he climbed in through the hatch and lay down on the twigs, pulling up his legs. So that's how it is, thought Maxim. It's not as simple as I thought. He felt worried. Gai didn't get his blast of radiation, we left the field almost two hours ago . . . He's lived in that field all his life . . . So maybe it's harmful for him to be without it? What if he falls ill? Of all the lousy things . . .

Looking in through the hatch at Gai's pale face, he felt more and more frightened. Eventually he couldn't stand it any longer, and he jumped down into the control bay, switched off the engine, dragged Gai out, and laid him on the grass beside the highway.

Gai slept, muttering something in his sleep and intensely shivering. Then he started shuddering as if he had a fever, hunching up and huddling tight, thrusting his hands in under his armpits as if he was trying to get warm. Maxim put Gai's head on his knees, squeezed Gai's temples with his fingers, and tried to concentrate. It had been a long time since he had given anyone a psychomassage, but he knew that the most important thing was to empty your mind of everything else and try to focus on including the sick person in your own healthy system. He sat there like that for ten or fifteen minutes, and when he surfaced, he saw that Gai was better: his face had turned pink, his breathing was regular, and he wasn't feeling cold any longer. Maxim made him a pillow of grass and sat there for a while, wafting away the mosquitoes, then remembered that they still had to travel on and on, and the reactor was leaking, which was dangerous for Gai, so he had to think of something. He got up and went back to the tank.

After some heavy fumbling and fiddling, he finally wrested several sheets of the side armor plating off their rusty rivets and packed these sheets against the ceramic partition separating the reactor and the motor from the control bay. He still had to attach the final sheet when he suddenly sensed that strangers had appeared nearby. When he cautiously stuck his head out of the hatch, all his insides turned cold and clenched up in a knot.

Standing on the highway, about ten paces in front of the tank, were three men, but he didn't immediately realize that they were men. Certainly, they were wearing clothes, and two of them were holding a pole on their shoulders, with a small hoofed animal that looked like a deer hanging from it and its bloodied head dangling down, and the third one had a bulky rifle of an unfamiliar type hanging across his pigeon chest from his neck. Mutants, thought Maxim. There they are—mutants . . .

All the stories and legends that he had heard suddenly welled up in his memory, seeming very believable. They skin people alive . . . cannibals . . . savages . . . animals. He clenched his teeth, jumped up onto the armor plating, and stood at his full height. Then the one with the rifle comically shifted his short little bowed legs but didn't move from the spot. He merely raised his terrifying hand with its two long, many-jointed fingers, gave a loud hiss, and then asked in a squeaky voice, "Hungry?"

Maxim parted his glued lips and said "Yes."

"You won't shoot?" the owner of the rifle inquired.

"No," said Maxim, smiling. "Absolutely not, no way."

15

Gai sat at the crude homemade table, cleaning his automatic rifle. It was about fifteen minutes after ten in the morning, the world was gray, colorless and dry, there was no place in it for joy, there was no place for the movement of life, and everything was lackluster and sickly. He didn't want to think, he didn't want to see or hear anything, he didn't even want to sleep—he wanted to simply lay his head down on the table, sink into despair, and die. Just die—that was all.

The room was small, with a single window that had no glass in it, looking out onto an immense grayish-brown wasteland cluttered with ruins and overgrown with wild bushes. The wallpaper in the room was faded, withered, and curled up at the edges— either from the heat or from age. The parquet flooring was dry and cracked, and in one corner it had been scorched into charcoal. Nothing from the former inhabitants remained in the room, apart from a large photograph lying under broken glass, in which, if you looked closely, it was possible to make out an old gentleman with idiotic sideburns, wearing a ludicrous hat that looked like a tin plate.

Gai wished his eyes had never seen any of this, he wished he could just die on the spot or howl like a desolate stray dog, but Maxim had told him, "Clean your gun!" "Every time," Maxim had said, tapping on the table with a finger of stone, "every time it starts getting to you, sit down and clean your rifle." So he had to clean it. It was Maxim, after all. If not for Maxim, he really would have lain down and died.

He had begged Maxim, "Don't leave right now, stay a while and treat me, help me with it." But no. Maxim had said that Gai must do it himself now. He'd said that it wasn't fatal, that it should pass, and it was bound to pass, but Gai had to brace himself, he had to cope . . . OK, Gai thought feebly, I'll manage. It's Maxim, after all. Not a man, not one of the Fathers, not a god, but Maxim . . .

And Maxim had also said, "Be angry! As soon as it starts tormenting you, remember where you got this from, who got you hooked like this and what for, and be angry, store up your hate. You'll need it soon—you're not the only one like this, there are forty million of you, duped and poisoned . . ." It was hard to believe, massaraksh, they'd spent all their life in formation, they'd always known what was what, who was their friend, who was their enemy, everything was simple, the path ahead was clear, they were all together, and it was good to be one of the millions, the same as everyone else. But no, he came along, made Gai love him, ruined Gai's career, and then literally tore him out of the ranks by the scruff of his neck and dragged him away into a different life with goals that were incomprehensible, and means for achieving them that were incomprehensible, and you had to think—massaraksh and massaraksh—about everything for yourself! Gai had never had any idea before of what that was like—thinking for yourself. There was an order, and everything was clear: think about the best way of carrying it out.

Yes . . . he dragged me out by the scruff of the neck, turned my face back toward my old nest, toward everything that was dearest of all to me, and showed me it was a garbage heap, a pile of shit, an abomination, lies . . . And when I looked, there really wasn't much that was beautiful about it; it made me feel sick to remember myself, to remember the guys, and as for Mr. Cornet Chachu! Gai angrily drove the breechblock into place and clicked the catch shut. And once again he was overwhelmed by weariness and apathy, and he didn't have any willpower left to load the magazine. He felt bad, oh so bad . . .

The warped, creaking door swung open, and an eager little face was thrust in—actually quite a pretty, likable face, if not for the bald cranium and the inflamed eyelids with no lashes. "Uncle

Mak said you should go to the square. Everybody's already gotten together, they're only waiting for you!"

Gai morosely squinted at her, at that spindly little body in a little dress of coarse sackcloth, at the abnormally thin little arms, like straws, covered with brown blotches, at the crooked little legs, swollen at the knees, and he felt nauseous, and he felt ashamed of his own revulsion—a child, and who was to blame? He looked away and said, "I'm not going. Tell him I don't feel well. I've fallen ill."

The door creaked, and when he looked up again, the little girl was gone. He flung his rifle onto the bed in annoyance, walked over to the window, and stuck his head out. The little girl was racing at ferocious speed along the hollow that used to be a street, raising dust between the remains of walls. A plump little toddler tagged along behind her, stumbled in pursuit for a few small steps, got hooked on something, flopped down onto the ground, raised his head, and lay there for while, then started roaring in a terrible, deep bass voice. The mother darted out from behind the ruins. Gai hastily staggered back, shook his head, and went back to the table. No, I can't get used to it. I'm obviously a despicable kind of person . . . Well, if I had the guy who's responsible for all of this in front of me, I wouldn't miss. But all the same, why can't I get used to it? Oh God, all the things I've seen in just this one month—enough for a hundred nightmares . . .

The mutants lived in small communities. Some of them roamed from place to place, hunting and searching for some-where a bit better, looking for roads to the north that skirted around the Guards' machine guns and the terrible areas where they went insane and died on the spot from attacks of horrendous headaches. Some of them lived a settled life on farms and in vil-lages that had survived after the battles and the detonation of three atomic bombs, one of which had exploded above this city, and two in the outskirts—there were miles-long bald patches of slag that gleamed like mirrors out there now. The settled farmers sowed small, degenerated strains of wheat, tended their strange vegetable patches in which the tomatoes were like berries and the berries were like tomatoes, and bred and raised hideous cattle that were frightening to look at, let alone to eat. They were a pitiful people: mutants, wild southern degenerates, about whom all sorts of crazy, fantastic stories were told and who talked all sorts of crazy, fantastic nonsense themselves—quiet, sickly, mutilated caricatures of people. The only normal ones here were the old folks, but very few of them were left; they were all sick and doomed to die soon. Their children and grandchildren also looked as if they weren't long for this world. They had a lot of children, but almost all of them died either at birth or in infancy. Those who did survive were weak and constantly plagued by unknown illnesses, and they were terribly ugly, but they all seemed obedient, quiet, and intelligent.

In fact, there was no doubt about it—these mutants had turned out to be decent people, kind and hospitable, peaceable . . . Only it was impossible to look at them. Even Maxim had been repulsed at first, until he got used to it, but he had gotten used to it quickly. It was easy for him—he was the master of his own nature . . .

Gai loaded the magazine into the rifle, propped his cheek on his palm, and started pondering. Yes, Maxim . . .

Of course, the venture Maxim was planning this time was clearly pointless. He had resolved to gather the mutants together, arm them, and drive the Guards back, at least beyond the Blue Serpent River just for a start. God, but it was funny. They could hardly walk, many of them died as they were simply walking along—one of them could die just from lifting a sack of grain—and Maxim wanted to go up against the Guards with them. Untrained, weak, timid—what good were they? Even if he gathered together those . . . those scouts of theirs, a single cornet would be enough to deal with their army if they didn't have Maxim. And even if Maxim was there, a cornet with a company would be enough.

I think Maxim himself understands that. But he spent an entire month rushing through the forest from village to village, from community to community, trying to persuade the old folks and respected people, the ones that the communities listen to. He ran around and dragged me around with him everywhere; it's impossible to calm him down. The old folks don't want to go, and they won't let the scouts go . . . And now I've got to go to this council meeting. I'm not going.

The world turned a bit brighter. It was no longer quite so sickening to look around, the blood started coursing through his veins a bit faster, and he felt a vague stirring of hope that today's meeting would fall through, that Maxim would come back and say, *That's enough, there's nothing more for us to do here*, and they would move on farther south, into the desert, where mutants were also said to live, but not such horrific ones, more like human beings, and not so sickly. It was even said that they had something like a state there, and even an army. Maybe it would be possible to reach some kind of realistic agreement with them . . . Of course, everything there was radioactive—the word was that bombs had been piled on top of each other there, especially to pollute the region . . . They even said there were special bombs to do it.

Remembering about the radioactivity, Gai reached into his duffel bag and took out a little box of yellow tablets. Popping two of them into his mouth, he winced and made a face at the intensely bitter taste. Damn it, what disgusting garbage, but I have to take them here—everything here's polluted too. And in the desert I'll probably have to suck them by the handful . . . But anyway, my thanks to the duke-prince; without these pills, I'd be a goner here. That duke-prince is a great guy, he doesn't get distressed or give in to despair in this hell, he treats people, he helps them, he makes his rounds, and he's organized an entire medication factory. And by the way, he said that the Land of the Fathers is only a small piece, merely the rump of our former great empire, and there used to be a different capital two hundred miles farther south—they say the ruins of it are still there, and they're magnificent too, so they say . . .

The door swung open and Maxim walked in, angry and naked, wearing nothing but his black shorts; he was lean and quick, and it was obvious that he was furious. When Gai saw him, he put on a sulky face and started looking out the window.

"Right, stop making things up," said Maxim. "Let's go."

"I don't want to," said Gai, "Damn them all. It turns my stomach. It's unbearable."

"Nonsense," Maxim retorted. "They're fine people, and they respect you a lot. Don't be such a little kid."

"Oh, sure, they respect me," said Gai.

"Yes they do, and how! The other day the duke-prince was asking if you could stay here. 'I'll die soon,' he said. 'I need a real man to take my place.'"

"Oh, sure, take his place . . ." Gai growled, but he could feel everything inside himself softening, even against his own will.

"And Boshku keeps pestering me too—he's afraid of approaching you directly. 'Let Gai stay here,' he says. 'He can teach people and protect them; he'll train up good kids . . .' Do you know the way Boshku talks?"

Gai blushed in pleasure, cleared his throat, and, still frowning and looking out the window, replied, "Oh, all right . . . Should I bring my rifle?

"Yes," said Maxim. "You can never tell."

Gai took his rifle under his arm and they walked out of the room—Gai leading, with Maxim close on his heels—then went down the crumbling staircase, stepped over a heap of little children messing around in the dust of the doorway, and set off along the street toward the square. Agh! *Street*, *square* . . . Nothing but words. The number of people who were killed here! They say there used to be a big, beautiful city here: theaters, a circus, museums, dog racing . . . and they say the churches here were especially beautiful—people used to come from all over the world to look at them—but now there's nothing but trash and no way of telling what used to be where. Instead of the circus there's a swamp with crocodiles in it, there used to be a subway system but now it's got ghouls in it, and it's dangerous to walk around in the city at night . . . They destroyed the country, the bastards.

And they didn't just kill people, they mutilated them too—and they bred all sorts of creatures of darkness here that were never here before. And not just here, either . . .

The duke-prince had told him that before the war animals that looked like dogs used to live in the forests. He had forgotten what they were called, but they were intelligent beasts, and very good-natured—they understood everything and they could be trained; they were a real joy. Well, so of course they started training them for military purposes: lying down under tanks with mines, dragging out the wounded, carrying dishes infected with plague over to the enemy, and all sorts of nonsense like that. And then a smart guy turned up who deciphered their language— it turned out that they did have a language, and quite a complex one. And in general they were very fond of imitating, and the way their larynx was formed meant that some of them could even be taught to speak a human language—not the entire language, of course, but they could remember about fifty or seventy words.

"Anyway, they were remarkable animals," the duke-prince had said. "We ought to have been friends with them, learned from each other, and helped each other—supposedly they were dying out. Ah, but no, they were used for fighting, trained to go to the enemy and collect military information. And then the war began and nobody had any more time for them, or for anything else either. And that's how we got the ghouls. They're mutants too, only not human but animal—very dangerous creatures." In the Special Southern District there was even an official order to wage an armed campaign against them, and the duke-prince had said quite bluntly, "We're all done for, and then there'll be nobody but ghouls living here . . ."

Gai recalled how one day in the forest Boshku and his hunters had brought down a deer that was being hunted by ghouls, and a fight had begun. But what kind of fighters are the mutants? They fired one shot each with their antiquated rifles, dropped their weapons, and sat down and put their hands over their eyes so they wouldn't see each other being torn apart, didn't they?

And, I must say, Maxim was at a loss too . . . Well, not exactly
at a loss, but somehow . . . he just didn't want to fight. So I had
to do the job for all of them. When my clip ran out, I used the
rifle butt. It was a good thing there weren't many ghouls, only
six of them. Two were killed, one got away, and three were
wounded and stunned—we tied them up and were going to take
them back to the village in the morning to be executed. But during the night I spotted Maxim stealthily getting up, and he went
over to them. He sat with them for a while, healing them the
way he knows how, by laying on his hands. Then he untied them
and, of course, not being stupid, they cut and ran, disappeared
in a flash. I said to him, "Why did you do that, Mak, what for?"
"I don't really know," he said. "I just feel we shouldn't execute
them. We shouldn't execute people," he said, "and we shouldn't
execute these either . . . They're not dogs," he said, "and they're
not any kind of ghouls . . ."

And it's not just the ghouls! The bats here are just incredible!
The kind that serve the Sorcerer . . . They're horror on wings,
not bats! And who is it that wanders through the villages at
night with an ax, stealing children? And he doesn't even come
into the house, but the children go out to him while they're
asleep, without waking up . . . Let's suppose all that's just lies,
but I've seen a few things for myself. I remember as if it were
yesterday the time the duke-prince took us to see the closest
entrance to the Fortress. We got there, and there was a peaceful, green little meadow, a little hill, and a cave in the hill. We
looked, and—Lord Almighty!—the entire meadow in front of the
entrance was piled high with dead ghouls, about twenty of them
at least, and they weren't mutilated or wounded—there wasn't a
single drop of blood on the grass. And then—the most amazing
thing of all—Maxim examined them and said, "They're not dead,
they're caught in some kind of seizure, as if someone hypnotized
them . . ." The question is, who?

Yes, these are uncanny places. A man can only go out in the
daytime here, and even then he has to be wary. If not for Maxim,

I'd have bolted out of here, shown the place a clean pair of heels. But if I'm really being honest, where would I run to? With this forest on all sides, and the forest's full of creatures of darkness, and the tank's sunk in a swamp . . . Run back to my own people? What could be more natural than to run back to your own kind? But they're not my own kind any longer, are they? If you think about it, they're monsters and puppets too, Maxim's right about that. What kind of people are they, if they can be controlled like machines? No, that's not for me. It's repulsive . . .

They walked out into the square, a large vacant lot with a black, half-melted monument to some long-forgotten public figure bizarrely jutting up at its center, and turned toward a small building that had survived, where the representatives usually gathered to swap rumors and consult about the sowing season or the hunting, or else simply to sit for a while, dozing and listening to the duke-prince's stories about the old times.

The men had already gathered in the small building, in a large, clean room. Gai didn't want to look at anybody here. Not even the duke-prince—supposedly not a mutant, just a man. Even he was mutilated: his entire face was covered in burns and scars. They walked in, greeted everyone, and sat down in the circle, right there on the floor. Boshku, sitting beside the stove, took his metal teapot off the coals and poured them each a cup of tea—strong and good, but without any sugar. Gai took his cup— an exceptionally beautiful, priceless piece of royal porcelain—and put it down in front of him, then set the butt of his automatic rifle on the floor between his feet, leaned his forehead against the ribbed barrel, and closed his eyes, in order not to see anyone.

The consultation was opened by the duke-prince. He was no prince, and no duke either, but he was a medical service colonel, the surgeon-in-chief of the Southern Fortress. When they started pounding the Fortress with atomic bombs, the garrison had mutinied and hung out a white flag (which their own side immediately pulverized with a thermonuclear bomb). The genuine prince and commander was torn to pieces by the soldiers, who got carried away and killed all the officers, and then suddenly realized that there was nobody to command, and they couldn't get by without a command structure: the war was still going on, the enemy was attacking, their side was attacking, and none of the soldiers knew the plan of the Fortress, so now it was a gigantic mouse-trap, and then the bacteriological bombs exploded—the entire arsenal of them—and plague broke out. Well, in short, half the garrison scattered every which way, three-quarters of the half who were left died, and the surgeon-in-chief accepted command of the remainder—the soldiers hadn't touched him during the mutiny—he was a doctor, after all. Somehow it became the custom to call him either "prince" or "duke," at first as a joke, and then everyone got used to it, and to avoid any confusion, Maxim called him the duke-prince.

"Friends!" said the duke-prince. "We have to discuss proposals from our friend Mak. These are very important proposals. Just how important they are, you can judge at least from the fact that the Sorcerer himself has come to join us and might perhaps talk to us . . ."

Gai raised his head. It was true: the Sorcerer himself was sitting in the corner, leaning back against the wall. It was terrifying to look at him, and impossible not to look. He was a remarkable personality. Even Maxim regarded him with respect, and he had told Gai, "The Sorcerer, brother, is an important figure." The Sorcerer was short, thickset, and neat, his arms and legs were short but strong, and in general he wasn't really very deformed, or at least the word *deformed* didn't suit him. He had an enormous cranium covered with coarse, dense hair that looked like silvery fur, and a small mouth with the lips folded in a strange manner, as if he were constantly preparing to whistle through his teeth, and in general his face was actually quite thin, but there were bags under his eyes, and the eyes themselves were long and narrow, with vertical pupils, like a snake's. He didn't talk much, only rarely appeared in public, and lived alone in a basement at the far end of the city, but he possessed enormous authority because of his amazing abilities.

First, he was very intelligent and he knew everything, although he was only about twenty years old and he had never been anywhere except this city. When questions of any kind came up, people went hat in hand to him for an answer. As a rule, he didn't give any answer, which signified that the question was trivial, and whichever way it was decided, everything would be fine. But if the question was vitally important—concerning the weather, or when to sow the crops—he always gave his advice, and he had never yet been mistaken. Only the elders went to see him, and they always kept quiet about what happened, but it was commonly believed that even when giving advice, the Sorcerer never opened his mouth. He just looked at you, and it became clear what had to be done.

Second, he had power over animals. He never asked the community for food or clothing; everything was brought to him by animals, various kinds of animals—forest beasts and insects and frogs—and his primary servants were huge bats. Rumor had it that he could talk to them, and they understood him and obeyed him.

Furthermore, people said that he knew the unknowable. It was impossible to understand what this unknowable was; in Gai's opinion, it was no more than a collection of empty words: the Black, Empty World before the birth of the World Light; the Black, Icy World after the extinction of the World Light; the Endless Void with many different World Lights . . . Nobody could explain what all of this meant, but Mak merely shook his head and murmured admiringly, "Now there's a real intellect!"

The Sorcerer sat there, not looking at anybody, with a half-blind night bird awkwardly shifting its feet on his shoulder. Every now and then the Sorcerer took little pieces of something out of his pocket and thrust them into its beak, and then it froze for a second, before throwing its head back and swallowing with an apparent effort, craning its neck.

"These are very important proposals," the duke-prince continued, "so I ask you to listen attentively. And you, Boshku, my old friend, brew the tea good and strong, because I can see that some of us are already dozing off. Don't doze off, you mustn't do that. Summon up your strength—maybe our fate is being decided at this very moment . . ."

The meeting started muttering in approval. A character with chalky-white irises was dragged away from the wall by the ears because he had arranged himself there for a doze, and was seated in the front row. "Why, I wasn't doing anything," the white-eyed character muttered. "It was only going to be, you know, just for a little bit. I mean, people shouldn't speak for so long, or else before they reach the end, I've already forgotten the beginning."

"All right," the duke-prince agreed. "Then we'll keep it short. The soldiers are driving us south, into the desert. They give no quarter and don't enter into negotiations. Of the families who have tried to get through to the north, nobody has returned. We must assume that they perished. This means that in ten or fifteen years they will finally squeeze us out into the desert, and we'll die there without any food and water. They say that people live in the desert too—I don't believe that, but many respected leaders do, and they claim that the inhabitants of the desert are every bit as cruel and bloodthirsty as the soldiers. But we are peace-loving people, we don't know how to fight. Many of us are dying, and we probably won't live to see the final outcome, but as of this moment we govern the people and we are obliged to think not just about ourselves but about our children . . . Boshku," he said, "please give our esteemed colleague Baker some tea. I think Baker has fallen asleep."

Baker was woken up and a hot cup was thrust into his blotchy hand. He burned his fingers and hissed, and the duke-prince continued: "Our friend Mak is proposing a way out. He came to us from the side of the soldiers. He hates the soldiers and says no mercy can be expected from them—they are all bamboozled by tyrants and burning with desire to exterminate us. At first Mak wanted to arm us and lead us into battle, but he realized that we are weak and we can't fight. So then he decided to make his way to the inhabitants of the desert—he believes in them too—reach an arrangement with them, and lead them against the soldiers. What is required from us? To give our blessing to this plan, allow the inhabitants of the desert to pass through our lands, and provide them with food while the war is going on. And our friend Mak also suggests that we should we give him permission to gather together all our scouts who wish to help, and he will teach them how to fight and lead them to the north to raise a rebellion there. So that, in brief, is how things stand. Now we have to decide, and I ask you to express your opinions."

Gai squinted sideways at Maxim. His friend Mak sat there with his legs drawn up under him, huge and brown, as motionless as a cliff—or not even a cliff but a gigantic battery, ready to discharge all its energy in a single moment. He was looking into the farthest corner, at the Sorcerer, but he immediately sensed Gai's glance and turned his head toward him. And then Gai suddenly thought that his friend Mak wasn't the same as he was before. He remembered that it had been ages now since Mak smiled his celebrated blinding-white, idiotic smile, it had been ages now since he sang his Highland songs, and his eyes had lost their former tenderness and genial humor—his eyes had become hard and glassy somehow, as if he wasn't even Maxim but Mr. Cornet Chachu. And Gai also remembered that it had been a long time now since Mak stopped dashing into all the corners like a jolly, curious dog; he had become reserved, and a kind of severity had appeared in him, a kind of single-minded purposefulness, an adult, practical focus, as if he was aiming himself at some target that only he could see. Mak had changed very, very much since the time when the full clip of a heavy army pistol had been emptied into him. He used to feel compassion for absolutely everybody, but now he didn't feel compassion for anybody. Well, maybe that was how it ought to be . . . But this was a terrible plan he had come up with. There would be slaughter, a huge massacre . . .

"There's something I don't understand here," piped up a bald freak, whose clothes suggested that he wasn't a local man. "What is it he wants? For the barbarians to come here? Why, they'll kill all of us. I know what the barbarians are like, don't I? They'll kill everyone—they won't leave a single man alive."

"They'll come here in peace," said Mak, "or they won't come at all."

"Then it's better if they don't come at all," the bald man said. "It's best to steer well clear of the barbarians. Better to go and face the soldiers' machine guns. At least that's still a bit like dying by your own hand. My father was a soldier."

"That's right, of course," Boshku mused. "But then, on the other hand, the barbarians could drive the soldiers away and leave us alone. Then things would be good."

"And why would they leave us alone all of a sudden?" the white-eyed man objected. "Since time out of mind no one's ever left us alone. Why would they start now, all of a sudden?"

"Well, he'll arrange things with them, won't he?" Boshku explained. *"Leave the forest folk alone*, he'll say, *and that's all, otherwise don't come*, he'll say . . ."

"Who will? Who'll arrange things with them?" asked Baker, swinging his head from side to side.

"Why, Mak will. Mak will arrange things."

"Ah, Mak . . . Well, if Mak arranges things with them, then maybe they really will leave us alone."

"Shall I give you some tea?" asked Boshku. "You're falling asleep, Baker."

"I don't want any of your tea."

"Come on, have some tea, just a cup, it's not like we're asking you to wash your neck, is it?"

The white-eyed man suddenly got up. "I'll be going," he said. "Nothing will come of this. They'll kill Mak, and they won't have any pity on us either. Why would they have any pity on us? We're all done for in ten years or so anyway. No children have been born in my community for two years now. Live in peace until we die, that's the long and the short of it. So you decide what you think is best. It's all the same to me."

He walked out, crooked and awkward, stumbling over the doorstep.

"Yes, Mak," said Leech, shaking his head. "Forgive us, but we don't trust anybody. How can we trust the barbarians? They live in the desert, they munch on sand and wash it down with sand. They're terrible people, all twisted together out of iron wire—they don't know how to cry or how to laugh. What are we to them? Moss under their feet. So they'll come, they'll beat the soldiers and settle here, and they'll burn down the forest, of course . . . What do they want with a forest? They love the desert. And we're done for again. No, I don't believe it. I don't believe it, Mak. Your idea's worthless."

"Yes," said Baker. "We don't need this, Mak. Let us die in peace, leave us alone. You hate the soldiers and you want to crush them, but what has that got to do with us? We don't feel hate for anybody. Feel compassion for us, Mak. Nobody has ever felt any compassion for us. Even you, although you're a good man—even you don't feel any compassion for us . . . You don't, do you, Mak, eh?"

Gai looked at Mak again and lowered his eyes in embarrassment. Maxim had blushed, blushed so hard that tears had sprung to his eyes. He hung his head and put his hands over his face. "It's not true," he said. "I do feel compassion for you. But not only for you. I—"

"Oh *nooo*, Mak," Baker insistently said. "Feel compassion *only* for us. We're the most unfortunate people in the whole world, after all, and you know it. Forget about your hate. Feel compassion, and that's all."

"But why should he feel any compassion?" piped up Filbert, smothered right up to his eyes in dirty bandages. "He's a soldier himself. When have soldiers ever had compassion for us? The soldier hasn't been born yet who would feel compassion for us."

"Dear friends, dear friends!" the duke-prince said in a stern voice. "Mak is our friend. He wishes us well—he wants to destroy our enemies."

"But the way it turns out is like this," said the bald freak who wasn't local, "even if we assume that the barbarians are stronger than the soldiers. They'll give the soldiers a drubbing, destroy their cursed towers, and occupy all of the North. Let them. We don't mind. Let them fight up there. But what good do we get out of it? That'll be the end of us; there'll be barbarians in the south, and barbarians in the north too, and more of the same barbarians on top of us. They don't need us, and since they don't need us, they'll just exterminate us. That's one thing.

"Now let's suppose that the soldiers fight the barbarians off. If they fight the barbarians off, the war will roll right over us to the south. And what then? We're finished that way too; soldiers in the north, soldiers in the south, and soldiers on top of us too. Well, and we know soldiers . . ."

The meeting started droning and buzzing, saying that was right, the bald freak had laid things out precisely and correctly, but the bald man wasn't finished yet.

"Let me finish!" he indignantly exclaimed. "Why have you started kicking up such a racket, really and truly? It could also happen that the barbarians kill all the soldiers, and the soldiers kill all the barbarians. That seems just right—we can carry on living. Ah, but no, that won't work either. Because there are still the ghouls. While the soldiers are alive, the ghouls hide, they're afraid of a bullet, the soldiers have been ordered to shoot ghouls. But when there are no more soldiers, that's total ruination for us. The ghouls will gobble us up, bones and all."

The meeting was extremely impressed by this idea. "He speaks true!" voices cried out. "Well, I never, what smart heads they have in the swamps . . ." "Yes, brothers, we forgot all about the ghouls . . . but they're wakeful all right, biding their time . . ." "We don't need anything, Mak, let things go on like they are . . ." "We've scraped by for twenty years, we'll hang on for another twenty, and then maybe another . . ."

"And we mustn't let our scouts go!" said the bald freak, raising his voice. "It makes no difference what they want . . . What's it to them? They don't live at home. Six Toes spends days and nights on the other side, shameful to say, robbing and drinking vodka. It's all right for them, they're not afraid of the towers, their heads don't hurt. But what about the community? The game animals are moving north—who's going to drive them back down to us from up there if not the scouts? We can't let him have them. And we need to clamp down hard on them, they've gotten spoiled rotten . . . They commit murders up there, they kidnap soldiers and torture them like some kind of beasts. We've can't let them go. They'll run completely wild."

"Don't let them go, don't let them go," the meeting affirmed. "How can we manage without them?" "And we've fed them, we bore them and raised them, they ought to realize that, but they don't care, they're always looking around for a chance to cut loose . . ."

The bald freak finally calmed down, took his seat, and started greedily gulping down his cold tea. The meeting calmed down too and went quiet. The old folks sat there completely still, trying not to look at Maxim.

Dejectedly nodding his head, Boshku said, "My, my, what an unhappy life we have! No salvation from anywhere. And what did we ever do to anyone?"

"We should never have been born, that's what," said Filbert. "They didn't think before they had us, it was the wrong time . . ." He held out his empty cup. "And we're wrong to have children. Just for them to die. Yes, yes, for them to die."

"The equilibrium . . ." a loud, hoarse voice suddenly declared. "I already told you that, Mak. You didn't want to understand me . . ."

They couldn't tell where the voice came from. Nobody said anything, keeping their eyes morosely lowered. Only the bird on the Sorcerer's shoulder carried on shifting its feet and opening and closing its yellow beak. The Sorcerer himself was sitting absolutely still, with his eyes closed and his thin, dry lips pressed together.

"But now, I hope, you have understood," the bird seemed to continue. "You wish to disrupt this equilibrium. Well now, that is possible. It lies within your power. But the question is: What for? Will anyone ask you to do it? You have made the correct choice, you have consulted with the most pitiful and the most unfortunate, the people who have drawn the most onerous lot of all in this equilibrium. But even they do not wish to see the equilibrium disrupted. Then what is it that motivates you?"

The bird ruffled up its feathers and tucked its head under its wing, but the voice carried on, and now Gai realized that it was the Sorcerer himself speaking, without opening his lips, and without moving a single muscle in his face. Gai found this very frightening, and so did everyone else in the meeting, even the duke-prince. Maxim was the only one who looked at the Sorcerer with a sullen and oddly challenging air.

"The impatience of an agitated conscience!" the Sorcerer declared. "Your conscience has been pampered by constant attention—it starts groaning at the slightest discomfort, and your reason respectfully bows down to it, instead of shouting at it and putting it in its place. Your conscience is outraged by the existing order of things, and with obedient haste your reason seeks ways to change this order. But the order has its own laws. These laws derive from the aspirations of immense masses of people, and they can only change with a change in those aspirations . . . And so on the one hand we have the aspirations of immense masses of people, and on the other hand your conscience, the embodiment of your own aspirations. Your conscience urges you to change the existing order—that is, to transgress the laws of this order, which are determined by the aspirations of the masses; that is, to change the aspirations of masses of millions of people to match the image and likeness of your aspirations. This is ludicrous and antihistorical. Your reason, clouded and deafened by your conscience, has lost its ability to distinguish the real good of the masses from the imaginary good dictated by your conscience. And reason that has ceased to distinguish the real from the imaginary is no longer reason. Reason must be kept pure. If you do not wish or are unable to do that, then so much the worse for you. And not only for you.

"You will tell me that in the world from which you came, people cannot live without a clear conscience. Well then, cease living. That is also not a bad solution—for you and for everyone else."

The Sorcerer stopped talking, and all heads turned to look at Maxim. Gai hadn't entirely comprehended what this pronouncement was all about. It was evidently an echo of some old argument. And it was also clear that the Sorcerer considered Maxim to be an intelligent but willful individual, who acted more out of caprice than out of necessity. That was hurtful. Maxim was a strange character, of course, but he never spared himself and always wished everyone well—not out of some kind of caprice but out of genuinely profound conviction. Of course, forty million people befuddled by radiation didn't want any changes, but they were befuddled, weren't they? It wasn't fair . . .

"I cannot agree with you," Maxim said in a cool voice. "With its pain, my conscience sets goals, and my reason realizes them. My conscience determines ideals; my reason seeks for the paths to them. That is the function of reason—to seek for paths. Without conscience, reason works only for itself, which means it works to no purpose. And as for the contradiction between my aspirations and those of the masses, there is a definite ideal: a human being should be free, both spiritually and physically. In this world the masses are not yet aware of this ideal, and the path to it is a painful one. But a start has to be made sometime. It is precisely those with an acutely sensitive conscience who must agitate the masses, not permit them to slumber in the brutish condition of cattle, and raise them up for the struggle against oppression. Even if the masses do not feel this oppression."

"Correct," the Sorcerer agreed with surprising readiness. "Conscience does indeed set ideals. But ideals are called ideals because they stand in stark contrast to reality. And therefore, when reason sets to work—cold, calm reason—it starts searching for the means to realize ideals, and it turns out that these means will not fit within the frameworks of the ideals, and these frameworks have to be expanded, and conscience has to be slightly stretched, adjusted, and accommodated . . .

"This is all that I wish to say, this is all that I repeat to you: you should not mollycoddle your conscience, you should expose it as often as possible to the dusty draft of new reality, and not be afraid that little blotches or a coarse crust might appear on it . . . But then, you understand this yourself. You have simply not yet learned to call things by their own names. But you will learn to do that too.

"Well, so your conscience has proclaimed a task: to overthrow the tyranny of these Unknown Fathers. Your reason has calculated how things stand and given you its advice: since the tyranny cannot be blown up from within, we shall strike at it from the outside, we shall throw the barbarians against it . . . Let the forest folk be trampled, let the channel of the Blue Serpent be dammed with corpses, let there be a great war, which might, perhaps, lead to the overthrow of the tyrants—all for the sake of a noble ideal. Well then, your conscience has said with a slight frown, I shall have to grow a little coarser for the sake of the great cause."

"Massaraksh . . ." hissed Maxim, redder and more furious than Gai had ever seen him before! "Yes, massaraksh! Yes! Everything is exactly as you say! But what else can be done? On the other side of the Blue Serpent forty million people have been transformed into walking blocks of wood. Forty million slaves . . ."

"That's right, that's right," said the Sorcerer. "But it's a different matter that the plan is inappropriate in and of itself: the barbarians will shatter against the towers and roll back, and in general our poor scouts are not capable of doing anything serious. But within the framework of this same plan, you could have contacted, for instance, the Island Empire . . .

"Although that is not what I mean to say. I'm afraid you simply arrived too late, Mak. You should have come here about fifty years ago, before there were any towers, before there was a war, when there was still some hope of conveying your ideals to the millions . . . But now there is no such hope, now the age of the towers has begun . . . unless you drag those millions here one by one, as you dragged this boy with a gun away . . .

"Only do not think that I am trying to dissuade you. I can see very clearly that you are a force. And your appearance here signifies of itself the inevitable collapse of the equilibrium on the surface of our little sphere. Act. But do not let your conscience hinder you from thinking clearly, and do not let your reason be embarrassed when conscience must be set aside . . . And I also advise you to remember this: I do not know how things are in your world, but in ours no power remains without a master for long. Someone always appears who will attempt to tame it and subordinate it to himself—either furtively or on some plausible pretext . . . That is all I wished to say."

The Sorcerer got to his feet with surprising agility, and the bird on his shoulder squatted down and spread out its wings. He slithered along the wall on his short little legs and disappeared through the door. And the entire gathering immediately set out after him. They walked away, moaning and groaning, still not having really understood what had been said but clearly pleased that everything had remained as it was, that the Sorcerer had forbidden the dangerous plan, that the Sorcerer had shown compassion for them, that he had stuck up for them, and now they could live out their lives in the way they had been doing. After all, they had an entire eternity still ahead of them—ten years, or even more than that.

The last to plod away was Boshku, with his empty teapot, and Gai, Mak, and the duke-prince were the only ones left in the room, apart from Baker, who was slumbering soundly in the corner, exhausted by his intellectual efforts. Gai's head felt bleary and confused, and so did his heart. The only thing he had clearly understood was this: My poor life, for the first half of it I was just a puppet, a wooden doll in somebody else's hands, and now I'll obviously have to live out the second half as a wanderer with no homeland, no friends, and no tomorrow . . .

"Are you offended, Mak?" the duke-prince asked with a guilty air.

"No, not really," Maxim replied. "More the opposite, in fact: what I feel is relief. The Sorcerer's right, my conscience isn't ready yet for undertakings like this. I probably need to do a bit more wandering and looking. Train my conscience a bit . . ." He gave a strangely disagreeable laugh. "What can you suggest to me, Duke-Prince?"

The old duke-prince got up with a grunt and started walking around the room, rubbing his stiff sides. "In the first place, I don't advise you to go on into the desert," he said. "Whether there are barbarians there or not, you won't find anything to suit your needs down there. Maybe it is worthwhile to take the Sorcerer's advice and establish contact with the Islanders, although, as God is my witness, I don't know how to do that. Probably you have to go to the sea and start from there . . . if the Islanders aren't just another myth, and if they want to talk to you . . .

"It seems to me that the best thing to do is go back and act on your own there. Remember what the Sorcerer said: you are a force. And everyone tries to put a force to use for his own purposes. In the history of our empire there have been numerous instances of bold and forceful individuals who have risen to the throne . . . of course, they were precisely the ones who created the most cruel traditions of tyranny, but that doesn't apply to you—you're not like that, and you are hardly likely to become like that . . . If I have understood you correctly, it is pointless to hope for a mass movement, which means that your path is not the path of civil war, and in fact not the path of war at all. You should infiltrate and act on your own, as a saboteur. After all, you are right, the system of towers must have a Center. And power over the North lies in the hands of whoever controls that Center. You need to take that lesson to heart."

"I'm afraid that's not for me," Maxim slowly said. "I can't say why just yet, but it's not for me, I can sense it. I don't want to control the Center. But you are right about one thing: there's nothing for me to do here or in the desert. The desert is too far away, and there is no base here for me to rely on. But there's still so much for me to find out, there's still Pandeia and Hontia, there are still the mountains, there's still the Island Empire somewhere . . . Have you heard about the white submarines? No? But I have, and so has Gai here, and we know a man who has seen them and fought against them. So that means they can fight . . ."

"Well all right." Maxim jumped to his feet. "No point in dragging things out. Thank you, Duke-Prince. You've been a great help to us. Let's go, Gai."

They walked out into the square and stopped beside the half-melted statue. Gai wistfully gazed around. On all sides the yellow ruins trembled in the heat haze, and the air was stifling and foul-smelling, but he no longer wanted to leave this place, this terrible but already familiar place, and go trudging through the forests again, subjecting himself to the will of all the dark, malicious coincidences lying in wait for a man there with every breath he took . . . He could go back to his own little room, play with bald little Tanga, finally make her the whistle he had promised to make out of a spent cartridge case—and, massaraksh, not begrudge firing a bullet into the air for the sake of the poor little girl . . .

"Where do you intend to go, after all?" the duke-prince asked, protecting his face from the dust with his battered, faded hat.

"To the west," Maxim replied. "To the sea. How far is it from here to the sea?"

"Two hundred miles," the duke-prince pensively said. "And you'll have to pass through badly polluted areas . . . Listen," he added. "Maybe we could do this . . ." He paused for a long time, and Gai had already begun impatiently stepping from one foot to the other, but Maxim wasn't in any hurry.

"Agh, what do I really need it for!" the duke-prince exclaimed at last. "To be quite honest, I was keeping it for myself. I thought that when things got really bad, when my nerves gave out, I'd just get in it and go back home, and then they could shoot me if they wanted . . . But what's the point now . . . It's too late."

"A plane?" Maxim quickly asked, casting a hopeful glance at the duke-prince.

"Yes. The *Mountain Eagle*. Does that name mean anything to you? No, of course not . . . Or to you, young man? No again . . . It was once an extremely famous bomber, gentlemen. His Imperial Highness Prince Kirnu's Quadruple-Golden-Bannered Personal Bombing Craft, the *Mountain Eagle*. I recall that the soldiers were forced to learn that by heart . . . *Private Such and Such, name the personal bombing craft of His Imperial Highness!* And the private would name it . . . Yes . . . Well then, I've preserved it. At first I wanted to evacuate the wounded in it, but there were too many. And then, after all the wounded died . . . Ah, what's the point in telling you about that . . . You take it, my friend. There's enough fuel to get halfway across the world . . ."

"Thank you," said Maxim. "Thank you, Duke-Prince. I'll never forget you."

"Never mind me," the old man said. "I'm not giving it to you for my sake. But if you should manage to do anything, my friend, don't forget these folks here."

"I'll manage something," said Maxim. "I'll manage, massaraksh! This has to work out, conscience or no conscience! And I'll never forget anybody."

16

Gai had never flown in an airplane before. In fact, this was the first time he had ever seen a plane. He had seen police helicopters and flying tactical platforms plenty of times and once had even been involved in an airborne raid—their section was loaded into a helicopter and landed on a highway, where a crowd of penal brigade soldiers who had rebelled because of the rotten food was surging toward a bridge. Gai's memories of this aerial assault maneuver were extremely unpleasant: the helicopter had flown very low, shuddering and swaying so badly that his guts were turned completely inside out, and on top of that there was the stupefying roar of the rotor, the stench of gasoline, and fountains of engine oil spraying out from everywhere.

But this was a different matter altogether.

Gai was totally flabbergasted by the Personal Bombing Craft of HIH, the *Mountain Eagle*. It was a genuine monster of a machine. It was absolutely impossible to imagine that it could rise up into the air: its narrow, ribbed body, decorated with numerous gold emblems, was as long as a street, and its gigantic, menacingly magnificent wings reached out so far, an entire brigade could have taken shelter under them. They were as far from the ground as the roof of a building, but the blades of the six immense propellers reached almost all the way back down. The bomber stood on three wheels, each several times the height of a man. The path to the dizzying height of the glittering glass cabin lay along the slim, silvery thread of a light aluminum ladder. Yes, this was a genuine symbol of the old empire, a symbol of a great past, a symbol of the former might that once extended across the entire continent.

Gai had thrown back his head to look, his legs trembling in awe, and Mak's words had struck him like a bolt of lightning:

"Well, what an old crate, massaraksh! . . . I beg your pardon, Duke-Prince, that just slipped out."

"It's the only one I have," the duke-prince coolly replied. "And by the way, it happens to be the best bomber in the world. In his time, His Imperial Highness made flights in it to—"

"Yes, yes, of course," Maxim hastily agreed. "It was just the surprise."

Up in the cockpit, Gai's delight reached the extreme limit of ecstasy. The compartment was made completely out of glass. An immense number of unfamiliar instruments, incredibly comfortable soft seats, incomprehensible levers and devices, bunches of different-colored wires, weird-looking helmets lying at the ready . . . The duke-prince hastily tried to impress something on Mak, pointing at instruments and wiggling levers, and Mak absentmindedly muttered, "Right, yes, I get it, I get it," but Gai, who had been seated in a chair so that he wouldn't get in the way, with his rifle on his knees so that he wouldn't—God forbid!—scratch anything, goggled wide-eyed, inanely turning his head in all directions.

The bomber was standing in an old, sagging hangar at the edge of the forest, and an even, gray-green field without a single hummock stretched out far in front of it. Beyond the field, about three miles away, the forest began again, and hanging over all of this was the white sky, which looked really close, within arm's reach, from here in the cabin.

Gai was very agitated. He didn't remember very clearly having taken his leave of the old duke-prince. The duke-prince had said something, and Maxim had said something, he thought they had laughed, and then the duke-prince had shed a few tears, and then the door had slammed . . . Gai suddenly discovered that he was secured to his seat by broad straps, and Maxim, sitting in the next seat, was rapidly and confidently clicking all sorts of little levers and switches.

Dials lit up on instrument boards, there was a loud crack, a thunderclap of exhaust fumes, the cabin started trembling, everything around him was filled with a ponderous rumbling sound, and far away down below, among the bushes lying flat and the grass that looked as if it were flowing along, the little duke-prince grabbed hold of his hat with both hands and backed away. Gai looked around and saw that the blades of the gigantic propellers had disappeared, they had fused into immense, blurred circles, and suddenly the entire wide-open field jolted and started creeping toward them, faster and faster—there was no more duke-prince, there was no more hangar, there was only the open field, impetuously tearing toward them, and the relentless, appalling shuddering, and the thunderous roaring, and when Gai turned his head with a struggle, he was horrified to discover that the gigantic wings were smoothly swaying up and down, seeming about to fall off at any moment, but then the shuddering disappeared, the field under the wings abruptly dropped away, and Gai was pervaded by a strange, cottony sensation all the way from his head down to his feet. And there was no field under the bomber any longer, and the forest had disappeared, transforming first into a blackish-green brush and then into an immense patched and repatched blanket, and then Gai guessed that he was flying.

He looked at Maxim in total ecstasy. His friend Mak was sitting in a casual pose, with his left arm resting on the armrest and his right hand gently jiggling the largest, and no doubt most important, lever. His eyes were narrowed and his lips were wrinkled up as if he were whistling. Yes, he was a great man. Great and incomprehensible. He can probably do anything at all, Gai thought. Here he is controlling this extremely complex machine that he's just seen for the first time in his life. It isn't some kind of tank, or a truck—it's an airplane, a legendary machine, I didn't even know any had survived—but he handles it like a toy, as if he'd spent all his life flying through the boundless aerial expanses. It's simply beyond all comprehension; it seems as if he sees so many things for the first time, but even so, he instantly gets the hang of them and does what has to be done . . .

And it's not just machines, is it? Machines aren't the only ones to acknowledge him as their master . . . If he wanted, even Cornet Chachu would stroll arm in arm with him . . . And the Sorcerer, who I'm afraid even to look at, regarded him as an equal . . . The duke-prince, a colonel and a senior surgeon-in-chief, an aristo-crat, you might say, he instantly sensed something special and exalted in Maxim too . . . He gave him this machine, entrusted it to him . . . And I wanted to marry Rada to him. What's Rada to him? He should have some countess, or a princess, say . . . But he's friends with me, how about that? And if he told me right now to throw myself out—well, I might very possibly do it, because he's Maxim! And I've learned and seen so many things because of him, more than you could learn and see in an entire lifetime . . . And I'll learn and see so many more things because of him, and learn so many things from him . . .

Maxim sensed Gai's glance, and his rapture, and his devotion, and he turned his head and gave a broad smile, the way he used to, and Gai barely managed to stop himself from grabbing hold of Maxim's powerful brown hand and pressing his lips against it in a kiss of gratitude. O my lord, my defense and my leader, com-mand me! Here am I before you, I am ready—hurl me into the fire, unite me with the flames . . . Against a thousand enemies, against the gaping muzzles, against millions of bullets . . . Where are they, your enemies? Where are those repulsive little men in abhorrent black uniforms? Where is that spiteful little officer who dared to raise his hand against you? Oh, you black scoundrel, I'll tear you apart with my nails, I'll bite your throat out . . . but not at this moment, no . . .

My lord is ordering me to do something—he wants something from me. Mak, Mak, I implore you, give me back your smile, why aren't you smiling anymore? Yes, yes, I am stupid, I don't under-stand you, I can't hear you, the roaring here is so loud, it's your obedient machine roaring . . . Ah, that's what it is, massaraksh, what an idiot I am, why of course, the helmet . . . Yes, yes, just a moment . . . I understand. It has an earphone in it, just like in a tank . . . I am listening, great one! Command me!

No, no, I don't want to come to my senses! Nothing's happening to me, it's just that I am yours, I want to die for you, command me to do something . . . Yes, I'll keep quiet, I'll shut up . . . It will tear my lungs apart, but I'll keep quiet, if you command me to . . .

The tower? What tower? Ah yes, I can see a tower . . . Those black villains, those villainous Fathers, those infamous dogs, they've stuck their towers up everywhere, but we'll sweep those towers away, we'll march, uttering fearsome cries, sweeping aside those towers, with our blazing eyes . . . Guide, guide your obedient machine straight at that abhorrent tower . . . and give me a bomb and I'll jump with the bomb, and I won't miss, you'll see! Give me a bomb, a bomb! Into the flames! Oh! . . . *Ohhh!* . . . *Ohhhh!"*

Gai breathed in with a struggle and tore at the collar of his coverall. His ears were ringing; the world was swimming and swaying in front of his eyes. The world was wreathed in mist, but the mist was rapidly dissipating, his muscles were aching, and he had an unpleasant tickling feeling in his throat. Then he saw Maxim's face, looking dark, gloomy, and even somehow cruel. The memory of something sweet welled up and immediately disappeared, but for some reason he felt a strong desire to stand to attention and click his heels. Only Gai realized that this was inappropriate and Maxim would be angry.

"Did I mess up somehow?" he guiltily asked, anxiously looking around.

"I was the one who messed up," Maxim replied. "I completely forgot about that crap."

"About what crap?"

Maxim went back to his chair, put his hand on the lever, and started looking straight ahead. "About the towers," he eventually said.

"What towers?"

"I set course too far to the north," said Maxim. "We took a hit from the radiation."

Gai suddenly felt ashamed. "Did I bellow out the hymn?" he asked.

"Worse than that," Maxim replied. "Never mind, from now on I'll be more careful."

Gai turned away, feeling immensely awkward, agonizingly straining to recall exactly what he had done, and started examining the world down below. He didn't see any tower, and of course he couldn't see the hangar or the field they had taken off from any longer. Down below the same patchwork blanket was still creeping by, and he could also see a river—a slim, dull, metallic snake, disappearing into the smoky haze far ahead, where the sea ought to rise up into the sky like a wall . . . What was I jabbering? Gai wondered. It must have been some kind of deadly nonsense, because Maxim is very annoyed and upset. Massaraksh, maybe my old Guards habits have come back and I insulted Maxim somehow? Where is that damned tower? This is a good opportunity to drop a bomb on it . . .

The bomber suddenly jolted. Gai bit his tongue, and Maxim grabbed hold of the lever with both hands. Something was wrong, something had happened . . . Gai apprehensively looked around and was relieved to discover that the wing was still there, and the propellers were still turning. Then he looked up. In the white sky above his head odd-looking, coal-black blotches were slowly expanding. Like drops of ink in water.

"What's that?" he asked.

"I don't know," said Maxim. "A strange business." He pronounced two unfamiliar words, and then, after a pause, he said, "An attack of sky stones. Nonsense, that just doesn't happen. The probability's zero point zero zero . . . Do I attract them or something?" He pronounced those unfamiliar words again and stopped talking.

Gai was about to ask what sky stones were, but then out of the corner of his eye, he spotted a strange movement down below on the right. He looked more closely. A clump of something yellowish was slowly and ponderously expanding above the dirty-green blanket of the forest. He didn't immediately realize that it was smoke. Then something glinted deep inside the clump, and a long, black form slid out of it, and at that very moment the horizon heeled over with hideous abruptness, becoming a wall, and Gai grabbed hold of the armrests. The automatic rifle slid off his knees and went tumbling across the floor. "Massaraksh . . ." Maxim hissed in the earphones. "So that's what it is! Ah, I'm an idiot!"

The horizon leveled up again, and Gai looked for the yellow clump of smoke, didn't find it, and started looking straight ahead, and suddenly a fountain of multicolored spray rose up above the forest directly in their course, and yellowish smoke ponderously swelled up in a clump again, and once again a long, black form rose up into the sky and burst into a blinding white sphere—Gai put his hand over his eyes. The white sphere rapidly faded, flooding with black and expanding into a giant blot. The floor started falling away under Gai's feet, he opened his mouth wide to gasp for air, and for a second he thought his stomach was going to leap out through his throat; the cabin turned dark, ragged black smoke slid toward them and flew off to the sides, then the horizon heeled over again, so that the forest was really close now on the left. Gai squeezed his eyes shut and cringed in anticipation of a blow, pain, or death—there wasn't enough air, everything around him was shuddering and shaking.

"Massaraksh . . ." Maxim's voice hissed in the earphones. "Thirty-three massarakshes . . ." And then there was an abrupt, furious hammering on the wall beside Gai, like someone firing a machine gun at point-blank range, an intense stream of icy-cold air struck him in the face, his helmet was torn off, and Gai huddled down, hiding his head from the roaring and the crosswind. This is the end, he thought. They're firing at us, he thought. Now they'll shoot us down and we'll burn up, he thought. But nothing happened. The bomber jolted a few more times, tumbled into several pits and rose back up out of them, and then the roaring of the engines suddenly stopped and an appalling silence set in, filled only with the whistling howl of the wind rushing in through the hole.

Gai waited for a little while, then raised his head, trying not to expose his face to the icy blast of air. Maxim was there. He was sitting in a tense pose, holding the control lever with both hands, glancing at the instruments and looking straight ahead by turns. The muscles under his brown skin were distended. The bomber was flying rather strangely somehow—holding its nose up high. The engines weren't working.

Gai glanced at the wing and was paralyzed with fear. The wing was on fire. "Fire!" he yelled, and tried to jump to his feet. The straps restrained him.

"Sit still," Maxim said through his teeth, without turning around.

"But the wing's on fire!"

"What can I do about it? I said it was an old crate, didn't I? Sit still and stay calm."

Gai got a grip on himself and started looking ahead. The bomber was flying very low. The alternating black and green patches down below flickered past, dazzling his eyes. And there, already rising up ahead of them, was the glittering, steely surface of the sea. We'll be smashed to hell, Gai thought with a sinking heart. That damned duke-prince and his damned bomber, massaraksh, a fine fragment of the old empire, we could quite simply have walked there and had an easy time of it, but now we'll burn up, and if we don't burn up, we'll be smashed to pieces, and if we're not smashed to pieces, we'll drown . . . It's fine for Maxim, he'll come back to life, but it's the end for me . . . I don't want that to happen.

"Don't get jumpy," said Maxim. "Hold on tight . . . Just a moment . . ."

The forest below them suddenly came to an end, and Gai saw a wavy, steel-gray surface rushing straight at him and closed his eyes . . .

A blow. A crunch. A terrifying hissing sound. Another blow. Everything was going to hell, all was lost, this was the end. Gai howled in terror. Some immense force grabbed him and tried to tear him out of the seat, together with the straps, together with all his innards, then flung him back in disappointment, everything all around him was cracking and smashing, there was a stink of burning, and lukewarm water was spraying about. Then everything went quiet. In the silence Gai could hear splashing and gurgling, something was hissing and crackling, and the floor began slowly swaying to and fro. Apparently he could open his eyes now and see what it was like in the next world . . .

Gai opened his eyes and saw Maxim, who was hanging down over him, unfastening his straps. "Can you swim?"

Aha, so we're alive then. "Yes," Gai answered.

"Then let's go."

Gai cautiously got up, expecting to feel sharp pain in his battered and broken body, but his body turned out to be all right. The bomber was gently swaying on low waves. Its left wing was missing, but the right one was still dangling on a latticework metal strut. The shoreline was right in front of its nose—the bomber had obviously been swung around when it landed.

Maxim picked up the automatic rifle, slung it behind his back, and opened the door. Water immediately rushed into the cabin, there was a repulsive smell of gasoline, and the floor under their feet started slowly heeling over.

"Forward," Maxim commanded. Gai squeezed past him and obediently plunked down into the waves.

He sank in over his head and surfaced, spitting out water, then swam for the shore. The shore was close, a firm shore that you could walk on, and even fall on without any danger to your life. Maxim swam beside him, silently slicing through the water. Massaraksh, he even swims like a fish, as if he was born in the water . . . Gai puffed and panted, working away as hard as he could with his arms and legs. It was tough swimming in his coverall and boots, and he was delighted when his foot touched the sandy bottom. The shoreline was still quite a long way off, but he got up and walked, raking his arms through the dirty, oil-slicked water in front of him. Maxim carried on swimming, overtook Gai, and emerged first onto the shallow slope of the sandy shore. When Gai staggered up to him, he was standing with his legs wide apart, looking up at the sky. Gai looked up at the sky too. Numerous black blots were spreading across it.

"We were lucky," said Maxim. "About ten of them were launched."

"Ten what?" asked Gai, slapping himself on the ear to shake out the water.

"Missiles . . . I completely forgot about them . . . They'd been waiting twenty years for us to fly past, and then we did . . . Why the hell didn't I suspect?"

Gai thought in annoyance that he could have suspected too, but he didn't. And two hours ago he could have said, *How can we fly, Mak, when the forest is full of missile silos?* Yes, thank you, of course, Duke-Prince, but it would have been better if you'd flown in your bomber yourself . . . He looked around at the sea. The *Mountain Eagle* was almost completely submerged, with the multiple airfoils of its broken tailplane pitifully protruding from the water.

"Right then," said Gai. "As I understand things, we're not going to reach the Island Empire now. So what are we going to do?"

"First of all," Maxim replied, "we'll take our medication. Get it out."

"What for?" asked Gai. He didn't like the prince's tablets.

"The water's very dirty," said Maxim. "My skin's stinging all over. Let's take four tablets each, or even five."

Gai hastily took out one of the bottles and shook out ten little yellow spheres onto his palm, and they shared the pills between them.

"And now let's go," said Maxim. "Take your rifle."

Gai took his rifle, spat out the acrid, bitter taste that had built up in his mouth, and set off along the shoreline after Maxim, with his feet sinking into the sand. It was hot and his coverall quickly dried out, but there was still water squelching in his boots. Maxim walked quickly and confidently, as if he knew exactly where they needed to go, although all around them there was nothing to be seen, apart from the sea on the left, the broad beach ahead and on the right, and, even farther away on the right, the high dunes about half a mile away from the water, with the tattered crowns of forest trees appearing above them from time to time.

They walked for about two miles, and all the time Gai kept wondering where they were going and where they were in general. He didn't want to ask, he wanted to figure it out for himself, but after recalling all the circumstances, he could only figure out that the estuary of the Blue Serpent River must be somewhere ahead, and they were walking north—but he couldn't understand where to and what for . . . He soon got fed up of trying to figure things out. Holding his rifle close, he caught up with Mak and asked what their plans were now.

Maxim quite readily replied that he and Gai didn't have any definite plans now, and they could only trust to chance. They could only hope that a white submarine would approach the shoreline and they would reach it before the Guards did. However, since waiting for that to happen while surrounded by dry sand was a dubious sort of pleasure, they had to try to walk to the Resort, which ought to be somewhere not far away. The city itself had been destroyed a long time ago, of course, but the springs must have survived, and in any case they would have a roof over their heads. They could spend the night in the city and then see what was what. Maybe they would have to spend twenty or thirty days on the seashore.

Gai discreetly remarked that this plan seemed rather strange to him, and Mak immediately agreed with that, and asked in a hopeful voice if Gai happened to have some other, cleverer plan in reserve. Gai said that unfortunately he didn't have any other plan, but they shouldn't forget about the Guard's tank patrols, which, as far as he knew, came a very long way to the south along the shoreline. Maxim frowned and said that was bad, and they would have to keep a sharp ear out and not let themselves be taken by surprise, after which he intensively interrogated Gai for a while about the tactics of the patrols. Having learned that the tank patrols focused on the sea rather than the shore, and that it was easy to hide from them by lying in the dunes, he calmed down and started whistling an unfamiliar march.

They tramped another mile or so to the strains of that march, and all the while Gai kept wondering how they ought to behave if a patrol did spot them after all, and after he thought of the answer, he expounded his ideas to Maxim. "If they discover us," he said, "we'll lie and say the degenerates kidnapped me and you pursued them and freed me, and the two of us have been wandering around in the forest, and today we reached this place."

"But what will that do for us?" Maxim asked, without any particular enthusiasm.

"What it will do for us," said Gai, starting to get angry, "is at least stop them from whacking us on the spot."

"Oh, no," Maxim firmly replied, "I'm not letting anyone whack me again, or you either."

"But what if it's a tank?" Gai asked in admiration.

"A tank—so what?" said Maxim. "A tank's no big deal . . ." He paused for a while and said, "You know, it would be good if we captured a tank." Gai could see that this idea was very much to his liking. "That's an excellent idea of yours, Gai," said Maxim. "And that's what we'll do. Capture a tank. As soon as they show up, you immediately fire a burst into the air from your rifle, and I'll put my hands behind my back, and you escort me straight toward them. And what happens after that is my concern, but you be careful to keep well out of it, don't get in the way of my hand, and especially don't do any more shooting."

Gai got all fired up at the idea and suggested walking along the dunes so that they could see the tanks from a distance. So that was what they did, climbed up onto the dunes. And immediately they spotted a white submarine.

Behind the dunes they saw a small, shallow bay, and the submarine was jutting up out of the water about a hundred yards from the shore. It actually didn't look anything like a submarine, especially not a white one. Gai thought at first that it was either the carcass of some gigantic two-humped animal or a freakishly shaped rock that had mysteriously risen up out of the sand. But Maxim immediately realized what it was. He even surmised that the submarine was abandoned, that it had been standing here for several years and had been sucked into the sand. And that was exactly the way it was. When they reached the bay and walked down to the water, Gai saw that the long hull and the two superstructures were covered with rusty blotches, the white paint had peeled away, the artillery platform was twisted sideways, and the gun was staring down into the water. There were gaping black holes with scorched edges in the metal plating—nothing could have remained alive inside it, of course.

"Is this definitely a white submarine?" Maxim asked. "Have you seen them before?"

"Yes, I think so," Gai replied. "I've never served on the coast, but they showed us photographs and mentograms . . . they described them . . . There was even an educational film, *Tanks in Coastal Defense*. This is a submarine. It obviously must have been carried into the bay by a storm, got stranded on a shoal, and then a patrol showed up . . . Do you see how battered it is? That plating's like a sieve . . ."

"Yes, it looks like that," Maxim murmured, peering at the vessel. "Shall we go and take a look?"

Gai hesitated. "Well, of course, we could," he hesitantly said.

"What's the matter?"

"Well, how can I put it . . ."

Yes indeed, how could he put it? Corporal Serembesh, a brave tank soldier, had once told Gai, in a dark barracks after lights-out, that it wasn't ordinary sailors who sailed in white submarines—dead sailors sailed in them, serving their second term, and some of them were cowards who had died in a state of fear, and they were serving out their first term . . . The sea demons groped about on the bottom of the sea, caught the drowned men, and filled the crews with them . . . Gai couldn't tell Mak something like that—Mak would laugh at him, and Gai didn't think this was a laughing matter . . .

Or take, for instance, acting private Leptu, demoted from officer's rank. When he got drunk in the canteen, he often used to say, "That's all just nonsense, guys—all those degenerates and mutants of yours, and the radiation, you can deal with all that, you can survive it—but you just pray that God never lands you on a white submarine. Better to drown outright, guys, than even touch the thing, I ought to know . . ." Nobody knew anything about why Leptu had been demoted, but previously he had served on the coast and commanded a patrol boat . . .

"You know," Gai fervidly said, "there are all sorts of superstitions, all sorts of legends . . . I won't tell you about them, but Cornet Chachu, for instance, said that all the submarines were infected and it was forbidden to board them . . . they say there's even an official order about that, about crippled submarines . . ."

"OK," said Maxim. "You stay here, and I'll go. Let's see what kind of contagion there is in there."

Gai didn't have time to say a word—before he could even open his mouth, Maxim had already jumped into the water. He dived and didn't reappear for long time—Gai even started gasping in anxiety as he waited for him—and then Maxim's black-haired head appeared alongside the flaking hull, directly below a shell hole. Nimbly and effortlessly, like a fly climbing up a wall, the brown figure scrambled up the slanting deck, flew up onto the bow superstructure, and disappeared. Gai convulsively sighed and loitered on the spot for a while before he started strolling back and forth along the water's edge, keeping his eyes fixed on the dead, rusty monster.

It was quiet; in this dead bay even the waves weren't murmuring. A blank white sky, lifeless white dunes, everything dry, hot, and absolutely still. Gai cast a look full of hate at the rusty carcass, unable to believe his sheer bad luck: other guys served for years and never saw any submarines, but he and Mak had just tumbled down out of the sky, strode along for an hour or so, and there it was: *Welcome* . . . How did I ever decide to do such a thing? It's all Mak's fault. When he says something, it all sounds so fine, as if there's nothing even to think about, and nothing to be afraid of . . . Or maybe I wasn't afraid because I imagined a white submarine as something alive and white, neat and trim, with sailors on the deck, dressed all in white . . . But this is an iron corpse . . . and this place is so dead, there isn't even any wind . . .

But there was a wind, I definitely remember: as we were walking along, the wind was blowing in my face, a refreshing little breeze . . . Gai longingly looked around, then sat down on the sand, laid his rifle beside him, and started indecisively tugging off his right boot. Can you believe this silence! And what if he doesn't come back at all? What if this lousy iron bastard has swallowed him up without leaving a single trace? . . . Oh, damn it, damn it, damn it!

He shuddered and dropped his boot; a terrifying, long, drawn-out sound had rung out across the bay, something between a howl and a screech, as if devils had scraped a rusty knife across a sinful soul. Oh Lord, it was just an iron hatch opening, a hatch that had rusted closed . . . Damn it, I've broken into a sweat! He opened a hatch, so now he'll climb out . . . No, he isn't climbing out.

For several minutes Gai craned his neck, looking at the submarine and listening. Silence. The same terrible silence, even more terrible after that rusty howl . . . Or maybe he . . . maybe the hatch didn't open but close? It closed itself . . . A vision arose before Gai's blank, lifeless eyes: a heavy steel door closing itself behind Maxim, and the heavy bolt sliding shut on its own . . . Gai licked his dry lips, gulped with a dry throat, and shouted, "Hey, Mak!" But it wasn't a shout . . . merely a hiss, that was all . . . Oh Lord, if I could just make some kind of sound! *"Heeey,"* he howled in desperation. *"Heeey . . ."* the dunes somberly replied, and everything went quiet again.

Silence. And he didn't have the strength to shout again . . .

Keeping his eyes fixed on the submarine, Gai groped for his rifle, released the safety catch with a trembling finger, and fired a burst into the bay without aiming at anything. There was just a brief, powerless crackling sound, as if he had fired into cotton. Little fountains spurted up on the smooth surface and circles started spreading out. Gai raised the barrel higher and pressed the trigger again. This time the sound was right: the rattle of bullets on metal, the whine of ricochets, the sharp smack of the echo. And then nothing. Not a single thing. Not another sound, as if he were here all alone, as if he had always been alone. As if he had ended up here in some mysterious way, been transported here, into this dead place, in a delirious dream, unable to wake up or shake off his trance. And now he would have to stay here alone forever.

Absolutely frantic, just as he was, in one boot, Gai waded into the water. Slowly at first, raising his feet high, until he was up to his waist in water, then faster and faster, almost starting to run, sobbing and swearing out loud. The rusty hulk came closer. Alternately plodding along, stroking his arms through the water, and flinging himself forward to swim, Gai reached the side of the vessel and tried to scramble up, but he couldn't. He circled around the stern of the submarine, grabbed hold of some cables or other, and scrambled up, skinning his hands and knees, onto the deck, where he stopped, weeping floods of tears. It was absolutely clear to him that Maxim was dead. *"Heeey,"* he shouted in a strangled voice. Silence.

The deck was empty; dried-out seaweed was stuck all over the perforated iron, as if it were overgrown with matted hair. The bow superstructure hung over his head like an immense spotted mushroom, and a wide, jagged scar gaped open in the armor plating to one side of him. With his boot clattering on the iron deck, Gai circled around the superstructure and saw iron rungs leading upward, still damp. Slinging his rifle behind his back, he started climbing. He climbed for a long time, for an eternity, in stifling silence, toward inevitable death, toward eternal death. He scrambled up and then froze there, on all fours.

The monster was already waiting for him. The hatch cover was wide open, as if it hadn't been closed for a hundred years and even the hinges had rusted in place again: *Do please come in!* Gai crawled to the black, gaping gullet, glanced in, and his head started spinning and he felt nauseous . . . Silence was welling up out of that iron throat in a compact mass, years and years of stagnant, musty silence, and Gai suddenly imagined his good friend Mak down there in the yellow, putrefied light, crushed under those tons of silence, fighting for his life, alone against them all, fighting with his final ounces of strength and calling out, "Gai! Gai!"—but the grinning silence languidly swallowed up those words, leaving not a trace behind, and kept bearing down on Mak, pinning him down, crushing him. It was absolutely unbearable, and Gai climbed into the hatchway.

Weeping, he tried to hurry, and finally he fell and went clattering downward, falling several yards before he landed on sand. He was in an iron corridor, feebly lit by widely spaced, dusty little lightbulbs; over years and years, fine sand had drifted in and built up at the bottom of the shaft. Gai jumped to his feet—he was still hurrying, still terribly afraid of being too late—and he ran without thinking about where he was going, shouting, "I'm here, Mak . . . I'm coming . . . I'm coming . . ."

"Why are you shouting like that?" Mak asked in a grouchy voice, seeming to thrust his head straight out of the wall. "What's happened? Have you cut your finger?"

Gai halted and dropped his arms. He was on the verge of fainting and had to lean against a bulkhead. His heart was furiously pounding, the blows thundered in his ears like a drum tattoo, and he couldn't control his voice.

Maxim looked at him in amazement for a moment, then he must have understood: he squeezed through into the corridor—the bulkhead door screeched again with a piercing note—walked up to Gai, took him by the shoulders, shook him, pulled him close, and hugged him, and for a few seconds Gai lay there on his chest in blissful oblivion, gradually recovering his wits. "I thought . . . you'd been . . . that you'd . . ."

"It's all right, it's all right," Maxim said in a soothing voice. "It's my fault, I should have called you at once. But there are some strange things in here, you know . . ."

Gai pulled away, wiped his nose with his wet sleeve, then wiped his face with his wet hand, and only then started feeling ashamed. "You were gone for ages and ages!" he furiously exclaimed. "I called, I fired my gun. . . Is it really so hard to answer?"

"Massaraksh, I didn't hear anything," Maxim guiltily said. "You know, there's a magnificent radio in here . . . I didn't know they could make such powerful ones in these parts."

"A radio, a radio . . ." Gai muttered, squeezing in through the half-open door. "You're amusing yourself in here, and meanwhile someone's almost gone insane worrying about you . . . What is all this?"

It was a rather spacious room with a rotted carpet on the floor and three semicircular lamps on the ceiling, only one of which was lit. A round table stood at the center of the space, with chairs around it. Strange-looking framed photographs and pictures were hanging on the walls, from which the tattered remains of velvet upholstery dangled. A large radio was crackling and howling in the corner—Gai had never seen one like it before.

"This is something like a mess room," said Maxim. "Walk around and take a look, there's plenty to look at in here."

"What about the crew?" asked Gai.

"There's nobody here. Neither alive nor dead. The lower compartments are flooded. I think they're all in there."

Gai looked at him in amazement, but Maxim turned away with a preoccupied expression on his face. "I have to tell you," he said, "it looks like it's a good thing that we didn't reach the

Empire in that plane. Just take a look, take a look . . ." He sat
down at the radio and started twisting the tuning knobs.

Gai looked around, not knowing where to begin, then walked
over to the wall and started examining the photographs hanging there. For a while he couldn't understand what they were
photographs of, then he realized that they were X-rays. Looking
out at him were nebulous skulls, all of them with identical grins.
Every image had an indecipherable inscription, as if someone had
signed them. Members of the crew? Celebrities of some kind or
other? Gai shrugged. Maybe Uncle Kaan could make some kind
of sense of this, but we're just simple folk . . .

In the farthest corner he saw a large, bright poster, a poster
in three colors that was quite beautiful, even though it had been
attacked by mold . . . The poster showed a blue sea and a handsome orange man in an unfamiliar uniform emerging from the
sea, with one foot already poised on the black shoreline; he
was very muscular, with a disproportionately small head, half
of which consisted of his powerful neck. In one hand the mighty
hero was clutching a scroll with an incomprehensible inscription,
and with the other he was thrusting a blazing torch into the land.
The torch was setting fire to a city, and repulsive-looking freaks
were writhing in the flames, while dozens of other freaks were
fleeing on their hands and knees in various directions. Something was written in large, orange letters in the upper part of
the poster; the letters were familiar, the same ones that Gai was
used to, but the words they made up were absolutely unpronounceable.

The longer Gai looked at the poster, the less he liked it.
For some reason he remembered a poster in their barracks that
showed a bold guardsman like a black eagle (also with a very
small head and powerful muscles) bravely shearing off the head
of a repulsive orange snake that had thrust itself up out of the
sea with a gigantic pair of scissors. He recalled that there were
words inscribed on the blades of the scissors: on one it said BATTLE
GUARDS, and on the other OUR GLORIOUS ARMY. "Aha," Gai said

to himself, casting a final glance at the poster. "We'll see about that . . . We'll see who singes who, massaraksh!"

He turned away from the poster and stopped dead.

Staring at him with glass eyes from an elegant varnished shelf was a familiar face—square, with light-brown bangs above the eyebrows and a conspicuous scar on the right cheek . . . Cornet Pudurash, a national hero, the commander of a company in the Dead but Unforgotten Brigade, the destroyer of eleven white submarines, who had perished while waging battle against overwhelming odds. His portrait, surmounted by a bouquet of immortelle flowers, hung in every barracks, his bust adorned every parade ground . . . but for some reason his shriveled head, with dead, yellow skin, was here. Gai stepped back. Yes, it was an absolutely genuine head. And there was another head—an unfamiliar, sharp-featured face . . . And another head . . . and another . . .

"Mak!" said Gai. "Have you seen this?"

"Yes," said Maxim.

"These are heads!" said Gai, "Genuine heads . . ."

"Look at the photo albums on the table," said Maxim.

Gai tore his eyes away from the appalling collection with an effort, turned around, and haltingly walked over to the table. The radio was shouting something in an unfamiliar language; music rang out, chimes jangled, and then somebody started speaking again—in a velvety, insinuating voice . . .

Gai picked up one of the albums at random and opened the hard, leather-bound cover. A portrait. A strange, long face with bushy sideburns that drooped from the cheeks right down to the shoulders, with hair shaved above the forehead, a hooked nose, and unusually shaped eyes. An unfamiliar uniform, with badges or medals of some kind arranged in two rows . . . What a weird character . . . Probably some kind of big shot. Gai turned the page. The same individual in a group of other individuals on the bridge of a white submarine, as dour as ever, although the others were grinning, displaying their teeth. In the background, out of focus—something like an esplanade, some unfamiliar-looking structures, vague silhouettes of either palm trees or cacti . . .

The next page took Gai's breath away: a burning Dragon with its turret twisted over to the side, the body of a Guards tank crewman hanging out of the hatch, another two bodies lying one on top of the other to one side, and the same character standing over them with his legs straddled—holding a pistol in his lowered hand and wearing a cap that looked like a pointed hood. The smoke from the Dragon was thick and black, but the area was familiar—it was this very shore, this sandy beach with the dunes behind it . . .

Gai completely tensed up as he turned over the page, and his expectations were met. A crowd of mutants, about twenty people, all naked, a whole heap of freaks, tied together with a single rope. Several brisk-looking pirates in pointed hoods, holding smoking torches, and that character again at one side, obviously giving an order, with his right hand extended and his left resting on the handle of a cutlass. How repulsive those freaks were, it was horrifying just to look at them . . . But what came next was even more horrifying.

The same heap of mutants, but already burned. The same character standing a short distance away, with his back to the corpses, sniffing a flower and chatting with another character . . .

A huge tree in the forest, hung all over with bodies. Some suspended by the hands, some by the feet—and these weren't freaks; one was wearing the check coverall of an educatee, another was in the black jacket of a guardsman.

A burning street, a woman with a baby lying in the road . . .

An old man tied to a post. His face was contorted, he was shouting, his eyes were squeezed shut. And the same character was right there, checking a medical syringe with a preoccupied air.

And then more hanged, burning, burned mutants, convicts, guardsmen, fishermen, peasants, men, women, old people, little children . . . an entire beach full of little children and the same character squatting down behind a heavy machine gun . . . women being dragged along . . . the same character again with a syringe, the lower half of his face covered by a white mask . . . a heap of severed heads, and the same character rummaging in this heap with a cane—in this image he was smiling . . . a panoramic shot: the line of the beach with four tanks on the dunes, all burning, and in the foreground two small figures in black with their hands raised . . .

Enough. Gai slammed the album shut and tossed it away, sat there for a few seconds, and then flung all the albums onto the floor with a curse.

"And you want to reach an agreement with them?" he yelled at Maxim's back. "You want to bring them here, to us? That butcher?" He jumped up, rushed over to the albums, and lashed out at them with his foot.

Maxim turned off the radio. "Don't get into a rage," he said. "I don't want anything to do with them anymore. And don't yell at me, you people are the ones to blame, you just let your world be destroyed, massaraksh, you devastated everything, plundered everything, sank to the level of vile, depraved animals. Now what can I do with you?" Suddenly he was there, close beside Gai, and he grabbed him by the sides of his chest. "Now what am I supposed to do with all of you?" he barked. "What? What? You mean you don't know? Come on, tell me!"

Gai shifted his neck about without speaking, feebly trying to push Maxim off.

Maxim let him go. "I know myself," he said morosely, "that I can't bring anyone here. We're surrounded by ravening beasts . . . We should be sending out armies against them . . ." He grabbed one of the albums off the floor and started jerkily turning the pages. "What a world you've fouled up," he said. "What a world! Here, look, what a world!"

Gai looked over his arm. In this album there were no horrors, only landscapes from various places, astoundingly beautiful and clear color photographs: blue bays framed in luxuriant greenery, blindingly white cities above the sea, a waterfall in a mountain gorge, a magnificent highway with a stream of different-colored automobiles on it. And ancient fortresses, and snowy mountain peaks above the clouds, and someone merrily hurtling down a snowy mountain slope on skis, and laughing girls playing in the sea surf.

"Where is all of this now?" Maxim asked. "What have you done with all of this, you damned children of those damned Fathers? Smashed it, befouled it, betrayed and exchanged it for iron . . . Ah, you . . . little people . . ."

He flung the album onto the table. "Let's go." He furiously fell against the door, it flew open with a screech and a squeal, and he strode off along the corridor.

On the deck he asked, "Are you hungry?"

"Uh-huh," Gai replied.

"OK," said Maxim. "We'll eat right away. Let's swim for it."

Gai clambered out onto the shore first, immediately took off his boot, got undressed, and laid out his clothes to dry. Maxim was still swimming around, and Gai felt alarmed as he watched him. His friend Mak was diving very deep and staying underwater for a really long time. He shouldn't do that, it was dangerous—how could he have enough air? Eventually Maxim came out, dragging a huge, powerful fish by the gills. The fish looked dazed, as if it just couldn't understand how it had been caught with bare hands.

Maxim tossed it away from himself into the sand and said, "I think that will do. It's hardly radioactive at all. Probably a mutant as well. Take your tablets, and I'll prepare it. We can eat it raw, I'll teach you how it's done—it's called *sashimi*. Never tried it? Come on, give me a knife . . ."

When they had eaten their fill of *sashimi*—Gai had to admit it had turned out pretty tasty—they stretched out naked on the hot sand, and after a long pause Maxim asked, "If we got picked up by the patrols and surrendered, where would they send us?"

"Where? They'd send you to your place of reeducation and me to my place of service . . . Why?"

"Is that certain?"

"It couldn't be more certain . . . The instructions of the commandant-general himself. But why do you ask?"

"Now we'll go and look for the Guards," said Maxim.

"To capture a tank?"

"No, we'll use your cover story. You were kidnapped by degenerates, and an educatee rescued you."

"Surrender?" Gai sat up. "But how can we? Me too? Go back into the radiation field?"

Maxim didn't say anything.

"I'll turn into a blockheaded dummy again . . ." Gai said in a helpless voice.

"No," said Maxim. "That is, yes, of course . . . but it won't be the same as it was before . . . Of course, you will be bit of a blockhead. But now you'll believe in something else, won't you? In something that's right . . . Of course, that's still not really very good . . . but it's still better, a lot better."

"But what for?" Gai shouted in despair. "What do you need to do it for?"

Maxim ran his hand over his face. "You see, Gai, my old friend," he said. "A war has broken out. Either we've attacked the Hontians, or they've attacked us . . . Anyway, in short, a war."

Gai looked at him in horror. A war means nuclear war—there isn't any other kind now . . . Rada . . . Oh Lord, why does this have to happen? Everything all over again from the beginning: the hunger, the grief, the refugees . . .

"We have to be there," Maxim went on. "General mobilization has already been declared, everyone's being called up, even the educatees are being amnestied and enlisted into the ranks . . . And we have to be together, Gai. You're a penal unit officer, after all . . . It would be good if I could end up under your command . . ."

Gai was hardly even listening to him. He swayed on his feet, clutching at his hair and repeating to himself, "What for, what for, damn you and curse you! Curse you, curse you thirty-three times over!"

Maxim shook him by the shoulder. "Come on, get a grip on yourself!" he said in a harsh voice. "Don't start falling to pieces. We'll have to fight now, there's no time for falling to pieces . . ." He got up and rubbed his face again. "Of course, with those cursed towers of yours . . . But a war means nuclear war! Massaraksh, no towers will be any help to them now . . ."

"GET A MOVE ON, FANK, GET A MOVE ON!"

"Get a move on, Fank, get a move on. I'm late."

"Yes, sir. Rada Gaal . . . She has been removed from the custody of the state prosecutor and is now in our hands."

"Where?"

"In your mansion the Crystal Swan. I regard it as my duty to express once again my doubts concerning the rationality of this action. A woman like that is hardly going to be of any help to us in controlling Mak. Her kind are easily forgotten, and Mak—"

"Do you think Egghead is stupider than you?"

"No, but—"

"Does Egghead know who kidnapped the woman?"

"I'm afraid that he does."

"All right, so he knows . . . That's all about that matter. Next?"

"Sandy Chichaku has met with Twitcher. Twitcher has apparently agreed to get him together with Brother-in-Law."

"Stop. Which Chichaku? Highbrow Chik?"

"Yes."

"I'm not interested in underground matters right now. Is that all you have on Mak's case? Then listen. This damn war has screwed up all our plans. I'm going away and I'll be back in thirty or forty days. In that time, Fank, you have to wrap up Mak's case. By the time I get back Mak must be here, in this building. Give him a job, let him work, don't restrict his freedom, but make it clear to him—very, very gently!—that Rada's fate depends on how he behaves . . . Under no circumstances allow them to meet . . . Show him the institute, tell him what we're working on . . . within reasonable limits, of course. Tell him about me, describe me as an intelligent, benign, just individual, a major scientist.

Give him my articles . . . apart from the top secret ones. Hint at my being in opposition to the government. He mustn't feel even the slightest desire to leave the institute. That's all I have to say. Any questions?"

"Yes. Security, guards?"

"None. It's pointless."

"Surveillance?"

"Very cautious . . . But better not. Don't frighten him off. The vital thing is that he mustn't want to leave the institute . . . Massaraksh, and I have to go away at a time like this! Well, is that everything now?"

"One final question. I'm sorry, Wanderer."

"Yes?"

"Just who is he, after all? What do you need him for?"

Wanderer got up, walked over to the window and, without looking around, said, "I'm afraid of him, Fank. He's a very, very, very dangerous man."

17

A hundred miles from the Hontian border, when the troop train was stuck for a long time on a siding at a dingy, scruffy station, newly appointed Private Second Class Zef, having come to an amicable arrangement with a security guard, ran to the station's water heater to get some boiling water and returned with a portable radio. He told everyone that there was absolute bedlam at the station: two brigades were entraining at the same time, and the two generals had started squabbling and swearing at each other and became careless, so he had mingled with the crowd of orderlies, valets, and adjutants surrounding the generals and borrowed this radio from one of them.

The heated freight car greeted this announcement with an outburst of loud, zesty, patriotic guffaws. All forty men immediately crowded around Zef, but they took a long time to get settled—someone got smacked in the teeth to stop him from shoving, someone else got poked with an awl in a soft spot, and they all cursed and complained about each other, until Maxim finally barked, "Quiet, you scumbags!" Then they all settled down. Zef switched on the radio and started tuning in to all the stations, one after another.

Certain curious things immediately came to light. First, it turned out that the war hadn't started yet, and the Voice of the Fathers radio station, which for the last week had been howling about bloody battles on their own territory, had been lying in a most blatant fashion. There hadn't been any bloody battles yet. The Hontian Patriotic League was clamoring in horror for the whole wide world to hear that these bandits, these usurpers of power, these so-called Unknown Fathers had capitalized on the acts of heinous provocation by their own hirelings in the form of the notorious so-called Hontian Union of Justice and were now concentrating their armor-clad hordes on the borders of poor, persecuted Hontia. In turn, the Hontian Union of Justice castigated the Hontian Patriots, those paid agents of the Unknown Fathers, in the most emphatic terms possible and recounted in exhaustive detail how someone's vastly superior forces had forced someone else's units, exhausted by preceding battles, across the border and were preventing them from returning, and this circumstance had provided the so-called Unknown Fathers with a pretext for a barbarous invasion, which could be expected at any moment. And in addition, both the League and the Union declared in almost identical terms that it was their sacred duty to warn the brazen aggressor that the counterblow would be devastating, and they hinted in vague terms at the use of atomic traps of some kind.

Pandeian radio summed up the situation in very calm tones and announced without the slightest embarrassment that any way in which this conflict developed would suit Pandeia. The private radio stations in Hontia and Pandeia amused their listeners with jolly music and ribald trivia games, while both of the Unknown Fathers' government radio stations continuously broadcast coverage of hate rallies, interspersed with martial music. Zef also picked up some broadcasts in languages that only he knew, and informed everyone that the principality of Ondol apparently still existed and was still carrying out piratical raids on the island of Hassalg. (Apart from Zef, not a single man in the railcar had ever heard of this principality or this island.) For the most part, however, the airwaves were choked with mind-boggling invective exchanged between commanders of the military units and formations straining hard to squeeze their way through to the Steel Staging Area along the slim threads of two rickety railroad lines.

"We're not ready for war this time either, massaraksh," Zef remarked, switching off the radio and opening the debate.

The others didn't agree with him. In the opinion of the majority, the immense force that was now lumbering on its way spelled the end for the Hontians. The criminal convicts thought the most important thing was to get across the border, and then every man would be his own master and every occupied city would be handed over to them for three days. The political convicts— that is, the degenerates—took a gloomier view of the situation and didn't expect the future to bring anything good; they openly declared that they were all being sent to the slaughter, to set off the atomic mines, that none of them would be left alive, so it would be a good idea to get as far as the border and go to ground there, somewhere where they wouldn't be found. The contesting viewpoints were so diametrically opposed that a genuine discussion failed to develop, and the patriotic debate very rapidly degenerated into monotonous abuse and revilement of the lousy, stinking creeps in the rear, who hadn't given the men any chow yesterday or today and had probably already stolen all the vodka that was due to the men. The military convicts were prepared to carry on talking about this subject right through the night, so Maxim and Zef elbowed their way out of the crowd and clambered up onto the crooked bunks that had been crudely cobbled together out of unplaned planks.

Zef was hungry and angry. He settled down to fall asleep, but Maxim didn't let him. "You'll sleep later," he sternly admonished him. "Tomorrow, maybe, we'll be at the front, and we haven't properly agreed about anything yet . . ." Zef grumbled that there was nothing to agree about, that they could sleep on it, that Maxim wasn't blind and he must be able to see for himself what deep shit they were in, that there was no way you could get any decent kind of operation together with this petty trash, with these thieves and bookkeepers. Maxim objected that they weren't talking about any kind of operation yet. It still wasn't clear what this war was needed for, and who needed it, and would Zef please be polite enough not to sleep when he was being spoken to, and to share his own considerations on the subject. Zef, however, had no intention of being polite, and he didn't conceal the fact. Why the hell, massaraksh, should he be polite, when he was so hungry and he was dealing with a snot-nosed kid who was incapable of drawing elementary conclusions and still insisted on trying to interfere in the revolution . . . He snarled, yawned, scratched, rewound his footcloths, and swore at Maxim, but after being goaded, exhorted, and lashed, he finally started talking and expounded his ideas concerning the causes of the war.

In his opinion, there were at least three possible causes of the war. Maybe they were all operating together, or maybe one of them was predominant. Or maybe there was a fourth cause that had not yet occurred to Zef. First of all, the economy. Information about the economic situation in the Land of the Fathers was kept strictly secret, but everybody knew that the situation was shitty, massaraksh and massaraksh, and when the economy is in a shitty condition, the best thing to do is to start a war with someone in order to immediately stop everybody's mouths. Wild Boar, who was an old hand and quite a specialist on the influence of economics on politics, had already forecast this war five years ago. Towers were all very well, but poverty was still poverty. You couldn't carry on for very long instilling into a hungry man's mind the idea that he's full—his mind couldn't take the strain, and there wasn't much fun in ruling a nation of madmen, especially since the insane were not susceptible to the radiation . . .

Another possible cause was ideological. State ideology in the Land of the Fathers was based on the idea of an external threat. At first this had simply been a lie, invented in order to impose discipline on the lawless anarchy of the postwar period, but then the individuals who had invented this lie had quit the stage, and their successors believed it and genuinely thought that Hontia was simply itching to get its hands on our wealth. And if you bore in mind that Hontia was a former province of the old empire that had declared independence in difficult times, then that added colonial ideas into the mix: bring the bastards back into the fold, after punishing them in exemplary fashion first . . .

And finally, the cause could be a matter of internal politics. The Department of Public Health and the military had been at each others' throats for many years now. It was a question of which one would gobble up the other. The Department of Public Health was a hideously ravenous, insatiable organization, but if these military operations were even marginally success-ful, the generals would bring this organization to heel. Of course, if the war failed to produce a result that was even slightly worth-while, it would be the gentlemen generals who were brought to heel, and therefore the possibility could not be excluded that this entire undertaking was a cunning act of provocation by the Department of Public Health. And by the way, it looked as if this was actually the case—judging from the disarray that was apparent everywhere, and also from what we had been yelling out loud to the entire world for a week already, when it turned out that the military action had actually not even started yet. And maybe, massaraksh, it wouldn't start at all . . .

When Zef reached this point, the couplers clattered and clanged and the car shuddered. They heard shouts, whistles, and tramping feet outside, and the train carrying the penal tank brigade set off. The criminal convicts broke into thunderous song: *"Once again there's no chow and no vodka for us . . ."*

"OK," said Maxim. "What you say sounds perfectly plausible. But then how do you see the war developing, if it does start after all? What will happen then?"

Zef aggressively growled that he was no general, and then plunged straight into telling Maxim how he saw the whole busi-ness. Apparently, during the brief respite between the end of the world war and the beginning of their civil war, the Hontians had managed to fence themselves off from their former overlords with a strong cordon of atomic minefields. And in addition, the Hontians undoubtedly also possessed atomic artillery, and their politicians had had enough wits not to make use of all this abun-dant wealth in the civil war but to save it for us. Which meant that the invasion could be envisaged as proceeding approximately as follows: The spearhead would be three or four penal tank bri-gades lined up in the Steel Staging Area, with an army corps propping them up from the rear. Following up behind the army

men, they would send in blocking detachments of guardsmen in
heavy tanks, equipped with mobile radiation emitters. The degenerates, like Zef, would all go rushing forward to escape from
the radiation blasts, the criminals and army men would go rushing forward in a fit of induced elation and enthusiasm, and any
deviations from this norm, which were bound to arise, would be
obliterated by fire from the Guards bastards. If the Hontians were
no fools, they would open fire on the blocking detachments with
their long-range guns, but it had to be assumed that they were
fools, and therefore it had to be assumed that they would engage
in mutual extermination—in this mayhem the League would turn
against the Union, and the Union would sink its teeth into the
backside of the League.

In the meantime our valiant troops would advance deep into
enemy territory, and the most interesting part would begin, but
unfortunately we wouldn't see that. Our glorious ironclad torrent
would lose its cohesion and start spreading across the country,
inevitably moving out of range of the mobile radiation emitters'
influence. If Maxim hadn't lied about Gai, the men who broke out
in this way would immediately start suffering from radiation hang-
over, which would be all the stronger because the Guards would
have spared no energy in whipping them on during the break-
through . . . "Massaraksh!" Zef howled. "I can just see those cretins
crawling out of their tanks, lying down on the ground, and begging to be shot. And the good-hearted Hontians, not to mention
the Hontian soldiers, driven berserk by this hideous outrage, won't
refuse them, of course . . . There could be unprecedented slaughter!"

The train was picking up speed and the car was energetically
rocking from side to side. In the farthest corner, criminal convicts
were shooting dice, the lamp was swaying up under the ceiling,
and on the lower bunks someone was monotonously muttering—he must have been praying. The air reeked of sweat, dirt,
and the bucket latrine. The tobacco smoke stung Maxim's eyes.

"I think they're taking that into account at General HQ," Zef
went on, "and so there won't be any whirlwind breakthroughs.

It will be a half-hearted positional war; the Hontians, for all their stupidity, will eventually realize what's going on, and they'll start hunting down the radiation emitters . . . Basically, I don't know what's going to happen," he concluded. "I don't even know if they'll give us any chow in the morning. I'm afraid they won't feed us again—why would they bother?"

They said nothing for a while. And then Maxim asked, "Are you certain that we've done the right thing? That our place is here?"

"Orders from HQ," Zef muttered.

"There might be an order," Maxim objected, "but we've got heads on our shoulders too. Maybe it would have been better to decamp with Boar. Maybe we would have been more use in the capital."

"Maybe," said Zef, "and maybe not. You heard that Boar is counting on atomic bombing—many of the towers would be destroyed, and free regions would emerge. But what if there isn't any bombing? Nobody knows anything, Mak. I can picture very clearly to myself the state of bedlam at our HQ . . . The rightists are strutting and swaggering; heads will roll in the government any day now, and those bastards will scramble for the free places . . ." He pondered, rummaging in his beard. "Boar spun us a line about the bombing. But I don't think that was why he headed for the capital. I know him, he's been creeping up on those leaderist types for a long time . . . so it's quite possible that heads will roll at our HQ too . . ."

"So it's bedlam at our HQ as well," Maxim slowly said. "So they're not ready either . . ."

"How could they be ready?" Zef protested. "Some of them dream of destroying the towers, but others dream of keeping them . . . The underground isn't a political party, it's like a mixed salad, with shrimp . . ."

"Yes, I know . . ." said Maxim. "A mixed salad."

The underground wasn't a political party. In fact, the underground wasn't even a front of political parties. Specific circumstances had split its HQ into two irreconcilable groups: categorical opponents of the towers and categorical supporters of the towers. All these people were more or less opposed to the existing order of things, but, massaraksh, their motivations diverged so widely!

There were "sociobiologists," who absolutely couldn't care less who was in power, whether it was Dad, who was a major dynastic financier, the head of an entire clan of bankers and industrialists, or a democratic union of representatives of the working strata of society. All they wanted was for the cursed towers to be razed to the ground and for everyone to be able to live like human beings, as they put it—that is, to live in the old, prewar manner.

There were aristocrats, the surviving remnants of the privileged classes of the old empire, who still believed that what was happening was merely a protracted, lingering misunderstanding, that the people still remained loyal to the legitimate heir to the imperial throne (a dismal, hulking brute of a man, who drank heavily and suffered from nosebleeds), and that it was only these absurd towers, the criminal brainchild of professors from His Imperial Highness's Academy of Sciences who had betrayed their oath of allegiance, that prevented our kind, simple-hearted people from manifesting their genuine, genial, simple-hearted devotion to their legitimate lords and masters.

The unconditional destruction of the towers was also supported by the revolutionaries—the local communists and socialists, such as Wild Boar, who had become well versed in theory and well seasoned in practice during the prewar class struggles. For them the destruction of the towers was merely an essential condition for a return to the natural course of history, a signal for the beginning of a series of revolutions that would eventually lead to a just social order. Siding with them were the rebelliously inclined intellectuals such as Zef or the late Gel Ketshef—simply honest people, who regarded the towers as a repulsive and dangerous venture, steering humankind into a dead end.

The leaderists, the liberals, and the enlighteners were in favor of keeping the towers. The leaderists—the extreme right wing of the underground—were, in Zef's estimation, simply a band of power-seekers who were desperate to obtain departmental appointments, and their efforts were sometimes successful. A certain Kalu the Swindler, who had managed to scramble his way into the Department of Propaganda, had once been a prominent leader of this fascist group. These political bandits were prepared to employ any means at all in their frenzied opposition to any government, if it was composed without their participation.

The liberals were in general opposed to both the towers and the Unknown Fathers. However, what they feared most of all was civil war. They were national patriots, extremely protective of the glory and might of the state, and apprehensive that the destruction of the towers might lead to chaos, a general desecration of sacred values, and the irretrievable disintegration of the nation. They were in the underground because they were all, to a man, supporters of parliamentary forms of government . . .

And as for the enlighteners, they were undoubtedly honest, sincere people, and far from stupid. They hated the tyranny of the Fathers and were categorically opposed to the use of the towers to deceive the masses, but they considered the towers to be a powerful means for educating the people. They regarded the modern individual as being both a savage and a beast by his very nature. Educating such individuals using the classic methods would require centuries and centuries. Burning out the beast in the human being, strangling the individual's animal instincts, teaching him to feel kindness and love for his neighbor, teaching him to hate ignorance, falsehood, and philistinism—that was a noble goal, and with the assistance of the towers, this goal could be achieved within a single generation.

There were too few communists, because they had almost all been killed during the war and the coup; nobody took the aristocrats seriously; the liberals were too passive and frequently didn't know themselves what they wanted. And so the largest and most influential groups in the underground were the socio-biologists, the leaderists, and the enlighteners. They had almost nothing in common, and the underground had neither a unified program, nor a unified leadership, nor a unified strategy, nor unified tactics . . .

"Yes, a mixed salad . . ." Maxim repeated. "It's sad. I had hoped that the underground was intending to somehow exploit the war . . . the potentially revolutionary situation . . ."

"The underground knows damn all," Zef morosely said. "How do we know what it's like—a war with radiation emitters right behind you?"

"You're all totally worthless," Maxim exclaimed, unable to hold back.

Zef immediately flared up. "Why, you!" he barked. "Ease up, now! Who are you to say what we're worth? Where did you spring from, massaraksh, to start demanding this and that from us? Do you want a combat mission? By all means. See everything, survive, go back, and report. Does that sound too easy for you? Excellent! So much the better for us . . . And that's enough. I want to sleep."

He demonstratively turned his back on Maxim and suddenly yelled at the dice players, "Hey, you grave diggers down there! Go to sleep! Onto your bunks."

Maxim lay down on his back, put his hands behind his head, and started looking up at the ceiling of the car. Something was crawling across the ceiling. The grave diggers were quietly and spitefully arguing as they settled down to sleep. The man to the left of him was groaning and whining in his sleep—he was doomed, and he was probably sleeping for the last time in his life. And the men around him—snoring, sniffling, tossing and turning—were probably sleeping for the last time in their lives. The world was a lackluster yellowish color, stifling and hopeless. The wheels hammered, the locomotive howled, a smell of burning blew in through the little barred window, and outside the window this weary, hopeless country went hurtling past, this country of cheerless slaves, this country of the doomed, this country of walking puppets . . .

Everything has rotted here, thought Maxim. Not a single living person. Not a single clear head. And I've ended up in a fine mess again, because I put my hope in someone or something. You can't count on anything here. You can't rely on anything here. Only on yourself. And what good am I on my own? I know that much history at least. A man alone ain't got no bloody chance . . .

Maybe the Sorcerer's right? Maybe I should abstract myself from it all? Calmly and coolly, from the height of my knowledge of the inescapable future, observe the raw material seething, boiling, and melting, the naive, clumsy, and amateurish fighters rising and falling; watch as time forges them into Damascus steel and plunges that steel into torrents of bloody filth to temper it, with the slag sprinkling down in showers of corpses . . . No, I don't know how to do that. Even thinking in categories like that is repugnant . . . It's a terrible thing—an established equilibrium of forces. But then, the Sorcerer did say that I am also a force. And there is a concrete enemy, which means there is a point to which the force can be applied . . .

I'll get whacked here, he suddenly thought. For certain. But not tomorrow! he firmly told himself. That will happen when I manifest myself as a force, and not before. And even then . . . we'll see . . .

The Center, he thought. The Center. That's what I have to search for, that's what the organization has to be directed against. And I'll direct them. I'll make sure that they do something real . . . And I'll make you do something real, my friend. Just listen to how loudly he snores! Snore on, snore on—tomorrow I'll drag you out of here . . .

OK, I have to sleep. But when will I ever get a proper sleep? In a big, spacious bed, in fresh sheets. What kind of habit is it they have here, sleeping over and over on the same sheet? Yes, in fresh sheets, and read a good book before I fall asleep, then retract the wall between me and the garden, turn out the light, and go to sleep . . . and in the morning have breakfast with my father and tell him about this railway car . . . I can't tell Mom about it, of course . . . Mom, you just remember that I'm alive, everything's all right, and tomorrow nothing's going to happen to me . . . And the train keeps on moving, there haven't been any stops for a long time, obviously somebody somewhere has realized that they can't start the war without us . . .

I wonder how Gai's getting along in his corporals' car? He probably feels pretty weird right now—they've got enthusiasm in there . . . I haven't thought about Rada for a long time. Why don't I think about Rada now . . . No, this isn't the time. OK, Maxim, my old friend, you lousy piece of cannon fodder, sleep, he told himself, and immediately dozed off . . .

He dreamed about the sun, the moon, and the stars. All of them at once; it was such a strange dream. He wasn't allowed to sleep for long. The train stopped, the heavy door swung open with a creak, and a strident voice bellowed, "Fourth company, out! Move it!"

It was five o'clock in the morning, it was just getting light, mist was hanging in the air, and a fine rain was sprinkling down. The military convicts started feebly clambering out of the railcar, convulsively yawning and shuddering in the chilly air. The corporals were there in an instant, spitefully and impatiently grabbing men by their feet, dragging them down onto the ground, giving the especially sluggish ones a thump, and yelling: "Separate into crews! Line up!" "Where do you think you're going, you dumb brute? Which platoon are you in?" "You, fat-face, how many times do I have to tell you?" "Where are you off to? You lousy, worthless mob!"

They raggedly sorted themselves out into crews and lined up in front of the railcars. A drunk who had lost his way in the mist ran around looking for his platoon, with abuse being barked at him from all sides. Zef, somber and short on sleep, with his beard bristling, gloomily and distinctly croaked, "Come on, come on, line us up, we'll wage you lots of war today . . ." A corporal running by smacked him on the ear, Maxim immediately stuck out his foot, and the corporal went tumbling over in the dirt. The crews roared in delighted laughter.

"Brigade, atten*tion!*" someone invisible roared. The battalion commanders started howling, straining themselves hoarse, the company commanders picked up the refrain, and the platoon commanders started dashing around. No one stood to attention; the military convicts huddled over with their hands stuck into their sleeves, skipping about on the spot, the fortunate rich ones smoked without trying to conceal it, someone relieved himself, politely turning his back to the gentlemen commanding officers, and little conversations rippled through the ranks about all the signs indicating that they wouldn't give the men anything to eat again, and they could go to hell with this damned war of theirs.

"Brigade, stand at ease," Zef suddenly shouted in a strident voice. "Dismissed! Fall out!" The crews gladly dispersed, but then the corporals started bustling about again, and suddenly guardsmen in gleaming black cloaks came running along the line of railcars, holding their automatic rifles at the ready and stretching out into a sparse cordon. A frightened silence ran along the line of railcars after them; the crews hastily lined up and leveled off, and out of old habit some of the army convicts put their hands behind their heads and spread their legs.

An iron voice from out of the mist said quietly but very clearly, "If any of you scoundrels opens his rotten mouth, I'll give the order to shoot." Everybody froze. The minutes wearily stretched out, filled with anticipation. The mist thinned a little bit, revealing a rather ugly station building, wet rails, and telegraph poles. On the right, at the head of the brigade, a dark group of men came into sight. Quiet voices could be heard coming from it, then someone querulously snapped, "Carry out the order!" Maxim squinted back over his shoulder—the guardsmen were standing motionless behind him, glaring out from under their hoods with expressions of suspicion and hatred.

A squat figure in a camouflage coverall separated off from the little group of men. It was the commander of the penal brigade, ex-colonel of tank forces Anipsu, who had been demoted and jailed for trading in government fuel on the black market. He brandished his cane in front of him, jerked up his head, and began his address: "Soldiers! . . . And that is not a mistake, I am addressing you all as soldiers, although all of us—including myself—are still just shit, the garbage of society . . . Blackguards and bastards! Be grateful that you have been permitted to go into battle today. In a few hours' time, almost all of you will be killed, and that will be good. But for those of you scumbags who survive, it will be the beginning of a glorious life. A soldier's rations, vodka, and all the rest of it. Now we shall move into position, and you will board your vehicles. This is a paltry job—just ride a hundred miles on caterpillar tracks. Making tank soldiers out of you is about as likely as making bullets out of shit, you know that yourselves, but everything that you can get your hands on is yours. Gobble it up. This is your own battle comrade, Anipsu, telling you this. There is no road back, but there is a road forward. If anyone backs down, I'll incinerate him on the spot. And that especially applies to the drivers . . . There are no questions. *Brigaaade! Rrright* turn! Forward . . . Close up! You blockheads, you centipedes! Close up, I told you. Corporals, massaraksh! Where are your eyes? . . . A herd of cattle! Separate out into fours . . . Corporals, sort these swine into fours! Massaraksh . . ."

With help from the guardsmen, the corporals managed to form up the brigade into a column four men wide, after which the command "Attention" rang out again. Maxim found himself not far away from the brigade commander. The ex-colonel was blind drunk. He stood there, swaying, with his backside perched on his cane, occasionally shaking his head and wiping his furious blue-gray face with the palm of his hand. The battalion commanders, also blind drunk, stayed behind his back—one was senselessly giggling, another was attempting with obtuse stubbornness to light a cigarette, and yet another kept clutching at the peak of his cap and probing the ranks of men with his bloodshot eyes. Men in the ranks enviously sniffed and a muttered murmur of flattering approval could be heard.

"Come on, come on . . ." Zef muttered. "We'll wage you lots of war today . . ."

Maxim irritably jostled Zef with his elbow. "Shut up," he said through his teeth. "I'm sick of hearing it."

At that moment two men walked up to the colonel: a cornet with a pipe clenched in his teeth and heavyset individual, a civilian, wearing a long raincoat with the collar raised and a hat. The civilian seemed strangely familiar to Maxim, and he started looking at the man more intently.

The civilian said something to the colonel in a low voice. "Hah?" the colonel exclaimed, turning his murky gaze toward the civilian. The civilian started talking again, pointing over his shoulder with his thumb at the column of military convicts. The cornet indifferently puffed on his pipe. "What for?" the colonel barked.

The civilian took out a piece of paper, and the colonel waved it aside with his hand. "I won't let you have him," he said. "Every last one of them has to croak . . ." The civilian insisted. "And I don't give a damn!" the colonel replied. "And I don't give a damn for your department. They're all going to croak . . . Aren't I right?" he asked the cornet.

The cornet didn't contradict him, but the civilian grabbed the sleeve of the colonel's coverall and jerked him toward himself, and the colonel almost fell off his cane. The giggling battalion commander broke into peals of idiotic laughter. The colonel's face darkened in indignation; he reached for his holster and pulled out a huge army pistol. "I'll count to ten," he announced to the civilian. "One . . . two . . ."

The civilian spat and walked away along the column, looking into the faces of the military convicts, but the colonel kept counting, and when he got to ten, he opened fire. At that point the cornet finally became alarmed and persuaded him to put his weapon away. "Everybody has to croak," the colonel declared. "Along with me . . . *Brigaaade!* On my command! On the double . . . *Forwaaard* march!"

And the brigade set off. Tramping along a sloppy trail rutted by caterpillar tracks, slipping and grabbing at each other, the military convicts descended into a marshy hollow, then turned and marched away from the railroad. Here the column was overtaken by the platoon commanders. Gai started walking along beside Maxim; he was pale-faced, working his jaw muscles, and he didn't say anything for a long time at first, although Zef immediately asked him what was new.

The hollow gradually broadened out, bushes appeared, and up ahead a patch of forest came into view. An immense, unwieldy tank of some ancient type was standing at the edge of the road, where one of its caterpillar tracks had foundered in a wet pothole; it was entirely unlike the patrol tanks of the coastal guard—it had a small, square turret and a little gun. Morose men in oil-stained jackets were tinkering with something beside the tank. The military convicts rambled along haphazardly with their hands stuck in their pockets and their rough collars raised. Many of them cautiously glanced around to see if they could cut and run. The bushes were very tempting, but dark figures with automatic rifles loomed up on the slopes of the hollow every two or three hundred paces.

Three tanker trucks came toward them, floundering through the potholes. The drivers were sullen faced and didn't look at the military convicts. The rain was growing stronger and the men's morale was sinking. They walked in silence, like cattle, looking around less and less.

"Listen, platoon commander," Zef growled, "are they really not going to give us any grub?"

Gai took a hunk of bread out of his pocket and handed it to him. "That's all," he said. "Until you die."

Zef submerged the bread in his beard and started precisely working away with his jaws. This is plain crazy, thought Maxim.

They all know they're going to certain death. But they keep walking. Does that mean they're hoping for something? Does it mean they have some kind of plan? Yes, right, they don't know anything about the radiation, do they . . . Every one of them is thinking, *Somewhere farther along the road, I'll turn off, jump out of the tank, and lie low, and let the other fools go into the attack . . .*

That's what we'll start the struggle against the rightists with. We have to write leaflets about the radiation, shout about it in public places, organize radio stations . . . although the radios only work on two wavelengths . . . but even so, we can break in during the pauses. No more wasting people on the towers—use them for counterpropaganda instead . . . But then, all that only comes later, later. I mustn't get distracted right now. Right now I have to take note of everything. Search for the slightest little cracks . . .

There were no tanks at the station, and no big guns either, only Guards sharpshooters everywhere. I have to bear that in mind. This is a good hollow, deep, and they'll probably remove the guards once we get through . . . But no, no, the guards are irrelevant—the entire crowd will go running forward just as soon as they switch on the radiation emitters . . . With incredible clarity he pictured to himself how it would all be. The radiation emitters are turned on. The military convicts' tanks go hurtling forward with a roar. The army men go surging after them in a great torrent. The entire area of the front line is emptied . . . It was hard to imagine how deep this area was, and he didn't know the effective range of the radiation emitters, but it had to be at least one or two miles. In a strip of territory one or two miles across, not a single man will be left with a clear head. Apart from me.

Ah, no, not just one or two miles. More than that. All the permanent installations, all the towers—they'll all be switched on, and probably at full power. The entire border zone will go insane . . . Massaraksh, what can I do about Zef? He won't be able to stand it . . . Maxim squinted at the rhythmically moving ginger beard, at the morose, dirty face of the world-famous scientist. Never mind, he'll cope. In a real emergency I'll just have to help him, although I'm afraid I'll be too busy for that. And then there's Gai—I mustn't take my eyes off him for a moment . . . Yes, I'll have my work cut out for me. OK. But in the final analysis, in this murky whirlpool, I'll still be completely in control, and nobody will be able to stop me, or even want to . . .

They passed the patch of forest, and immediately heard the combined rumbling of loudspeakers, crackling of exhaust pipes, and angry shouts. Up ahead of them, on a shallow, grassy slope rising toward the north, the tanks were standing in three rows. Men were wandering between them, and layers of grayish-blue smoke were hovering in the air. "Look, there are our coffins!" someone at the front exclaimed in a loud, jolly voice.

"Just look what they're giving us," said Gai. "Prewar tanks, imperial junk, old tin cans . . . Listen, Mak, are we really going to croak here, then? This is absolutely certain death . . ."

"How far is it to the border?" Maxim asked. "And in general, what's over there—behind the crest of hills?"

"A plain," Gai replied. "As smooth as a tabletop. The border's about two miles away, then the hills begin, and they reach all the way—"

"Is there no river?"

"No."

"Any ravines?"

"N-No . . . I don't remember. Why?"

Maxim caught hold of his hand and tightly squeezed it. "Don't lose heart, boy," he said. "Everything's going to be fine."

Gai looked up at him with desperate hope in his sunken eyes; the skin was stretched taut over his cheekbones. "Really?" he said. "Because I can't see any way out at all. They've taken away our guns, the tanks have blanks instead of live shells, and there aren't any machine guns. There's death ahead of us, and death behind us."

"Aha!" Zef said with malicious spite, picking his teeth. "Wet your pants, have you? This isn't as simple as smacking convicts in the teeth."

The column filed into a gap between the rows of tanks and halted. It became hard to talk. Huge loudspeakers had been set up right there on the grass, and a velvety tape-recorded bass voice was pontificating: "There, beyond the ridge of this hollow, is the perfidious enemy. Forward. Only forward. Pull the levers right back—and forward. Against the enemy. Forward . . . There, beyond the ridge of this hollow, is the perfidious enemy. Pull the levers right back—and forward . . ." Then the voice broke off midword and the colonel started yelling. He was standing on the radiator of his off-road vehicle with the battalion commanders holding him by the legs.

"Soldiers!" the colonel yelled. "Enough idle chatter! You see before you your tanks. Everyone to their vehicles! And the drivers above all, because I couldn't give a damn about the rest of you. But anyone who stays behind . . ." He took out his pistol and showed it to all of them. "Is that clear, you rotten, lousy pigs? Company commanders, lead the crews to their tanks."

The men started shoving and jostling. The colonel, swaying like a pole on his radiator, carried on shouting something, but he could no longer be heard, because the loudspeakers had once again started hammering home the message that the enemy lay ahead, and therefore—pull the levers right back. All the military convicts went rushing to the third row of tanks. A fight broke out and steel-tipped boots started flying. The huge, gray crowd slowly seethed around the tanks in the back row. Some tanks started moving and men came scattering down off them. The colonel turned completely blue from the strain of yelling and finally started shooting over the men's heads. A black line of guardsmen came running out of the patch of forest.

"Let's go," said Maxim, taking a firm grip of Gai's and Zef's shoulders and leading them to the vehicle on the end of the front row—a sullen, blotchy tank with a flaccidly drooping gun barrel.

"Wait," Gai jabbered in confusion, looking around. "We're the fourth company, we're over that way, in the second row . . ."

"Go on, go on, then," Maxim angrily said. "Maybe you want to command a platoon for a while too?"

"A soldier through and through," said Zef. *"Cool it, mama . . ."*

Someone grabbed hold of Maxim's belt from behind. Without turning back, Maxim tried to free himself, but he couldn't, and he glanced around. Dragging along behind him, tenaciously clinging on with one hand and wiping his bloodied nose with the other, was the fourth member of the crew, a criminal convict nicknamed Hook.

"Ah," said Maxim, "I forgot about you. Come on, come on, don't fall behind . . ." He noted to himself with displeasure that in the hurly-burly he had forgotten about this man, who had actually been given quite an important role in his plan.

At that moment the Guards' machine guns started roaring out, bullets started jumping off armor plating with a mewling whine, and they had to double over and run at top speed. Maxim ran in behind the end tank and stopped. "Listen to my orders," he said. "Hook, start her up. Zef, into the turret; Gai, check the lower hatches—and check them thoroughly, or I'll have your head!"

He set off around the tank, examining the tracks. There was shooting and yelling and the monotonous droning of the loudspeakers on all sides, but he had promised himself that he wouldn't be distracted, and he wasn't distracted, he simply noted to himself: The loudspeakers. Gai. Mustn't forget him. The tracks were in tolerable condition, but the leading wheels gave cause for concern. Never mind, that's OK, I don't have to ride in it for long . . .

Gai agilely crawled out from under the tank, already dirty, with his hands all scratched. "The hatches are rusted," he shouted. "I didn't close them—they have to stay open, right?"

"There, beyond the ridge of this hollow, is the perfidious enemy!" the tape-recorded voice pontificated. "Forward. Only forward. Pull the levers right back . . ."

Maxim grabbed Gai by the collar and pulled him close. "Do you love me?" he asked, staring into those dilated pupils. "Do you trust me?"

"Yes!" gasped Gai.

"Listen to nobody but me. Don't listen to anybody else. Everything else is lies. I'm your friend, only me, nobody else. I'm your commander. Remember that. I give the orders—remember that."

Dumbfounded Gai kept nodding rapidly, soundlessly repeating: "Yes, yes. Yes. Only you. Nobody else . . ."

"Mak!" someone yelled right in his ear.

Maxim looked around. Standing there in front of him was that strangely familiar civilian, wearing a long raincoat, but no hat any longer. Massaraksh. A square face with peeling skin, and red, puffy eyes . . . It was Fank! With a bloody scratch on one cheek and a split in his lip . . .

"Massaraksh!" Fank yelled, trying to shout above the noise. "Have you gone deaf or what? Do you recognize me?"

"Fank," said Maxim. "What are you doing here?"

Fank wiped the blood off his lip. "Let's go!" he shouted. "Quick!"

"Where?"

"To get the hell out of here. Let's go!" He grabbed hold of Maxim's coverall and pulled.

Maxim flung off his hand. "They'll kill us!" he shouted. "The Guards!"

Fank shook his head. "Let's go! I've got a pass for you!" And then, seeing that Maxim wasn't moving, "I've searched the entire country for you! Thought I'd never find you! Let's go immediately!"

"I'm not alone," Maxim shouted.

"I don't understand."

"I'm not alone," Maxim bawled. "There are three of us! I won't go alone!"

"Rubbish! Don't talk nonsense. What kind of fatuous nobility is this? Are you tired of living?" Fank choked on his own shout and started violently coughing.

Maxim looked around. Pale-faced Gai was looking at him with his lips trembling, holding on to his sleeve—of course, he had heard everything. Two guardsmen were hammering a bloodied military convict into the next tank with their rifle butts.

"One pass!" Fank yelled in a strained voice. "One!" he held up one finger.

Maxim started shaking his head. "There are three of us!" He held up three fingers. "I'm not going anywhere without them!"

Zef's massive ginger beard was thrust out of the side hatch like a twig broom. Fank licked his lips—he clearly didn't know what to do.

"Who are you?" Maxim shouted. "What do you want me for?"

Fank briefly glanced at him and started looking at Gai. "Is this one with you?" he shouted.

"Yes! This one too!"

Fank's eyes turned wild. He stuck his hand in under his raincoat, pulled out a pistol, and aimed the barrel at Gai. Maxim struck Fank's hand with all his strength from below, and the pistol went flying high into the air. Still not understanding what had happened, Maxim pensively watched it go. Fank doubled over and stuck his injured hand under his armpit.

Gai dealt him a brief and precise blow to the neck, just like in the drills, and he collapsed facedown. Guardsmen suddenly appeared close by, sweaty and grinning with bared teeth after their work, looking haggard in their fury.

"Into the tank!" Maxim barked at Gai, bending down and grabbing Fank under the arms. Fank was bulky and he just barely fit through the hatch. Maxim dived in after him, receiving a blow from a rifle butt to his backside in farewell.

Inside the tank it was as dark and cold as in a crypt, with an intense stench of diesel oil. Zef dragged Fank away from the hatch and laid him out on the floor. "Who's this?" he barked.

Maxim had no time to answer. Hook, who had been tormenting the starter for a long time with no success, finally got the tank started. Everything began shaking and rattling. Maxim gestured with his hand, clambered into the turret, and stuck his head out. There was nobody left between the tanks apart from guardsmen. All the tanks' engines were working, there was a hellish roaring, and the slope was enveloped in a stifling cloud of exhaust fumes.

Some tanks were moving, here and there heads were jutting out of turrets, and the military convict who was protruding from the turret of the next tank was making signs to Maxim and contorting his bruised, swollen features. Suddenly he disappeared, the engines started roaring with redoubled volume, and all the tanks simultaneously rushed forward, clanging and clattering up the slope.

Maxim felt himself grabbed across the torso and pulled downward. He bent down and saw Gai's idiotically goggling eyes. Like the other time, in the bomber, Gai kept trying to catch Maxim in his arms, all the time muttering something. His face had become repulsive; there was neither boyishness nor naive courage left in it—only obdurate imbecility and the readiness to become a killer. It's started, thought Maxim, squeamishly attempting to push the hapless young man away. It's started, it's started . . . They've turned on the radiation emitters, it's started . . .

The tank scrambled up onto the crest, shuddering, with clods of turf flying out from under its caterpillar tracks. The blue-gray smoke obscured everything behind it, but ahead a gray, clayey plain suddenly opened up, and in the distance the flat hills on the Hontian side heaved into view, with an avalanche of tanks hurtling toward them, maintaining their speed. There were no rows any longer—all the tanks were rushing along, racing each other, brushing against each other, senselessly rotating their turrets . . .

A caterpillar tread flew off one tank traveling at full speed and the tank started spinning around on the spot and overturned; its other caterpillar track flew off and went soaring up into the sky like a heavy, glittering snake, the lead wheels kept on furiously spinning, and two little figures in gray popped out of the lower hatches, jumped down onto the ground, and ran forward, waving their arms around—forward, only forward, at the perfidious enemy . . .

There was a flash of fire, the sharp crack of a shot from a tank gun burst through all the clanging and roaring, and all the tanks started firing at once; long, red tongues of flame shot out of their gun barrels, the tanks squatted back and jumped up again, they

were enveloped in the dense, black smoke of coarse gunpowder, and a minute later everything was obscured by a blackish-
yellow cloud, and Maxim kept watching, unable to tear his eyes
away from this spectacle that was so colossal in its criminality,
patiently peeling away Gai's tenacious hands, while Gai kept pulling at him, calling out, imploring, craving to shield Maxim from
every danger with his own chest . . . Men, windup dolls, savage
beasts . . . Men.

Then Maxim came to his senses. It was time to take over the
controls. Holding on to the metal rungs, he went down inside,
on the way slapping Gai on the shoulder—Gai started thrashing
about in hysterical ecstasy. Maxim looked around in the cramped,
lurching box, almost choking on the stench of gasoline, made out
Fank's deathly pale face, with its eyes rolled up and back, and Zef
huddled up under a shell crate. He shoved aside Gai, who was
devotedly clinging to him, and squeezed through to the driver.

Hook was jerking the levers back, putting on as much speed
as he could. He was singing, yelling in such an appalling voice
that he could actually be heard, and Maxim even made out the
words of the Song of Thanksgiving. Now he had to somehow
pacify Hook, take his place, and find a convenient ravine, or a
deep hollow, or some kind of hill in all this smoke, so they would
have somewhere to take shelter against atomic explosions . . .

But things didn't go to plan. The moment he started cautiously unclasping Hook's fists, which had frozen onto the levers,
his devoted slave Gai, seeing his lord being defied, pushed his
way in from the side and dealt the crazed Hook a terrible blow
on the temple with a huge spanner. Hook slumped down, went
limp, and let go of the levers. With savage fury, Maxim flung Gai
aside, but it was already too late, and there was no time to feel
horror and sympathy. He dragged the corpse out of the way, sat
down, and took the controls.

He could see almost nothing through the observation hatch,
just a small patch of clayey soil with a sparse covering of blades
of grass, and beyond that a blank shroud of bluish-gray fumes.

Finding anything in that was out of the question. There was only one thing left to do—slow down and keep cautiously moving while the tank traveled deeper into the hills. However, slowing down was dangerous too. If the atomic mines started exploding before he reached the hills, he could be blinded, or even completely incinerated.

Gai rubbed up against him from the right and the left, peering into his face, petitioning for orders. "It's all right, old buddy . . ." Maxim muttered, elbowing him away. "It will pass . . . Everything will pass, everything will be fine . . ." Gai saw that Maxim was talking to him and shed a mortified tear, because once again, like the time in the bomber, he couldn't hear a word.

The tank shot through a dense trail of black smoke—on their left a tank was on fire. They hurtled past it and had to abruptly swerve to the right, to avoid driving over a dead man squashed flat by caterpillar tracks. A crooked border sign emerged from the smoke and disappeared again, followed by tattered, crumpled tangles of barbed wire. A man in a strange white helmet stuck his head up for a moment out of an inconspicuous little ditch, furiously waved his fists in the air, and immediately disappeared, as if he had dissolved into the ground.

The shroud of smoke ahead thinned out a little, and Maxim saw round, brownish hills, very close, and the mud-spattered side of a tank that for some reason was creeping diagonally across the general movement, and then another blazing tank. Maxim steered away to the left, aiming his tank into a deep saddle, overgrown with bushes, between two of the slightly higher hills. He was already close when flames came spurting out toward him, and the entire tank rang from a terrible blow. In his surprise, Maxim switched to full speed ahead, the bushes and the cloud of white smoke hanging over them leaped toward him, he glimpsed white helmets, faces contorted in hatred, raised fists, and then something gave a metallic crack as it broke under his tank's caterpillar tracks.

Maxim gritted his teeth, made a steep turn to the right, and drove his tank as far away as he could from that spot, moving across the slope, sharply heeling over, almost overturning, skirting around the hill, and finally drove into a narrow hollow overgrown with small, young trees. Here he stopped, threw back the front hatch, thrust himself out to the waist, and looked around. This was a suitable spot—the tank was closely surrounded on all sides by high, brownish slopes. Maxim turned off the engine, and immediately Gai started howling some kind of devoted nonsense in a high falsetto voice, something absurdly rhymed, a kind of homespun ode in honor of his greatest and most beloved Mak—the kind of song a dog might compose about its master if it learned to use human language.

"Be quiet," Maxim ordered. "Drag these men out of here and lay them out beside the tank . . . Stop, I haven't finished yet! Do it carefully, these are my beloved friends—our beloved friends."

"But where are you going?" Gai asked in horror.

"I'll be here, close by."

"Don't go away," Gai whined. "Or allow me to go with you."

"You're disobeying me," Maxim sternly said. "Do as I told you. And do it carefully—remember that these are our friends."

Gai started whining, but Maxim wasn't listening any longer. He clambered out of the tank and ran up the slope of the hill. Somewhere not far away tanks were still moving, their engines strenuously roaring, their caterpillar tracks clanging, their guns occasionally booming. A shell whistled high into the sky. Hunching over, Maxim ran up onto the summit of the hill, squatted down among the bushes, and commended himself once again for making such a shrewd choice.

Down below, a mere stone's throw away, there was a broad corridor between the hills, and an unbroken torrent of tanks was pouring through that corridor, streaming into it from the smoke-covered plain—low, squat, powerful tanks, with huge, flat turrets and long guns. These weren't the military convicts, it was the regular army driving by. Deafened and stunned, for several minutes Maxim observed this spectacle, as appalling and improbable as a historical movie. The air oscillated and shuddered from the furious rumbling and roaring, the hill trembled under his feet like a frightened animal, yet somehow it seemed to Maxim that the tanks were moving in somber, menacing silence. He knew perfectly well that inside them, behind the armor plating, crazed soldiers were hoarsely croaking in delirious enthusiasm, but all the hatches were tightly sealed, and each tank seemed to be a solid ingot of inanimate metal . . .

When the final tanks had passed by, Maxim looked back and down at his own tank, heeled over to one side among the trees, and it seemed to him like a pitiful tin toy, a decrepit parody of a genuine battle machine. Yes, a Force had passed by below . . . on its way to encounter another, even more terrible Force. Recalling that other Force, Maxim hastily slithered back down into the grove of trees.

He rounded the tank and stopped.

They were lying in a short row: Fank, so white that he was almost blue, looking like a dead man; Zef, huddled up and groaning, clutching his ginger thatch with dirty-white fingers; and merrily smiling Hook, with a doll's dead eyes. Maxim's order had been carried out to the letter.

But Gai was also lying there a short distance away, all tattered and covered in blood, with his dead, offended face turned away from the sky and his arms flung out wide; the grass around him was crushed and trampled, and there was a flattened white helmet covered in dark blotches, and someone else's feet in boots were sticking out of the smashed and broken bushes. "Massaraksh," Maxim murmured in horror, picturing to himself how only a few minutes ago two snarling, howling dogs had fought to the death here, each striving for the glory of its own master . . .

And at that moment, that other Force struck its counterblow.

This blow caught Maxim on the eyes. He snarled at the pain, squeezed his eyes shut with all his might, and dropped down onto Gai, already knowing that he was dead but nonetheless trying to shield him with his own body. It was a pure reflex response; he didn't have time to think about anything or even feel anything except for the pain in his eyes—he was still falling when his brain switched itself off.

When the world around him became tolerable for human perception once again, his awareness switched back on. Probably only a very short time had passed by, only a few seconds, but Maxim came around covered in copious sweat, with a dry throat, and his head was ringing as if he had been struck on the ear with a plank of wood. Everything around him had changed: the world had turned crimson, the world was piled high with leaves and broken branches, the world was filled with incandescent air, and there were bushes, torn up by the roots, burning boughs of trees, and lumps of hot, dry earth raining down from the red sky. And a ghastly, ringing silence.

The living and the dead had been rolled aside. Gai was lying facedown about ten paces away, covered with leaves. Zef was sitting beside him, still holding his head with one hand and covering his eyes with the other. Fank had gone slithering down the slope, getting jammed in a rain gully, and now he was scrambling around in it, scraping his face against the ground. The tank had also been swept lower and overturned. And dead Hook was now leaning back against a caterpillar track, still merrily smiling . . .

Maxim jumped to his feet, casting aside the branches heaped over him. He ran over to Gai, grabbed hold of him, lifted him up, looked into his glassy eyes, pressed his own cheek against his friend's, cursed this world and cursed it thrice again, a world in which he was so alone and so helpless, where the dead became dead forever, because there was no way, nothing with which to return them to life . . . He thought that he wept, hammered his fists on the ground, and trampled the white helmet, and then Zef started screaming in long, drawn-out screeches of pain, and Maxim came to his senses and, without looking around, no longer feeling anything except hate and a yearning to kill, trudged back up the slope to his observation post . . .

Everything had changed here too. There weren't any bushes any longer, the baked clay was steaming and cracking, and the slope facing northward was on fire. In the north the crimson sky merged into a sheer wall of blackish-brown smoke, and rising up above that wall, swelling up even as he watched, were strange, bright orange, oily, greasy storm clouds. And a light, damp wind, like a draft drawn into the ash pan of this hellish furnace that had been constructed by misfortunate fools for other misfortunate fools, was blowing toward that spot where thousands of thousands of tons of incandescent ash, and hopes of surviving and living, all cremated and reduced to atoms, were soaring up toward the firmament of heaven, which had snapped under the blow.

Maxim looked down into the corridor between the hills. The corridor was empty; the clay, plowed up by caterpillar tracks and seared by the atomic blast, was smoking, with thousands of little fires dancing on it—smoldering leaves and torn-off branches burning out. And the plain to the south seemed very broad and very deserted; it was no longer obscured by powder fumes, it was red, under a red sky, with solitary, motionless little boxes on it—the wrecked and ruined tanks of the military convicts—and a sparse, jagged line of strange machines was already moving across it, approaching the hills.

They looked like tanks, only at the spot where the artillery turret should have been, each of them had a tall latticework cone with a dull, rounded object at its summit. They were traveling fast, gently swaying over uneven sections of ground, and they weren't black like the tanks of the unfortunate military convicts, or grayish-green like the army's assault tanks— they were yellow, the bright, jolly yellow of the Guards patrol vehicles . . . The right flank of the line was already out of sight behind the hills, and Maxim only had time to count eight radiation emitters. He seemed to sense the insolence in them, these masters of the situation. They were going into battle but didn't consider it necessary to conceal or camouflage themselves; they deliberately made an exhibition of themselves with their bright coloring, and their ugly five-yard-high humps, and the absence of any normal weapons.

The men driving these vehicles and controlling these machines must consider themselves perfectly safe. But then, they probably weren't even thinking about that, they were simply hurrying forward, their radiation whips lashing on the iron herd that was stampeding through hell at that moment, and they almost certainly knew nothing about those whips, just as they didn't know that those whips were lashing them too . . .

Maxim saw that the radiation emitter on the left flank of the line was heading into the hollow, and he set off down the slope of the hill to meet it. He walked at his full height. He knew that he would have to extract the black cattle-herders out of their iron shell by force, and he wanted that. Never in his life had he wanted anything so badly as he now wanted to feel living flesh under his fingers . . .

When he reached the bottom of the hollow, the radiation emitter was already very close. The yellow machine came hurtling straight at him, blindly staring with the glass lenses of its periscopes, its latticework cone ponderously swaying, unsynchronized with the bobbing of the vehicle, and now he could see the silvery sphere, bristling with close-set, glittering needles, that was swaying on its summit.

They never even thought of stopping, and Maxim stepped out of the way, letting them pass, ran along beside them for a few yards, and jumped up onto the armor plating.

PART V

THE
EARTHMAN

18

The state prosecutor was a light sleeper and the purring of the telephone immediately woke him. He picked up the receiver without opening his eyes. The rustling voice of his night secretary notified him, as if apologizing, "Seven thirty, Your Excellency . . ."

"Yes," said the prosecutor, still not opening his eyes. "Yes. Thank you."

He switched on the light, threw back the blanket, and sat up. For a while he sat there, staring at his own pale, skinny legs and thinking with sad amazement that here he was, already in his sixth decade, but he couldn't remember a single day when he had been allowed to get a good sleep. Somebody had always woken him up. When he was a cornet, he had been woken after a drinking bout by his doltish brute of an orderly. When he was the chairman of an extraordinary tribunal, he had been woken by his fool of a secretary with documents that hadn't been signed yet. When he was a grammar school boy, his mother used to wake him so that he would go to his lessons, and that was the most heinous time—those were the most repulsive awakenings. And they had always told him *You have to.*

You have to, Your Excellency . . . You have to, Mr. Chairman . . . You have to, my little son . . . And now he was the one who told himself "You have to . . ." He got up, pulled on his robe, splashed a handful of eau de cologne on his face, put in his teeth, glanced into the mirror, massaging his cheeks with a hostile grimace, and walked through into his office.

The warm milk was already sitting on the desk, and the saucer of salty biscuits was lying under a starched napkin. They had to be drunk and eaten, as medication, but first he went over to the safe, pulled the door open, took out a green folder, and put it on the desk beside his breakfast. Crunching on a biscuit and sipping the milk, he thoroughly examined the folder until he was certain that nobody had opened it since yesterday evening. How much has changed, he thought. Only three months have gone by, but how everything has changed!

He mechanically glanced at the yellow telephone, and for a few seconds he couldn't take his eyes off it. The telephone remained silent, as bright and elegant as a jolly toy . . . as appalling as a ticking time bomb that is impossible to defuse . . . The prosecutor convulsively gripped the green folder between his finger and thumb and squeezed his eyes shut. He felt the fear growing and hastily checked himself: no, this was no good, right now he had to remain absolutely calm and reason absolutely impassively . . . I have no choice in any case. So it's a risk . . .

Well, then take the risk. There has always been a risk and always will be, it just has to be reduced to the minimum. And I shall reduce it to the minimum. Yes, massaraksh, to the minimum! . . . You appear not to be convinced of that, Egghead? Ah, you have doubts? You always have doubts, Egghead, that's a certain quality that you have—and good for you . . .

Well then, let us try to dispel your doubts. Have you heard of a man by the name of Maxim Kammerer? Have you really heard about him? You just think that you have. You have never heard about this man before. You are going to hear about him right now for the first time. And I ask you please to hear me out and reach the most objective, most unprejudiced judgment possible concerning him. It is very important to me to know your objective opinion, Egghead—you know, at this point in time the very integrity of my skin depends on it. The pale skin with blue veins that is so very dear to me . . .

He finished chewing the final biscuit and drained the milk in a single gulp. Then he said out loud, "Let us begin."

He opened the folder. This man's past is hazy. And that, of course, is a poor start when getting to know someone new. But you and I know not only how to deduce the present from the past but also how to deduce the past from the present. And if our Mak's past really is so necessary to us, when all is said and done we can always do that, deduce it from the present. This is called extrapolation . . .

Our Mak begins his present by escaping from penal servitude. Suddenly. Unexpectedly. At the very moment when Wanderer and I are reaching out our hands for him. Here is the panic-stricken report from the commandant-general, a classic howl from an idiot who has messed things up and has no hope of escaping punishment: he is not to blame for anything, he did everything according to his instructions, he did not know that the individual concerned had voluntarily joined the suicide sappers, but the individual concerned did join them and got himself blown up in a minefield. He didn't know . . . And Wanderer and I didn't know that, either. But we ought to have known! The individual concerned is an unpredictable kind of person—you ought to have anticipated something of the kind, Mr. Egghead . . . Yes, at the time I was staggered by the news, but now we understand what happened: someone explained about the towers to our Mak, he decided that there was no point hanging around in the Land of the Fathers, and he took off to the South, feigning his own death . . .

The prosecutor lowered his head into his hands and feebly rubbed his forehead. Yes, that was when the whole business started . . . That was the first screwup in my series of screwups: I believed that he had been killed. But how could I not have believed it? What normal man would go running off to the South, to the mutants, to certain death? Anybody would have believed it. But Wanderer didn't.

The prosecutor picked up the next report. Oh, that Wanderer! That smart Wanderer, that brilliant Wanderer . . . That was how I should have acted—the way he did. I was certain that Mak had been killed: the South is the South. But he flooded the territory beyond the river with his agents. Fat Fank—ah, I didn't get to him when I should have. I didn't get my claws into him! That fat swine with the peeling skin even lost weight running around the country, nosing around, keeping his eyes open, and his agent Chicken died of a fever on Highway 6, and his Tapa the Cock was captured by the Highlanders, and then Fifty-One—I don't know who he is—got captured by pirates way out on the coast, but still managed to report back just in time that Mak had shown up there, surrendered to the patrols, and been sent back to his penal colony . . . That's the way people with brains do things: they don't believe anything and they have pity on nobody. And that's the way I should have acted at the time. Dropped all my other business and focused only on Mak—after all, even then I realized what a terrible force Mak is, but instead I got into a scrap with Twitcher and lost, and then I got involved with this idiotic war and lost again.

And I would have lost again now too, but I've finally had a stroke of luck. Mak has turned up in the capital, in Wanderer's lair, and I've found out about it before Wanderer. Yes, Wanderer, with your gristly ears, yes, now you're the one who has lost. How terrible that you just had to go away again at this precise moment! And do you know, Wanderer, I'm not even offended by the fact that once again it remains entirely unknown where you went to and what for. So you went away—fine! Of course, you relied on that Fank of yours in all of this, and your Fank brought you Mak, but then—what a disaster!—Fank collapsed after all his military adventures. He's lying unconscious in the Palace Hospital—such an important individual, people like him are only ever put in the Palace Hospital!—and I shan't botch things up this time around; now he'll stay lying there for as long as I need him to. So you're not here, and Fank isn't here, but our Mak is, so things have turned out really well . . .

Noticing the onset of an incipient feeling of joy, the prosecutor immediately extinguished it. Emotions again, massaraksh. Calmly now, Egghead. You are making the acquaintance of a new individual by the name of Mak—you have to be very objective. Especially since this new Mak is nothing at all like the old one; he

is very grown-up now, he knows what finance and juvenile criminality are now. Our Mak has grown wiser and sterner . . . Look
at the way he has broken through into the underground's Central
HQ (on the recommendations of Memo Gramenu and Allu Zef),
descending on them like a bolt from the blue with his proposal
for counterpropaganda. And Central HQ wailed and lamented,
because it meant revealing the true function of the towers to
the rank-and-file membership—but Mak convinced them, didn't
he? He frightened them, entangled them in his arguments, and
they accepted the idea of counterpropaganda and assigned Mak to
develop it . . . He figured out the situation very quickly, quickly
and correctly. And they understood that—they realized just who
they were dealing with. Or they simply sensed it . . .

And here is the latest report: the faction of enlighteners
invited him to participate in discussion of the program of reeducation, and he was delighted to accept. He immediately suggested
a whole heap of ideas. Pretty useless ideas, but that's not the
point—reeducation is idiotic nonsense in any case—the important
thing is that he is no longer a terrorist, he does not want to blow
anything up, and he does not want to kill anyone; the important
thing is that he has turned to political activity, that he is actively
building up his authority at Central HQ, making speeches, criti-
cizing, climbing upward; the important thing is that he has ideas
and is just yearning to put them into practice, and that is precisely
what we want, Mr. Egghead . . .

The prosecutor leaned back in his chair.

And here's another thing that we need: reports on his way
of life. He works a lot—both in the laboratory and at home—he
is still pining for that woman, for Rada Gaal, he exercises, has
almost no friends, doesn't smoke, hardly drinks at all, and eats
very moderately. On the other hand, he displays a clear inclina-
tion for luxury in his daily life and is well aware of his own worth:
he accepted the automobile to which he is entitled by his position
as an automatic given, while expressing his dissatisfaction with
its low power and ugly appearance; he is also dissatisfied with his

two-room apartment—he considers it too cramped and lacking
in basic comforts; he has decorated his home with original paint-
ings and antique works of art, spending almost his entire advance
on them . . . well, and so on. Good material, very good material . . . And by the way, how much money does he have, what
resources does he possess now? *Riiight*, a project coordinator in
the chemical synthesis laboratory . . . salary paid in a blue envelope . . . his own car . . . a two-room apartment on the grounds
of the Department of Special Research . . . They've set him up
pretty well. And they've probably promised him even more.

I'd like to know how they explained what it was that Wanderer
needed him for. Fank knows, the fat swine, but he won't tell,
chances are he'll croak anyway . . . Ah, if only I could somehow drag everything that he knows out of him! What pleasure I
would take in terminating him after that—the amount of trouble
that he has caused me, that mangy brute . . . He stole that Rada
from me too, and she would be really useful to me right now.
Rada . . . What a weapon she is for dealing with pure, honest,
courageous Mak! But then, right now perhaps it's not really such
a bad thing . . . I'm not the one keeping your beloved under lock
and key, Mak, it's Wanderer—it's all that odious blackmailer's
scheming . . .

The prosecutor shuddered: the yellow telephone had quietly
tinkled. Merely tinkled, and nothing more. Quietly, even melodi-
cally. Come to life for a split second and then frozen again, as if
simply reminding him it was there . . . Keeping his eyes fixed on
it, the prosecutor ran his trembling fingers across his forehead.
No, it was a mistake. Of course, a mistake. It could have been
anything—a telephone is a complicated device, some spark or
other simply jumped the wires inside it . . .

He wiped his fingers on his robe. And the phone immediately
gave a thunderous roar. Like a shot at point-blank range . . . Like
a saber slash across the throat . . . Like a sudden fall from the
roof to the asphalt . . . The prosecutor picked up the receiver.
He didn't want to pick up the receiver, he didn't even know

that he was picking up the receiver, he even imagined that he wasn't picking up the receiver but was quickly tiptoeing into the bedroom, getting dressed, driving the car out of the garage and racing off at top speed . . . But where to?

"State prosecutor," he said in a hoarse voice, and coughed to clear his throat.

"Egghead? It's Dad speaking."

There . . . This is it . . . Now it will be *We're expecting you in about an hour* . . .

"I realized," he helplessly said. "Hello, Dad."

"Have you read the communiqué?"

"No."

Ah, you haven't? Well, come over, and we'll read it to you . . .

"It's over," said Dad. "They've botched up the war."

The prosecutor gulped. He needed to say something. He urgently needed to say something, best of all to crack a joke. Crack a subtle joke . . . Oh God, help me crack a subtle joke!

"Nothing to say? But what did I tell you? Steer clear of that mess, stick with the civilians, the civilians and not the military men! Oh, Egghead . . ."

"Well, you are Dad," the prosecutor managed to force out. "And children always disobey their parents, don't they?"

Dad giggled. "Children . . ." he said. "Remember that saying: 'If your child disobeys you . . .'? How does it go on, Egghead?"

My God, my God! ". . . wipe him off the face of the earth." That was what he said that time: "Wipe him off the face of the earth," and then Wanderer picked up a heavy black pistol off the table, slowly raised it, and fired two shots, and the child clutched his shattered bald head in his hands and toppled over onto the carpet . . .

"Lost your memory?" Dad asked. "Oh, Egghead. What are you going to do, Egghead?"

"I made a mistake . . ." the prosecutor wheezed. "A mistake. It was all because of Twitcher . . ."

"You made a mistake . . . All right, then, think, Egghead. Ponder on it for a while. I'll call you back . . ."

And that's all. He's gone. And I don't know where to call him to weep and implore . . . That's stupid, stupid. That has never done anyone any good . . . OK . . . Hang on . . . Just hang on, will you, you bastard!

He swung his open hand and smashed it hard against the edge of the desk—to make it bleed, to make it hurt, to make it stop trembling . . . That helped a bit, but he still leaned down, opened the lower drawer of the desk with his other hand, took out a flask, tugged out the cork with his teeth, and took several swallows. He felt a rush of heat. That's the way . . . Calmly, now . . .

We'll see about this. This is a race—we'll see who runs faster. You can't do away with Egghead that easily; it will cost you a bit more effort than that. Egghead can't instantly be summoned just like that. If you could have summoned him, you would have . . . It's all right that he called. He always does that. There's still time. Two days, three days, four days . . . "There is still time!" he shouted at himself. "Don't get jittery." He got up and started walking around the office in circles.

I do have a hold over you. I have Mak. I have a man who is not afraid of the radiation. For whom no barriers exist. Who wishes to change the order of things. Who hates you. A man who is pure and, therefore, open to all temptations. A man who will trust me. A man who will want to meet with me . . . He already wants to meet with me as it is—my agents have told him many times that the state prosecutor is benevolent and just, a great expert on the laws, and a genuine guardian of law and order, that the Fathers dislike him and only tolerate him because they don't trust each other . . . My agents have shown me to him, in secret, in advantageous circumstances, and he liked my face . . . And, most important of all, they have hinted to him, in the strictest secrecy, that I know where the Center is located. He has excellent control of his face, but it was reported to me that just at that moment he gave himself away . . . That's the kind of man I have—a man who really wants to seize the Center and who can do it—the only one out of all of them . . . That is, I don't actually have this man just yet, but the nets have been cast, the bait has been swallowed, and today I'll strike and hook him. Or I'm finished. Finished . . . Finished . . .

He abruptly swung around and glanced in horror at the yellow telephone.

He couldn't control his imagination any longer. He saw that cramped room, upholstered in dark red velvet, a stifling, musty room, with no windows, a dingy, bare desk, and five gilded chairs . . . And the rest of us were all standing there: me, Wanderer, with the eyes of a ravenous killer, and that bald butcher . . . that bungler, that blabbermouth, he knew where the Center was, didn't he, he destroyed so many people to find out where the Center was, and then—the windbag, the drunk, the braggart—how could he go talking to anybody about such things? Let alone to relatives . . . And especially to relatives like that. And he was the head of the Department of Public Health, the eyes and ears of the Unknown Fathers, the armor and the battle-ax of the nation . . . Dad scowled as he said, "Wipe him off the face of the earth," Wanderer fired twice at point-blank range, and Father-in-Law grumbled, "Now the upholstery's all splattered again . . ." And they started arguing again about why the room stank like that, and I stood there with my legs turned to rubber, thinking, Do they know or don't they? and Wanderer stood there, grinning like a hungry predator, and looking at me, as if he could guess . . .

He didn't guess a damn thing. But now I understand why he always took such pains to make sure nobody could penetrate the mystery of the Center. He always knew where the Center was and was just looking for a way to take it over himself . . . Too late, Wanderer, too late . . . And you'll be too late as well, Dad. And you, Father-in-Law. And as for you, Twitcher, you're not even in the running . . .

He jerked open a curtain and pressed his forehead against the cold glass. He had almost smothered his fear. And in order to finally trample it underfoot, to extinguish the final spark, he pictured Mak bursting into the instrument room of the Center and taking it by storm . . .

Blister could have done that too, with his personal bodyguard, with that gang of his brothers, cousins, nephews, blood brothers, and protégés, with those appalling scum who have never even heard of the law, who have only ever known one law—shoot first . . . Wanderer had had good reason to raise his hand against Blister—that very evening he had been attacked right outside the gates of his mansion, his car was riddled with bullets, his driver and secretary were killed, and in some mysterious way the attackers were all killed themselves, right down to the last man, all twenty-four of them with two machine guns . . . Yes, Blister could have burst into the instrument room too, but he would have gotten bogged down there, without going any farther, because then comes a barrier of depressive radiation, and maybe now there are even two barriers, although one would be enough. No one can get through there: a degenerate will collapse in a faint from the pain, and a simple, loyal citizen will just drop to his knees and start quietly weeping in mortal anguish . . .

Only Mak will get through there, and he will sink his skilled hands into the generators, and first of all switch the Center, and the entire system of towers, to a depressive field. And then, entirely unopposed, he will walk up into the radio studio and put on a tape with a previously recorded speech for cyclical repeat transmission . . . The entire country, from the Hontian border to beyond the Blue Serpent, will be in a state of depression, millions of fools will be just lying there in floods of tears, with no desire to even to stir a finger, and the loudspeakers will be roaring at the tops of their voices that the Unknown Fathers are criminals, reviling them for this and castigating them for that, and saying they are here, and they are there, kill them, save the country, it is I who am telling you this, Mak Sim, a living god on earth (or something else, like the legitimate heir to the imperial throne, or the great dictator—or whatever he likes the best) . . . To arms, my guardsmen! To arms, my army! To

arms, my subjects! And meanwhile he'll go back to the instrument room and switch the generator to a field of heightened
attention, and then the entire country will listen open-mouthed,
straining not to miss a single word, learning the message by
heart, repeating it to themselves, and the loudspeakers will keep
roaring, the towers will keep working, and it will go on like that
for another hour, and then he will switch the radiation emitters
to enthusiasm, just half an hour of enthusiasm—and that's the
end of the broadcasts . . .

And when I come around—massaraksh, an hour and a half of
hellish agony, but I'll just have to put up with it, massaraksh—
there won't be any more Dad, none of them will be left, there
will only be Mak, the great god Mak, and his faithful adviser the
former state prosecutor, now the head of the great Mak's government . . . Ah, never mind about the government, I shall simply
be alive, and nobody will be threatening me, and then we shall
see . . . Mak isn't the kind to abandon useful friends—he doesn't
even abandon his useless friends—and I'll be a very useful friend.
Oh, what a friend I shall be to him!

He abruptly broke off, went back to the desk, squinted at
the yellow phone, laughed, picked up the receiver of the green
phone, and asked for the deputy head of the Department of
Special Research.

"Brainiac? Good morning, this is Egghead. How are you feeling? How's your stomach? Well, that's excellent . . . Is Wanderer
still not back yet? . . . Uh-huh . . . Well, OK . . . I got a call from
upstairs, instructing me to inspect you a bit . . . No, no, I think
it's purely a formality, I understand damn all about what you
do anyway, but you should draw up some kind of a report . . .
the draft conclusions of an inspection visit and what have you.
And make sure that everybody's where they should be this
time, not like last year . . . Huh . . . About eleven o'clock, probably . . . Arrange things so that I can leave with all the documents
at twelve . . . Well, I'll see you then. Let's go and suffer . . . Do
you suffer too? Or perhaps you long ago invented a form of

defense? Only you're hiding it from the bosses? All right now, I'm only joking . . . See you."

He put down the receiver and glanced at his watch. It was a quarter to ten. He gave a loud groan and dragged himself off to the bathroom. This nightmare again . . . half an hour of nightmare. Against which there is no defense. From which there is no salvation . . . Which destroys the very desire to live . . . How very annoying it is that I'll have to spare Wanderer.

The bath was already full of hot water. The prosecutor flung off his robe, tugged off his nightshirt, and stuck a painkiller under his tongue. The same thing all my life. One twenty-fourth of my entire life is hell. More than 4 percent . . . And that's not counting the summonses from on high. Well, the summonses will end soon, but this 4 percent will remain until the very end . . . But then, we'll see about that. When everything is settled, I'll deal with Wanderer myself . . . He clambered into the bath, arranged himself as comfortably as possible, relaxed, and started thinking about how he would deal with Wanderer. But he didn't have time to think of anything. The familiar pain struck him on the top of his head, traveled down along his spine, sinking a claw into every cell and every nerve, and started fiercely and methodically shredding him to pieces, in time to the wild jolting of his heart.

When it was all over, he continued lying there for a while in languid exhaustion—the torments of hell also had their compensations: a half hour of nightmare presented him with several minutes of heavenly bliss—then he climbed out, rubbed himself down in front of the mirror, opened the door a little, accepted some clean underwear from his valet, got dressed, went back into his office, drank another glass of warm milk, this time mixed with medicinal water, ate some sticky mush with honey, simply sat there for a little while, finally recovering his wits, then called his day secretary and ordered the car to be made ready.

The way to the Department of Special Research lay along the Government Highway, which was empty at this time of day. It was lined with curly trees that looked as if they were artificial.

The driver drove hard, without stopping at the traffic lights, occasionally turning on a booming, bass siren. They drove up to the tall iron gates of the department at three minutes to eleven. A guardsman in dress uniform walked up to the car, leaned down, glanced in, recognized the prosecutor, and saluted. The gates immediately swung open to reveal a view of a rich, green park with white and yellow blocks of apartment buildings, and behind them the gigantic glass parallelepiped of the institute. They slowly drove along the narrow road with its forbidding warnings about speed, past a children's playground, past the squat building of the swimming pool and the cheerful, brightly colored building of the restaurant. And all of this was surrounded by greenery, billowing clouds of greenery, and wonderful, absolutely pure air and—massaraksh!—what an amazing smell hung in the air here; there was nothing like it absolutely anywhere else, not in any field or any forest . . .

Oh, that Wanderer—all of this is his initiative, immense damned sums of money have been blown on all of it, but how everyone loves him here! This is the right way to live; this is the right way to set yourself up. Immense damned sums of money were blown on it and Stepfather was terribly displeased, and he's still displeased now . . . Risk? Yes, of course there was a risk, but Wanderer took the risk, and now his department is his own, the people here won't betray him, they won't try to squeeze him out . . . He has five hundred people here, most of them young, they don't read the newspapers, they don't listen to the radio; they have no time, you see, they have important scientific research work . . . so here the radiation misses the target completely, or rather, the target it strikes is a completely different one.

Yes, Wanderer, if I were you, I would drag out the development of those protective helmets for a long time. Perhaps you are dragging it out? You almost certainly are. But damn it all, how can I get a serious grip on you? Now, if only a second Wanderer would just turn up. . . But there isn't another mind like that one in the entire world. And he knows it. And he keeps a very close watch on any man with even a modicum of talent. He takes him in hand when he's still young, coddles him and estranges him from his parents—and the parents, the fools, are utterly delighted!—and there, look, he has another little soldier in his ranks . . . Oh, what a great thing it is that Wanderer isn't here right now, what a stroke of luck!

The car stopped and the day secretary swung the door open. The prosecutor clambered out and walked up the steps into the glass-walled vestibule. Brainiac and his minions were already waiting for him. With an appropriate expression of boredom on his face, the prosecutor flaccidly shook Brainiac's hand, glanced at the minions, and allowed himself to be escorted to the elevator. They entered the cabin in regulation order: Mr. State Prosecutor, followed by Mr. Deputy Head of the Department, followed by the state prosecutor's minion and the deputy head of the department's senior minion. They left the others in the vestibule. They entered Brainiac's office in regulation order too: the state prosecutor was followed in by Brainiac, and Mr. Prosecutor's minion and Brainiac's senior minion were left outside the door in the reception office. The prosecutor immediately lowered himself into an armchair in a state of exhaustion, and Brainiac immediately started fussing about, pressing buttons at the edge of the desk with his fingers, and when an entire mob of secretaries came running into the room, he ordered tea to be served.

The prosecutor spent the first few minutes amusing himself by studying Brainiac. Brainiac was looking incredibly guilty. He avoided looking the prosecutor in the eyes, kept smoothing down his hair, pointlessly rubbing his hands together, unnaturally coughing, and making a large number of meaningless, fussy movements. He always looked this way. His appearance and behavior were his main assets. He constantly roused suspicions that he had a guilty conscience and drew down constant, thoroughgoing checks and audits on himself. The Department of Public Health had studied his life hour by hour. And since his life was irreproachable, and each new check merely confirmed this

rather unexpected fact, Brainiac's rise up the professional ladder
had proceeded at record speed.

The prosecutor knew all of this perfectly well—he himself had
personally checked Brainiac three times, each time in the most
thorough manner possible, and each time raising him one rung
higher—and nonetheless at this moment, as he amused himself
by scrutinizing Brainiac, he suddenly caught himself thinking that,
by God, Brainiac, the artful rogue, knew where Wanderer was
and was terribly afraid that this information would be dragged
out of him now. And the prosecutor couldn't resist it. "Greetings
from Wanderer," he casually said, tapping his fingers on the armrest of his chair.

Brainiac cast a quick glance at the prosecutor and immediately looked away. "Mm . . . uh . . . yes," he said, biting his lip and
clearing his throat. "Um . . . In just a moment . . . um . . . they'll
bring the tea . . ."

"He asked you to give him a call," the prosecutor said even
more casually.

"What? *Uhhh* . . . OK . . . The tea today will be quite exceptional. My new secretary is a genuine connoisseur of teas . . . That
is . . ."—he cleared his throat again—". . . where should I call him?"

"I don't understand," the prosecutor said.

"No, well, it's just that . . . um . . . in order to call him, I have
to know the . . . the telephone number . . . but he never leaves a
number . . ." Brainiac suddenly started fussing about, blushing in
his distress, and slapping his hands around on the table. He found
a pencil and asked, "Where did he say I should call?"

The prosecutor backed off. "I was joking," he said.

"Eh? What?" A range of suspicious expressions instantly
started flickering across Brainiac's face in rapid succession. "Ah!
Joking?" He guffawed in sham laughter. "You really caught me
there . . . How amusing. And I was thinking . . . Ha-ha-ha! And
here's the tea!"

The prosecutor accepted a glass of hot, strong tea from the
pampered hands of the pampered secretary and said, "OK, I was

just joking, enough of that. There's not much time. Where's your piece of paper?"

After performing a whole heap of unnecessary movements, Brainiac extracted the draft of a certified report of inspection from the desk. If the way in which he shrank and cringed as he did this was anything to go by, the draft simply had to be crammed absolutely full of false information that was intended to lead the inspector astray, and in general must been composed with subversive intentions.

"*Riiight* then," said the prosecutor, smacking his lips on a small lump of sugar. "What's this you have here? 'Report of Verificatory Investigation' . . . *Riiight* . . . The interference phenomena laboratory . . . the spectroscopic research laboratory . . . the integral radiation laboratory . . . I don't understand a thing, can't make head or tail of it. How do you make any sense out of all this?"

"Well, I . . . hmm . . . You know, I don't really know anything about it either—after all, my professional background is as . . . a manager, I don't interfere in these matters." Brainiac kept hiding his eyes, biting on his lip, and vigorously ruffling up his hair, making it absolutely clear beyond the slightest possible doubt that he wasn't any kind of manager but a Hontian spy with specialized higher education. Well, what a character!

The prosecutor turned his attention back to the report. He made a profound remark about the excessive expenditure of the power amplification group, asked who Zoi Barutu was, and whether he was related to Moru Barutu, the well-known propaganda writer, passed a reproachful comment with regard to the lensless refractometer, which had cost absolutely crazy money although they hadn't even gotten a handle on it yet, and summed up the work of the radiation research and improvement sector by saying that there was no substantial progress to be observed (and thank God, he added to himself), and that his opinion on this point definitely must be included in the final draft of the report.

He looked through the section of the report dealing with protection against radiation even more casually. "You are merely marking time," he declared. "In terms of physical protective measures, absolutely nothing had been achieved, and in terms of physiological protective measures, even less than that . . . In any case, physiological measures aren't what we need at all: why would I want to let myself be hacked to pieces, you could reduce me to an idiot . . . But the chemists have done well—they've won us another minute. A minute last year, and a minute and a half the year before last . . . What does that mean? It means that now I can take a pill, and instead of thirty minutes, I'll be in agony for twenty-two. Well, now that's not bad. Almost thirty percent . . . Make a note of my opinion: increase the tempo of work on physical protection and pay the staff of the chemical protection division an incentive bonus. That's all."

He tossed the sheets of paper across to Brainiac. "Have a clean copy typed out . . . and my opinion too . . . And now, strictly pro forma, show me around . . . well now, let's say . . . uh . . . I visited the physicists last time, take me to see the chemists, I'll have a look at what they're up to."

Brainiac jumped to his feet and pressed more buttons, and the prosecutor got up with an air of extreme exhaustion.

Accompanied by Brainiac and his own day secretary, the prosecutor took a leisurely stroll through the laboratories of the division of chemical protection, politely smiling at people with a single chevron on the sleeve of their white coats, sometimes slapping on the shoulder those who didn't have any chevrons, and halting beside those who had two chevrons to shake their hands, sagely nod his head, and inquire if they had any complaints.

There weren't any complaints. They were all apparently working, or pretending to work—in this place you couldn't tell. Little lights were blinking on various instruments, liquids were boiling in various vessels, there was a smell of some kind of garbage, and in some places they were torturing animals. Everything here was clean, bright, and spacious, the people looked well fed and calm, and they didn't manifest any enthusiasm, behaving perfectly correctly with the inspector—but without any warmth at all, and in any case without the appropriate obsequiousness.

And hanging in almost every room—whether it was an office or a laboratory—was a portrait of Wanderer: above a desk, beside tables of figures and graphs, above a door, sometimes under glass on a desk. The portraits were amateur photographs and pencil or charcoal sketches, and one of them was even painted in oils. In this place you could see Wanderer playing ball games, Wanderer giving a lecture, Wanderer gnawing on an apple, Wanderer looking severe, thoughtful, weary, or infuriated, and even Wanderer laughing his head off. These sons of bitches even drew cartoons of him and hung them in the most obvious places! . . . The prosecutor imagined himself walking into the office of the junior counselor of justice, Filtik, and discovering a caricature of himself there. Massaraksh, it was unimaginable, absolutely impossible!

He smiled, slapped shoulders, and shook hands, but all the time he was thinking that this was the second time he had been here since last year, and everything seemed to be the same as before, but previously he somehow hadn't taken any notice of it all . . . But now he had. Why only now?

Ah, that was why! What was Wanderer to me a year or two years ago? Formally, he was one of us, but in actuality he was merely an armchair presence who had no influence on politics, no place of his own in politics, and no goals of his own in politics. However, since then Wanderer had succeeded in doing a great deal. The statewide operation for the elimination of foreign spies was his initiative. The prosecutor had conducted those trials himself and had been astounded at the time to find that he was not dealing with the usual sham degenerate spies but with genuine, seasoned intelligence agents, planted by the Island Empire to gather scientific and economic information. Wanderer had fished them all out, every last one, and after that he had become the regular chief of special counterintelligence.

And moreover, it was Wanderer who had exposed the conspiracy led by bald Blister, an appalling character, who had been very firmly entrenched and vigorously and dangerously undermined Wanderer's stewardship of counterintelligence. And he had whacked Blister himself—he didn't trust anybody else to do it. He always acted openly, never used any kind of camouflage, and only acted alone—no coalitions, no unions, no temporary alliances. In this way he had brought down three heads of the Military Department, one after another—they were summoned to the top before they even had an inkling of what was happening—and then managed to get Twitcher, a man whose fear of war amounted to panic, appointed . . .

It was Wanderer who had hacked down Project Gold a year ago, when it presented to the top level by the Patriotic Union of Industry and Finance . . . At the time Wanderer had seemed to be on the verge of being toppled himself, because the project had aroused Dad's enthusiasm, but Wanderer had somehow managed to persuade him that all the advantages of the project were strictly temporary, and in ten years' time there would be a general epidemic of insanity and a total collapse . . .

He always somehow contrived to persuade them; nobody else could ever persuade them of anything, only Wanderer could. And basically it was clear why. He was never afraid of anything. Yes, he did spend a long time sitting in his office, but eventually he realized his own true worth. He realized that we needed him, whoever we might be, and no matter how fiercely we might fight among ourselves. Because only he can create protection, only he can free us from our torments . . . And snot-nosed kids in white coats draw caricatures of him, and he allows them to do it . . .

The day secretary opened the next door for the prosecutor, and the prosecutor saw his Mak. Wearing a white coat with a single chevron on the sleeve, Mak was sitting on the windowsill looking out. If a counselor of justice took the liberty of lounging on the windowsill and counting crows during work hours, he could with a clear conscience be dispatched under armed guard to the labor camps as an obvious idle parasite and even a saboteur. But in this particular case, massaraksh, it was quite impossible to say anything. Take him by the scruff of the neck and he would tell you, *I beg your pardon! I am conducting a thought experiment here! Go away and don't interfere!*

The great Mak was counting crows. He briefly glanced at the men who had come in and returned to this occupation, but then he turned back and looked more closely. You recognized me, thought the prosecutor. You did, my smart fellow . . . He politely smiled at Mak, slapped the young lab assistant who was twirling the handle of an arithmometer on the shoulder, stopped in the middle of the room, and looked around.

"Well now . . ." he said into the space between Mak and Brainiac. "What do we have going on here?"

"Mr. Sim," said Brainiac, blushing, blinking, rubbing his hands together, and clearing his throat, "explain to the inspector what you . . . uh . . . hmm . . ."

"But I know you, don't I?" said the great Mak, somehow or other popping up with startling suddenness only two steps away from the prosecutor. "Forgive me if I'm mistaken, but aren't you the state prosecutor?"

Yes, dealing with Mak wasn't easy—the entire thoroughly thought-out plan had immediately gone up in smoke. Mak hadn't even thought of trying to hide anything, he wasn't afraid of anything, he was curious, and from the elevation of his own immense height, he peered down at the prosecutor as if he were examining some kind of exotic animal . . . The prosecutor had to regroup and think on his feet.

"Yes," he said in a tone of cold surprise, ceasing to smile. "As far as I am aware, I am indeed the state prosecutor, although I don't understand . . ." He frowned and peered into Mak's face. Mak gave a broad smile. "Ah!" the prosecutor exclaimed. "Why, of course . . . Mak Sim, also known as Maxim Kammerer! However, pardon me, but I was informed that you had been killed while serving penal labor . . . Massaraksh, how did you come to be here?"

"It's a long story," Mak replied with a casual wave of his hand. "And as it happens, I was also surprised to see you here. I never supposed that our activities were of any interest to the Department of Justice."

"Your activities are of interest to the most surprising people," said the prosecutor. He took Mak by the arm, led him to the window farthest away, and inquired in a confidential whisper, "When are you going to let us have the pills? The real pills, for the full thirty minutes."

"Why, are you really also—" Mak began. "But then, yes, naturally . . ."

The prosecutor woefully shook his head and rolled up his eyes with a heavy sigh. "Our blessing and our curse," he said. "The good fortune of our state and the wretched misfortune of its leaders . . . Massaraksh, I am terribly glad that you're alive, Mak. I ought to tell you that the case in which you were tried is one of the few in my career that has left me with a sense of nagging dissatisfaction . . . No, no, don't try to deny it—according to the letter of the law you were guilty, so from that point of view everything is in good order . . . you attacked a tower and I think killed a guardsman; that sort of thing doesn't earn you a pat on the head, you know. But in essence . . . I confess that my hand trembled when I signed your sentence. As if I were sentencing a child—please don't be offended. After all, in the final analysis, it was more our initiative than yours, and the entire responsibility—"

"I'm not offended," said Mak. "And you're not so very far from the truth: the escapade with that tower was puerile . . . In any case, I'm grateful to the state prosecutor's office for not having us shot at the time."

"It was all that I was able to do," said the prosecutor. "I recall that I was very upset when I heard that you had been killed . . ." He laughed and squeezed Mak's elbow in a friendly fashion. "I'm devilishly glad that everything has turned out so well. And devilishly glad to make your acquaintance . . ." He looked at his watch. "But tell me, Mak, why are you here? No, no, I'm not going to arrest you, it's none of my business, the military police can deal with you now. But what are you doing in this institute? Are you really a chemist? And apart from that . . ." He pointed to Maxim's chevron.

"I'm a little bit of everything," said Mak. "A little bit of a chemist, a little bit of a physicist . . ."

"A little bit of an underground operative," the prosecutor said with a good-natured laugh.

"Only a very little bit," Mak decisively replied.

"A little bit of a conjuror," the prosecutor said.

Mak looked at him intently.

"A little bit of a fantasizer," the prosecutor continued, "a little bit of an adventurer."

"But those are not professions," Mak objected. "They are, if you like, simply the qualities of any decent scientist."

"And any decent politician," said the prosecutor.

"An uncommon combination of words," Mak remarked.

The prosecutor cast a quizzical glance at him, then caught on and laughed again. "Yes," he said. "Political activity does have certain specific characteristics. Politics is the art of washing things clean with very dirty water. Never descend into politics, Mak, stick with your chemistry." He looked at his watch and said in annoyance, "Ah, damn it, I have absolutely no time, and I really did want to have a chat with you . . . I've looked at your file, you're a highly intriguing individual . . . But you're probably very busy too."

"Yes," said the clever fellow Mak. "But, of course, not so very busy as the state prosecutor."

"Well now," said the prosecutor, laughing once again. "Your bosses assure us that you work day and night . . . But I, for instance, cannot say the same for myself. A state prosecutor does sometimes find himself with a free evening . . . It will surprise you to hear that I have a whole heap of questions for you, Mak. I must admit that I wanted to have a talk with you back then, after the trial. But work, work, work, there's never any end to it."

"I'm at your disposal," said Mak. "Especially since I also have a few questions for you."

Oh, come on! the prosecutor mentally rebuked him. Don't be so open about things, we're not alone here. Out loud he replied, beaming brightly, "Excellent! I'll do everything I can . . . And now, please pardon me, I have to run . . ."

He shook the enormous hand of his Mak, the Mak he had already caught, the Mak who had already conclusively taken the bait. He played along quite excellently, he undoubtedly does want to meet, and now I'll sink the hook home . . .

The prosecutor halted in the doorway and clicked his fingers, and looked back: "Let me see now, Mak, what are you doing this evening? I've just realized that I have a free evening today . . ."

"Today?" said Mak. "Well, why not? Of course, I have—"

"Bring someone along!" the prosecutor exclaimed. "That's even better, I'll introduce you to my wife, it will be a splendid evening . . . Eight o'clock—does that suit you? I'll send a car to pick you up. Agreed?"

"Agreed."

Agreed, the prosecutor triumphantly thought as he walked around the final laboratories in the division, smiling, slapping shoulders, and shaking hands. *Agreed*! he thought as he signed the report in Brainiac's office. "Agreed, massaraksh, agreed!" he triumphantly shouted to himself on the way home.

He gave the driver his instructions. He told his secretary to inform the department that the prosecutor was busy—nobody was to be received, the phones were to be disconnected, and in general they should all clear out and go to hell, but in a way that meant they would still remain within easy reach all the time. He summoned his wife and kissed her on the neck, recalling in passing that it had been ten days since they saw each other, and asked her to make arrangements for a good dinner, something light and delicious for four, to behave herself at the table and prepare herself to meet a very interesting man. And plenty of wines, various kinds and all of the very best quality. . .

After that he locked himself in his office, laid out the contents of the green folder on his desk again, and started thinking everything through once more from the very beginning. He was only disturbed once, when a Military Department courier brought the latest communiqué from the front. The front had fallen apart. Someone had tipped off the Hontians that they should focus on the blocking detachments, and last night they had bombarded the radiation emitter tanks with atomic shells, destroying up to 95 percent of them. No more information had been received concerning the fate of the army that had broken through. This was the end. This was the end of the war. It was the end of General Shekagu and General Odu. It was the end of Four-Eyes, Teapot, Stormcloud and other, more minor figures. It could very possibly be the end of Father-in-Law and Stepbrother. And of course, it would have been the end of Egghead, if only Egghead weren't such a smarty pants . . .

He dissolved the report in a glass of water and started walking around the office in circles. He felt a tremendous sense of relief. Now, at least, he knew for certain when he would be summoned to the top. They would finish off Father-in-Law first, and then spend at least twenty-four hours choosing between Twitcher and Tooth. Then they would have to waste a bit of time on Four-Eyes and Stormcloud. That was another twenty-four hours. Well, they would casually whack Teapot in passing, and then just dealing with General Shekagu would take them at least forty-eight hours. And after that, and only after that . . . After that they wouldn't have any "after that."

He didn't leave his office until the very moment when his guest arrived.

The guest made a quite exceptionally pleasant impression. He was magnificent. He was so magnificent that the prosecutor's wife, who was a cold woman, sophisticated in the most formidable meaning of the word, and had long ago ceased to be a woman in his eyes but was his old battle comrade, shed twenty years at the first sight of Mak and acted in a devilishly natural manner—she could not have acted any more naturally even if she had known the part that Mak was destined to play in her fate.

"But why are you alone?" she asked in surprise. "My husband ordered dinner for four."

"Yes, indeed," the prosecutor put in. "I thought you would come with your lady friend—I remember the young woman, she almost came to grief because of you."

"She did come to grief," Maxim calmly replied. "But with your permission, can we talk about that later? Which way would you like me to go?"

They sat over dinner for a long time, in a cheerful atmosphere, laughing a lot and drinking a little bit. The prosecutor recited the latest lines of gossip—those that had been approved and were recommended for release by the Department of Public Health. The prosecutor's wife very charmingly cracked indiscreet little jokes, and Mak described his flight in the bomber in humorous tones. As the prosecutor laughed at the story, he thought in horror about what would have become of him if even a single missile had hit the target . . .

When everything had been eaten and drunk, the prosecutor's wife made her excuses, suggesting that the men prove their ability to survive without a lady for at least one hour. The prosecutor combatively accepted this challenge, grabbed Mak by the arm, and drew him into the study to regale him with a wine that only thirty or forty people in the country had ever had a chance to try.

They settled into soft armchairs on each side of a low table in a very cozy corner of the study, took a sip of the precious wine, and looked at each other. Mak was very serious. This smart fellow Mak clearly knew what the conversation would be about, and on a sudden impulse the prosecutor abandoned his initial plan for a discussion that would be artful and wearying, constructed out of veiled allusions and designed to facilitate gradual mutual revelations. Rada's fate, Wanderer's intrigues, the Fathers' machinations—all that was not of the slightest importance. With breathtaking clarity that induced a sense of desperation, he acknowledged that all his mastery in conversations of that kind would be redundant with this man. Mak would either agree or refuse. It was absolutely simple, as simple as the fact that the prosecutor would either carry on living or be splatted in a few days. Hastily setting down his little glass on the little table with trembling fingers, he began without any preliminaries:

"I know, Mak, that you are an underground activist, a member of Central HQ, and a passionate enemy of the existing order of things. In addition to which, you are also a fugitive convict and the killer of the crew of a special forces tank . . . And now about me. I am the state prosecutor, a trusted agent of the government who has access to the highest state secrets, and also an enemy of the existing order of things. I am proposing that you should depose the Unknown Fathers. When I say 'you,' I mean you and only you, in person—this does not concern your organization. I ask you to please understand that any intervention by the underground can only make a hash of the job. I am proposing a conspiracy with you, based on my knowledge of the most important state secret of all. I shall inform you of that secret. Only the two of us must know it. If any third person discovers it, we shall be eliminated in the very, very near future. Don't forget that the underground and its HQ are teeming with agent provocateurs. Therefore, do not even think of putting your trust in anybody—especially in your close friends."

The prosecutor drained his little glass in a single gulp, without even tasting the wine.

"I know the location of the Center. And you are the only man who is capable of capturing this Center. I am proposing to you a complete, detailed plan for seizing the Center and the actions to follow that. You carry out this plan and become the head of the state. I remain as your political and economic adviser, because you know absolutely damn all concerning matters of that kind. I am familiar with the general outline of your political program: use the Center for reeducating the people in a spirit of humane values and elevated morality, and on that basis build a just society in the absolute shortest term possible. I don't have any objections. I accept it—simply because nothing could be worse than the present situation. That's all I have to say. You have the floor."

Mak didn't say anything. He remained silent, twirling the precious glass of precious wine in his fingers. The prosecutor waited. He couldn't feel his own body. It seemed to him that he wasn't here, that he was dangling somewhere in the celestial void, looking down at the softly lit, cozy little corner, with Mak sitting in the armchair beside him, saying nothing—a vision of something that was dead and stiff, neither speaking nor breathing . . .

And then Mak asked, "What are my chances of staying alive if I capture the Center?"

"Fifty-fifty," said the prosecutor. Or rather, he imagined that he had said it, because Mak knitted his brows and repeated his question in a louder voice.

"Fifty-fifty," the prosecutor hoarsely said. "Perhaps even better than that. I don't know."

Mak remained silent for a long time again.

"All right," he eventually said. "Where is the Center located?"

19

At about noon the phone rang. Maxim picked up the receiver and the prosecutor's voice said, "Mr. Sim, please."

"I'm on the line," said Maxim. "Hello."

He immediately sensed that something bad had happened. "He's arrived," said the prosecutor. "Start immediately. Is that possible?"

"Yes," Maxim said through his teeth. "But you promised me a few things."

"I haven't had a chance to do anything," the prosecutor said, his voice tinged with a slight note of panic. "And now I won't get a chance. Start immediately, at once—we can't wait for even a single minute. Do you hear, Mak?"

"All right," said Maxim. "Is that all?"

"He's coming to see you. He'll be there in thirty or forty minutes."

"I understand. Now is that all?"

"Yes. Go on, Mak, get on with it. Go with God!"

Maxim hung up and sat there for a few seconds, gathering his thoughts. Massaraksh, everything is going down the drain . . . But I still have a chance to think . . . He grabbed the phone again. "Professor Allu Zef, please."

"Yes," Zef roared.

"This is Mak."

"Massaraksh, I asked you not to pester me today—"

"Shut up and listen. Come down into the lobby immediately and wait for me there."

"Massaraksh, I'm busy!"

Maxim grated his teeth and squinted at the lab assistant. The assistant was assiduously calculating something on an arithmometer.

"Zef," said Maxim. "Come down to the lobby immediately. Do you understand me? Immediately!" He cut off the call and dialed Wild Boar's number. He was lucky: Boar was home. "This is Mak. Go outside and wait for me—some urgent business has come up."

"All right," said Boar. "I'm on my way."

Maxim dropped the receiver, reached into his desk, pulled out the first folder he came across, and started leafing through the pages while feverishly trying to weigh up whether everything was ready. The car was in the garage, the bomb was in the trunk, the tank was full of fuel . . . he didn't have a gun, but to hell with it, he didn't need a gun . . . the documents were in his pocket, Boar was waiting . . . It was smart of me to think of Boar . . . Of course, he could refuse . . . No, he's not likely to refuse, I wouldn't refuse . . . That's all. I think that's all . . .

He told the lab assistant, "I've been called to a meeting, say I'm at the Department of Construction. I'll be back in an hour or two. See you later."

He tucked the folder under his arm, walked out of the laboratory, and ran down the stairs. Zef was already striding around the lobby. When he saw Maxim, he stopped, clasped his hands behind his back, and scowled.

"What the hell, massaraksh—" he began before Maxim had even reached him.

Without dawdling, Maxim grabbed him by the arm and dragged him toward the exit. "What the hell's going on?" Zef muttered, digging his heels in. "Where to? What for?" Maxim shoved him out through the door, then dragged him along the asphalt path and around the corner to the garages. There was no one around, only a lawnmower chattering away on the lawn in the distance.

"Will you tell me just where you're dragging me off to?" Zef yelled.

"Be quiet," said Maxim. "Listen. Get all our guys together immediately. Everybody you can get hold of . . . To hell with any questions. Listen! Everybody you can get hold of. With weapons. There's a pavilion just beside the gates, know it? Hole up in there. Wait. In about thirty minutes—Are you listening to me, Zef?"

"Well come on, then," Zef impatiently said.

"In about thirty minutes, Wanderer will drive up to the gates—"

"So he's come back, then?"

"Don't interrupt. In about thirty minutes—maybe—Wanderer will drive up to the gates. If he doesn't, that's good. Just sit there and wait for me. But if he does drive up, shoot him."

"Have you gone wacko, or what?" asked Zef, stopping dead. Maxim kept on walking and Zef ran after him, cursing and swearing. "They'll kill all of us, massaraksh! The guards! And cops all over the place!"

"Do the best you can," said Maxim. "Wanderer has to be shot."

They reached the garage. Maxim heaved on the bolt and rolled the door aside.

"This idea's totally insane," said Zef. "What for? Why Wanderer? He's a perfectly decent kind of guy, everyone here likes him."

"Suit yourself," Maxim said in a cold voice. He opened the trunk, felt for the primer and the timing mechanism through the oil-impregnated paper, and slammed the lid shut again. "I can't tell you anything right now. But we have a chance. Our one and only chance . . ." He got into the driver's seat and put the key in the ignition. "And don't forget this: if you don't whack this perfectly decent kind of guy, he'll whack me. You don't have very much time. Go to it, Zef."

He switched on the motor and backed out of the garage. Zef was left standing in the opening of the door. It was the first time in Maxim's life that he had ever seen Zef looking that way— frightened, stunned, at a loss. "Good-bye, Zef," he said to himself, just in case.

The car rolled up to the gates. The guardsman unhurriedly noted down the number, opened the trunk, glanced in, closed the trunk, went back to Maxim, and asked him, "What are you taking out?"

"A refractometer," said Maxim, holding out his pass and the permit to remove the equipment.

"Who signed the permit?"

"I don't know . . . Brainiac, probably."

"You don't know . . . If he'd signed it a bit more clearly, everything would be in order."

The guardsman finally opened the gates. Maxim drove out onto the highway and squeezed everything he could out of his set of wheels. If it doesn't come off, he thought, and I'm still alive, I'll have to run for it . . . That damned Wanderer, he sensed something, the son of a bitch, and came back.

But what am I going to do if it does come off? Nothing's ready, I don't have any plans of the palace—Egghead didn't get a chance to do anything, and he didn't get me any photos of the Fathers either . . . The guys aren't prepared, there isn't any plan of action . . . That damned Wanderer—if not for him, I'd have another three days to work out a plan . . . Probably I should do things in this order: the palace, the Fathers, the central telegraph office and telephone exchange, an urgent dispatch to the labor camps telling General to gather all our guys together and get the hell out of there . . . Massaraksh, I don't have a clue about how to seize power . . . And then there are still the Guards . . . and there's the army . . . and our HQ, damn it! They're the ones who'll immediately spring into action! I have to start with them. Well, that's Boar's job. He'll be glad to deal with it; he knows all about that side of things . . . And the white submarines are still hovering somewhere on the horizon . . . Massaraksh, that means another war!

He switched on the radio. Through the strains of a brisk march, a hoarse-voiced announcer was shouting: ". . . time and time again the infinite wisdom of the Unknown Fathers has been clearly demonstrated to the whole world—and on this occasion it is their military wisdom. It is as if the strategic genius of Gabellu

and the Iron Warrior had come back to life! As if the glorious
spirits of our invincible warrior ancestors had risen once again,
racing into the action to take their place at the head of our tank
columns! The Hontian provocateurs and fomenters of conflict
have suffered such a crushing defeat that henceforth they will
never again dare to poke their noses across our borders, never
again will they covet our sacred land! The woefully inept Hontian military launched a massive armada of many thousands of
bombers, rockets, and guided missiles at our cities, but here too
the victory went not to the strategy of brute force and predatory aggression but to the wise strategy of infinitely subtle cal-
culation and constant preparedness to repel the enemy. Yes, it
was to good purpose that we endured deprivations, contribut-
ing the final coppers in our pockets to the consolidation of our
defenses, to the creation of an impenetrable antiballistic shield!
'Our ADT system has no equals in the world,' retired field mar-
shal and recipient of two Golden Banners Iza Petrotsu declared
only six months ago. And you were right, old warrior! Not a
single bomb, not a single rocket, and not a single missile fell on
the sacred ground of the Land of the Fathers! 'The insuperable
network of steel towers is not only our indestructible shield, it
is a symbol of the genius and preternatural astuteness of those
to whom we owe everything—our Unknown Fathers,' writes
today's edition of—"

Maxim switched off the radio. Yes, the war seemed to be
over. But then, who could tell what else they were concocting
now . . . Maxim turned off the main street onto a narrow side
street between gigantic skyscrapers of pink stone, drove over the
cobblestones past a long line for a bread shop, and pulled up at
a dilapidated, blackened little house. Boar was already waiting,
smoking a cigarette and leaning back against a streetlamp. When
the car stopped, he flung his cigarette butt away, squeezed in
through the little door, and sat down beside Maxim.

He was as calm and cool as always. "Hello, Mak," he said.
"What's happened?"

Maxim turned the car around and drove back out onto the main street. "Do you know what a thermobaric bomb is?" he asked.

"I've heard about them," said Boar.

"Excellent."

For a while they drove in silence. The traffic was heavy and Maxim switched off, concentrating on how to cut in, work his way forward, and squeeze his way through between the immense trucks and old, stinking buses without scraping anybody or letting anybody scrape him so that he could catch the green light and then catch the next green light without sacrificing any of the pitiful speed that they already had, and eventually their car broke out onto Forest Boulevard, the familiar highway lined with huge, branching trees.

It's amusing, Maxim suddenly thought. I drove into this world along this very road—or, rather, poor old Fank drove me into it, and I didn't have a clue about anything, I thought he was a specialist in aliens. And now maybe I'm driving out of this world along the same road, and maybe even out of the world altogether, and I'm carrying a good man away with me . . . He squinted sideways at Boar. Boar's face was absolutely calm; he was sitting there with the elbow above his false hand sticking out of the window and waiting for when he would be given an explanation. Maybe he was surprised, maybe he was agitated, but it wasn't obvious, and Maxim felt proud that a man like this trusted him and relied on him without the slightest hesitation.

"I'm very grateful to you, Boar," he said.

"How's that?" Boar asked, turning his dry, yellowish face toward Maxim.

"Do you remember, at one of the HQ sessions you called me aside and gave me some sensible advice?"

"I remember."

"Well then. I'm grateful to you for that. I took your advice."

"Yes, so I noticed. You even disappointed me a bit by doing that."

"You were right back then," said Maxim. "I listened to your advice, and now as a result of that, things have turned out so that I have a chance to get into the Center."

Boar gave a sudden jolt. "Right now?" he quickly asked.

"Yes. I've got to hurry, I haven't had a chance to prepare anything. I might be killed, and then it will all have been in vain. That's why I've taken you with me."

"Tell me."

"I'll go into the building, you'll stay in the car. After a while the alarm will be raised, and maybe shooting will break out. But it shouldn't involve you. You keep sitting in the car and waiting. You wait for . . ." Maxim thought for a moment, calculating . . . "You wait for twenty minutes. If you get a jolt of radiation during that time, it means everything has worked out fine. You can pass out with a happy smile on your face . . . If not—get out of the car. There's a bomb in the trunk with a synchronous fuse set for ten minutes. Unload the bomb onto the road, activate the fuse, and drive away. There'll be a panic. A very great panic. Try to squeeze everything you can out of it."

Boar pondered for a while. "Will you just let me call a couple of places?" he asked.

"No," said Maxim.

"You see," said Boar. "If they don't kill you, then as I understand it, you're bound to need men who are ready for a fight. If they do kill you, then I'll need them. That's what you took me along for, in case they kill you . . . But on my own I can only make a start, and there won't be much time, and the men have to be warned in advance."

"HQ?" Maxim asked in a hostile tone.

"Absolutely not. I've got my own group."

Maxim didn't say anything. A five-story building with a stone wall running across its pediment was already rising up ahead of them. That building. Somewhere inside it Fish was wandering along the corridors and the infuriated Hippopotamus was yelling and sputtering. And the Center was in there. The circle was closing.

"All right," said Maxim. "There's a pay phone at the entrance. When I go inside—but not before—you can get out of the car and make your calls."

"OK," said Boar.

They were already approaching the turn off the highway. For some reason Maxim remembered Rada and imagined what would happen to her if he didn't come back. Things would be bad for her. Or maybe, on the contrary, they would let her go. But anyway, she'll be alone, with Gai gone, and me gone . . . The poor little girl . . .

"Do you have a family?" he asked Boar.

"Yes. A wife."

Maxim bit his lip. "I'm sorry things have turned out so awkward," he muttered.

"Never mind," Boar calmly said. "I said good-bye. I always say good-bye when I leave the house . . . So this is the Center, then? Who would ever have thought it? Everybody knows that the television center and the radio center are here, and now it turns out that *the* Center is here too . . ."

Maxim stopped in the parking lot, squeezing in between a dilapidated little old car and a luxurious government limousine.

"Well, this is it," he said. "Wish me luck."

"With all my heart," said Boar. His voice broke and he started coughing. "So I've lived to see this day after all," he murmured.

Maxim laid his cheek on the steering wheel. "It would be good to survive this day," he said. "It would be good to see the evening." Boar looked at him in alarm. "I really don't feel like going," Maxim explained. "Oh, I don't feel like it at all . . . By the way, Boar, don't forget to tell your friends that you don't live on the inner surface of a sphere. You live on the outer surface of a sphere. And there are many such spheres in existence on which people live far worse than you do, and some on which they live far better. But nowhere do they live more stupidly . . . You don't believe me? Well, to hell with you anyway. I'm going."

He swung open the door and clambered out. He walked across the asphalt surface of the parking lot and started walking up the stone steps, one step at a time, fingering in his pocket the entry pass that the prosecutor had had made for him. It was hot and the sky was shimmering like aluminum—the impenetrable sky of the inhabited island. The stone steps burned his feet through the soles of his shoes, or maybe he was just imagining it.

It was all stupid. The entire undertaking was amateurish. Why the hell should he do all of this when they hadn't had a chance to properly prepare . . . What if there are two officers sitting there instead just one? Or even three officers sitting there in that little room, waiting for me with their automatic rifles at the ready? Cornet Chachu shot me with a pistol, the caliber's the same, only there'll be more bullets, and I'm not the same man I used to be; it's really worn me down, this inhabited island of mine. And this time they won't just let me just creep away . . . I'm a fool. I always was a fool and I still am. Mr. State Prosecutor snared me, hooked me on his rod . . . But how could he have trusted me? It doesn't make any sense . . . It would be good to slope off and head for the mountains right now, breathe some pure mountain air—I've never had a chance to visit the mountains here . . . And I really love mountains . . . Such a clever, distrustful man—and he trusted me with such a valuable thing! The greatest treasure of this world. This abominable, repulsive, iniquitous treasure! Curse and confound it, massaraksh, and three more massarakshes, and another thirty-three massarakshes!

He opened the glass door and held out his pass to the guardsman. Then he walked across the vestibule—past the girl in glasses, who was still stamping pieces of paper, past the administrator in the peaked cap, who was bawling somebody out on the phone—and at the entrance to the corridor he showed his internal pass to another guardsman. The guardsman nodded to him—they were already acquainted, you could say: Maxim had come here every day for the last three days.

Onward.

He walked down a long corridor without any doors and turned left. This was only the second time he had been here. The first time had been the day before yesterday, by mistake. ("Where is it that you are actually trying to get to, sir?" "I'm actually trying to get to room number sixteen, Corporal." "You've taken a wrong turn, sir. You need the next corridor." "Sorry, Corporal, I beg your pardon. Yes, indeed . . .")

He handed the corporal his internal pass and squinted at the two beefy guardsmen with automatic rifles standing motionless at each side of the door facing him. Then he glanced at the door that he was about to enter: SPECIAL TRANSPORTATION DIVISION. The corporal carefully examined the pass and then, still examining it, pressed a button in the wall, and a bell rang on the other side of the door. Now he had readied himself, that officer who was sitting in there beside the green curtain. Or two officers had readied themselves. Or maybe even three officers . . . They're waiting for me to walk in, and if I panic at the sight of them and dart back out, I'll be met by the corporal, and the guardsmen guarding the door without a plaque on it, which no doubt has a whole pack of soldiers lurking behind it.

The corporal handed back his pass and said, "Please go through. Have your credentials ready."

Taking out a piece of pink cardboard, Maxim opened the door and stepped into the room.

Massaraksh. Just as he had feared.

Not one room. Three. An enfilade. And at the end—the green curtain. And a carpet runner stretching from under his feet all the way to the curtain. At least thirty yards.

And not two officers. Not even three. Six.

Two in army gray—in the first room. They had already aimed their automatics.

Two in guardsmen's black—in the second room. They hadn't aimed yet, but they were also ready.

Two in civilian clothes—one at each side of the green curtain in the third room. They had their heads turned and were looking off to one side.

Right then, Mak!

He went hurtling forward. It was something like a hop, skip, and jump from a standing start. He just managed to think, I'd better not rupture any tendons. The air firmly struck him in the face.

The green curtain. The civilian on the left was looking off to the side, his neck was exposed. A blow with the edge of the hand.

The civilian on the right was probably blinking. His eyelids were motionless, half-lowered. A blow up across the sinciput— and straight into the elevator.

It was dark in the elevator. Where's the button? Massaraksh, where's the button?

An automatic rifle started stuttering slowly and sonorously, and immediately a second one started up. Well now, excellent reactions. . . . But they're still firing at the door, at the place where they saw me. They still haven't realized what happened. It's merely a reflex response.

The button!

A shadow slowly crept across the curtains, moving diagonally downward—one of the civilians was falling

Massaraksh, there it is—in the most obvious place.

He pressed the button and the cabin started moving downward. It was a high-speed elevator and the cabin crept down quite fast. But then, that wasn't important now . . . Massaraksh, I've broken through!

The cabin stopped. Maxim darted out and rumbling and clanging immediately erupted in the elevator shaft, and chips of wood started flying. They were firing at the roof of the cabin from above with three barrels. OK, OK, fire away . . . Now they'll realize that they don't need to shoot, they need to get the elevator back up and come down themselves . . . They missed their chance, got flummoxed.

He looked around. Massaraksh, stymied again. Not one entrance but three. Three absolutely identical tunnels . . . Ah, but they're simply duplicate generators. One's working, the others are on preventive maintenance. Which one of them is working now? I think it's that one . . .

He dashed toward the middle tunnel. Behind his back the elevator started growling. Oh, no, too late already . . . Too slow, you won't get here in time . . . although, I must say, this is a long tunnel, and my foot hurts . . . Now here's a turn, and now there's no way you can get me . . .

He ran up to the generators, rumbling on a deep bass note under a steel slab, stopped, and rested for a few seconds with his arms lowered. Right, three-quarters of the job is already done. Even seven-eighths . . . What's left is a mere trifle, no more than a half of one thirty-fourth . . . now they'll come down in the elevator and plunge straight into the tunnel, about which they definitely know damn all, and the depressive radiation will drive them back out again . . . What else can happen? They could fling a gas grenade along the corridor. Not likely—where would they get them from? They've probably already raised the alarm.

The Fathers could have switched off the depressive barrier, of course . . . Oh, they wouldn't decide to do that, and they won't have time, because the five of them need to get together, with five keys, come to an agreement, figure out whether this is a stunt by one of them, a provocation . . . And really, who in the world can break his way in here through the radiation barrier? Wanderer, if he has secretly invented a protective device? He would be detained by the six men with automatics . . . There isn't anybody else . . . All right, while they squabble, look for answers, and try to figure things out, I'll get the job finished . . .

Around the corner in the tunnel automatics yammered into the darkness. That's permitted. I don't object . . . He leaned down over the distribution device, carefully removed the cover, and flung it into a corner. Mm-hmm, an extremely primitive little item. It's a good thing I thought of reading up a bit on their electronics here . . . He lowered a finger into the circuit assembly . . . What if I hadn't thought of doing that? And what if Wanderer had come back the day before yesterday? Mm-hmm, gentlemen . . . Massaraksh, that current is really intense . . . Yes, gentlemen, I would have found myself in the position of an embryomechanic who has to urgently figure out . . . I don't even know what . . . a steam boiler? An embryomechanic would have figured that out. A camel harness? Yes, a camel harness. Eh? OK then, embryomechanic, would you have figured it out? I don't think it's very likely . . .

Massaraksh, why don't they have any insulation on anything? Ah, so that's where you are . . . Right, go with God, as Mr. State Prosecutor says!

He sat down right there on the floor and wiped his forehead with the back of his hand. The job was done. An immensely powerful field of depressive radiation had descended on the entire country—from south of the Blue Serpent all the way to the Hontian border, from the ocean all the way to the Alabaster Mountain Range.

The automatics around the corner have stopped firing. The gentlemen officers are feeling depressed. Now I'll take a look at what that's like: gentlemen officers in a depressed state.

For the first time in his life the state prosecutor is delighted to feel a burst of radiation.

The Unknown Fathers, who haven't yet managed to figure things out and understand what's happening, are writhing in pain, with their toes turned up, as Cornet Chachu used to say. And Cornet Chachu, by the way, is also in a state of deep depression, and the thought of that delights me.

Zef and the guys are also lying stretched out with their toes turned up. Sorry, guys, but it's necessary.

And Wanderer! Now, isn't that great? The terrible Wanderer is also lying there with his toes turned up, and his huge ears spread out across the floor—the hugest ears in the whole country. Or maybe he has already been shot. That would be even better.

Rada, my poor little Rada is lying in a fit of depression. Never mind, little girl, it probably isn't painful, and it will all be over and done with soon . . .

Boar . . .

He jumped up. How much time had gone by? He went dashing back through the tunnel. Boar must also be lying with his toes turned up, but if he had heard the shooting, his nerves might have given way . . . Of course, that was highly doubtful—what nerves did Boar have?

He ran up to the elevator, pausing for a moment to glance at the gentlemen officers in their depressed state. It was a painful sight: all three of them had dropped their rifles and were weeping—they didn't even have the strength to wipe away their tears and snot. Fine, weep a bit, it's good for you. Weep over my Gai, weep over Bird . . . over Gel . . . over my Forester . . . I guess you haven't wept since you were kids, and in any case you never wept over the people you killed. So weep a little bit at least before you die . . .

The elevator shot him up to the surface. The enfilade of rooms was full of people: officers, soldiers, corporals, guardsmen, civilians, all of them armed, all lying or sitting there lamenting, some wailing at the top of their lungs, some muttering, shaking their heads, and hammering one fist against their chests . . . and this one here had shot himself. Massaraksh, what a terrible thing it is, this Black Radiation, no wonder the Fathers were saving it for a rainy day.

He ran out into the vestibule, leaping over the feebly stirring people, almost flying head over heels down the stone steps, and stopped in front of his own car, relieved to be able to catch his breath. Boar's nerves had held out. He was slumped in the front passenger seat with his eyes closed.

Maxim lugged the bomb out of the trunk, freed it from the oil-impregnated paper, carefully set it under his arm, and went back to the elevator without hurrying. He thoroughly examined the fuse, activated the timer, placed the bomb in the elevator cabin, and pressed the button. The cabin fell down and away, carrying with it a lake of fire that would be unleashed in ten minutes—or, rather, nine minutes and a number of seconds.

He ran back.

In the car he sat Boar up more or less straight, got in behind the wheel, and drove out of the parking lot. The gray building towered up over them, oppressive, grotesque, and doomed, chock full of doomed people incapable of moving or of understanding what was happening.

It was a nest, a hideous nest of vipers packed with the very choicest garbage, deliberately and thoughtfully selected garbage, and this garbage had been collected together here especially in order to transform into garbage everybody who was within reach of the hideous sorcery of radio, television, and radiation from the towers. All of them in there are enemies, and none of them would pause for even a second before riddling us with bullets, before betraying and crucifying me, Boar, Zef, Rada, and all my friends and dear ones.

And it's a good thing that I've only just remembered this now; any earlier that thought would have been a hindrance to me. I would immediately have remembered Fish . . . The only human being in the doomed nest of vipers, and that human being happens to be a Fish. But what about Fish? he thought. What do I actually know about her? That she taught me to speak their language? And made up my bed after me? Come on now, leave Fish out of it, you know perfectly well that it's not just a matter of Fish.

The point is that as of today you're coming out to fight seriously, to the death, the way everybody else here fights, and you'll have to fight against blockheads—against malicious blockheads, who have been reduced to dummies by the radiation; against cunning, ignorant, ravenous blockheads who directed that radiation; against benevolently motivated blockheads who would be glad to use the radiation to transform rabid, brutalized puppets into amiable, quasi-benign puppets . . . And they will all do their best to kill you, and your friends, and your cause, because—and remember this very well, master this lesson now for the rest of your life!—because in this world they don't know any other way to change the opinion of those who don't share their views.

The Sorcerer said, *Do not let your conscience prevent you from thinking clearly; let reason learn to stifle your conscience when it is necessary.* That's right, thought Maxim. The truth of it is bitter, a terrible truth . . . They call what I have just done a heroic deed. Boar has lived to see this day. And Forester, Bird, Green, and Gel Ketshef all believed in this day like a heartwarming fairy tale, and so did my Gai, and hundreds and thousands of people whom I have never seen . . . But even so, I feel bad about it. And if I want people to trust me in the future, I must never tell anyone that the greatest feat of courage I performed wasn't when I cavorted about under a hail of bullets but right now, when there is still enough time to go back and defuse the bomb but I'm driving this car as hard as I can push it, away from that cursed place . . .

He drove hard along the straight highway, the same road along which Fank had driven him six months earlier in his luxurious limousine, trying to overtake the endless column of armored trucks, hurtling along the road in order to hand Maxim over to Wanderer . . . and now it was clear why . . . Could he really have already known that the radiation didn't affect me, that I didn't understand anything and I could be turned and twisted any way at all? He must have known, that damned Wanderer did know. And that means he really is a devil, the most terrifying man in the country, and maybe on the planet.

"He knows everything," the state prosecutor told me, fearfully glancing back over his shoulder . . . But no, not everything—you have outsmarted Wanderer, Mak, you have beaten the devil. And now you have to finish him off before it's too late, before he has time to bounce back. Or maybe he has already been finished off—right in front of the gates of his own lair . . . Oh, I don't believe it, I don't believe it, the guys aren't up to that job. Blister had twenty-four relatives with machine guns . . .

Massaraksh. It's true that I don't know how revolutions are made. I didn't make any preparations for seizing the telegraph office, the telephone exchange, and the bridges right at the very outset, I have hardly any men at all, the rank-and-file underground

members don't know me, Central HQ will be against me . . . I
didn't even manage to inform General in the penal labor camp
to get ready to rouse the political prisoners and shoot them up
here on a special train. But no matter what happens there, I have
to finish Wanderer off. I have to be able to finish Wanderer off
and hold out for a few hours until the army and the Guards are
knocked out by radiation deprivation. None of them know about
radiation deprivation, do they? Even Wanderer probably doesn't
know—how could he know? After all, in the entire country, Gai
is the only one who has ever been removed from the radiation
field—by me.

There were lots of cars on the highway, all of them standing
in chaotic disarray—across the roadway, at a slant, slumped over
into the roadside ditches. The drivers and passengers, crushed
by depression, were sitting, dolefully lamenting, on the running
boards, helplessly slouching off the seats, and lying around at
the edge of the road. All of this was a hindrance; Maxim constantly had to brake, doubling back and driving around blockages, and he didn't immediately notice that moving toward him
from the direction of the city, also doubling back and driving
around blockages, was a low, flat, bright yellow government
automobile.

They met on a relatively clear section of the highway and shot
past each other, almost colliding, and Maxim had time to spot a
naked cranium, round green eyes, and immense, protruding ears.
He cringed bodily, because suddenly everything had gone down
the tubes again . . . Wanderer! Massaraksh! The entire country is
lying around in a state of depression, and that bastard, that devil,
has wormed his way out of things again! So he did invent his
protective device after all . . . And I don't have a gun . . .

Maxim looked in the mirror: the long yellow car was turning
around. Well then, I'll have to get by without a gun. At least this is
something that my conscience won't torment me about . . . Maxim
stepped on the accelerator. Speed, speed . . . come on, come on,
sweetheart, more . . . The flat yellow hood was moving closer,

growing larger, Maxim could already see the intent green eyes above the steering wheel . . . Right, Mak!

Maxim splayed out his legs to brace himself, barricaded Boar in place with one arm, and stamped down on the brake with all his strength.

With an ear-shredding howling and squealing of brakes, the yellow hood smashed into Maxim's trunk, grinding and crunching, crumpling up into a concertina and standing up on end. Glass showered everywhere. Maxim kicked open the door and tumbled out of his car. The pain was terrible—there was pain in his heel, pain in his smashed knee, pain in his skinned arm—but an instant later he forgot about it, because Wanderer was already standing there in front of him. It was impossible, but it was true. A long, lean devil, with his hand menacingly drawn back to strike . . .

Maxim flung himself at Wanderer, putting everything he had left into that leap. He missed! And then there was a terrible blow to the back of his head . . . The world tilted over and Maxim almost fell, but he didn't after all, and then Wanderer was back in front of him again, with his naked cranium, intent green eyes, and hand drawn back to strike . . . Stop, stop, he's going to miss . . . Aha! . . . What's he looking at? . . . Come on, you can't fool us like that . . . With his face frozen still, Wanderer was staring over Maxim's head; Maxim pounced again and this time he hit the target. The long, black man doubled over and slowly collapsed onto the asphalt. Then Maxim looked around.

The gray cube of the Center was clearly visible from here, but it was no longer a cube. It was caving in as he watched, heaving up and collapsing into itself; a trembling haze of sultry air, steam, and smoke was rising up from it, and something blindingly white, hot even at this distance, was peeping out in appalling merriment through the long vertical cracks and the window holes . . . OK, so everything's in order there.

Maxim triumphantly turned back to Wanderer. The devil was lying on his side, clutching his stomach in his long arms, and his eyes were closed. Maxim cautiously moved a little bit closer.

Boar stuck his head out of the crumpled little car. He wriggled and squirmed around as he tried to clamber out. Maxim stopped beside Wanderer and leaned down, trying to figure out how to strike to instantly finish this. Massaraksh, his damned hand refused to strike at a man on the ground . . .

And then Wanderer half-opened his eyes and said in a hoarse voice, *"Dummkopf! Rotznase!"*

Maxim didn't immediately understand him, and when he did, his legs almost buckled underneath him.

Fool . . .

Snot-nose . . .

Fool . . .

Snot-nose . . .

Then he heard Boar's voice speak out of the gray, echoing void, "Just move away, Mak, I've got a pistol."

Without even looking, Maxim grabbed hold of his hand.

Wanderer sat up with a struggle, still clutching his stomach. "Snot-nosed kid . . ." he hissed, straining to speak. "Don't just stand there stock-still . . . go find a car . . . move it, move it. Don't just stand there like that, look around!"

Maxim obtusely looked around. The highway was coming to life. There was no more Center, it had been transformed into a puddle of molten metal, into steam and stench, the towers weren't working any longer, the puppets had ceased to be puppets. As they came to, dumbfounded people were sullenly gazing around, shuffling their feet beside their cars, trying to figure out what had happened to them, how they had ended up here, and what to do next.

"Who are you?" asked Wild Boar.

"None of your business," Wanderer replied in German. He was in pain, groaning and gasping for breath.

"I don't understand," said Boar, raising the barrel of his pistol.

"Kammerer . . ." Wanderer exclaimed. "Shut your terrorist's mouth . . . and go find a car . . ."

"What car?" Maxim dim-wittedly asked.

"Massaraksh . . ." Wanderer croaked. He raggedly struggled to his feet, still hunching over and pressing his hand against his stomach, staggered over to Maxim's little car, and climbed inside.

"Get in . . . quickly . . ." he said from behind the steering wheel. Then he glanced back over his shoulder at the pillar of smoke illuminated by flames. "What did you plant in there?" he asked in a despairing voice.

"A thermobaric bomb."

"In the basement or in the vestibule?"

"In the basement," Maxim said.

Wanderer groaned and sat there for a moment with his head thrown back, then switched on the engine. The car gave a shudder and started rattling. "Get in will you, at last!" he yelled.

"Who are you," asked Boar. "A Hontian?"

Maxim shook his head, tore open the door that was jammed shut, and told him, "Climb in."

He himself walked around the car and got in beside Wanderer. The car jerked, and something inside it started squealing and crunching, but it was already rolling down the highway, grotesquely wobbling along, jangling its doors that wouldn't close properly and loudly backfiring.

"What are you intending to do now?" Wanderer asked.

"Wait . . ." Maxim asked him. "At least tell me who you are."

"I work as a Galactic Security agent," Wanderer said in a bitter voice. "I've been here for five years. We're working on trying to save this unfortunate planet. Painstakingly, taking into account all the possible consequences. All of them, do you understand? And who are you? Who the hell are you to go meddling in somebody else's business, ruining all our calculations, blowing things up, shooting—who the hell are you?"

"I didn't know," Maxim said in a crestfallen voice. "How could I have known?"

"Yes, of course you didn't know. But you did know that independent interference is forbidden—you're an employee of the FSG . . . You ought to have known . . . Back on Earth his mother's going insane over him . . . Some girls or other keep calling all the time . . . His father's abandoned his job . . . What were you intending to do next?"

"I was intending to shoot you," said Maxim.

"*Whaaat?*" The car swerved.

"Yes," Maxim humbly said. "And what was I supposed to do? I was told that you were the head villain here, and . . ."—he chuckled—". . . and it wasn't hard to believe it."

Wanderer dubiously squinted at him with a round, green eye. "Well, OK. And what then?"

"Then the revolution was supposed to start."

"And why should it?"

"But the Center is destroyed, isn't it? There's no more radiation."

"So what?"

"Now they'll immediately realize that they're being oppressed, that their life is wretched, and they'll rise up—"

"Where will they rise up to?" Wanderer sadly asked. "Who will rise up? The Unknown Fathers are still alive, and thriving, the Guards are alive and well, the army is mobilized, the country is on a war footing . . . What exactly did you calculate would happen?"

Maxim lowered his head. Of course, he could have told this sad monster about his plans, his intentions for the future and the rest of it, but what was the point, since nothing was ready, since things had turned out like this . . .

"They'll do their own calculating." He pointed over his shoulder at Boar. "Let this man do the calculating, for instance . . . My job was to give them a chance to calculate a few things for themselves."

"Your job . . ." Wanderer sputtered. "Your job was to sit in a corner and wait for me to catch you."

"Yes, probably," said Maxim. "Next time I'll bear that in mind."

"You're going straight back to Earth today," Wanderer harshly said.

"I'll see you burn first!" Maxim protested.

"You're going straight back to Earth today," Wanderer repeated, raising his voice. "I've got enough trouble on this planet without you. Collect your Rada and be on your way."

"You have Rada?" Maxim eagerly asked.

"Yes, she's been with me for a long time. Alive and well, don't worry."

"For Rada—thank you," said Maxim. "Thank you very much."

The car drove into the city. On the main street a monstrous traffic jam was honking and pouring out smoky fumes. Wanderer turned onto a side street and started driving though the slums. Everything here was dead. Military policemen jutted up like columns on the corners, their hands clasped behind their backs, their faces surmounted by battle helmets. Yes, they had rapidly responded to events. A general alarm and everyone was at their posts. As soon as they recovered from the depression. Maybe I shouldn't have blown everything up immediately— maybe I ought to have followed the prosecutor's plan? No, no, massaraksh, let everything go on just as it is now. I don't want to hear his pointless rebukes. Let them figure out what's what for themselves—they're sure to figure things out, after all, just as soon as their heads clear . . .

Wanderer turned back out onto the main highway. Boar delicately slapped him on the shoulder with the barrel of his pistol. "If you don't mind, let me out here. Right over there, where the men are standing . . ."

The men were standing beside a newspaper kiosk, with their hands thrust deep into the pockets of their gray raincoats—about five of them—but apart from them there was nobody out on the sidewalks; the local residents had obviously been badly frightened by the depressive radiation strike and had all hidden away in various places.

"And what do you intend to do?" Wanderer asked, slowing down.

"Breathe a bit of fresh air," Boar replied. "The weather's really glorious today."

"He's one of ours," Maxim told him. "You can say anything in front of him."

The car halted at the roadside. The men in raincoats went behind the kiosk, and Maxim could see them peeping out from there.

"One of ours?" asked Boar. "Who are they, ours?"

At a loss, Maxim looked at Wanderer. Wanderer had no intention of trying to help him out.

"Anyway, OK," said Boar. "I trust you. We're going to deal with HQ now. I think HQ is the right place to start. There are people there—you know who I'm talking about—who need to be gotten out of the way, before they can put a halter on the movement."

"Good thinking," Wanderer suddenly growled. "And by the way, I think I recognize you. You are Tik Fesku, otherwise known as Wild Boar. Is that right?"

"Exactly right," Boar politely said. Then he told Maxim, "And you deal with the Fathers. It's a difficult job, but it's just right for you. Where can I find you?"

"Wait, Boar," said Maxim. "I almost forgot. In a few hours the whole country will collapse for days from radiation deprivation. Everybody will be absolutely helpless."

"Everybody?" Boar doubtfully asked.

"Everybody except the degenerates. We need to make good use of that period of several days."

Boar thought and raised his eyebrows. "Well now, that's excellent," he said. "If it's true . . . As it happens, it's degenerates that we'll be dealing with. But I'll bear it in mind. So where can I find you?"

Before Maxim could reply, Wanderer spoke for him. "At the same phone number," he said. "And the same place. And I'll tell you this. Set up your committee, since that's how things have worked out. Reestablish the same organization that you had

under the empire. Some of your people work for me in the institute . . . Massaraksh!" he suddenly hissed. "We have no time, and
none of the people we need are close at hand . . . Damn you to
hell, Mak!"

"The most important thing," said Boar, setting his hand on
Maxim's shoulder, "is that there isn't any more Center. Well
done, Mak. Thank you . . ." He squeezed Maxim's shoulder and
awkwardly clambered out of the car, grappling with his artificial hand. Then suddenly his feelings broke through. "Lord," he
exclaimed, standing beside the car with his eyes closed, "is it really
and truly gone? That's . . . it's . . ."

"Close the door," said Wanderer. "Harder, harder . . ."

The car sped away. Maxim looked back. Boar was standing in
the middle of the small group of men in gray raincoats and saying
something, waving his good arm around. The men were standing
there without moving. They still hadn't understood what had
happened. Or they didn't believe it.

The street was empty. Armored personnel transports carrying
guardsmen came trundling toward them along the edges of the
sidewalks, and far up ahead, where the turn for the department
was, trucks were already parked across the road and little figures
in black were running across it. And suddenly a sickeningly familiar orange-yellow patrol vehicle with a long telescopic antenna
appeared in the column of personnel transports.

"Massaraksh," Maxim murmured. "I completely forgot about
those gizmos!"

"You forgot about lots of things," Wanderer growled. "You
forgot about the mobile radiation emitters, you forgot about the
Island Empire, you forgot about the economy . . . Are you aware
that there is inflation in this country? Do you even have any idea
what inflation is? Are you aware that famine is imminent, that
the land is infertile? Are you aware that we have not had time to
establish reserves of bread or reserves of medical supplies here
yet? Do you know that in twenty percent of cases this radiation
deprivation of yours leads to schizophrenia? Huh?"

He wiped his mighty forehead with the receding hair at the temples. "We need doctors . . . twelve thousand doctors. We need protein synthesizers. We need to decontaminate a hundred million hectares of polluted soil—just for a start. We need to halt the degeneration of the biosphere . . . Massaraksh, we need at least one earthman on the Islands, in that black-guard's admiralty . . . Nobody can stay in place there—none of our men can even get back and tell us for certain what's going on there . . ."

Maxim didn't say anything. They reached the vehicles blocking the way through, and a dark-faced, stocky officer, waving his arm in a strangely familiar manner, walked up to them and demanded their documents in a croaking voice. Wanderer angrily and impatiently thrust a glittering ID card under his nose. The officer morosely saluted and glanced at Maxim. It was Mr. Cornet—no, now already Mr. Brigadier of Guards Chachu. His eyes opened wide. "Is this man with you, Your Excellency?" he asked.

"Yes. Order them to let me through immediately."

"I beg your pardon, Your Excellency, but this man—"

"Let me through immediately," Wanderer barked.

Brigadier Chachu sullenly saluted, swung around, and waved to the soldiers. One of the trucks moved aside and Wanderer hurled the car into the gap that opened up.

"That's the way it is," he said. "They're ready; they were always ready. And you thought it was all *Abracadabra* and it's done. Shoot Wanderer, hang the Fathers, disband the cowards and fascists at your HQ, and the revolution will be over."

"I never thought that," said Maxim. He was feeling very miserable, crushed, helpless, and hopelessly stupid.

Wanderer squinted at him and gave a crooked grin. "Well, all right, all right," he said. "I'm just angry. Not with you—with myself. I answer for everything that happens here, and it's my fault that things have turned out this way. I simply couldn't keep up with you." He grinned again. "You guys in the FSG are quick on your feet."

"No," said Maxim, "don't torment yourself like that. I'm not tormenting myself—I'm sorry, what's your name?"

"Call me Rudolf."

"Yes . . . I'm not tormenting myself, Rudolf. And I don't intend to. I intend to work. And make a revolution."

"You'd better intend to go home," said Wanderer.

"I am home," Maxim impatiently said. "Let's not talk about that any more . . . I'm interested in the mobile radiation emitters. What can be done about them?"

"Nothing has to be done about them," Wanderer replied. "You'd do better to think about what can be done about inflation."

"I'm asking about the radiation emitters," said Maxim.

Wanderer sighed. "They work on batteries," he said. "And they can only be recharged at my institute. In three days' time they'll croak . . . But in a month's time an invasion is due to begin. Usually we manage to throw the submarines off course so that only a few of them reach the coast. But this time they're assembling an armada . . . I was counting on the depressive radiation, but now we'll simply have to sink them . . ." He paused for a moment. "So you're at home, are you? Well, let's suppose you are . . . Then what precisely do you intend to do now?"

They were already approaching the department. The heavy gates were tightly closed, and there were black gun ports that Maxim had never seen before in the stone wall. The department had become like a fortress, ready for battle. But three men were standing in front of the pavilion, and Zef's ginger beard blazed as brightly as an exotic flower among the greenery.

"I don't know," said Maxim. "I'm going to do what well-informed people tell me to do. If I have to, I'll deal with inflation. If I have to, I'll sink submarines . . . But I know my most important task now: as long as I'm alive, nobody will ever be able to build another Center. Not even with the very best intentions in the world."

Wanderer didn't say anything to that. The gates were very close now. Zef scrambled through the hedge and walked out into the road. His automatic rifle was hanging behind his shoulder, and it was obvious from a distance that he was angry, and now he would start cursing and demanding explanations for why, massaraksh, they had dragged him away from his work, filled his head with all sorts of nonsense about Wanderer, and left him hanging around here among the flowers for more than an hour like a little kid.

AFTERWORD

BY BORIS STRUGATSKY

It is known with absolute certainty when this novel was conceived—on June 12, 1967, the following entry appeared in our work journal: "We need to compose a proposal for an optimistic story about [first] contact." And immediately thereafter:

> We have composed the proposal. The story *The Inhabited Island*. The plot: Ivanov crash-lands. The situation. Capitalism. Oligarchy. Control via psychowaves. Sciences only utilitarian. No progress. The machine is controlled by votaries. A means of ideal propaganda has just been discovered. Unstable equilibrium. Infighting in the government. The people are pulled from one side to the other, depending on who can reach the button. The psychology of tyranny: What does a tyrant want? It's not push-button power; what's wanted is sincerity, great deeds. There is a percentage of the population on whom the rays have no effect. Some of them eagerly strive to join the oligarchs (the oligarchs are also not susceptible). Some of them flee to the underground to avoid elimination as recalcitrant material.

Some of them are revolutionaries like the Decembrists and the Narodnik populists. Following trials and tribulations Ivanov finds himself in the underground.

It is curious that this emphatically cheerful entry is situated precisely between two profoundly somber ones—06/12/67: "B. has arrived in Moscow in connection with the rejection of ToT by Detgiz"; and 06/13/67: "Offensive snub at Young Guard with ToT."* This double blow stunned us, uncoupling us from reality for a while. We were left, so to speak, in a state of "artistic punch-drunkenness."

I remember very clearly how, discouraged and angry, we said to each other, "Ah, you don't want satire? You don't need Saltykov-Shchedrins any longer? Contemporary problems no longer perturb you? *Aaall right!* You'll get an empty-headed, harebrained, absolutely toothless, entertaining novel about the adventures of spunky kid, a twenty-second-century Young Communist . . ." We humorous lads seemingly intended to punish someone among the holders of power for rejecting the serious themes and problems we were offering. Punish Comrade Farfurkis with a frivolous novel! Laughable. It is laughable and a little embarrassing to remember it now. But at that time, in the summer and autumn of 1967, when all the editorial offices who were friendliest to us had, one after another, rejected *Tale of the Troika* and *Ugly Swans*, we failed to see anything amusing in what was happening.

We set about *The Inhabited Island* without enthusiasm, but very soon the work enthralled us. It turned to be a damned thrilling occupation—writing a toothless, strictly entertaining novel! Especially since quite soon it stopped seeming so very toothless to us. The radiation towers, and the degenerates, and the Battle Guards—everything fell into place like cartridges slipping into the

---

* Translator's Note: "B." is Boris Strugatsky; "ToT" is the Strugatsky novel *Tale of the Troika*. "Detgiz" is Detskoe Gosudarstvennoe Izdatelstvo, the State Publishing House for Children's Literature, and Young Guard is Molodaya Gvardiya, another Russian publishing house.

magazine, everything found its prototype in our adorable reality, everything proved to be a vehicle for a subtext. Moreover, it happened quite regardless of our will, seemingly of its own accord, like the multicolored candy crumbs in some magical kaleidoscope that transforms chaos and a random mishmash into an elegant, coherent, and entirely symmetrical little picture.

It was splendid, inventing a new, fantastic world—and it was even more splendid endowing it with highly familiar attributes and various realia. I'm looking through the work journal at the moment: November 1967, the Komarovo Writers' House, we only worked during the day, but how we worked: seven, ten, eleven(!) pages a day. Not fair copy, of course, but draft text, created and extracted out of nothing, out of oblivion! At that rate we finished the draft in only two passes, 296 pages in thirty-two working days. The clean copy was written even faster, twelve to sixteen pages a day, and in May the completed manuscript was taken off to Detgiz in Moscow and, almost simultaneously, to the Leningrad journal *Neva*.

Thus the novel (an unprecedentedly thick Strugatsky novel for that time) was written in a period of six months. Its entire subsequent history is an agonizing story of polishing, smoothing out, ideologically deburring, adapting, and adjusting the text to conform to the various and often absolutely unpredictable demands of the Great and Mighty Censoring Machine.

"What is a telegraph pole? It's a well-edited pine tree." They failed to reduce *The Inhabited Island* to the condition of a pole—in fact the pine tree remained a pine tree, despite all the ingenious efforts of the delimbers in plainclothes—but nonetheless a more than ample hash was made of things, with even more authorial blood set boiling and authorial nerves frayed. And this grueling struggle for definitive and irreproachable ideological decontamination went on for very nearly a year.

Two factors played an absolutely essential role in this battle. First, we (and the novel) were damn lucky with our editors—both at Detgiz and at *Neva*. At Detgiz the novel was handled by Nina Matveevna

Berkova, an old friend and defender of ours, a highly experienced editor who had been through hell and high water, who knew the theory and practice of Soviet literature from A to Z, who never gave way to despair, who knew how to retreat and was always ready to advance. And in *Neva* we were overseen by Samuil Aronovich Lurie, a supremely subtle stylist and natural-born literary scholar, as intelligent and vitriolic as the devil, a connoisseur of the psychology of Soviet ideological bosses in general and the psychology of A. F. Popov, the editor-in-chief of *Neva* at the time, in particular. If not for the efforts of these friends who were our editors, the fate of the novel could have been different—it would either not have appeared at all or would have been so badly mutilated as to be unrecognizable.

Second, the general political context of that time. It was 1968, "the year of Czechoslovakia," when the Czech Gorbachevs were desperately attempting to prove to the Soviet monsters that "socialism with a human face" was possible and even inevitable. At times it seemed that they were pulling it off, that at any moment the Stalinists would retreat and give way. No one knew what would happen in a month's time—whether freedom would triumph, as in Prague, or whether everything would finally come full circle, back to remorseless ideological glaciation, perhaps even to the total triumph of the proponents of the GULAG.

With one accord the liberal intelligentsia expressed their opposition, all eagerly trying to convince each other (in their kitchens) that Dubček was certain to win, because it was impossible to strike down the ideological rebellion by force—that would be against the mood of the times, this wasn't Hungary in 1956, and all these Brezhnev-Suslovs were too spineless, they didn't have the good old Stalinist tempering, they didn't have enough fire in their bellies, and the army these days wasn't what it used to be. "Yes it is, our army's still what it used to be," the cleverest of us objected. "And their bellies have enough fire in them, don't you worry. You can be sure the Brezhnev-Suslovs won't flinch, and they'll *never* give way to any Dubčeks, because it's a matter of the Brezhnevs' own survival."

And there was deadly silence from those few individuals who generally could not be directly contacted, who already knew in May that the matter had been decided. And, of course, nothing was said by those who didn't know anything for certain but sensed it, sensed it with their very skin: everything will be as it should be, everything will be the way it's supposed to be, everything will be the way it always has been—the midlevel bosses, naturally including the junior officers of the ideological army, and the editors-in-chief of journals, the handlers of the Party's regional committees and city committees, the staff of Glavlit* . . .

The scales were wavering in the balance. No one wanted to make the final decisions; everyone was waiting to see which way the drawbar of history would turn. Those in positions of responsibility tried not to read any manuscripts at all, and when they did, they put forward mind-boggling demands to authors, and when those had been taken into account, they put forward others, even more mind-boggling.

In *Neva* they demanded that we: shorten it; take out words such as "homeland," "patriot" and "fatherland"; it wasn't permissible for Mak to have forgotten what Hitler was called; clarify the role of Wanderer; emphasize the presence of social inequality in the Land of the Fathers; replace the Galactic Security Commission with a different term, with different initials† . . .

At Detgiz (to begin with) they demanded that we: shorten it; take out the naturalism in the description of war; clarify the role of Wanderer; obfuscate the social order of the Land of the Fathers; emphatically exclude the very concept of "Guards" (replace it, say, with "Legion"); emphatically alter the very

---

* TRANSLATOR'S NOTE: "Glavlit" is short for Glavnoe Upravlenie po Delam Literatury i Izdatelstv (the Central Directorate for Literary and Publishing Matters), the original name of the main Soviet censorship body. Though the organization was renamed several times, it was still commonly known as Glavlit.

† TRANSLATOR'S NOTE: In Russian, "Galactic Security Commission" is "Komissiya Galakticheskoy Bezopasnosti," or KGB.

concept of "Unknown Fathers"; remove terms such as "social democrats," "communists," etc.

However, as Vladimir Vysotsky sang in those years, "but that was just for starters." The full implications were waiting for us up ahead.

In early 1969 the serial version of the novel appeared in *Neva*. Despite the general toughening up of the ideological climate as a consequence of the Czechoslovak "disgrace," despite the sacred horror that had seized the obsequiously and fearfully trembling ideological bosses, despite the fact that at that precise moment several articles berating the Strugatsky brothers' science fiction had all simultaneously drawn to a head and burst—despite all of this, we managed to publish the novel, and with only limited, in effect minimal, losses. This was a success. Indeed, you could say it was a victory that had seemed unlikely and that no one had expected.

At Detgiz things also seemed to be going well. In mid-May Arkady wrote that *The Inhabited Island* had been allowed through unscathed, without a single remark. The book had gone off to the printers. Furthermore, the production department had promised that, although the book was planned for the third quarter, a chink might possibly be found in order to bring it out in the second, i.e., in June or July.

However, the book did not appear in either June or July. Moreover, in early June an article entitled "Leaves and Roots" appeared in the journal *Soviet Literature*, renowned for its incisive, one might even say extreme, national-patriotic tendency. In this article our *Inhabited Island* was held up as an example of literature without any roots. At the time this part of the article seemed to me (and not only to me) to be "stupid and vacuous" and therefore in no way dangerous. Big deal, so they berate the authors because they let a null-transmitter overshadow the people, and because the novel doesn't contain any genuine artistic images. What else is new? We had heard worse things than that about ourselves! Back then we were far more alarmed by a denunciation received at the same time by the Leningrad Regional Committee of the Communist Party of the Soviet Union from a certain true-believing candidate of sciences,* physicist, and colonel all in one. With the directness of a military man and Party member, the physicist-colonel quite simply, without any fuzziness or equivocation, accused the authors of the novel published in *Neva* of mockery of the army, anti-patriotism, and other such barefaced anti-Soviet propaganda. It was suggested that measures be taken.

It is not possible to give a definite answer to the question of precisely which straw broke the camel's back, but on June 13, 1969, the passage of the novel through Detgiz was halted by an instruction from on high, and the manuscript was confiscated from the printing house. The period of the Great Stand of the Detgiz version of *The Inhabited Island* began.†

There is no point in listing all the rumors, or even the most plausible of them, that appeared at the time, migrated from mouth to mouth, and vanished into oblivion without a trace, not having received even the slightest solid substantiation. The correct interpretation of events was probably expressed by those commentators who judged that the *quantity* of scandals around the name of the brothers Strugatsky (six vituperative articles in the central press in six months) had finally made the transition to *quality*, and it had been decided by someone somewhere to turn the screws on the recalcitrant rebels and apply exemplary punishment. However, even this hypothesis, which explains rather well the opening and middlegame of the chess match that played out, in no way explains the relatively successful endgame.

After six months of frostbitten standoff, the manuscript suddenly reappeared in the authors' field of view—directly from Glavlit, covered all over with multitudinous notes and accompanied

---

* TRANSLATOR'S NOTE: The Russian degree of candidate is effectively equivalent to a doctorate.

† TRANSLATOR'S NOTE: A reference to Great Stand on the Ugra River, in which the forces of Ivan the Great faced off against the Great Horde of Akhmat Khan on opposite sides of the Ugra River from October to November 1480.

by instructions, which in the appropriate fashion were immediately brought to our notice through the agency of the editor. It was difficult at the time and is now quite impossible to judge which precise instructions had issued from the inner depths of the censorship commission and which had been formulated by the management of the publishing house. On this point there were, and still are, differing views, and this mystery will never be solved now. In essence, the instructions for us to carry out boiled down to a requirement to remove from the novel as many as possible realities of Soviet life (ideally all of them, without exception) and, first and foremost, the Russian surnames of the characters.

In January 1970 we got together at our mother's place in Leningrad, and over four days we performed the titanic task of cleaning up the manuscript, which could actually be more correctly be described as *polluting* it, in the unappetizing sense of nocturnal pollution.

First to fall victim to this stylistic self-repression was the Russian Maxim Rostislavsky, who henceforth became, forever and always, to the end of time, the German Maxim Kammerer. Pavel Grigorievich (a.k.a. Wanderer), became Rudolf Sikorsky, and in general the novel acquired a slight but distinct German accent: tanks were transformed into *Panzerwagen*, military offenders into *Blitzträger*, "snot-nosed fool" became *"Dummkopf! Rotznase!"* The following terms disappeared from the novel: "foot-cloths," "convicts," "salad, with shrimp," "tobacco and eau de cologne," "medals," "counterintelligence," and "sugar candy," as well as certain proverbs and sayings, such as "God marks the scoundrel." The interlude "There's a Bad Kind of Smell Here . . ." disappeared completely, without a trace. And the Unknown Fathers Dad, Father-in-Law, and Stepbrother were transformed into the Fire-Bearing Creators Chancellor, Count, and Baron.

It is not possible to list all the corrections and expurgations here; it is not even possible to list the most substantial of them. Yuri Fleishman, in carrying out the quite incredibly finicky task of comparing the final manuscript with the Detgiz publication, discovered 896 variations—corrections, abridgements, insertions, substitutions . . . eight hundred and ninety-six!

But this was, if not yet the end of the story, then at least its culmination. The corrected version was passed back to Glavlit at Nogin Square, and before five months had passed (on 05/22/70) I received a brief epistle from Arkady:

> Nogin Square has finally released *II* from its sharp-clawed paws. Permission to publish has been given. The reason for such a long delay has become clear, by the way, but more about that when we meet. It has simply been realized that we are regular Soviet guys and not slanderers or detractors of any kind, it's just that our attitude is overly critical and sensitive, but that's okay; with a light guiding hand on our shoulder, we can and should carry on working. . . . It has been calculated that if everything goes smoothly (in production), the book will come out sometime in September.

The book, naturally, didn't come out in September; it didn't even come out in November. This saga, the cautionary tale of the publication of a cheerful, absolutely ideologically consistent, purely entertaining little story of a twenty-second-century Young Communist, conceived and written by its authors primarily for the sake of the money, finally ended in January 1971.

It's an interesting question who actually won in this hopeless battle of writers against the state machine. In the end the authors did, after all, manage to launch their creation into the world, if only in a badly mutilated form. But did the censors and bosses succeed at all in achieving their aim of eradicating from the novel the "free spirit" of allusion, the "uncontrollable associations," and every possible kind of subtext? To some extent—indisputably. Beyond any doubt, the acuity and satirical orientation of the mutilated text suffered badly, but to my mind the bosses did not succeed in completely castrating it. For a long time all manner of "well-wishers" carried on eagerly taking swipes at the novel. And although their critical inspiration rarely rose above accusing the authors of "disrespecting Soviet cosmonautics" (what they had in mind was Maxim's disdainful attitude toward working in the Free Search), the bosses' warily hostile attitude to *The Inhabited Island*, even in its "corrected" modification, remained distinctly discernible. But then, more likely than not, that was simply inertia.

In the present edition the original text of the novel has in large measure been restored. Naturally, it was not possible to give Maxim Kammerer, né Rostislavsky, his "maiden" name back—in the twenty years that have passed he has become the hero of several stories, in which he's featured rather as Kammerer. It was either change the name everywhere or nowhere. I preferred nowhere. Several changes, made by the authors under pressure, nonetheless proved so felicitous that it was decided to retain them in the restored text—for instance, the bizarre-sounding "educatees" instead of the banal "convicts," and "Cornet Chachu" instead of "Captain Chachu." But by far the greatest portion of the nine hundred distortions have, of course, been corrected, and the text has been brought to its canonical form.

I have just reread all of the above and suddenly feel a vague anxiety that I will be misunderstood by the contemporary reader, the reader of the end of the twentieth century and beginning of the twenty-first.

First, the reader might have gotten the idea that all this time the Strugatskys did nothing else except run around editorial offices, begging them for pity's sake to print the book, and sobbing into each other's waistcoats, mutilating their own texts as they sobbed. Well, naturally, all that really did happen—we ran, and sobbed, and mutilated—but it only took up a small part of our working time. After all, it was during these months that our first (and last) science fiction detective novel (*The Dead Mountaineer's Inn*) was written, the story *Space Mowgli* was begun and finished, our "secret" novel *The Doomed City* was begun and the draft of three parts was finished, and *Roadside Picnic* was conceived and begun. So, for all the sobbing, both life and work carried on as usual, and we had no time to hang our heads and wring our hands "in violent grief."

And now for "second." Second, I recall what the well-known writer Svyatoslav Loginov ("the instant patriarch of Russian fantasy") said about his recent talk to present-day schoolkids, when he attempted, inter alia, to astound them with the incredible and ludicrous difficulties that a writer encountered in the mid-1970s and suddenly heard a bewildered question from the rows of seats: "If it was so hard to get printed, why didn't you organize your own publishing house?" The present-day reader simply can't imagine what we writers of the 1960s and '70s had to deal with, how ruthlessly and talentlessly the all-powerful Party and state press suppressed literature and culture in general, what a narrow, flimsy little bridge any self-respecting writer had to make his way across: A step to the right and there waiting for you is Article 70 (or 90) of the Criminal Code, trial, prison camp, the nuthouse; in the best-case scenario you are blacklisted and excluded from the literary process for ten years or so. A step to the left and you're clutched in the embrace of vulgar slobs and talentless botchers, a traitor to your own work, an elastic conscience, a Judas, counting and recounting your vile pieces of silver. The present-day reader is evidently no longer capable of understanding these dilemmas. The psychological gulf between him and people of my time gapes wide, and you can hardly expect to fill it with texts like my commentaries—but, then, no other means exists, does it? Freedom is like the air or good health: while you have it, you don't notice it and don't understand how bad things are without it or outside it.

One school of thought, it is true, holds that no one actually even needs freedom—all they need is to be liberated from the need to make decisions. This opinion is quite popular just at present. For it has been said, "It is often the best kind of liberty—liberty from care." Possibly, possibly . . . But, then, that is a subject for an entirely different conversation.